Acting on Faith

Jann Rowland

This is a work of fiction, based on the works of Jane Austen. All of the characters and events portrayed in this novel are products of Jane Austen's original novel, the author's imagination, or are used fictitiously.

ACTING ON FAITH

Copyright © 2013 Jann Rowland

Cover art by Dana Rowland

Published by One Good Sonnet Publishing

ISBN: 0992000009
ISBN-13: 978-0992000004

To Tomoko, *my* Elizabeth Bennet.
Without her support, this work would have been impossible.

ACKNOWLEDGEMENTS

There are many who deserve thanks and recognition for their contributions to this work.

Thanks to my sister Dana, who not only provided commentary and proof-reading skills, but also created the wonderful art which graces the front cover of this book. It was my shared interest with Dana which provided the genesis for my entrance into the world of writing.

I am grateful to Lelia, for becoming my partner in crime, and for graciously undertaking the task of making sure that all my commas were in the right place and that my grammar would pass muster.

My wife and children, who have put up with my absence while I hunkered down in front of the computer more often than they would have liked.

A special thanks to my mother, who received the first copy of this work for Christmas, bound into a folio. It was she who gave me my best review, and provided the impetus to take the plunge and publish it.

And to all others who have provided encouragement and commentary along the way, and have made the writing and publishing of this work to be truly worthwhile.

Chapter I

*F*itzwilliam Darcy sat in the study of his London townhouse staring out the window, the letter in his hands almost forgotten as he held it, turning it over and over, while his mind actively avoided considering what he suspected lay within. The weather was unusual for early October, being unseasonably warm and humid. Somewhere in the distance, he could just make out the rumbling of thunder, and his thoughts turned morosely to the introspection which had been his constant companion these last, long months. It struck him that thunder was a very close analogy to his mood of late—he had alternated between quiet and thoughtful periods interspersed with dark and stormy tempests of railing against fate.

Sighing, he glanced down at the letter, his eyes taking in the familiar messy and careless penmanship of his closest friend. It had arrived two days earlier, and although he was aware of the news it likely contained, Darcy had avoided opening it up to this point, unable to bear the ecstatic effusions of happiness from his good friend while his own situation was still very much in doubt.

Darcy sighed and dropped the letter on the desk, while leaning back in his chair. A hand passed over his face to stop on his temples, massaging them briefly before he opened his eyes and stared at the letter. It was the height of selfishness, he knew, to begrudge the happiness of a friend, regardless of the state of his own emotions. Deep down he knew he did not resent his friend for his suspected joyous news—after all, no one deserved such happiness more than Bingley, especially after the many months he had spent pining over his lost love. Keenly aware of the misjudgment which had led to Bingley's abandonment of Jane Bennet at the point when the neighborhood had expected an engagement, Darcy could not have imagined when he had made that recommendation to his friend that he was in a most direct way affecting his own future happiness.

Of course, by then the damage had already been done. "Not handsome enough to tempt me."

A bitter laugh escaped his lips as he considered the absurdity of the statement made in a fit of pique almost a full year before. Not handsome enough indeed! Intriguing, mesmerizing, and utterly bewitching was far closer to the mark!

Now, Darcy had no particular knowledge from the woman in question that she had overheard his ill-judged remark, but Elizabeth was nothing if not rational, sensible, and amiable. For her to have taken such a decided dislike of him from the outset of their acquaintance, she must have had some provocation. And try as he might (as he had indeed been trying for months), he could not think of any other instance early in their acquaintance when he would have offended her. Although they had shared many lively and contrary discussions while at Netherfield and even before, nothing could account for her developing such animosity, and he was almost certain, upon reexamining their interactions and his newly bought insight into her character and moods, her distaste for him had preceded those days when they had dwelt under the same roof at Netherfield.

No, it must have been the first evening at the assembly, although Wickham's interference later, when he had told her his falsehoods about the Kympton living, had almost certainly prejudiced her even further against him. Of course, again, by Darcy's reckoning, the damage had already been done. For, long before Darcy's thoughtless and unintended slight toward Elizabeth, Wickham had, by attempting to elope with Georgiana, laid the groundwork for Darcy's ill humor, which had resulted in the slight ever being uttered. He could not in good conscience blame Wickham for his choice of words—no, he had only himself to blame for not controlling his tongue and for behaving in such an un-gentlemanlike manner—but that Wickham had put him in such a mood in the first place was undeniable.

Wickham! Even when absent, the cad intruded on his life—he was a blight against the very Darcy name! When Wickham had poisoned Elizabeth against Darcy, he had unknowingly wreaked greater and more profound revenge against his old nemesis than he had obviously intended.

Darcy snorted in bitter amusement, not unaware of the irony of the situation. He had spent his entire adult life—as well as much of his youth—wishing to be free of any connection with Wickham, while now, he would do almost anything to enter into a much closer one. It was a bitter pill, to be certain, yet Elizabeth was worth it—his time in reflection these past months had taught him that if nothing else.

Which brought him back to his present dilemma—what were Elizabeth's feelings toward him now? Had her opinion of him changed enough for him to entertain the hope of her regard? As much as he wanted to rush back to Hertfordshire and declare himself—as much as he had wanted to declare himself during his recent stay there—his former arrogant assurance had given way to caution, forcing him to retreat into his customary reserve and observe events as they occurred around him. She had been silent and grave, not her usual effusive and outgoing self when they had been in company, and they had rarely exchanged more than a few words. Could the fact that it had been his mistaken pride and arrogance which had allowed her youngest sister's elopement and attachment to a man without morals or principle, have crushed any warmth of regard that their interactions at Pemberley had wrought?

Knowing he would only work himself into a headache if he continued with his present jumbled thoughts, Darcy let out a sigh and forced himself to consider the situation rationally. That he had been mistaken—horribly mistaken—in Elizabeth Bennet's opinions and state of mind so many times in the past did not escape him, but in the absence of any encouragement on her behalf, it was all he had.

How had she felt about him at Pemberley? Her demeanor, while embarrassed at their unexpected meeting, had encouraged him, as she had seemed to have borne him no ill will regarding the past. Had he mistaken her change of feelings for her natural vivacious spirit and generous nature?

As he pondered the question, bits and pieces of memories—times they had spent in one another's company and the little things which had passed between them—flitted across his memory. He remembered walking with her in the gardens of Pemberley, the introduction to his sister, and above all, the long look they had shared in the music room the night she and her aunt and uncle had dined at Pemberley. When he contrasted her demeanor then with what he had witnessed in Hertfordshire, the paradox was confusing at best. Had he been mistaken during that time in Derbyshire? Had his desire to earn her good opinion blinded him yet again to her reaction to him?

No, it could not be. He had learned through painful experience exactly what constituted her disapproval. Whereas she had been argumentative, impertinent, and overtly hostile—as he now knew—during the months of their first acquaintance, in Derbyshire she had been charming and pleasant, although a little embarrassed and quiet in his presence. In other words, her behavior in Derbyshire had been what he had mistaken her original behavior in Hertfordshire to be. And yet, when contrasted with what he had witnessed when he had returned to Hertfordshire only the previous week, his confidence left him once again forcing him to face an agony of indecision. The one encouraged him and filled him with the longing to press his suit with her again, only in a proper manner, where he courted Elizabeth with the greatest respect and attention, as she deserved. The other made him want to slink back to Derbyshire to lick his wounds in private, fearing she would never have anything to do with him again.

It was a convoluted mess, to be certain, but one he wished—and feared in equal measure—to unravel.

A commotion in the hallway caught his attention, and he heard loud voices, among them the unmistakable bellowing of his Aunt Catherine. Sighing at the unwelcome intrusion into his solitude, Darcy rose to his feet and crossed the room to his door. Whatever business his aunt had in invading his home, the quickest and surest way of ensuring his and Georgiana's comfort and peace was to deal her and send her on her way as quickly as possible.

Out in the hallway, his aunt was striding toward the doorway in which he had just appeared, his butler trailing after her in an attempt to deflect her attention long enough for him to announce her. His aunt, however, was having none of it. Her countenance was as black as a thunder cloud, and her swift, determined stride, combined with the way she sized him up as she approached, caused a sinking feeling to settle in his stomach—whatever she was about, this was certainly no social visit.

Catching his butler's eye, Darcy shook his head slightly, freeing the man from the odious presence of Darcy's least favorite aunt. Breathing a sigh of relief, the harried butler stopped and bowed slightly in his master's direction before beating a swift retreat, leaving Darcy alone with Lady Catherine.

Calmly bowing and bidding her his welcome, Darcy stepped aside and invited her to precede him into the study. With barely a word of response or thanks, Catherine swept past him into the room and sat in the chair in front of his desk in a manner as grand as if she was the queen herself. Praying for patience, Darcy crossed the room and sat in his own chair, wondering for perhaps the thousandth time that his own sweet and angelic mother could have been sister to this loud and obnoxious high-born lady. Whatever bee she had in her bonnet, Darcy knew with an instinctive certainty that this visit would not be pleasant and that his aunt would likely leave it disappointed, if not in high dudgeon.

Darcy immediately addressed his aunt, asking her business, a query to which no reply was forthcoming. They sat in silence for several moments, each eyeing the other, and while his aunt looked as if she had swallowed a rancid pill and did not know as of yet how to expel it, Darcy merely regarded her calmly, unwilling to begin the conversation. Whatever she had come here to say would be said without any encouragement from him.

At length, she dropped his gaze and peered around the room. "I was somewhat surprised, yet still gratified, to find you at home today, Nephew."

Whatever he had been expecting, this was not it. "I had business today, Aunt," said Darcy, hoping his abrupt manner would help her to come to the point.

Sniffing at his words, she directed her attention back upon him, peering at him with the stern, severe expression he remembered from his childhood, the one which had never failed to cow him into obedience. It appeared she was unaware of the fact that the small boy had grown into a man who was decidedly unimpressed by her draconian and controlling ways.

"Well, it is good to know you still know your duty — in this instance at least."

Darcy narrowed his eyes, his suspicion of her motives now giving way to certainty as to her errand. He was still confused as to why now, of all times, she should make a sudden and unannounced trip to London, which she had never done before, and entreat him on a matter which had been discussed ad nauseum, not to mention been resolved in his mind. Still, he would not discuss it with her unless she insisted, and when she did, he was determined to end all further discussion on the subject once and for all.

"You can be certain, Aunt, that I am very aware of my duties and am perfectly willing to fulfill them to the best of my abilities. Now, will you kindly state your business so I may return to mine? I have much to accomplish."

Silence again descended upon the room, and Darcy was unwilling to break it. Let his aunt make the first move. In this, he would not have long to wait.

"Tell me, Darcy, do you honor the memory of your mother?"

"I am surprised you even have to ask, Aunt," responded he after a moment's pause. Though she had never before opened this particular conversation in such a manner, he immediately knew to what she was referring.

"You have not answered the question."

"Lady Catherine, as you well know, I hold my mother's memory in the deepest of respect and devotion. My mother was dear to me."

"And yet you have still not done your duty and engaged yourself to your cousin, the one whom your mother chose for you! At the age of eight and twenty, you have still not done your duty and honored your mother's wishes, and you have the audacity to sit there and claim a willingness to perform your duties. Why is it, then, that my daughter remains unmarried?"

Darcy ignored her reference to his mother and concentrated on her never-ending insistence in the matter of his marriage. "Lady Catherine, I have told you repeatedly, and I shall do so once again—I will not marry Anne."

"You know we planned your union while you were yet in your cradles—"

"I know of no such thing," interrupted Darcy. "I hardly think it likely, considering the difference in our respective ages, that you and my mother hovered over us while we were *both* lying in our cradles, planning an event so far in the future. Regardless, the matter is of little import—I have no intention of ever yielding in this matter, so there is little to be gained by continuing to importune me."

"And what of Anne?" spat she in response. "If you refuse to marry her, what is to become of her? You know she has been waiting for you these many years—waiting for you to finally do your duty and make her an offer. Have you considered how heartbroken she will be when the man for whom she has waited since she was a girl casts her aside? Where will her prospects for marriage be then?"

"Lady Catherine," said Darcy, his anger at this obstinate woman beginning to rise, "perhaps before coming into my home in a lather, making demands and accusations, you should first speak *with* your daughter and understand her feelings on the matter rather than presuming to speak *for* her. Anne and I spoke on this subject many years ago and decided that we would not marry, regardless of what you—or anyone else—has to say on the matter."

"But Darcy, surely you must see Anne is formed for you. Your situation in life, your splendid fortune on both sides of the family—these are all circumstances highly in favor of your making a splendid match."

"And our dispositions are so similar we should be bored with each other within six months."

"What nonsense are you speaking? What do your dispositions have to do with the matter? We are speaking of matters of dynastic succession, not some young schoolboy infatuation."

"Which is exactly why you and Sir Lewis enjoyed such . . . *felicity* in marriage," responded Darcy, thinking about how his uncle had truly been the perfect match for his aunt, by her reckoning. Lewis de Bourgh had been as arrogant and meddling as his termagant of a wife.

As he could have predicted, his barb was completely misunderstood by Lady Catherine. "That is exactly what I am saying. You and your cousin are both of a quiet, reserved disposition, which would benefit you most excellently in your future marriage."

Darcy brought his hand up yet again to massage his temples, where a most unpleasant aching sensation had started to build as his discussion with his aunt continued.

"I believe you have mistaken my meaning, Lady Catherine. I was not speaking of our felicity; I was speaking of our characters being too similar. I am very much of the opinion that two reserved, quiet persons such as myself and Anne would suit each other very ill indeed. We both require lively partners who will help us become more open and engaging—we two would only cause the other to become more introverted than the reverse."

As he said this, Darcy, in his mind's eye, was remembering a pair of fine, lively eyes which had bewitched him at first glance. A man could lose himself in those eyes and not care whether he was ever found. *She*, at least, would never allow him to become more reclusive than he already was—her very nature would forbid it and would draw him out in the process.

Lady Catherine, though, was clearly not amused. Barely suppressed rage now filled her countenance as she glared back at him. "So it is true then."

Startled, Darcy stared back at his aunt. "I beg your pardon?"

"This rumor I have heard about you and that . . . that . . . little minx from Hertfordshire."

Although surprised, Darcy was able to keep his head. If Aunt Catherine had heard a rumor connecting him to someone other than Anne, it was of little wonder she had descended upon him in such a fury, determined to "make him see reason." And most peculiarly, the only person she could know from Hertfordshire other than her parson's wife was Elizabeth Bennet. He wondered at the possibility of such a report existing, and he could not account for anyone coming to such a conclusion based on what their dealings before the people of the neighborhood had been. However, in order to determine his best response to her charge, he needed to know exactly of what the rumor consisted.

"I beg your pardon, madam, but I have not the faintest idea of what you speak."

"I hardly believe that," said Lady Catherine, her voice rising in response. "There can be no other explanation on the matter."

"Perhaps if you would share this rumor to which you refer, I can either confirm or deny it."

Her responding glare was filled with disdain, but his aunt nonetheless responded. "Two days ago, I received an alarming report which contained, among other things, Miss Jane Bennet's most advantageous engagement to your friend Bingley and the rumor of your imminent engagement to her younger sister, Miss Elizabeth. Although I deemed it a report openly circulated by those Bennets in an attempt to entrap you, I instantly set off with the express purpose of contradicting this nefarious scheme."

Darcy was struck dumb. How such a report could have come to be was beyond his present capacity to understand—his dealings with Elizabeth in Hertfordshire had always been characterized by such rancor that he was certain she would not have been secretive in her disapproval of him to those of the neighborhood. His recent visit there had resulted in no more than the briefest and most desultory of conversations—certainly not enough to incite speculation. As uneasy as he was pertaining to the source of the rumor, he could not help be curious. Who had seen through him?

"And who was the source of this rumor?" asked Darcy.

"I really have not the faintest idea," replied Lady Catherine. "I do not know the particulars, only that such a rumor was in existence through my clergyman, Mr. Collins. If you recall, Mrs. Collins is from the neighborhood—I can only presume they received the news through a letter from Mrs. Collins's family in Hertfordshire."

"Yet you did not substantiate this rumor yourself?"

She shrugged. "Why should I need to? The mere whisper of such a thing on the lips of my clergyman was all the confirmation I required. After all, you know that where there is smoke, there is fire. Your standing in society could be adversely affected by such a report if you do not take a stand immediately."

"If you will quote pithy sayings, then let me say that the existence of one engagement often breeds rumors of another. Did you not perhaps think this could be nothing more than idle speculation regarding one sister due to the engagement of another?"

"Why should I take it to be so?" demanded Lady Catherine. "I am well aware of people of their type; they are grasping, artful people, looking only to improve their connections and increase their fortune. Should I not have acted such to protect you from such inferior connections?"

By now, Darcy's disdain for this meddling woman had reached unprecedented heights. "I assure you, madam, I am very capable of looking out for my own future as well as my connections. Somehow, though, I do not think you have fully grasped the implications of what you have *accomplished* with your ill-judged mission today. You have set out from Rosings to confront me on the basis of a mere *rumor*! You have undertaken this journey and insulted me and my adherence to duty on an unsubstantiated piece of gossip, one which you felt could not contain any truth whatsoever. Considering our longstanding disagreement regarding my exact relationship with Anne, I wonder at your blindness to the implications of such an application. You do realize that if word of this interview were ever to reach the ton, rather than prevent such a thing—as is I presume your purpose here today—it might blow this mere *rumor* into the proportions of scandal, where I might be *forced* to make Miss Elizabeth an offer if only to save our reputations. How could you have failed to consider that?"

Throughout his declaration, his aunt had turned a shade of red due to his manner of speaking to her, which quickly turned an unbecoming shade of white once the implications of his diatribe had become clear to her. Yet she quickly gathered herself and continued her assault, causing him to reflect that whatever else she was, she was certainly not slow of wit or bereft of courage.

"Do not be a fool, Darcy. You and I are alone in this room and no one else knows of my presence. If your servants are as well trained as they were when my sister was mistress of this house, no word of our meeting shall reach the ears of others."

"The servants, *dear* Aunt Catherine, are as well trained and loyal as ever. And yet you are here, where you usually disdain to be, in favor of the comforts of Rosings, and it is not outside the realm of possibility that someone may have seen you as you exited the carriage and entered my home, or may have noticed the de Bourgh family crest on your coach as it passed through the city. From there, it is not a great leap to guess the nature of our conversation, given your repeated tendency to wax poetic on the subject of my so-called *engagement* to your daughter. When coupled with our conversation here today, which has lasted already for longer than a mere social call, what do you think the effects of this rumor should be if it were to make its way to London? Miss Bennet could very well be seen to be engaged to me to cause such an action from you, and her reputation ruined if no engagement were forthcoming."

"And what is it to me? What should it be to you if her reputation should be ruined? It is her own doing and that of her family. If she should become embroiled in a scandal, who should feel the effects of it but herself? She should not think to quit the sphere in which she was born in the first place—if she should reach for the heights and fall in the process, what should it be to you?"

"First of all, I am not convinced this rumor has originated with Miss Elizabeth or any of her family," retorted Darcy. "I was in Hertfordshire not a week ago, and I can assure you there were no whisperings of an engagement between us at the time."

"Then they have begun to spread them since you came away to town!"

"That I cannot believe! I am acquainted with Miss Elizabeth's character, and I fancy I know her well enough to understand she would never spread rumors of such a gross falsehood, especially when they concern her most intimately. The other thing you should consider is I am by no means the sort of man who does not take his obligations seriously. If such a report did exist, and Miss Elizabeth's reputation was to suffer as a result, I would have no choice but to do the *honorable* thing and marry her."

Lady Catherine was speechless as she regarded him, the expression on her face almost comical in its mixture of utter fury and complete consternation. Eventually, however, she found her voice, and once again the diatribe began.

"How can you say such a thing?" she cried. "She is obviously spreading these rumors herself, undoubtedly with the active participation of her family. She can have no claim whatsoever on your honor."

"As I have already stated more than once, madam, I suggest you verify the rumors, as well as their source, before you make such inflammatory, unchristian statements. Miss Elizabeth Bennet is a lady of the highest character and morality, and as such, she is deserving of your respect. Until I know with certainty that she or her family are responsible for the tidings you bring today, I shall reserve judgment."

"It is true then!" screeched Lady Catherine as she rose from her seat and faced him, her hands gripping the edge of his desk. "You mean to have the little country tart in the face of the family's objections, against all decency, and against the wishes of your late, revered mother!"

"Lady Catherine!" bellowed Darcy as he rose to face her down. "I will not have you bring my mother, the family, or any of your misguided notions of decency into this discussion. I have made my intentions clear on the matter of my supposed engagement to Anne many times, and you will not slander Miss Elizabeth or any other innocent person due to your disappointment over my unwillingness to oblige your fantasy."

"I thought better of you, nephew!" rasped Lady Catherine, irrationally causing him to hope she had, for once, lost her voice. "I had thought you better than to be taken in by a mere country miss searching for a fortune. How could you have forgotten yourself? How could you be contemplating this engagement while turning your back on your cousin Anne, who would make you a most proper and eligible match?"

Sitting down heavily, Darcy sighed and looked up at his aunt. "Lady Catherine, again you are wrong, as no such engagement exists."

"Of this, I am aware," said Lady Catherine, once again taking her seat.

Darcy peered at his aunt intently, suspecting there was something she was still not telling him. Before he could pursue the matter, she was speaking once again.

"And what will you do about the report?"

"Nothing," was his blunt statement. "I am unaware as to the contents of the report to which you refer or the particulars of its disbursement, but I do not believe the Bennets can have caused it to be circulated. At this time, the only thing I can state with a certainty is that there is no understanding between Miss Elizabeth and myself—I have not been graced with the honor of her hand, nor have I approached her father for permission to marry her. You see, Lady Catherine, it appears this excursion of yours has been for naught."

It was nothing less than the truth, of course. He had *not* had the honor of the acceptance of his proposals, nor had he spoken with her father, nor did the event seem likely at this point. It was clear he would have to return to Hertfordshire now, if for no other reason than to determine the extent of this rumor and what should be done to contain it. What the likelihood of Elizabeth actually accepting him now was, he could not say. He knew enough of her disposition, however, to understand that whatever she might feel for him, being force marched to the altar due to a scandal would not be the ideal way to enter into the marriage state. It was more like being sentenced to the gallows.

"Nephew," said Lady Catherine, interrupting his thoughts, "I am happy to see there is no engagement between you and that girl, but mark my words—she means to have you."

"I fear you could not be further from the truth if you tried, madam," responded Darcy. His head ached and he wanted nothing more than to end this interview and return to his contemplations.

"Come, Nephew, do not be so naïve. She and her family have obviously spread these rumors—if there is no engagement, then there can be no other explanation."

"Unless it is nothing more than idle speculation as I stated from the outset."

"These things always have a grain of truth at their core, Darcy. Surely you know this."

Darcy almost laughed out loud—Lady Catherine certainly had no idea exactly how much of a grain of truth this particular rumor actually contained. For although he could not be certain of Elizabeth's point of view on the subject, he knew he would be ecstatic if this report were ever to be proven correct by her acceptance of his suit.

"Hear me, Darcy," continued his aunt when he made no response, "she means to have your wealth and draw you in. She is nothing more than an adventuress—a fortune-hunting young woman who should be left to her fate. You must publicly repudiate this insidious rumor and distance yourself from all further acquaintance with her. It would also be best if you severed all relationship with that Bingley fellow as well. Surely you can do without him—his wealth merely comes from trade. Really, you should take greater care with whom you count your friends. How is Georgiana to make a good marriage if you insist on consorting with riffraff such as that Bingley fellow and those Bennets?"

Incensed though he was by her snobbish characterization of Bingley and the Bennets, Darcy held his temper and took a few moments to calm himself before making his response.

"If she is a fortune hunter such as you claim, then why did she not accept my proposal when I made it to her back in April?"

Silence reigned over the room as Lady Catherine struggled to comprehend his meaning. Darcy smiled grimly at the reflection that he had finally found a way to induce his aunt to speechlessness. Unfortunately, her silence was destined to be short-lived.

"You offered for her in April?" she queried, disbelief coloring her voice. "Darcy, how could you?"

"Lady Catherine . . ." he warned, but his aunt was not to be deterred.

"And she refused?"

"Most emphatically. I believe the words, 'the last man on earth I could ever be prevailed upon to marry' figured prominently in her rejection."

"Most astonishing!" exclaimed the lady. "I fear I have overestimated her scheming nature if she would reject such an advantageous offer of marriage. Surely she must be a simpleton!"

"Come now, Lady Catherine, a simpleton! You have met her and crossed verbal swords with her—whatever her faults may be, weak understanding cannot be among them. She knew exactly what she was doing when she rejected me, and the blame can rest on none other than my shoulders. My proposal was ill considered and not one which would induce a worthy woman such as Miss Bennet to accept it. And perhaps even more importantly, I completely misjudged her opinion of me. I was indeed most humbled by her, to my betterment, I might add."

"But Nephew," she continued, "do you not see? Somehow her mother, eager as she obviously is to marry off her daughters to wealthy men, has discovered this and has prevailed upon her to change her mind. Believe me—Mr. Collins has told me all about the Bennets and their artful ways. Since they have no expectation of another offer, they must resort to stratagem and trickery to entrap you into a marriage so advantageous to their family fortunes."

Darcy shook his head in amazement at his aunt's continued willful blindness and stubborn nature. "Considering she was not *prevailed upon* to marry the very Mr. Collins to whom you refer, do you really think she could now be prevailed upon to accept and actively entrap a man whom she had previously refused? You yourself have waxed poetic on many occasions about how foolish she was for rejecting an eligible match to your sycophantic and senseless parson which would have secured her family's future. I can imagine what kind of vindictive and jealous nonsense he has been spouting in your ear. Your arguments are not sound, Lady Catherine—I know Miss Elizabeth, and whatever she is, she is no fortune hunter."

"So what will you do?" Her words, while seeming offhand, were delivered with such a studied air of nonchalance that Darcy instinctively understood her motive for the question—she hoped to force him to promise the end of his connection with the Bennets and any possible engagement with Miss Elizabeth, all the while hoping that she would eventually be able to wear him down and force him to marry Anne. He was not of a mind to allow her any triumph in this cursed conversation.

"I intend to return to Hertfordshire at my earliest opportunity and discover the situation for myself. If Miss Elizabeth's reputation has not suffered due to this rumor you have so kindly brought to my attention, then nothing further needs to be done. If, however, she suffers due to this idle report, then I shall know my duty and act accordingly."

"So you mean to have her then?"

Darcy sighed. "I have said no such thing, but I shall not lie to you. If I can convince Miss Elizabeth of the constancy of my feelings for her—and can somehow excite the same feelings in response—then, yes, I mean to do everything in my power to secure her hand. If, on the other hand, I fail in my endeavor, I shall bow out gracefully."

Lady Catherine was aghast. "You mean to tell me you would debase yourself and offer for a woman who has refused you once?"

"If there was the slightest chance of her acceptance? Yes."

"How could you do such a thing?" she asked, her voice once again rising to the level of a shriek. "Where is your pride, your sense of duty and honor?"

"Changed, directed toward something better. My pride has never done me any favors in the past."

"And this is your final word?"

"Lady Catherine, I would advise you to let go of your argument and step back. I have stated my feelings very clearly, both on the subject of Anne and Miss Elizabeth."

She rose in a fury. "Very well, then, I shall know how to act."

"Lady Catherine," Darcy interrupted as she made her way to the door, "I have the highest respect for you as my aunt and the sister of my mother, but I will not tolerate any further interference from you. Please do the entire family a favor and cease your useless attempts to meddle in my affairs."

"Insolent boy!" she retorted. "The earl shall hear about this. *He* will make you see sense!"

"I highly doubt it," Darcy responded, a wry quality entering his voice. "As you are well aware, the earl himself has made a love match. I doubt he will be anything but happy for me if I should have the good fortune to accomplish the same."

To this Lady Catherine was momentarily speechless, and Darcy knew he had won a significant point—Lady Catherine knew her brother very well, and their differences of opinion and disputes were legendary. The earl would in no way support his sister over his nephew in this matter.

All of these thoughts crossed Lady Catherine's face as clearly as if they had been written upon her brow.

"I am sincerely happy your mother did not live to witness such willful disgrace," she finally bit out with some venom. "To know you have fallen in such an infamous manner would have caused her the greatest of heartbreak."

"And what would you know of the matter?" Darcy spat in response, highly incensed at her continued obstinacy and vindictiveness. "Perhaps I should tell you of my final conversation with my mother—which I had concealed, knowing you would be highly offended. Your behavior here today would have embarrassed her far more than mine."

"Do you think I did not know my sister?" she demanded.

"It is clear you did not, madam. On her death bed, my mother asked me to attend her and told me that this day would come—that you would use every weapon in your arsenal to attempt to force me into marriage with Anne. She made me promise I would not give in to your demands unless it was my desire to unite with my cousin. So you see, your arguments concerning my mother are groundless at best, gross falsehoods at worst. I would highly appreciate your never referring to my mother in such a manner in my presence again. I have endured your scheming and your controlling ways for the entirety of my life, but depend upon it, madam, I shall do so no longer."

"How dare you?" she screamed, raising her walking stick at him menacingly.

Darcy merely stared back at her coldly, unimpressed by her display of displeasure. "In much the same manner as you dare, I would imagine."

"It must be a falsehood—my sister and I planned your union from the time you were a child!"

"Another fantasy she repudiated to me. This dream has existed in your mind and in your mind alone. If you doubt my word, perhaps I should show you the clause in my mother's will known only to my father and I. Therein, she confirmed the supposed engagement between Anne and I was never agreed to by herself. She provided proof in the event you should try to convince me with some trumped-up evidence of an arrangement between you two."

The expression on his aunt's face told Darcy he had guessed near enough to the mark to determine what his aunt's plans had been. She was so apoplectic with fury that for several moments she could not say a word. At length, she appeared to gather control over herself, and she regarded him, still in the heights of fury, but with a look of utmost disdain etched upon her haughty features.

"Very well, then. I wish you all the misery in the world with your artful little adventuress, Darcy. Don't expect me or anyone from the family to ever recognize her."

"Good day, Lady Catherine," he responded firmly, unwilling to rise any further to her bait.

The slamming of the door and the rapping of her cane against the floor tiles signaled her final exit from his domain, causing Darcy to exhale with the greatest of relief. Although he had known this day would come and had anticipated an extremely unpleasant confrontation, the actuality of the event had exceeded his expectations.

At once, he was able to return his attention to the issue at hand—it was now inconceivable for him to stay away from Hertfordshire for any length of time. His aunt's intelligence had rendered his return a moot point—he must go back and ascertain the situation before he would know how to act.

The letter lying on his desk once again caught his eye, and as he thought about his reasons for not opening it before, they all seemed so childish compared with this new information he possessed—Elizabeth needed him, and he would be damned if he would allow her to be hurt in any way.

Grasping the letter, he broke the seal and scanned the contents, noting through the scribbled lines and blots that the information contained was essentially what he had believed it to be, coupled with an invitation to return to Netherfield at any time convenient. Chuckling at the predictability of his friend, Darcy immediately set his pen to paper and composed a letter accepting his friend's invitation and stating his business would be complete in three days, after which he would join his friend and celebrate his newfound happiness. After all, Darcy now knew he had business of his own to attend to in Hertfordshire.

Once the letter was complete, he sealed it and rang for his butler to send it to

Netherfield by express immediately. He then leaned back in his chair to think of the events of the day. He still had no clue whatsoever about the state of Elizabeth's mind. However, one fact was beyond refute — if this rumor was nothing more than an idle report, he could do nothing other than to try to persuade Elizabeth of his change of heart. In the end, the chance that she would ultimately accept him outweighed the heartache of rejection by a rather wide margin.

Chapter II

*T*he unseasonably warm weather which hung over London was also making its presence felt to the north in Hertfordshire, a circumstance which suited Miss Elizabeth Bennet remarkably well.

The situation in Longbourn house had not been an easy one for the family, and although everything had turned out well in the end, the long succession of events had made it seem as if peace at Longbourn—always a difficult thing—had departed, never to return. The family had indeed weathered a series of storms, from Lydia's elopement and Mrs. Bennet's histrionics, to Lydia's subsequent discovery and marriage, to the visit of the newly married Wickhams—not to mention the upheaval and uncertainty which had plagued Jane's long saga with respect to the attentions—and lack thereof—of Mr. Bingley. Some of the recent events had provided pleasure to certain members of the party, but to most, they had been nothing more than one disaster after another, and even though Lydia was now somewhat respectably married and settled, the more discerning members of the family understood her life would not be easy. Even if the miraculous were to occur and Wickham were to completely change and become a model soldier and citizen, he was still an officer in the army and could hardly keep Lydia in the lifestyle to which she was accustomed—and which even a modest country gentleman such as her father could provide. Needless to say, no member of the family with a modicum of sense expected Wickham to suddenly reform.

Admittedly, the situation had improved since then. The benefits of the Wickhams' departure could not be underestimated due to the tranquility it brought to most of the party. And with Mr. Bingley's return and subsequent proposal to Jane, it seemed as if the fortunes of the Bennets were once more on the rise. Indeed, the society gossips of the area, such as they were, now spoke of the family in glowing tones, remarking on their good fortune and respectability, whereas only a month before they had been full of whispers about impropriety, sadly shaking their heads and remarking that the whole family was held under the darkest of clouds.

Of course, Bingley's proposal, although a greatly desired and celebrated event, was not one which could possibly preserve the tranquility and peace of the country manor. In fact, quite the opposite occurred—not only did the air of excitement pervade the entire family, but it was an inexhaustible source of conversation and action for the Bennet matron, who had already, merely a se'nnight after its accomplishment, begun to dream of and plan an elaborate wedding feast which would surpass anything the small community had ever before seen.

The members of the family party each had their own ways of dealing with the constant stream of excited prattle which erupted from Mrs. Bennet's mouth. Mr. Bennet, of course, retreated to his bookroom most mornings, disappearing faster than the money in Wickham's purse—or at least he did so on the mornings in which he did not shoot with Bingley or ride out on estate business. Mary had her pianoforte, and when that was not enough, a book of sermons and an out-of-the-way corner in the far reaches of Longbourn's park were enough for her. Kitty, it appeared, had become adept at avoiding her mother, identifying with alacrity exactly when the woman would go into her planning mode (which was nearly always) and disappearing at the first sign of trouble. Most of the family had no idea what became of Kitty on those occasions, and when asked, Kitty responded in a calm (for Kitty) tone of voice that she had found something with which to occupy her time. Her father and Elizabeth, although they looked on with knowing smiles, said nothing. Jane, of course, was the one member of the family who had the greatest tolerance for her mother's incessant schemes, yet when she was beginning to feel fatigued, her fiancé was generally available, and Mrs. Bennet was only too happy to shoo her daughter out the door to spend time with the young man. After all, it would not do to have Bingley grow tired of her before the wedding. The engagement must be preserved at all costs!

As for Elizabeth, her method of escape from an overly excitable parent was much the same as had been her wont all of her life—a good book and an invitation to her father's bookroom or a long walk along the paths near her family home. And even though it was early October, the aforementioned unseasonably warm weather was a boon in that it allowed her to continue her practice of walking out every day, whereas in a normal year, the weather would be chancy at this time, prone to rain and other unpleasantness which would make her walks difficult and dirty at best, and impossible at worst.

Thus, it was with a grateful heart that she departed from Longbourn early on the first Sunday in October, eager to feel the bright morning sun on her face before the family attended church later that morning. The cook, as always, had a few of her favorite pastries and breads from the kitchen ready for her consumption, and after wrapping them in a kerchief, Elizabeth made her escape from the estate and set out along her favorite paths.

The world was a wondrous thing that morning. The early morning frost which coated the landscape mocked the warmth in the air, knowing its dominance was only a matter of time and a change in the weather. Elizabeth shook her head at the fanciful thoughts which appeared to have taken hold of her mind that morning and glanced around at the foliage which was coated in the pure white substance, rendering the entire scene uncommonly lovely. The frost patterns on the windows of her home had always fascinated her in their pure beauty and intricacy, and Elizabeth, not being formed for gloomy or melancholy thoughts, chose to perceive such beauty as it was and not as a harbinger of the approaching season of cold and dreary weather which would confine her to the house more often than not.

The pathways of her home were well known to her, and she walked without conscious thought of her destination, so confident was she in her ability to navigate the sometimes confusing myriad of trails, roads, and animal paths surrounding her home.

She took her time, stopping here and there, intent on enjoying her surroundings, the vistas of the area which would soon be closed to her for another season. In the back of her mind, thoughts and impressions threatened to burst forth, a cacophony of recent memories and experiences, all of them demanding that she sort through them and try to gain some understanding of the changes her life had undergone. Still, she ignored them, choosing instead to dwell on her surroundings, content in the knowledge that such thoughts would intrude in force when she had reached her destination.

She stopped more than once to take stock of the views along the way, and although she had seen every one of them many times in the past, she still marveled at the pure beauty and serenity of the scenes while comparing them to the few other places she had visited in the course of the past year. While Kent had been much like Hertfordshire in both its features and landscape, the air held a perpetual hint of the salty tanginess of the sea, refreshing in both mind and body. And Derbyshire, although quite different from her home, contained beauties of its own—from the stark and barren glory of the peaks to the wild and rocky beauty of the valleys. She had to admit the beauties of that county had been as pleasing as any she had seen before. The only other place she had visited was her aunt and uncle's house in London, which of course could not compare to the beauties of the country in the mind of a young country miss such as Elizabeth Bennet.

Of course, such thoughts of sceneries and paths far from her home brought forth other thoughts, namely the ones which she had been endeavoring to avoid. Shaking her head, she smiled and reflected that one could not always control one's thoughts, and no matter what was done, such thoughts often intruded upon one's consciousness, whether willed to do so or not.

By this time, she had arrived at the base of Oakham Mount, and welcoming the exertion which would keep her thoughts at bay for just a few more precious moments, she began to climb. It was not a difficult climb—Oakham Mount was more of a large hill than any true mountain—but it afforded the finest view of the area, being wooded only to the north side. The other three sides were barren and afforded remarkable views—on a clear day, Elizabeth could see not only her own home, nestled in amongst the trees, but also the manor house of Netherfield, a jewel in the green pastures of the estate. It was that manor house, and more specifically its inhabitants, to which her thoughts had threatened to return during the entirety of her walk.

Sighing, Elizabeth stopped and gazed around, reveling in the familiar views laid out before her. It was for this sense of peace and belonging she maintained her habit of solitary walks, much to her mother's distress and her father's amusement.

At length, her stomach reminded her rather forcibly that it had as yet gone unfilled and that she possessed a kerchief filled with delicacies from cook waiting to be consumed.

Making her way to the large boulder which protruded from the summit of the hill and which comprised her normal resting place when she visited Oakham Mount, she doffed the old travel shawl she had brought and spread it out on the boulder to protect her dress from becoming soiled. Once she had situated herself comfortably, she opened her prize and—selecting a tasty morsel—began to consume her breakfast.

As she ate, her eyes wandered over the scenery, while her mind, this morning at its most recalcitrant, began to travel on the course which it had tried several times already that morning. The thoughts of the beauty of the morning forgotten, she once again considered all which had occurred.

The events of the previous month—indeed, the events which had taken place since her visit to Kent the previous spring—now almost seemed surreal to Elizabeth. She was aware of the very great changes which had occurred—and which were about to occur with Jane's wedding—and wondered how the arrival of two rich young men—and one fortune-seeking snake—could have turned the sometimes chaotic world of the Bennets of Longbourn even further on its head.

Elizabeth reflected on Mr. Bingley—her most beloved sister was happy, so what more could Elizabeth want? Sensible, serene Jane was now engaged to a most handsome and eligible young man, and Elizabeth could not be happier for her sister. In fact, the engagement seemed to have changed Jane in Elizabeth's eyes, something which only one with as intimate a knowledge of her sister as Elizabeth possessed would even notice. Jane was still as calm and sensible as ever—she held her emotions and thoughts as guarded as she ever had—but now Elizabeth was able to detect a happiness in Jane, a contentment with the world which perhaps had not always been there, although Elizabeth had certainly not noticed it before. It appeared Jane had found her place in the world and was happy to immerse herself in her new role as a fiancée and later wife, future mother, and mistress of her own house. Elizabeth was happy for her.

She was also happy for Mr. Bingley. The man had been somewhat easily led, not only by his superior and overbearing sisters, but also by his friend, and although Elizabeth thought she detected Mr. Darcy's influence once again in Bingley's return to Hertfordshire and Jane, she was also certain Bingley had finally determined to take control of his own life. She had no knowledge of what had passed between the two friends, but she fancied she could detect a new confidence in Mr. Bingley's manner, as if he had finally discovered that his opinions and understanding had value in and of themselves—that he was not necessarily required to defer to his friend in all things—and had subsequently gained a heightened understanding because of it. She could not be certain, but the way they had interacted while in company, the way Bingley had often expressed his opinions, sometimes contradicting Mr. Darcy's, bespoke a newfound self-assurance which came from within rather than showing the artificial buoyancy which had until so recently indicated Mr. Darcy's influence over him. Perhaps some good had come from the interference of his sisters and his friend if the result she thought she detected was any indication. An independent and confident husband could only bode well for Jane's future felicity, something about which Elizabeth knew she would have worried had Jane married him last fall as they had all hoped.

Of the second instance of recent attachment in their family, Elizabeth could not think without abhorrence and some measure of guilt. After all, Elizabeth herself had been led down the garden path by Mr. Wickham, and if she was so easily fooled by the libertine, an empty-headed flirt such as her sister could not hope to be immune to the man's charms. She knew there was an excellent chance that Lydia would not have believed her if she had revealed her knowledge of Wickham's past and that her father still would have ignored her advice, believing in Lydia's immunity from fortune hunters due to her lack of fortune. Still, Elizabeth bitterly regretted her silence on the matter, knowing she would feel better about herself if she had at least made the attempt to make her family aware of Wickham's conduct. If nothing else, perhaps Kitty would have—because of her jealousy of her younger sister—made their father aware of Lydia's partiality in time for him to have done something to prevent the elopement which had so nearly ruined their family's good name.

But she had kept her own counsel, never connecting the fact that although the thought of Wickham's absence soon after her return from Kent seemed a justifiable reason to keep her knowledge quiet, her sister had only days later been invited to spend the summer months with a most unsuitable chaperone in the Colonel's wife. She knew intellectually that the blame rested with the silver-tongued serpent to whom her sister was now shackled for the rest of her life, but her heart still wished she had done something more to protect her family from him and others of his ilk. It was a bitter pill, as she knew her sister would never be happy with Wickham, although Lydia would perhaps never have the sense to understand her own predicament. For now, being married was all Lydia concerned herself with, and if her conduct during her visit to Hertfordshire had been any indication, Elizabeth suspected she would be content at least for the time being.

Lydia was not even sensible enough to understand why her family, outside of her mother, and to a lesser extent Kitty, did not want to hear about her wedding. After all, she had been the first of the five daughters to marry—surely that was a happy occasion, was it not? The silly and stupid remarks Lydia had continued to make, regardless of any reprimand or censure from anyone in her family, still had the power to annoy Elizabeth days after the event. In particular, one of their conversations stood out in Elizabeth's mind.

"I wish *all* my sisters had accompanied me to Brighton," prattled Lydia, unmindful as usual to the various expressions of disinterest on her sisters' faces. Jane of course, was as calm and patient as ever, and only one as close to her as Elizabeth could have noticed the tightness in her eyes and the slight downturn to her lips indicating her disapproval. Elizabeth wore a look of complete disgust, while even Kitty seemed to sense for once that her sister was far from proper. Mary seemed to be the most intelligent of them all by the simple fact that she had refused to accompany her sisters and listen to Lydia's endless crowing.

"Why ever would you wish for such a thing?" asked Elizabeth, certain that for once her sister would sense her bored tone and desist.

The depths of Lydia's obliviousness, however, had yet to be tested.

"Why, so that we all could have returned with husbands, of course," stated she as if it were the most obvious thing in the entire world. "There were so many handsome officers, so many balls and parties . . . I daresay I could have found husbands for you all—even Mary, dull as she is." Lydia giggled, delighted with her own wit. "We would have been such a merry party, all coming home with handsome officers."

"I thank you for my part," responded Elizabeth, her voice laced with derision. "But I believe I must decline, as I do not particularly like your way of finding a husband. I am certain that if I wanted to marry in such a way, any man would do. All I would have to do would be to throw myself on him in a most improper manner and steal away in the dead of night without telling anyone. I daresay my father and uncle would then have to come and *persuade* my paramour to marry me. Is that not what you have done to secure your husband?"

Lydia halted and turned to peer at Elizabeth intently, a fierce glower on her face—even Lydia could not be so ignorant as to miss the insult in her sister's words. To Elizabeth's side, Jane looked on, open-mouthed in surprise that her closest sister would speak to her youngest in such a manner, while Kitty stared on in consternation. Elizabeth found she did not care—she was done coddling her stupid sister, who had not the wit to understand exactly what kind of man to whom she had pledged herself.

Lydia was silent for several moments in seeming disbelief—Elizabeth was certain she had never been spoken to in such a manner, what with her father's disinterest and her mother's penchant for indulging and spoiling her in almost everything. However, it was not long before a sly smile appeared on Lydia's face, and she sneered at Elizabeth in a most unpleasant manner. At that moment, Mr. Wickham cantered by on his horse, doffing his hat at the assembled sisters with an arrogant smirk affixed to his features—the smirk which had not disappeared the entire time the Wickhams had been at Longbourn. Elizabeth was struck by the similarity in their expressions—they appeared to be two peas in a pod, the way they flouted propriety and laughed at others with more sense and manners.

"Why, Lizzy," said Lydia with a laugh, "I do believe you are envious of me."

"Envious?" responded Elizabeth with a snort of derision. "Of you? Whatever caused that silly notion to enter your head?"

"Was my Wicky not once a favorite of yours? Yes, I believe you envy me, dear Lizzy, for snapping up the man you wanted. Come, sister, you need not feel that way—after all, I think *I* am a better match for him than *you* would ever be. You should concentrate on finding your own husband now rather than pining away for mine."

Elizabeth stared at her brazen sister, shocked that the silly chit would ever voice such a thing in front of her sisters. Still, it was better than saying it in front of the servants—or worse yet, in front of their neighbors and acquaintances, something of which Elizabeth knew Lydia was entirely capable. And she was undoubtedly correct—Lydia *was* a better match for the scoundrel than Elizabeth could be. Silently, she said a prayer to the Lord on high, thanking him for the interference of Mr. Darcy and for his strength and fortitude in making her aware of Mr. Wickham's true character.

"You may as well remove that thought from your head. I assure you—whatever slight inclination I once felt toward your *husband* has dried up in light of his . . . other proclivities, of which I believe it is best to be silent. You are welcome to him, Lydia—I believe I should prefer a man who would court me in the light of day and ask my father for permission before whisking me off with nothing more than a letter to tell the story of my fate."

"Then you shall end an old maid and be forced to watch those of your sisters who were more successful in finding husbands."

"Better than being bound to such a man for the rest of my life," replied Elizabeth, forcing her tone to remain even.

"Why do you hate me, Lizzy?" asked Lydia, tears suddenly appearing in the corners of her eyes. "Is it because I married your favorite, or simply because I am married before you, even though I am younger?"

At that moment, Elizabeth was distracted as Wickham once again rode his stallion past the small group. But whereas he had been all charm and geniality before, now his eyes were hard as he peered at Elizabeth, no doubt wondering what had passed between the sisters.

Elizabeth was struck by a feeling of sudden loathing for this libertine of a brother-in-law, indignation filling her being for his very existence. He had lived a life of privilege and ease, one which he had not earned for himself but had been provided by a man who had loved him though he had not deserved such notice. That good and noble man had provided him opportunities which he had squandered—opportunities which would most certainly not have been extended for any reason other than the purest regard and affection. Even the familiarity in which he rode his horse could not have been obtained without his patron's generosity, something which he had trampled underfoot and wasted in pursuit of his baser instincts.

But Elizabeth had to admit to herself that though she was filled with indignation, she really could not take it out on her sister—Lydia had been spoiled and indulged all her life, and therefore part of the blame must be laid on her parents' shoulders. Elizabeth certainly did not want to part with Lydia in such acrimonious terms.

Feeling ashamed at her words and actions, Elizabeth stepped forward and engulfed her sister in an embrace, one which was returned with equal fervor. Lydia must truly be upset to respond in such a manner—they had never been the other's favorite sister and had found themselves at odds more often than not.

Speaking lowly so they would not be overheard, Elizabeth said, "I do not hate you, Liddy—indeed, I do not. I cannot lie and say I agree with this marriage you have entered into, but I do wish you the best in it. I simply hope and pray you will be happy with him, though I fear very much that you will not."

Lydia pulled back at this statement and peered into Elizabeth's eyes, a questioning expression on her face. But for Elizabeth, the heartache of the past weeks was too much to bear, and she was not about to elucidate to her sister the type of man Wickham truly was. Hopefully, her life would not be too hard, though Elizabeth held little hope for her future.

"I do wish you the best," she repeated, feeling tears gather in her own eyes. "I am sorry, but I feel a little fatigued. I shall return to the house and lie down before dinner."

She turned and walked away from her sisters, feeling Jane fall in beside her. A glance back showed Lydia watching them, her expression unreadable. Such thoughts could not hold Lydia's verbosity in check for long, however, and she soon shrugged and turned back to Kitty.

"I daresay I do not know what upset her, but it is of little matter. Come, Kitty, let me tell you of my wedding . . ."

It was later that afternoon, while Elizabeth was sitting alone in the little garden behind the house, reflecting on the conversation she had had with her sister, when her solitude was interrupted by a most unwelcome visitor.

"Sister," intoned a voice, startling her out of her reverie.

Elizabeth glanced up to see Wickham staring down at her with an expression of some seriousness, something which she could never remember ever seeing on his face before. She gazed back at him, noting his slightly dark look and the way he sized her up; being the object of his scrutiny caused Elizabeth to feel slightly uncomfortable.

She tilted her head to the side, waiting for him to speak—she would not initiate any conversation with him if she could help it.

"I was wondering if I could join you for a moment," said he, a hint of his old playfulness appearing yet again in his countenance and in his voice. "You and I have not spoken much since our arrival and I should very much like to continue our acquaintance."

Elizabeth gestured dismissively at the other side of the bench upon which she sat, not caring whether he stayed or left. "Indeed, I have no objection to you joining me, Mr. Wickham."

His artful and engaging smile once again stole over his face, and he sat, more toward the center of the bench and far closer to her than she would have liked. Elizabeth attempted to respond with a smile of her own as she waited for him to speak.

He was silent for several moments, and although Elizabeth felt he had something he wished to say to her, he appeared to be casting about for the best way to voice whatever was on his mind. She stayed resolutely silent.

"I understand from the Gardiners that you spent some time in Derbyshire and actually saw Pemberley while you were in the north."

Suspecting his motive to be the discussion of his grievances with the Darcys yet again, Elizabeth made no answer, merely acknowledging his comment with a nod of assent.

"Ah, it is a beautiful county, would you not agree?"

When Elizabeth allowed that it was, he continued, "And Pemberley is a jewel among estates. Indeed, I find myself missing its hills and valleys, the woods and the fields . . . But I suppose it is a vain hope to ever see the scenes of my youth again."

Elizabeth suspected he was attempting to sound poetic for whatever reason, but she was not about to be drawn into a discussion of the many injustices perpetrated against him by the Darcys—not since she knew the truth of his dealings with them.

"I suppose not, Mr. Wickham. After all, given your relationship with the current master of Pemberley, I should expect that even if you were in the area and in a position to view the estate, you would be denied admittance."

"True enough," Wickham responded, his tone dismissive. "But I should love to have my Lydia see it some day. After all, I did grow up there, and one does appreciate the opportunity to show loved ones the sights of their childhood. Would you not agree?"

"Indeed, I believe that would be very agreeable."

Again, he was silent for several moments, but his eyes were fixed upon her most disturbingly

"My dear sister, have I done something to offend you?" he suddenly asked, his eyes never leaving his face.

Elizabeth did not respond; she merely raised an eyebrow in his direction, wondering that he would have the audacity to ask such a question.

"You continue to call me 'Mr. Wickham,' though we are now brother and sister, and your very looks announce your reproach and unfriendliness. If I have done something to offend you, I would very much appreciate the opportunity to apologize and move beyond it."

Shaking her head at the man's impudence, Elizabeth looked away even as she began to speak. "Really, Mr. Wickham, you are either most brazen in your arrogance or utterly stupid in your lack of understanding. My sister might be blind to any improprieties, but I assure you I am not."

"But we are now married—is that not cause for celebration?"

The scathing expression she now directed at the man could not be mistaken any more than the scorn-laced words which issued from her mouth. "Celebration for you, perhaps, but not for us, I assure you. Why would we celebrate the fact that a snake has burrowed its way into our family to steal my uncle's money and ruin our family's reputation? I assure you, sir, your marriage is not cause for approbation."

"And I suppose the Darcys are the means of this changed attitude toward me," growled Wickham.

"You have stolen my young and impressionable sister, who is not yet sixteen, away from her family in the deepest night, hidden yourself away from her relations and only agreed to marry her once my uncle provided you with a pecuniary incentive. And this is not the first time you have attempted this. Trust me, *sir*; I am well able to see the impropriety of your actions without Mr. Darcy's assistance."

His returning smile was practically feral, but he surprised her by once again changing the subject. "I noticed earlier that my wife was upset due to some words she exchanged with you. Might I ask what you were discussing?"

"Would you have me relate every disagreement I have with any of my sisters, Mr. Wickham?" was her arch response. "You must allow us to keep *some* of our secrets."

"Perhaps, but now she is my wife and under my care. I would not have her importuned by any . . . unsubstantiated rumors which may disturb her peace of mind."

"In that case, sir, I can assure you that nothing which passed between my sister and I will disturb her peace of mind. I cannot vouch for her future peace of mind, you understand."

With that, Elizabeth stood and turned her back on him. However, she was unable to part from him without offering another barb in his direction. "Mr. Wickham, I would appreciate it if our future interactions could be confined to those necessitated by our mingling in the same company. I assume you do not wish to be subjected to my impertinent opinions, and I can assure you I have no desire to again be importuned by any stories of your misfortunes. It is time to leave well enough alone."

A sense of relief stole over Elizabeth as she walked away from him, content with their final conversation and determined to never repeat it. Still, until she turned the corner, the uncomfortable sensation of his eyes upon her back filled her with uneasiness.

Looking back on the conversations, Elizabeth had to admit she had been somewhat foolish to react the way she had to the pair, but she had been unable to help it. That evening, she had been called into her father's bookroom and cautioned against allowing her indignation to color her interactions with her new brother. A shocked Elizabeth had quickly realized that the bench upon which her little tête-à-tête with Wickham had occurred was situated directly below her father's bookroom, and as the window had been open at the time, her father had heard the entire exchange. He confided in her that he had almost intervened a number of times, concerned as he was for Elizabeth's safety and uncertain as he was concerning how Wickham would respond to her open disdain.

The rest of the visit had passed far too slowly for Elizabeth's taste, and although she had paid as much attention to her silly sister as she was able, she had confined her comments to the husband to what was passing in the room at the time while ensuring she was never in a position to be alone in his company. He had never importuned her again, although she had at times felt his gaze upon her. The entire family, outside of her mother, was vastly relieved when the Wickhams finally quit the place and proceeded to Newcastle to join his new regiment.

Elizabeth shuddered and turned her musings on the "happy couple" away, content as she was due to their departure. Of course, thoughts of Mr. Wickham automatically engendered thoughts of the third young man who had turned their world upside-down, although her feelings regarding *him* were by no means as decided as those toward her new brother. It was ironic, considering her early interactions with both young men. But regardless of the fact that she would have gladly avoided thinking about him indefinitely, her mind had other ideas, and she found herself falling into the memories and thoughts of Mr. Darcy of Derbyshire.

Simply put, Elizabeth's feelings for him were in upheaval. She had at last realized what an honor it had been for such a man to single her out the previous year in Hertfordshire and later during his proposal to her in Kent. He was a man of much social prominence, sought after by the highest levels of society, not only because of his riches and availability in the marriage market, but also due to his understanding and liberality, his knowledge of estate affairs, and his ability to offer advice, as he had so ably done with Mr. Bingley. She wondered that she had never seen it before, but knowing their early interactions—and specifically his slight of her the night of their first acquaintance—it was perhaps unsurprising that she had been unwilling to accept any knowledge of his good character. She understood now that her initial resentment had been largely unfounded and that a lifetime of hearing constant comparisons between Jane's beauty and her own lack thereof had found their target that night. She had long thought her indifference toward such unkind comments to be able to withstand any such attacks, yet her vanity and pride had taken that one admittedly unkind phrase and had formed a barrier between them which had prevented her from acknowledging any good thing about the young man.

Then Wickham had of course spewed his evil lies and slander, finding fertile ground in her already offended sensibilities and causing the barrier between them to grow until it was almost its own physical entity. How she wished now she had been more temperate in her thoughts and allowed herself the ability to see him in another light.

Thus it was that even at this late date, Elizabeth did not understand her own feelings for Darcy. The time they had spent in one another's company and their interactions while she had visited Derbyshire had led her to believe they could build a different kind of relationship than had existed in the past. She felt that they were both beginning to see past their previous thoughts and actions to understand who the other truly was.

But that had been severed by Lydia's ill-judged actions, and she had been forced to flee his presence, but not until after the humiliation of knowing his thoughts and opinions of her family were entirely founded in fact. She almost wished he had not come upon her as he had, that he had never discovered the particulars of Lydia's infamous elopement, and that he could have continued in his high opinion of her. It had been obvious after their short time together in Derbyshire that his high opinion of her had persisted despite all that had occurred between them.

And yet what would have happened if they had continued as they had been? What if he had still held tender feelings for her, and then he had proposed and married her, only to find out that his new brother-in-law was now the nefarious devil from his childhood . . . that he now had a close connection to the man he rightly despised and wished to never again lay eyes upon? How would he then react?

Elizabeth was certain she knew—their marriage would be over at that point, for although they would had no choice but to continue to be joined in the eyes of the law, there was no possibility he would continue to respect and love her after such an acute betrayal.

No, it was better this way—better that his opinion of her family was confirmed before he was connected to them for the rest of his life. Now that she had come to respect him, she could only wish him joy in his future life, though it could no longer include her. She knew this to be true but wished she could have somehow kept his good opinion in spite of it.

All this left Elizabeth feeling unsettled. She did not know she wanted Mr. Darcy to be anything more than he was now to her—her feelings for him were so unsettled as to defy all attempts at sorting them out.

What she did know was that her own situation was about to become even murkier and that she was not certain how to proceed. As much as she loved her father and enjoyed the time she spent with him, Jane had always been the rock in her life—the one in the family in whom she could fully confide and lean upon. That rock was about to be removed, and she did not know how she would react to the event.

Should she stay at Longbourn? How would her relationship with her mother change? Elizabeth was not certain she could bear Longbourn without Jane's constant calming presence to check her mother's ways. Would Mrs. Bennet turn her attention on Elizabeth as her next project in the marriage market, or would she let the matter go, complaining all the while about Elizabeth's unmarriageable wildness?

Living with Jane was out of the question. Though she was certain Jane and Bingley would take her in without a moment's hesitation, the thought of intruding upon the home of the newly married couple was not palatable in the slightest.

Equally unpalatable was the thought of staying with her aunt and uncle in London. Again, they would be happy to allow her to stay with them, but she knew her uncle had his own family to raise, and the thought of living with them seemed more and more like an imposition, unless of course she assisted them by acting as a governess to the children, which she knew she could not do, as her uncle would then insist upon paying her. She would not accept both board as well as payment from them, of that she was certain.

Thus, she was left with only the path of finding a partner in life or finding work as a governess or a lady's companion—those were the only options available to a young woman of gentle birth. Elizabeth was aware of her situation and had long wondered if she was even marriageable at all—she was not beautiful or possessed of a sweet disposition as Jane was. Were her own limited charms of beauty enough of a replacement for the more worldly charms that most highborn women possessed? Were they enough to entice a young man to offer for her in spite of her lack of dowry and connections? Recent history aside, common sense suggested they were not.

Perhaps she had been wrong in dismissing out of hand the two proposals she had received. Perhaps she should have maintained more of Charlotte's philosophy and accepted one of them, knowing that Mr. Collins' inelegantly voiced words were no more than the truth—she *was* unlikely to receive many eligible offers of marriage. Perhaps she *had* been wrong.

Yet it was not in her to behave in such a manner. Prudence was all well and good, but Elizabeth could not imagine a worse fate than that of her parents'. If a marriage to a young man whom she respected and loved could not be obtained, then it would be better for her to live out her days as an old maid, looking after children who were not her own, rather than end up tied to a man such as William Collins. She was not Charlotte.

Sighing, Elizabeth rose from her makeshift seat and took her old shawl, shaking the dust from it, before starting back down the path to her home. She had indulged in her thoughts for long enough—soon, it would be time to attend church. Her future, whatever it was to be, would take care of itself, and she did not need to decide on anything that moment.

As she walked, Elizabeth forced herself out of her gloomy thoughts and gazed about in appreciation, allowing her love of her home to carry her away to better contemplations.

Later that same afternoon, a carriage was seen to be entering the village of Meryton. It was a handsome vehicle pulled by a team of dark brown carriage horses, and it was clearly the property of someone of affluence. The dark cherry wood was polished until it gleamed in the bright sunlight, the springs were well-oiled and maintained, and the family crest emblazoned on the back was intricate and imposing—and known to the people of the small country village. It appeared Mr. Darcy had returned to Meryton.

However, if the good people of Meryton could have looked inside the dim confines of the mostly shaded windows, they would have seen a far different scene than the one they would have imagined. For although it was true the coach belonged to Mr. Darcy of Hertfordshire, he was not the occupant. At that very moment, Mr. Darcy was engaged in activities which were anything but as tranquil as merely riding in a carriage through a country village.

As for how the coach came to be travelling through the small town of Meryton, it had all transpired the previous evening. Having sent a response by express to Charles Bingley indicating his willingness to attend his friend as soon as his business had been completed, Darcy, the very next morning, received a response himself thanking him for his letter and requesting a small favor. It seemed the Bingley carriage had developed a minor fault on the journey into Hertfordshire and was even now being repaired in Meryton after a delay of some days. While this was not of consequence to Bingley due to his fondness for his horses, it was a rather large imposition to his sister, who was scheduled to join him that very morning. The Bingley coach would be ready by Monday or Tuesday at the latest, but as Bingley was to entertain his friend later in the week, he was concerned about his sister arriving and not having time to prepare for the arrival of her brother's guest.

Darcy could have cheerfully done without Miss Bingley's presence in Hertfordshire altogether, yet he knew his friend needed a proper hostess, and as he was not yet married, Bingley's older sister was the closest thing he had until the marriage actually took place. So long as he was not required to actually travel in the coach with the young huntress, Darcy was not put out by the request in the slightest. After all, he had several carriages, and the inconvenience of having one of them occupied for the day was truly negligible. Besides, the exercise would not hurt his team of horses. It was by no means certain they would have been out that day, and their enforced confinement over the past ten days meant a day's travel would do them a world of good.

So after sending a reply back to Bingley by the same method, Darcy instructed the driver of his carriage, along with the appropriate footmen, to proceed to the Bingley townhouse, convey Miss Bingley to Hertfordshire, and then return. After his friend's request was fulfilled, he thought no more of the matter—greater events were afoot which would occupy his attention for the remainder of the day and, indeed, for most of the rest of the week.

Of course, the young lady he had just assisted had no such means of occupation and spent the entirety of the journey brooding over the fact that the owner of the carriage had not accompanied her on her journey, cursing the stupidity of her brother and his weakness for a pretty face, and lamenting the fact that she was returning to Netherfield, perhaps the one place on the face of the earth which she had the least desire to ever visit again. Her maid said nothing the entire way, aware of her mistress' moods as she was and understanding Miss Bingley was not one for pleasant conversation with a servant in general—in Miss Bingley's present mood, she knew that to interrupt her mistress was to invite mistreatment.

And Caroline did brood, trying to understand how her careful plans and manipulations had gone so awry. A mere two months previous, she had been in an unusual level of excitement, anticipating her visit to Pemberley, the one place on earth she truly coveted, and secure in the knowledge she had separated her brother from the clutches of his latest infatuation. Surely seeing her at Pemberley would spur the man to finally end her waiting and offer to make her the mistress of the great estate, she had thought. How could it have gone any other way?

But it had all unraveled so quickly—mere moments after their arrival, in fact. Learning that Elizabeth Bennet, the despised sister of the upstart her brother was set to marry, was in Lambton had filled her with rage. She was certain the little minx had purposely set herself in the way of *Caroline's* Mr. Darcy for the express purpose of trying to entrap him into marriage. Miss Eliza was obviously required to resort to such stratagems, as she was unable to tempt *any* man due to her lack of dowry and deficiency of accomplishments. But of course, Caroline was unable to say anything, unable to refuse admission to the house which was to be *her* home— not until she became mistress of it in fact. Once that was accomplished, the woman who fancied herself a rival would be banned from Pemberley forever.

Unfortunately, one avenue to greater consequence and social standing had been removed. Her brother had been destined to marry an heiress, someone who was of the highest circles, someone who could pave the way for her family's entrance into that high society Caroline had craved all her life. She had chosen Georgiana Darcy as her brother's future wife, in part due to her reasoning that one marriage in the family might facilitate another, and in part because they were already on intimate terms with the family. That Georgiana was a mousey little thing, easily dominated, was nothing more than an additional benefit. However, it was always understood by Caroline that it did not have to be Georgiana—anyone would do, as long as she possessed the proper connections, dowry, and standing in society. This would in turn make Caroline more marriageable to Darcy and bring her closer to the prize she had sought since learning of her brother's fortunate friendship with the man.

Caroline was not stupid—she was well aware of the opinions of those around her and understood that some considered her delusional to have set her sights so high. Pemberley was not in need of a cash infusion, which complicated matters, and the highest to whom a tradesman's daughter such as herself could normally aspire was some young landowner of the middle circles, someone who needed her dowry much more than he needed her connections. A marriage by her brother to someone of the first circles such as Georgiana Darcy would bring Caroline the much-needed connections which would make an alliance with her that much more enticing.

And now such hopes were dashed by this imprudent match with which her brother had saddled himself. His marriage rendered the accomplishment of *her* goals much more difficult.

In truth, Caroline was well aware of the fact that if she was to consider Jane Bennet alone, the match was quite eligible indeed. Charles, after all, was the son of a tradesman, with the stench of new money firmly attached to his fortune. While Mr. Bennet was not the proprietor of a large estate or possessed of a title, he *was* a gentleman, and as such, his daughter, on a purely societal scale, was above Charles—it was a marriage acceptable to many because of her status and his money.

Yet to Caroline, it was a serious blow to all her plans and schemes. Even discounting the hopes she had entertained for her brother's future partner in life, Jane Bennet's relations—one uncle in trade and the other a country attorney— brought the specter of trade, the origins she had tried her whole life to escape, more firmly into the consciousness of those of society whom she most desperately wanted to impress. If only Jane Bennet's uncles had been gentlemen themselves, then Caroline could forgive, if not accept, her brother's most imprudent match.

But it was all too late. The engagement had been finalized, not only by Jane's acceptance of her brother's suit, but also by the announcement Charles had been quick to place in the London society papers. Caroline was well aware of the social consequences of a broken engagement. No, the only path available to her was to smile pleasantly and act as if she were delighted with the match. She had no doubt she would be able to convince these savages of her sincerity, although those important players—such as Jane Bennet and some members of her loathsome family—would not be drawn in. Too much had passed for that to happen, and Caroline's pointed severing of her acquaintance with Jane Bennet the previous spring could not be misunderstood. Still, Jane was of such a sweet and temperate disposition that as long as Caroline maintained the appearance of civility, she was sure Jane would accept the gesture as such and return the favor.

Privately, the thought of having to move aside for the little country miss who possessed no accomplishments and who would undoubtedly fail when confronted with the responsibility of acting as mistress to her brother's home was a bitter pill to swallow, but it also promised future amusement at the expense of her future sister. How Caroline would laugh when her brother came to her, bemoaning the fact that his little wife could not manage his home. She hoped that by then Mr. Darcy would have come to his senses, and she would be ensconced in Pemberley, running a household which was double the consequence of her brother's. Mrs. Bennet was proof of Jane's unsuitability—Caroline was certain her mother could have taught Jane nothing of what she would need to know.

Yet in the back of her mind, a little niggling concern had been worrying its way through her consciousness. Caroline *knew* her abilities and accomplishments were substantial and perfectly suited to the running of Mr. Darcy's vast home—she had spent countless hours bettering herself, determining the man's likes and dislikes, molding herself into the perfect partner for his life. But though she had done all of this, Darcy still dithered and delayed when he should have been securing her hand. Caroline did not know what to do to make herself more desirable.

And even more than that, a part of her whispered in the back of her consciousness that what she had seen between Darcy and that chit Eliza Bennet while at Pemberley that summer boded very ill indeed for her future ambitions. The disgusting manner in which the chit had thrown herself at Darcy at every opportunity, the way in which she had forced her acquaintance on poor Georgiana—it all bespoke her desperation to cheat Caroline of her rightful place.

She tried to tell herself that Darcy had merely tolerated the presence of an acquaintance—that he had behaved properly, with civility and decorum. Yet part of her remembered the looks they had exchanged, the words they had spoken, the way they had almost seemed to communicate *without* words. And the way Darcy had flung his words of admiration back at Caroline the night Eliza and her loathsome relations had dined at Pemberley, saying that *she* was among the handsomest women of his acquaintance . . . It had been all a mortified Caroline could do not to gag at the thought that the little country miss could possibly outshine Caroline Bingley.

And then Miss Eliza had left Derbyshire in haste, canceling an invitation in the process. Caroline had neither known nor cared what had caused her abrupt departure, but at the time it had seemed a godsend. Now, she had thought with glee, she would have Darcy and his sister all to herself without the interference of the scheming Eliza Bennet — she could not fail to capture him!

But then, another disaster had befallen — the man himself had departed, citing some urgent business which had suddenly come up. Caroline, although she had graciously offered to remain at Pemberley to provide companionship to Georgiana during Darcy's absence, had nevertheless been bundled off to stay with her relations in Scarborough, banished as if she were some indifferent acquaintance. It was not to be borne!

The truth which Caroline was loath to admit even to herself was that she was afraid — deeply afraid. She could not imagine what the Bennet chit could offer a man like Darcy, but she feared the girl had managed to accomplish what Caroline herself had not. Deep within her, Caroline was afraid that Miss Eliza Bennet was at the center of whatever had prompted Darcy to depart in such haste, and if she was, then the game might already be up.

It was with these musings that Caroline passed a most exhausting journey, her mind running over and over her fears, hopes, and dreams.

But as all things must come to an end, so too did Caroline's journey. The horses pulled up to Netherfield, and Caroline alighted from the carriage, assisted by her brother.

"Caroline," stated Bingley, his voice emotionless and distant.

Hurriedly greeting him, she climbed the stairs into the manor, immediately pleading fatigue and a need to rest and refresh herself before dinner. At this point, her ruminations had drained her, and she could not take the trouble to find out what had happened to her normally cheerful and ebullient brother — there would be time for that later. And knowing that the engagement could not be undone now, Caroline was determined to present the best front to those with whom she would prefer never to meet again. The world would never say that Caroline Bingley was anything but a proper, perfect hostess!

That evening, Caroline entered the dining room, pleased to find that it was only the two of them for dinner, as it would take time for her to prepare herself for the upcoming ordeal.

The two had just begun on their soup when Charles turned to her and began to make small conversation.

"I hope your journey was not too tiring, Caroline. It is good to see you again."

"Mr. Darcy's carriage was wonderful, Charles, but the expedition was a little draining. I will be very happy to seek my bed tonight."

Charles nodded his head in commiseration before turning back to his meal. "I hope you recover quickly, dear sister — I would like to begin again to fulfill my societal obligations immediately."

"Charles, I have only just arrived. I would appreciate a few days to recuperate."

"And you shall have them."

"When will Mr. Darcy arrive?"

The question was voiced in as calm and nonchalant a manner as Caroline was able, but she still felt the weight of her brother's gaze on her. Regardless, it was of no concern — she suspected Charles was aware of her ambitions toward his friend, but he was so easily led that she feared no intrusion from him.

"His original letter said he would arrive on Tuesday, but it appears that something has come up since then. I still expect him some time this week. Exactly when remains unclear. In the meantime, I have accepted an invitation for an evening with the Lucases for Tuesday, where we shall be in the company of many of the prominent families in the neighborhood."

Caroline almost snorted at the thought that there were any *prominent* families in this desolate hole, but she held herself in check, aware that it would not endear her to her brother. "Really, Charles, could we not put it off until I have had time to recover?"

His lips set in a disapproving line, Charles' response was stern. "Caroline, I do not intend to slight our neighbors—people who will be my neighbors and associates for the foreseeable future. I know of your distaste for the society in Meryton, but I hope you will curb your dissatisfaction and perform your duties without rancor. I will be married shortly; then my dear Jane will free you from the responsibility—surely you can accommodate me until that time."

"I assure you, Charles, I have no intention of performing my duties with anything other than the utmost in propriety and devotion."

"Very well," was his only reply.

The ensuing conversation was stilted and desultory, but Caroline did not mind at all—her brother was not the most titillating conversationalist, and after a draining journey, she wanted nothing more than to retire to her room and prepare herself for the realization of her dreams.

But Caroline had decided one thing throughout the course of that long and dreadful day—the game was not over. Caroline promised to herself that whatever it took, she would not be bested by the likes of Eliza Bennet. She would continue to fight for what was rightfully hers and emerge victorious. There was no other option, no other possible outcome.

Caroline determined to do whatever it took to ensure that no matter what happened, she would not allow Eliza to marry Darcy herself. Whether Caroline was successful or not, the thought of being bested by the little adventuress was more than she could bear.

Chapter III

*L*ord Henry Fitzwilliam, the fifteenth Earl of Matlock, was somewhat of an oddity among the British nobility.

The second son of the previous earl, Henry, as a young lad, had never expected to inherit his father's position, and being a pragmatic young man, he had planned out his life to suit his own needs rather than those of society. His own needs in no way included the running of the large family estate, nor did they include the pressures and privileges of being a member of the peerage; instead, they centered around finding a good woman with whom to share his life, tending to the small estate which his father had set aside for his eventual inheritance, and indulging in his own love of books and scholarly pursuits. Thus, when his older brother had died after being thrown from his horse, Henry—then but two and twenty years of age—although resigned to the fact that he now had no choice but to assume his position as his father's heir, resolved to face his future on his own terms.

On his grand tour of the continent when news of his brother's passing reached him, Henry immediately set off for home and immersed himself in his new role, gleaning everything he could from his father regarding the running of the estate and his duties in the House of Lords. Yet though he had been trained for the running of an estate—he *was* after all, the son of an earl, and he had been reared at his father's knee—the running of the small family estate for which he had been prepared was a completely different matter from the running of Highfield Hall, his family's ancestral home. Regardless, he took to his new life as if he had been born to it. And though the political aspect of his new position was one for which he had never been prepared, he quickly discovered he had some natural talent for that as well.

However, although he had taken up the position with little or no concern, his father had had much less success in changing his son's views, which were, to be blunt, somewhat radical to someone of strict moral and noble upbringing. Henry's older brother had in truth been precise and proper (or a stick in the mud, as Henry preferred to refer to him), but Henry had never felt much of a desire to be so himself. He was not improper, but many of his viewpoints, if examined strictly from a traditional point of view, could be considered to be so.

One of the many things about which he disagreed with not only his father but also most of the family was the proper attributes which must be considered in the choice of a bride. His mother and father had paraded him through season after season in London, hoping he would choose a bride from amongst the highest of society. Surely a future earl could have his choice of eligible young women from any family of the same social level—or perhaps even aspire to the daughter of a duke! In so doing, he would secure the demands of dowry, gentility, and status, while also providing heirs which would carry on the family name.

Henry, though, had different ideals. Dowry and status were all well and good, but they would not provide the companionship which Henry felt was the main reason for entering into the marriage state. It did not take long for the beautiful and well-dowered yet insipid and annoying heiresses of London to completely bore the young heir, and all of his parents' efforts went for naught.

It was not until his six and twentieth year that Henry, already largely running the estate in his father's stead (his father having married late and already approaching his seventieth year), by chance attended an event in London—where he did not normally venture—and met the woman for whom he was certain he had been waiting.

Miss Constance Farrington was a proper, genteel, and attractive young lady, and she would be considered a most eligible match for most on the marriage market—after all, her father was a man of some means, being the landowner of a large estate in Northamptonshire, with an income of more than 7,000 pounds per annum. That—along with the fact that as her father's only child, she was also his sole heir—meant that she was much sought after by many members of society, particularly those younger brothers without estates of their own looking to elevate themselves to the rank of landed gentlemen. All of these things were highly in Constance's favor.

What was not in her favor was the fact that her father, although a gentleman, had no title to his name, no relations closer than second cousins, and no worthwhile connections to bring to his daughter's marriage. Beyond this, the reason he owned the estate at all was because his great-grandfather had built up a family business to the point that his son was able to sell it and purchase the estate as well as some of the land surrounding it with the proceeds, thereby creating the current property. Thus, the stench of trade was far too strong in the opinion of those to whom such things mattered.

Henry, however, was not one of those people. Upon meeting in the ballroom, he and Constance had immediately detected a kindred soul in one another, and not heeding what he knew others would say of the match, Henry had immediately set out to pursue her to the exclusion of all others. Henry's father had been livid, berating his son, reminding him of his duty to marry not only to increase his family's fortune and standing but also to increase their political power through connections to others of high society. And while most of his family had joined in the chorus, they were eventually forced to yield, as Henry would not be dissuaded—he had led Constance to the altar less than nine months after their first meeting.

His nephew, Fitzwilliam Darcy, knew all this about his uncle. Henry Fitzwilliam was a man of convictions and beliefs, but unlike his sister Catherine, he was by no means overbearing and did not impose his opinions on those around him. He *was*, however, rather loquacious when prompted to share his story and convictions with his young relations. Thus, Darcy had been encouraged to follow his own heart when asking for his uncle's advice but warned not to discount the advice of his father. And though George Darcy would not have counseled his son to completely ignore the demands of society for the contents of his heart, still, his views were much more aligned with those of his uncle than that of most of his peers. He too had made a love match with Anne Fitzwilliam, much to the delight of her brother.

Since the debacle of his proposal the previous April, Darcy had had cause more than once to lament the lost and forgotten lessons of his youth. He could not remember exactly how it had come about, but somewhere in the five years since the death of his father, he had left the advice and teachings received at his father's and uncle's knees behind. He had become puffed up in his pride in his position, family name, and fortune, and he had somehow forgotten that there was more to life than the trappings so frequently sought out by the highest of society. He had no doubt he could have avoided the mistakes which had led to that fateful evening in Kent if he had only remembered the ideals by which he had been raised. Then he would not find himself beset by this uncertainty and might already find himself married to the woman who had stolen his heart.

Still, such thoughts were not conducive to the serene state of mind which he knew he would need as he confronted the lioness in her den. Or in his uncle's den, to be more precise.

A slight smile lit up his face as the carriage rolled to a stop outside Lord Matlock's London townhouse—whatever his aunt was, she was most certainly not bereft of audacity. But in light of the thoughts which had just been running through Darcy's mind of his uncle's character and convictions, which had never been in any doubt, Darcy wondered if she had taken leave of her senses. She had been one of the most outspoken and vitriolic dissenters against Matlock's marriage, and he had ignored her—how could she possibly expect he would support her in the same matter regarding his nephew? Darcy shook his head.

This, however, would be the end. He would tolerate no further meddling in his affairs, a truth of which he intended to make abundantly clear. He would sever all ties with her, if necessary, to get her attention.

As he exited the carriage, he glanced up at the house to see his cousin the colonel standing outside the door, a smirk already plastered on his features. Darcy nearly groaned out loud—the last thing he needed was his overly teasing cousin to make sport with him over their aunt's ridiculousness.

"Cousin, you have certainly stirred up a hornet's nest!" greeted Richard, undoubtedly intending to be droll.

Darcy scowled at his cousin, who, seeing the reaction he had engendered, smiled even more broadly, if that was even possible.

"Richard, I hardly see how this can be an occasion for jokes and witty repartee."

"*That* is because you are always too ready to see the worst in a situation. Come, Darcy—let loose your hidden lighter side. Indulge in a sense of morbid fascination and amusement in the wonder of overbearing impropriety that is our aunt. At times like this, one can only remember the sage words: 'You cannot choose your relations.' It is the truth, is it not?"

"I am certain you cannot," replied Darcy with a wry grin, grateful in spite of himself for Richard's ability to relieve the tension of almost any situation. "For if we were able, I am certain Lady Catherine would *not* have been chosen—by any of us."

"That is the spirit, old man!"

Richard led him inside, but rather than carry on into the main inhabited part of the house, he deflected them toward a small anteroom near the entrance. Slapping Darcy on the back in good-natured affection, he immediately walked to the small side table and poured them each a goodly measure of brandy and then handed one to his cousin while sipping his own.

"Brandy so early in the day, cousin?" asked Darcy, raising an eyebrow.

"If you had had to put up with Lady Catherine's shrill voice all morning, you would have taken to drink as well."

Laughing, Darcy lifted his glass in salute and swallowed a measure of the amber liquid.

"Spare me not, cousin—what has she been saying?"

"Oh, come now, Darcy. Surely you can imagine it yourself. In between rants about the recalcitrance and lack of respect afflicting the younger generation, she has waxed long and eloquent about you in particular, me for supporting you, my father for marrying below himself, my mother for being the daughter of a mere country gentleman with ties to trade, and the world for not standing up and ensuring that everything she desires is done with alacrity. Of course, she has not neglected to regale us all with tales about her agreement with your mother that you should marry her daughter, about how splendidly the two of you would do together, and about how your 'little minx' has drawn you in and made you forget your duty. And if she had had the time in between all these disparate tirades, I'm certain she would have rebuked me for not yet defeating Napoleon—or perhaps she has not worked her way up to that particular complaint."

Trust his overly clever and flippant cousin to put the situation in the most humorous of manners. Regardless, Darcy found himself vastly amused at the way his aunt was portrayed. It was *much less* than she deserved, he was certain.

"And what of Anne? How is she dealing with the harridan?"

"Anne retired to her bedchambers as soon as they arrived and has not been seen since. She has refused to see anyone other than my mother and Georgiana, which is another thing that has Aunt Catherine fit to be tied. Still, my father has put down his foot and forbidden Lady Catherine from forcing her way into Anne's room. You know how she takes being forbidden *anything*.

"I must say, cousin, I expected Lady Catherine's rage to become almost incandescent when you finally put your foot down regarding the matter of your future partner in life, but she has outdone herself. And I cannot begin to tell you how shocked I was to discover it was our lovely friend from Hertfordshire who had captured you and denied our aunt the fulfillment of her fondest dream. Do you care to elaborate on what has happened between you and the pretty Miss Elizabeth Bennet?"

Darcy groaned, wishing to put up with almost anything other than his cousin's teasing about Elizabeth — the wounds were still too raw, the situation too unsettled and uncertain for that.

"And what of your father?" responded Darcy, ignoring the question for the moment.

"Father is as he ever was, although he is quite curious about Miss Bennet in his own right," replied the colonel, refusing to be put off. "He asked to see you as soon as you had arrived.

"In fact, I think I must insist you do so, Darcy," he continued with a grin. "It would not do to keep an earl waiting, after all."

"In a moment, Richard," said Darcy, brushing him off. "First, I would like to have a brief conversation with Anne. She is as much at the center of this firestorm as I or Miss Bennet, and I would hear her opinion before we proceed."

He met Richard's piercing stare with an implacable one of his own, finally forcing his cousin to shrug his shoulders in apparent unconcern. "Very well then, Darcy. I shall stall father while you visit Anne. But we shall have a full accounting of your relationship with your lady."

"Of course, Richard — you shall have it. But I would prefer to avoid having to repeat myself in this matter — I shall tell you both at once, so you may have your curiosity sated in the matter of my personal life."

"Excellent!" agreed the colonel with a grin on his face. "I suggest you take the back stairs up to Anne's room — less chance of meeting the harridan that way, you know."

Thanking his cousin for the advice, Darcy made his way to Anne's room as Richard had recommended, taking the stairs two at a time. He was not precisely concerned over Anne's reaction — they had agreed on this matter more than ten years earlier, and not once had either of them wavered in their determination — but he *was* worried over Anne's condition. He was also hopeful her mother's histrionics had not made her finally capitulate due to a desire to finally silence the woman. Her refusal to see Lady Catherine was an indication that all was still right with their pact, but he wanted to confirm it for himself. Given his hopes for his future with Elizabeth, the last thing he needed was to have Anne pressure him into submitting to her mother's schemes.

Darcy knocked at the door to her usual suite somewhat diffidently, still not confident in the reception he was to receive. When the maid opened the door, he announced himself, requesting to speak to Anne, and he was immediately admitted when the sound of his cousin's voice forestalled the maid's response.

Anne was seated on a settee by the fireplace, and although her face was her normal pale shade, the hint of a rosy color in her cheeks and the playful smile upon her face told him all he needed to know about her state of mind. She was amused! Whether it was due to her mother, his predicament, or the state of his heretofore secret relationship with the very eligible Miss Bennet, he was not certain, but his fears of her relenting to her mother's fuming were immediately put to rest by her countenance.

"Come in, cousin," beckoned she.

Somewhat sheepishly, Darcy entered the room, and responding unconsciously to her grin, he seated himself and looked on her, noting that she appeared remarkably well considering what she had had to endure over the past several days.

"Well, was it everything you imagined?"

"Your mother's reaction?"

At Anne's nod, he laughed and continued, "I don't think any of our speculations or flights of fancy could have possibly prepared us for the realization of your mother's wrath. I must confess I cannot think of another person who could have continued on in such a vein and without any rest for this length of time. You mother is certainly a marvel."

"Agreed, cousin!" responded Anne with a laugh. "Yesterday when she left your house and rejoined me in the carriage, her face was a most peculiar shade of red. I declare I thought she would suffer apoplexy right in front of me in the carriage—I do not think I have ever witnessed such a thing in my entire life."

"Anne," said Darcy with a reproving tone, "she is your mother."

"Aye, she is, cousin. But that does not mean I am blind to her faults or that I cannot find her antics amusing. I *do love* her, although she has rarely given me reason for my continued devotion."

Satisfied she was not suffering emotionally from her mother's behavior, Darcy peered closely at Anne, alert for any physical suffering. Her dainty size and frail constitution had made her entire family overly protective of her well-being, and although he knew it annoyed her at times, he was worried that the excitement and travel had had an adverse affect on her health.

Before he could voice his concerns, Anne, noticing his glances, sighed in exasperation and affixed him with a stern look.

"Do not stare at me so, Fitzwilliam," admonished she. "I am perfectly well."

"Are you?"

"A little tired, perhaps, but, yes, I am well. In fact, I think the excitement and exercise has done me a world of good—it is far better than being cooped up in that dreadfully depressing manor while my draconian mother limits my movements 'for my own good.'" This last was said in an imitation of Lady Catherine's voice which caused Darcy to chuckle at her irreverence and ability to effectively mimic her mother's condescending tones.

"No, Darcy, I am well and ready to assert my independence. I will not return to Rosings with my mother."

Darcy raised his eyebrow in surprise at such words of open rebellion, but she appeared unmoved.

"I should have done this long ago—you know it as well as I! But unfortunately, I could not be bothered to challenge her, nor did I have the strength to endure her displeasure. And now we come to this due to our unwillingness to put her to rights many years ago. No, I will not be moved on this—I think the best thing for us both is to distance ourselves from my mother for a time. She needs to get used to the fact that the world will not bow down to her and accede to her desires—let her do so in solitude."

"In that case, my dear cousin, I believe we will need to come up with alternate arrangements for your future residence," responded Darcy, a little bemused at his cousin's newfound assertiveness.

"Very well, then." Anne waved him from the room. "I understand our uncle wished to speak to you — you would do well not to keep him waiting."

Entering his uncle's inner sanctum, Darcy approached his relations, who were sharing another beverage while peering at him with almost identical smirks on their faces. Darcy almost sighed — having previously seen them wear that expression, he was well aware of the potential consequences of *both* of them sharing it. Sometimes, it was unnerving exactly how alike his uncle and cousin were. Richard was perhaps more cheeky and irreverent than Uncle Henry, but both were lively and playful — in short, nothing like Darcy himself. They made for truly pleasurable company, but at times, they became a little trying for the staid and serious Darcy.

"Come in, come in," his uncle boomed, motioning Darcy to a nearby chair with a negligent wave of his hand. "Let us gather around and plot our next move, like pirates stalking a fat merchant ship."

"We had best keep our perfidy to ourselves, father," Richard chimed in. "We do not want the fire-breathing dragon to know what we are up to, after all."

Taking a seat in front of his uncle's desk, Darcy shook his head. "I presume it would be a waste of energy to request that the two of you comport yourselves with the appropriate level of seriousness due the situation."

"Completely useless to suggest such a thing," murmured Richard while grinning at Darcy.

"Come, Darcy," admonished Uncle Henry, "the entire family has waited for this day with anticipation. Surely you do not mean to deprive us of the pleasure this august event imparts by forbidding our enjoyment."

"I would by no means suspend any pleasure of yours, uncle," said Darcy, remembering a time when he had spoken almost the same words to his love and cursing the tone and manner in which he had delivered them. "Is there anything I can do to further entertain you?"

The earl turned to his son. "See, I told you he could find humor in the situation."

"It's not the humor in the situation which eludes me," said Darcy. "I am merely concerned as to how we should respond."

"Oh, very well — I suppose we shall have to indulge you."

"But I had not finished," protested Richard, practically falling off his seat in his mirth. "I must take the full measure of my cousin, as I think I shall rarely have such an opportunity again!"

"Now, Richard," chastised the earl, "I believe Darcy is correct. Perhaps it is time to discuss this in a serious manner."

His eyes twinkled, and the corners of his mouth twitched upwards as he continued, "Much as I am loath to let this go . . ."

Darcy said nothing, letting the rolling of his eyes speak volumes as to his opinion of his relations' inability to remain serious.

"Well, then, Darcy," the earl eventually said, "what say you? We have heard my sister and her opinion of the matter — shall we not now hear your own?"

"I believe you know my opinion, Uncle. Have I not expressed my view regarding this delusion of Aunt Catherine's in excruciating detail? Anne and I are united in this — we will not allow her to impose her will upon us in this or any other matter. There is little more to be said."

"Very admirable, nephew, and I know of your determination with regard to her demands, but this is not of what I speak. Your aunt has bellowed loud and long of your . . . How did she refer to the lady, son?"

Richard grinned and took a sip of his drink. "I believe she referred to Miss Bennet as an 'impertinent country adventuress, intent upon entrapping a man far above her sphere.'"

"Yes, that is it," responded Matlock with a grin.

Apparently, the earl recognized the pinched look of displeasure Darcy knew adorned his face, as the man sighed and rose to his feet, retrieved the bottle of brandy, and after gathering another snifter, refilled his own drink and poured a substantial amount for his nephew.

"Fitzwilliam, I will not continue to sport with you—I apologize. It is merely difficult to be serious when confronted with such absurdities as my sister presents in abundance. We have all anticipated this day with a certain amount of dread, but when faced with the actuality of her displeasure, I find that she is so ridiculous as to defy all attempts to view her with any degree of seriousness."

Darcy nodded and drank a generous portion of his uncle's brandy, fortifying himself against the sudden urge to beat his aunt about the head with her own cane.

"As I was saying—your aunt has gone on and on about the young miss to whom you seem to have attached yourself, and since I know better than to take her account at face value, it is up to you to ensure I have a complete understanding of the situation.

"And I must confess, I am curious about this young lady and concerned about some of the things my sister has said. Is it true the young lady has no dowry and no connections of which to speak?"

Darcy was aghast. "Surely *you of all people* would not judge Miss Bennet in such a manner—you who married my aunt against the wishes of your father *and* my aunt, whom we discuss in so blithe a manner?"

"Of course not, Fitzwilliam," responded the earl. His voice was even, and his eyes focused on Darcy, indicating that he was approaching this conversation with sobriety completely at odds with his previous irreverence. "Richard has told me of your young lady, and she sounds like a lovely young woman. But in Constance's case, she at least had money of her own—I knew she was not a fortune hunter. I do have every confidence in your ability to identify and avoid entrapment from any young lady after nothing more than your fortune. Have you not fended off that fellow Bingley's sister all these years?"

A quiet chuckle met his declaration, and some of the tension in the room dissipated, as was almost certainly his intent. "Come, Darcy. I merely want to confirm for myself that your lady is worthy of this devotion you appear to hold for her."

"Would a fortune hunter refuse an offer of marriage?"

"Certainly not . . ." began the earl before his eyes widened and he stared back at Darcy, his expression incredulous. The colonel's expression mirrored his father's, as he had as yet not heard this news either.

"Surely she did not," Richard finally stated.

"I assure you she most certainly did," affirmed Darcy.

The earl appeared to be torn between amusement and disbelief. "Then you had best assuage our curiosity, nephew. This seems to be a most intriguing story, and one which I would very much like to hear."

"Then you shall, uncle."

Some time later, when Darcy had finished recounting the history of his acquaintance with Elizabeth Bennet, he sat back and observed the reaction of his relations to the tale. Even Richard, who had known part of it, was stunned by the twists and turns the relationship had taken, the entirety of which seemed worthy of recounting in a novel.

"Extraordinary!" Henry exclaimed at last. "A young woman with no fortune and connections refusing you, of all people!"

"She *is* quite a singular lady, father," interjected Richard. "I believe I must say I have never met her like."

Darcy peered at his cousin, wondering if there were more to his words than he had stated. However, the chagrin over his behavior to his beloved quickly overcame his thoughts of Richard, and he responded to his relations. "Quite properly, uncle. As I have said, my proposal to her was most insulting to the lady and all her family. She was quite within her rights to respond as she did."

The earl was still shaking his head in wonder. "Is she a simpleton? For a woman of no fortune or connections to refuse the offer of a gentleman such as yourself without even a by-your-leave . . . Have you fallen for someone of some mental deficiency?"

"Trust me, father, mentally deficient is not in any way descriptive of Miss Elizabeth," answered Richard. "A sharper young lady I have never had the good fortune to meet."

"Indeed? In that case, I must commend her for her sensibilities and convictions, even while I wonder at her lack of prudence—such a marriage proposal cannot come to one of her station every day, after all.

"I am afraid I still do not understand," continued the earl, leaning back in his chair with his brandy snifter in one hand. "You became acquainted with the young lady in Hertfordshire, followed her to Kent—"

"I did not *follow* her, uncle," Darcy exclaimed.

Lord Matlock waved him off. "Mere semantics, my boy. You *encountered* her in Kent," he continued with a teasing grin, "proposed to her, were rejected, met her again at Pemberley 'completely by chance,' left to apprehend her sister and that scoundrel Wickham, you paid the man off to marry her silly sister, and you have since seen her a handful of times."

Although Darcy was somewhat embarrassed to have his history with Elizabeth described so summarily, he allowed it to be so.

"What *I* don't understand, Darcy," interrupted the colonel with an implacable glare, "is why you didn't call me when you found Wickham. I would cheerfully pay the libertine back for what he did to Georgiana, and then you would not have had to bear the mortification and expense of paying him off. Surely we could have come up with some story of the girl's travels which would have satisfied the rumors."

"Cousin, you know how vicious the gossips can be. Arranging the marriage was the only way to ensure the family's reputation—I could not allow Miss Bennet to suffer when it was in my power to prevent it, especially when the illumination of Wickham's character to the right authorities would have prevented the elopement from ever taking place."

"Yes, yes," said the earl. "We fully understand and commend you for your honor and integrity, Darcy. I still do not understand why you would go to the trouble. After all, the lady had already refused you . . ."

He trailed off and peered at Darcy closely until a large grin suffused over his face, and he broke out into laughter.

"You still hope to persuade her to accept your suit!" he chortled.

"I do," stated Darcy seriously.

"Amazing! I am simply astonished that you would hold out hope that she would accept a second proposal from you. I am hardly able to account for it!"

Darcy was not to be dissuaded. "Uncle, much of what passed between us in the initial stages of our relationship was based on misunderstanding and outright falsehood. Her manner at Pemberley was so changed—I felt her opinion of me had improved once she knew the truth, and there was hope for a satisfactory ending. I maintain we are well suited for one another."

Standing, the earl walked around the desk and squeezed Darcy's shoulder in affection. "Well, then, if your devotion to this lady is so steady, the only thing I am left to wonder is when I might meet this wondrous creature."

Finally smiling in appreciation for his uncle's support, Darcy responded, "I will ensure a meeting as soon as I am able, uncle. Hopefully, the delay will not be of long duration."

"See that you do, nephew," said the earl with a laugh before returning to his chair. "I only hope she proves worthy of your unstinting dedication."

"Believe me, uncle," Darcy replied quietly, "Miss Elizabeth Bennet is worth all this and more."

"That she is," murmured the colonel, draining the last of the brandy from his glass.

Darcy was disturbed at his cousin's comment. Did Richard admire the lady as well?

"Be that as it may," his uncle interrupted his thoughts, "though we now have the why, we still do not have the how, specifically in regard to what to do with your aunt and your cousin. Your aunt has already expressed her displeasure for your attachment and refusal to marry Anne—we cannot leave Anne to suffer her displeasure alone."

"Agreed," stated Darcy. "I have just come from speaking with Anne, and she is adamant she will not return to Kent with Lady Catherine. Between the two of us, I believe we can come up with an alternative for her."

"Take her into our own homes?"

"Yes. Anne is close to Georgiana and gets along famously with Aunt Constance—she could stay with each of us in turn. This would get her out from under Aunt Catherine's thumb and give her a much better environment in which to live. Perhaps we can even employ a competent doctor to see if we can determine what ails her. Perhaps some time at Pemberley or Highfield would do her some good."

"Brilliant idea, Fitzwilliam! I should have thought of it myself."

"Cousin," interrupted the colonel once again, "I know you have spoken with Anne and she refuses to go back to Kent, but perhaps before you and my father map out the rest of her life, you should speak to her and ask her what *she* wishes rather than dictating *to* her how she will live her life."

"Very good advice, son," replied the earl. "Now if you two will excuse me, I must speak to my wife." His eyes twinkled as he leered at Darcy. "There are . . . *events* afoot which will entertain her as much as they have entertained me."

With that, he quit the room.

Sitting in companionable silence, Darcy and his cousin continued to sip their drinks while Darcy thought about his situation and brooded over the coming ordeal. But more than that, he was concerned about the colonel's comments concerning Elizabeth. He had wondered if Richard had liked Elizabeth in a more than friendly manner when they had been in Kent, but the failed proposal, the separation, and the events surrounding her younger sister had quite driven the matter from his mind. He stole a few glances at Richard, noting his quiet, introspective manner and distracted air—it was somewhat unusual for his generally more garrulous cousin.

"Richard, I would like to ask you about your comments regarding Miss Bennet," Darcy finally said, unwilling to bear the silence any longer.

"You need not concern yourself with me, Darcy," replied Richard with somewhat of a resigned sigh. "I admit that I was intrigued by her when we were in Kent—who would not be? But I have no designs on your young lady—I never did, although if my situation were different, then my reaction may have been very different as well. If I were so inclined to attempt the feat, I imagine it would be very easy to love her."

"Very easy, indeed."

"I suppose I should congratulate you, old man. She is a wonderful woman and particularly suited to you, I should think. Life will never be dull with her."

"That is assuming I can convince her to accept me," responded Darcy, feeling his morose mood of the past several months once again descending upon him.

"Therein lies the rub," agreed Richard in what Darcy considered an entirely inappropriate joviality. It appeared Richard's good humor had been restored, causing him to revert to his usual playful banter.

"Listen to me, cousin," he continued in a more sober tone, "my advice to you would be to simply be Fitzwilliam Darcy—it would behoove you to hide nothing from her. You have spent so much time since you inherited Pemberley concealing yourself behind your mask to protect yourself against the predators of society. I daresay she does not know the true Fitzwilliam Darcy, and if she is to eventually return your feelings, she must see the real you."

"I hope that our interactions in Derbyshire and Hertfordshire since that time have shown her the real me, but your advice is well-judged."

"Then that is all you can do," responded the colonel before he rose and slapped his cousin on the back. "I wish you the best of luck, cousin. She will be very good for you."

Draining his glass, Richard quit the room, leaving Darcy to his thoughts.

Dinner that evening at the Fitzwilliam London house was tense, with none of the usual banter and pleasantries which would be exchanged during a normal meal with Darcy's Fitzwilliam relations.

Lady Catherine kept a running monologue all throughout the meal, complaining about the younger generation's lack of propriety, Darcy's lack of respect and stubborn refusal in agreeing to the marriage which *his mother* had planned for him, Anne's own recalcitrance, and the world in general for not obliging her whims. Although the comments were not directed at anyone in particular, they were loud and obnoxious, disturbing the tranquility of the room and setting everyone else on edge.

His uncle, whom Darcy quickly determined seemed to have the patience of a saint, tried to quiet her, appealing to her sense of propriety and decorum, but Lady Catherine would have none of it, so caught up was she in her own disappointment and anger.

Having nothing else to do and lacking the possibility of any open conversation while his aunt ranted on, Darcy spent his time at dinner talking in a low voice with Anne and Georgiana, who were situated to either side of him.

Anne reaffirmed her determination to remain in London while her mother returned to Kent. Furthermore, she had surprised Darcy with a request to accompany him to Hertfordshire, citing his hope of persuading Elizabeth to respond positively to his addresses and telling him she wished to become better acquainted with his future wife. Since she did not doubt his powers of persuasion, as she cheekily informed him herself, she assumed Elizabeth would eventually capitulate and marry him, after which they would be much closer relations and would both benefit by a closer friendship.

For her part, Georgiana had also expressed an interest in joining him at Netherfield, with the express purpose of furthering her own acquaintance with the young lady. Eager for his sister to become better acquainted with the woman he hoped to make his bride, Darcy had immediately acquiesced and agreed to write Bingley, requesting an invitation for both Georgiana and Anne. The only reason to refuse the request was the presence of Wickham, which should already be alleviated—if their original schedule held firm, Darcy knew the Wickhams should already have departed for Newcastle. Georgiana was recovering nicely from her experience with the cad, but Darcy did not want to risk her recovery by allowing her to be in his company. That simply would not do.

Of course, no one had as of yet undertaken the responsibility of informing Lady Catherine of the fact that not only would her daughter not accompany her back to her home and into her sphere of control, but that said daughter would be visiting the detested young lady who had dared to catch the eye of her nephew. Darcy and Anne had determined that an already uncomfortable situation would quickly become unbearable if Lady Catherine were to be informed, so until the invitation was obtained from Bingley and their plans were settled upon, the secret would be kept from the irascible woman. Anne had even agreed to plead an inability to face the trip back to Rosings as an excuse for keeping them in town, and although Darcy despised the falsehood, in this case he agreed there was no reason to upset his aunt any further.

The only downside to the plan was the necessity of moving his departure to Netherfield back until all the arrangements could be made. He was distressed at the thought of having to leave Elizabeth to the wolves and gossip hounds of Hertfordshire society, but given Bingley's silence on the matter, he was somewhat mollified, hoping that the rumor had been contained, while at the same time disappointed that he could not use that as an avenue to secure her hand. Then again, that possibility was not a particularly palatable one as he well knew, having experienced with excruciating detail the sharpness of Elizabeth's tongue when she was truly displeased. The thought of leading her to the altar with anything less than her enthusiastic agreement was surely a short road to a long life of acrimony and discord.

Chapter IV

An evening at Lucas Lodge was by no means as agreeable a prospect after Charlotte's departure from Hertfordshire as it had been before.

It was at times like these when Elizabeth felt the absence of her friend most keenly. Lady Lucas was all that was polite and kind, if a little silly like Elizabeth's own mother; Maria was sweet and angelic; the other children were polite and well-behaved; and even Sir William, although likely to drone on about his presentation at St. James' court, was affable and eager to please his guests. But the inescapable fact was that they were not Charlotte.

Elizabeth's discontent stemmed more from the absence of one of her only truly close friends and from the situation in which Charlotte had inserted herself in by means of her marriage to Elizabeth's odious cousin. Even after all the time which had passed since the marriage and the short period spent with them the previous spring, Elizabeth could not help but feel that all that Charlotte had lost outweighed whatever she had managed to gain. Certainly a life spent in the company of such a tedious man as Mr. Collins, not to mention Mr. Darcy's snobbish and meddlesome aunt, was nothing of which to be envious.

But to Lucas Lodge they had been invited, and to Lucas Lodge they must go, along with many other prominent families in the neighborhood—including the Bingley party, which, if Elizabeth's intelligence were correct, now included at least one of the superior sisters among its company. Of the Hursts, there had been no mention as of yet, but Miss Bingley had apparently arrived a mere two days earlier. How her brother would have received her, Elizabeth could not guess. But knowing, as Elizabeth suspected he did, of her interference in his affairs with Jane, she hoped Mr. Bingley had at least warned his sister from sticking her nose into his business again, thereby protecting Jane from Caroline's vitriolic tongue. Elizabeth could only hope.

As the carriage pulled up to the front of the manor, Elizabeth's gaze ran over the familiar sights of Lucas Lodge, and a feeling of discontent welled up within her. Elizabeth herself could not be certain as to the precise source of her restlessness, but in that moment she felt herself unequal to an evening spent in the company of those among whom she had spent her entire life. She wished for nothing more than to order the carriage to return her to Longbourn, where she could pass away the evening in solitary reflection. But knowing her mother's reaction if she should even consider such a course, Elizabeth gathered her fortitude and resigned herself to the evening.

They disembarked from the Bennet carriage and made their way toward the house, entering to be greeted by the elder Lucases, who were engaged in greeting their guests as they arrived. As always, Lady Lucas was flighty and overly happy, greeting Elizabeth's mother particularly with loud exclamations, laughing embraces, and congratulations for Jane's recent engagement, while Sir William was affable yet laborious in his greetings to the entire Bennet party.

"Lizzy! So good to see you — it has been far too long!"

The loudly spoken words caught Elizabeth unawares, and she peered toward the owner of the voice, her face assuming an expression of polite neutrality.

"Mr. Lucas," responded Elizabeth, though she tried to conceal her lack of enthusiasm in order to maintain the illusion of politeness. "I am sorry — I had not realized you had returned. Welcome home."

Samuel Lucas was Sir William's eldest son and heir. Being somewhat less than three years older than Elizabeth, and owing to the fact that Elizabeth had been more interested in boys' activities as a young girl, they had at times been playmates growing up. Although not what Elizabeth would have called a close friend (certainly nothing like what Charlotte had been to Elizabeth), she and Samuel had spent some hours together running in the fields, climbing trees, or engaged in mock sword fights which had invariably ended up with one of them getting hurt. Surprisingly enough, it had been Samuel who had run home crying more frequently than Elizabeth, something for which he had always appeared to resent her.

However, Samuel had been absent from Lucas Lodge since the time he had entered his teen years. First, he had attended school, next he had gone to university — although the Lucases certainly did not have the resources to send him to an exalted campus such as Cambridge or Oxford — and then, once he had completed his studies, he had spent some little time touring the continent. Elizabeth could not remember precisely, but she guessed that she had not seen Samuel in more than three years. When questioned, his parents had declared that he was too engrossed in his studies and acquaintances to come home and that he spent his summers at friends' estates or traveling.

What they had never said — and which Elizabeth had inferred on her own — was that Lucas Lodge had become too small for the likes of Samuel Lucas, who had always had grandiose dreams for his future. Thus, his last visit — which she now recalled had been a week during the summer after his second year of university — had been all he could stand before he was off on another of his journeys, no doubt to carouse with his friends, drinking far more than he ought and perhaps even engaging in other less savory activities.

This was another secret Elizabeth had never shared with any of her acquaintances—during the time he had last been there, Elizabeth had detected some hints which told her that he had become too engrossed in his reveling and had turned into somewhat of a womanizer. Of course, Elizabeth could not know this directly, given the fact that he was not likely to broach such subjects with a woman of gentle birth, no matter what he had become. It was more his manner and the way his eyes had raked over her that she, an innocent young woman of seventeen summers, had found disturbing and uncomfortable.

Much the same as what was happening at that very moment.

"'Mr. Lucas?'" queried Mr. Lucas, his eyebrow raised. "Since when have I been merely 'Mr. Lucas' to you, Lizzy? You used to call me 'Sammy.'"

"That was when we were young and carefree," responded Elizabeth, endeavoring to keep her voice as even as possible as she remembered they had had almost this exact conversation three years previous. She was uncomfortable in his presence—not even Mr. Darcy's scrutiny (although she now knew that to be in admiration rather than criticism) had made her feel as uncomfortable as the Lucas heir was making her feel at that very moment. Still, she would be polite and not allow her feelings to betray her.

"Now we are older, and proper conduct requires us to address each other with more formality than we have in the past. Anything less would be unseemly."

His eyebrow crept up further, even as his lips tightened into an amused leer. "So, you would have me call you 'Miss Bennet' now, would you?"

"I think it is best, Mr. Lucas," replied she. "We are acquaintances and friends who have not, after all, seen one another for many years and who are not married or engaged."

Immediately, Elizabeth cursed her loose tongue when she saw him smile sagaciously at her, his leer raking her body from head to toe and making her feel even more uncomfortable than before.

He ignored the comment, causing Elizabeth no small amount of relief. "Well, then, *Miss Bennet*, how have you been? It has been some time, has it not?"

"It has," replied Elizabeth. "The last time I saw you, you were still in university."

"Indeed, I believe you are correct. But you still have not answered my question."

"I have been well. Life in Hertfordshire has continued on in your absence, and a great many changes have occurred. I was surprised when you did not return for your sister's wedding in January."

He had the grace to look slightly embarrassed. "I would have liked to be here," he prevaricated, "but unfortunately, other matters arose which demanded my attention.

"But I can see that much has changed since I was last in Hertfordshire. Indeed, I hardly recognized you. You are looking very well—very well indeed."

Elizabeth nodded her head in thanks for the compliment, secretly wanting nothing more than to be out of his company. "I thank you for your comments, Mr. Lucas. I believe I should like to go and greet my sister's betrothed, so if you will excuse me . . ."

"But of course, Miss Bennet," stated he with a grandiose bow. "Please allow me to extend my congratulations in the matter of your eldest sister's engagement."

"I thank you, sir."

"Very well, then," said Mr. Lucas with one final smoldering look. "I thank you for your time and look forward to once again continuing our acquaintance."

Elizabeth curtseyed and walked away from him, feeling his eyes on her back as she left. The manner in which he had insolently obliged her and hidden his nature behind a veneer of propriety sickened her; she was reminded of Wickham and his insincere flattering ways. She determined then that though she was not as confident of her ability to see another's character as she had once been, she would not fall prey to a scoundrel of Wickham's ilk again!

For the rest of the evening, Elizabeth moved from one conversation to another, renewing acquaintances, catching up on the latest news of the area, and, in general, trying to enjoy herself as much as she possibly could, considering her distinct lack of enthusiasm for even being present at the event. And of course, she spent her time engaging herself in simply being busy so as to better avoid being drawn into conversation with her erstwhile childhood companion.

Many times throughout the evening, she found herself experiencing the uncomfortable sensation of being watched, and when she looked, invariably she found Samuel's eyes fixated upon her. He seemed to be observing her to the extent that she found it unlikely that he was able to engage in any other activities.

Other than her discomfort with the Lucas heir, the evening progressed as much as it would at any gathering in Hertfordshire. The only exceptions were the fact that Charlotte was not there for her to engage in conversation and the fact that Lydia was not there to make a spectacle of herself.

Elizabeth had determined that once the event of Lydia's elopement had occurred, she would take Kitty under her wing and show her the proper way of comporting herself among company. Of course, Jane had been willing to assist in this endeavor and had even begun before Elizabeth's arrival from Derbyshire. But now, Jane, being engaged and completely enthralled by her betrothed, did not have as much time to spend in the endeavor of improving Kitty's manners. This did not trouble Elizabeth overmuch—she was far too happy for her sister to feel any other emotion—and she had determined to help Kitty as much as she was able without Jane's assistance when need be.

It was slow progress, to be sure—Kitty, being the natural follower which she was, *had* been under the influence of her younger sister for quite some time, after all. But the important thing was that Elizabeth had seen the young woman make progress. Even her father had commented on her comportment and way of expressing herself—she was less insipid and more likely to speak her opinion in a calm and rational manner rather than running amok and demanding the attention of the company, much as Lydia had always done. They still had a distance to traverse before Kitty could be considered a truly proper young lady, and she still did fall back on her old ways from time to time, but Elizabeth was satisfied for the moment.

Of course, that in and of itself led to more exasperation for Elizabeth. Her father, having seen the effects of his neglect in the event of Lydia's behavior, had determined upon his return from London that Kitty needed to be taken in hand and shown how to behave. With Elizabeth's influence now so visible in Kitty's demeanor, it had taken very little for him to wash his hands of the matter and allow his second eldest to be responsible for Kitty's reformation. Although she loved her father dearly, Elizabeth could not help but wish he could be moved from his bookroom to take a more active role in his family rather than abrogating his responsibilities and taking the path of least resistance. Still, it was nothing more than she would have expected, and Kitty was easily led once her attention had been gained.

As usual, they had not been at Lucas Lodge for long before Mary felt the need to exhibit, and she could soon be found ensconced at the pianoforte, serenading the company with her favorite concertos and sonatas. Mrs. Bennet was loud and effusive in her proclamations while eagerly basking in the congratulations which poured in from the ladies of the neighborhood regarding the marriage of her youngest and engagement of her eldest. And Mr. Bennet, of course, was engaged in his favorite activity (outside the confines of his bookroom) of drinking punch with the men of the neighborhood and laughing at the antics of his wife and some of his children. In all, it was a typical night for the Bennet family members who remained.

Then there was the dour and unhappy presence of Miss Bingley. She hid her displeasure to all but the most astute of the company, but to the observant viewer, her displeasure at once again being in company with the "savages" of Hertfordshire was evident in the pinched lines around her mouth and the narrowed gaze she directed at anyone who addressed her.

To Elizabeth, she had been frostily polite, inquiring after her family — as if they were not at the party themselves — and then saying no more than propriety demanded. And although Elizabeth would not spend any more time in her company than she could politely avoid, Miss Bingley's arrogance did shine forth on one occasion.

Bingley and Jane had drifted off to speak with some of the other ladies of the area, leaving Miss Bingley and Elizabeth alone, and in complete silence, as Elizabeth could not imagine two people who had less to say to one another than herself and Miss Bingley. Elizabeth was about to quit her presence when Miss Bingley suddenly turned to her and addressed her in a tone which was more than usually insolent and condescending:

"Pray, Miss Eliza, your *family* from *Gracechurch Street* . . . are they well?"

It did not escape Elizabeth's attention that the words were spoken out of the hearing of her brother, causing Elizabeth to once again wonder exactly what had transpired between brother and sister upon Miss Bingley's arrival. At the very least, it appeared she was not willing to risk her brother's displeasure by insulting his fiancée's family if there was any possibility that he would overhear.

Elizabeth could not help but be amused at the woman's behavior, reflecting that on a true societal scale, she herself was above Miss Bingley in standing, if not in consequence, by virtue of her status as the daughter of a gentleman. Strictly speaking, Miss Bingley was merely the daughter of a tradesman and could be considered to be below Aunt Gardiner, who was the *wife* of a tradesman, although Elizabeth knew Miss Bingley would rather be mauled by rabid dogs than to admit such a truth.

In the face of such rudeness, Elizabeth determined the only response was to be politely distant. However, Elizabeth *would not* allow the woman in front of her to disparage her family without some manner of response.

"Very well, thank you very much," responded Elizabeth in as lofty a tone as she could manage. "Your brother and Mr. Darcy both asked after them as well. I believe we have made a *very dear* friend in Mr. Darcy—and his wonderful sister of course. They were both very kind for those few short days we spent in Lambton, and their abilities as the consummate hosts were without peer. I very much look forward to continuing my acquaintance with him and dear Georgiana through my new connection to your brother. Indeed, I find that we are fortunate to have made the acquaintance of both Mr. Darcy and your brother—they are both very good men indeed."

Miss Bingley's reaction to Elizabeth's statement did not disappoint, as she appeared to acquire a hint of green to her skin tone at the thought of Elizabeth continuing her acquaintance with the illustrious Mr. Darcy, making Elizabeth even more convinced the woman's dislike for her person had been founded in jealousy. Miss Bingley paused in the act of taking a sip of her drink and lowered her glass, piercing Elizabeth with a stare of utter scorn and menace.

"They are both good men, though I flatter my brother by speaking so of him. Indeed, I find it most refreshing that Mr. Darcy would *condescend* to associate with those of . . . *lesser standing* in society than himself. It is one of the attributes which truly allows his greater qualities and character to shine forth. Your aunt and uncle are *very fortunate* that he has taken notice of them."

Elizabeth nearly gasped at Miss Bingley's derisive comments, maintaining her composure at the insult only by the strength of her resolve. The audacity of such a woman of no more consequence than twenty thousand pounds and the friendship of her brother with a member of the first circles was beyond the pale!

"I believe, as I have said, that we are *all* very fortunate that Mr. Darcy is the man that he is. After all, *your brother* could hardly aspire to the attention he receives without Mr. Darcy's patronage, now could he?"

If Elizabeth had thought Caroline's color to be unattractive before, the almost orange hue her face acquired—which oddly enough nearly matched her gown—put that idea to rest. She was almost shaking in rage as she stared back at Elizabeth.

"And of course, you yourself benefit from Mr. Darcy's standing as well," continued Elizabeth, taking great care to appear oblivious to Miss Bingley's displeasure. "After all, it is your connection to Mr. Darcy, through your brother, which allows you the ability to move in more . . . polite society now, is it not Miss Bingley?"

"Quite," managed Miss Bingley through clenched teeth, clearly unwilling to say any more.

"Indeed, I find myself hoping that my nieces—daughters of Mrs. Gardiner—have equal luck in finding a patron of the stature of Mr. Darcy, much as you have done. In that manner, as the *daughters of a tradesman*, they could hope to aspire to the same society which you have. Indeed, you are very *fortunate*."

Miss Bingley's eyes were almost bulging out of her head by this time, and she appeared to have swallowed her tongue.

"I understand Mr. Darcy will be returning to Netherfield shortly," continued Elizabeth along blithely, aware of and amused by the fact that Miss Bingley was nearly apoplectic with rage at being reminded of her humble origins. "I am most desirous of his return—pray tell me when he will return to your brother's house."

"I cannot say," Miss Bingley finally responded after a few moments of composing herself. "Charles merely stated that he would be returning some time this week, due to some business in London which had delayed his arrival."

"That is a true shame," stated Elizabeth, fully enjoying this encounter. "I so wish to continue my acquaintance with him and thank him again for the enjoyable time we spent at Pemberley. I cannot remember a time when I passed the hours so agreeably; and Pemberley certainly is a gem, is it not?"

Though she now appeared to be attempting to swallow a riding crop, Miss Bingley, in as short a manner as possible, allowed it to be so.

"Well, then, I suppose that we shall have to content ourselves with one another until he returns," said Elizabeth, motioning at the entire company, while she resisted the temptation to laugh out loud.

"Regardless, Miss Bingley, it has been a *true pleasure* to speak with you, but I believe I have not greeted Maria Lucas yet, so I shall bid you good evening. I truly hope we are able to continue to have such . . . *fascinating* discussions again in the near future."

Without a backward glance, Elizabeth stepped away from Caroline, inwardly laughing at the woman's disregard and obvious dislike for her person. Let the conceited woman think Elizabeth had set her cap for Mr. Darcy—the scheming that such knowledge would doubtlessly engender would keep her tongue in check and prevent her from insulting too many of her brother's neighbors. Although Elizabeth could not care two figs if Miss Bingley were to embarrass herself with her airs and supercilious manners, she did wish to avoid having Jane's time with Bingley ruined by the bitter woman.

The evening was moving along apace, with very few incidents to incite Elizabeth's mortification and concern—in general, her family appeared to be behaving themselves with far more decorum than she had ever had any reason to expect. Lydia's absence certainly appeared to be a godsend at that moment!

Dinner was a pleasant affair with five courses (Lady Lucas, regardless of whatever faults she possessed, was as accomplished a hostess as Elizabeth's own mother), and the separation after dinner was appreciated by Elizabeth as a means of escaping Samuel's ever-wandering eyes.

The men had just returned from the dining room when Elizabeth's peace was shattered by the person of the man she had been attempting to avoid all evening. Their conversation was short and somewhat one-sided, but once Elizabeth had managed to extricate herself from the unwanted tête-à-tête, a disaster of a different sort made its presence felt.

Heretofore, Mrs. Bennet had been basking in the attention which she apparently felt was her due, what with Jane's engagement to the handsome young man who was in the process of making himself even more agreeable to the assembled neighborhood. But seeing Elizabeth talking with Samuel had apparently started her imagination soaring at the prospect of perhaps having another daughter married.

Now, it must be said that although Mrs. Bennet had been quite offended for some time after Elizabeth's refusal of Mr. Collins, she had now largely forgotten the disappointment of that day. She still did tend to rail about "those artful Lucases" having stolen the future position of mistress of Longbourn, which she felt rightfully belonged to one of *her* daughters, but her resentment of Elizabeth had largely subsided.

However, Elizabeth certainly did not even for an instant think that her mother had given up her scheming. Her machinations and ambitions for her remaining unattached daughters were as prevalent as they had been prior to the family's unexpected good fortune, and it now appeared that Elizabeth was to once again feel the full force of her mother's grandiose plans in earnest.

Elizabeth had left Samuel's side and was making for Jane and Bingley's company when her mother's voice rang out over the company:

"Lady Lucas, did you see Elizabeth speaking with Samuel? Weren't they as thick as thieves when they were younger?"

"I believe you are correct, Mrs. Bennet. Perhaps that prior preference has carried over to the present."

"They appear to be very handsome together indeed. Would it not be wonderful to join our families together by means of your son with my eldest remaining unattached daughter?"

"*Very* agreeable, my dear Mrs. Bennet. Elizabeth is such a pleasant, charming young lady—I imagine she would grace the home of any young man. We would be vastly pleased to welcome her into our family as the next mistress of the estate."

"You know that one marriage often breeds rumors of another," declared one of the other ladies of the neighborhood. "In the case of your youngest, it seems that it has bred several."

Elizabeth's mother simpered and smirked and basked in the approbation of the assembled ladies. "Well, I daresay Elizabeth will make Samuel a fine husband, for she has a sweet disposition and has been raised to manage the household matters of any estate. I have trained her myself, you know, as I have trained all the girls for their eventual roles as mistresses and wives.

"I am certain now she had this all planned out," continued she, not noticing the expression of humiliation which now adorned Elizabeth's face. "I was so distressed when she would not accept her *previous suitor*." Even her mother was not senseless enough to mention Mr. Collins's previous attentions at Lucas Lodge, whatever other improprieties might spew from her mouth. "But it appears she knew what she was doing all the time. If she had informed me of her partiality for Samuel, it would have saved me so much distress on my poor nerves, and perhaps I could have directed . . . Well, never mind that now. I for one am delighted!"

Her cheeks still burning with mortification, Elizabeth surreptitiously glanced around the room, certain that just about everyone within hearing range had heard her mother's statements and had been witness to her humiliation. Surprisingly, it appeared that few in the room had paid any attention, likely because they were all so accustomed to the Bennet matron's outbursts. However, Elizabeth did catch the expressions on a few of the assembled—Bingley and Jane appeared concerned, while Sir William looked on with surprising pity for her embarrassment. The most disturbing was Samuel's smirk of self satisfaction, a sight which spurred her to action. Even now, her mother was continuing her comments for the whole room to hear—she had to be stopped!

Feeling as if every eye in the room were affixed upon her, Elizabeth quickly crossed the floor and confronted her mother.

"Mother!" hissed Elizabeth. "Please cease this at once!"

"Why should I, Lizzy?" cried Mrs. Bennet. "The whole neighborhood knows of your history with young Samuel—do you not think he is everything a suitor should be?"

"He is *not* my suitor, mama! And if we keep up this line of conversation and tone of voice, I will never be able to find another one either. For heaven's sake, mama, can you not lower your voice?"

"And what shall you do, Lizzy? I suppose you mean to refuse Samuel, like you did Mr. . . . the last man to make an offer for you? You would do well to listen to me for a change—I suppose young people nowadays think they know everything and do not need to listen to their elders. I am telling you, Miss Lizzy—if you continue to turn your nose up at *every* young man who shows an interest in you, you will end an old maid, and I do not know what I shall do with you.

"I suppose since your sister has made such a good match, you could live with her—you are very close to her, after all."

"*Mama!*"

"Mrs. Bennet!"

Elizabeth started when Bingley suddenly appeared at her side, his stern expression directed at the Bennet matriarch and completely incongruous with his usually placid and agreeable demeanor.

"I must insist you stop this immediately! Whether there is anything between Miss Elizabeth and Mr. Lucas or not, speaking in such a manner for the whole room to hear is not seemly."

Mrs. Bennet's jaw dropped, and she gazed at Mr. Bingley, apparently stunned that he would speak to her in such a manner. Elizabeth, who knew her mother well, could tell from the expression on her face that indignation was warring with the need to avoid offending her eldest daughter's fiancé, to whom she was *not as of yet* married.

Eventually, the latter won over, and she directed an imperious glare at her second daughter. "Very well, then, Mr. Bingley; I shall not discuss the matter any further.

"I do not know what I have done to deserve such an . . . ungrateful daughter," muttered Mrs. Bennet, pointedly turning her back on Elizabeth.

At this juncture, Elizabeth wanted nothing more than to quit the gathering and return to her home to hide her shame in her own room. She glanced up at Jane to see a look of mixed distress for her mother's words and pity for her sister. Jane took Elizabeth's arm and began directing her toward another corner of the room, followed by her handsome suitor. Elizabeth desperately attempted to avoid the gaze of the company and was successful, but for one member. Miss Bingley's sneer of disgust bored into her, communicating every ounce of the woman's scorn.

She scowled at Bingley's sister but allowed herself to be led to the corner, where Jane and Bingley endeavored for the rest of the evening to cheer her up and protect her from hearing any further outbursts.

The evening for Caroline Bingley was torture in its purest sense. The noise of these people, their sheer lack of comportment and manners, and their lack of breeding made her want to scream with frustration. Her brother had never been especially choosy about the company he kept—how he had managed to become an intimate friend of Mr. Darcy she would never know—but she did not think him so lost to propriety as to welcome the attention of these insipid savages. Yet there he was, prancing around the room with Jane Bennet on his arm, oblivious to the failings of the *cattle* with whom he had surrounded himself. Their father must be turning in his grave at the level to which his son had sunk.

It was an evening of increasingly low events for the young woman. The conversation was insipid, the comportment of the assembled company abysmal, and the dinner was not fit to grace the trough of a pig, let alone fine society. How she would ever survive the weeks until her brother signed away the rest of his life by marrying Jane Bennet, she could hardly imagine. She would admit that Jane was lovely and carried herself well—in terms of compatibility and temperament, it was a good match indeed. Still, there were other young ladies of the ton who possessed similar qualities—and dowries and connections to go with them. He could have done so much better.

Her conversation with that odious young adventuress was infuriating in the extreme. If not for her brother and the need to stay on his good side, she would have cut Miss Eliza directly and severed all acquaintance with her. The nerve of the little chit!

There was one high point to the evening. Caroline was situated less than fifteen feet from the gaggle of ladies gossiping and congratulating Mrs. Bennet for her daughter's conquest, and she therefore heard every word which issued from the odious woman's mouth regarding the detested Miss Eliza and Samuel Lucas. Caroline knew it was not proper comportment for a young woman to take enjoyment in the humiliation of another, but she also knew that one must take one's small victories when they are presented. Fine eyes indeed! Nothing could overcome the consequence of having a mother-in-law like Mrs. Bennet, not even the finest eyes in the entire world. Her brother would eventually discover this, much to his chagrin.

What had surprised her was Charles' response. She had rarely known him to raise his voice—whether to servants, his siblings, or anyone of his acquaintance, really. For him to openly and loudly defend his future sister's honor—to her mother, no less—was nothing short of astonishing.

It also made Caroline nervous. Her brother had always been of such an agreeable and malleable disposition that it had been a simple matter for her to manipulate him into anything she wanted.

It seemed that his engagement to Jane Bennet had had the unexpected consequence of improving his confidence. Her brother had finally discovered his backbone, and Caroline knew her days of influencing him in whatever manner she wanted were likely gone. His future wife was now the one in control of his life, and Caroline knew she could do nothing to change matters back to her own favor. It was done.

And how had he come to be back in this neighborhood anyway? The agreement with Mr. Darcy was that they would keep Charles out of Hertfordshire to help him forget about Jane, and then Mr. Darcy would advise him to give up the place entirely once his separation was complete. Had seeing Eliza Bennet at Lambton and Pemberley given him hope that his suit was not as hopeless as he had feared? But she could hardly have seen him making such a large decision without seeking Mr. Darcy's advice. Had the man betrayed them?

No, that could not be. Whatever Mr. Darcy was, he was proper, and these people were hardly proper, regardless of the attention he had shown to Eliza at Pemberley.

The situation highlighted one thing for Caroline—with Charles's marriage, it was now imperative to secure Mr. Darcy at the first opportunity. There was no other choice!

It was not long after her detested rival's humiliation that the night entered its lowest point for the Caroline, giving rise to all her fears. Caroline was watching Eliza Bennet as she was being comforted by Jane and Caroline's brother when she happened to overhear a discussion not two feet from her.

Sir William Lucas was one of the locals she detested most of all. His pompous statements regarding St. James's court and his self-important pronouncements had the ability to infuriate her. To think that a simpleton such as him, in a gathering such as this, had thought Caroline Bingley to be in need of assistance in society and require an invitation to court was beyond the pale! He held a special place of loathing in her heart, right alongside the space marked for one Eliza Bennet.

Her feelings were only made worse when she heard a few of his comments to one of his neighbors.

"You know, it is all simply rubbish, this talk about Miss Elizabeth Bennet and my Samuel."

"Why do you say that, Sir William?"

"Why, they have not seen one another in years. Miss Elizabeth has grown into a fine young woman, and Samuel . . . Well, let us just say that he still has some learning and growing to do."

"You censure your own son?"

Sir William waved his hand. "Do not misunderstand me. Samuel has made me proud, but he has become a little too fond of the bottle and carousing with his friends from the university to which I sent him. That is the reason I called him home—it is high time he left his youth behind. I would have him learn the management of the estate and settle down with a nice young lady."

"But was he not close to Miss Elizabeth as a youngster?"

"They were friends, but that was before Miss Elizabeth herself began to settle down—they played as young boys do, climbing trees and wading in ponds. I cannot tell you the number of times he came running home, having received the short end of the stick—quite literally, I can tell you!—during one of their mock sword battles. She was quite the spirited girl—still is."

"So, is she not perfect for him?"

"Believe me, if she were to turn her head toward him, I would be happy to have her as a daughter. She is as fine a young lady as any I have ever seen, St. James's court or not."

Caroline almost snorted at the thought. It was another case of Sir William showing his complete misunderstanding of exactly *what* made a truly accomplished and fine woman. Yet this account of Miss Eliza could prove useful—after all, Caroline remembered the disgust Mr. Darcy had felt for the girl's muddied petticoats and her scamper across the country to visit her ill sister. To know that she had been such a hoyden as a young girl had to show Darcy that she was not fit to be mistress of such a fine estate as Pemberley.

But then, the conversation took a turn for the worse.

"Then why do you not encourage the match?" asked Sir William's companion.

The jolly man looked around furtively and leaned closer to his companion, causing Caroline to unconsciously inch closer, morbidly curious to see why the man did not desire a closer connection despite all of his misconceived notions of propriety and compatibility.

"I believe that Miss Elizabeth has caught the eye of another, one far more illustrious than my son could ever hope to be."

"Truly? She has another suitor?"

"Indeed. If my conjectures are true, I suspect another has feelings for her."

"And who is this mystery man?"

"None other than Mr. Bingley's good friend."

The shock which appeared on the face of the other gentleman mirrored the surprise and horror which Caroline knew must be etched upon her own face. With no other recourse available to one overhearing a conversation between others, she could only hang onto every word which issued from the odious man's lips.

"Surely not! Mr. Darcy was well-known in his disdain for the neighborhood and his contempt for her beauty. Did he not slight her so horrendously at their first meeting?"

"Ah, yes, the infamous slight. It is true—he did slight her. But did you not see his behavior toward her from that moment forward?"

"I must admit, it quite escaped my notice. Please, do tell."

"Well, it was not a fortnight later, in this very room, no less, that Mr. Darcy *did* ask Miss Elizabeth to dance. I can assure you that although he was prompted to do it, it most certainly did not look like an imposition.

"Then there is the manner in which his eyes follow her whenever she moves about a room and how they have always seemed to challenge one another—I have been witness to more than one of their conversations, and I can tell you they seemed to be evenly matched, wit for wit!

"And then, do not forget the ball Mr. Bingley held at Netherfield last year. Tell me, do you remember who Mr. Darcy's dance partners were that evening?"

When the other man admitted he could not recall, Sir William continued with a look of glee upon his face.

"Well, then I shall tell you. Mr. Darcy danced exactly three dances that evening, although he did not partner for the first, the last, or the dinner dance. In fact, after dinner, I do not recall seeing much of the man at all. However, he did dance with Mrs. Hurst and Miss Bingley as was proper, given their status as sisters of his host. Can you guess who else he danced with? It was none other than our Miss Elizabeth Bennet!"

"Now that you mention it, I do recall that dance. It does shed a new light on my perspective of it all."

"Indeed, it does. Mr. Darcy, who would be pleased with none of the young ladies in attendance, who seemed to find society in our little village lacking in essentials, danced with only one who was not formerly a member of his party. When you add it all up, it leads to only one thing—Mr. Darcy admires Elizabeth Bennet!"

"But would you wish such a proud and disagreeable man on such a wonderful young woman? Would someone such as your son not be a better and far more agreeable match for her? She did not seem to return Darcy's affection, after all— they seemed to part after that dance with acrimony, as I recall."

"Too true, too true. But there are certain things you must understand about Mr. Darcy. I have been presented at court, as you well know, and I must admit that there were times that I felt small and out of place there. To a gentleman of Mr. Darcy's stature and consequence, I can imagine how our little assemblies and gatherings might seem quaint and lacking. He is, after all, accustomed to the finest society of the ton and is, I understand, related to the nobility.

"I do not consider him so much disagreeable in company, as simply uncomfortable walking into a room where every lady knows his consequence within minutes of his entrance.

"And you must understand that Miss Elizabeth never gave any consequence to his stature and treated him much the same as she would any other young man, which must be, to a man such as Darcy, intriguing and puzzling. He is, you know, sought after by many for his connections and his status as a single young man of magnificent fortune."

"Well, when you put it that way, I suppose we must wish Miss Elizabeth the best of luck in securing him."

"If that is what she means to do. My Charlotte has told me of her romantic ideals and wishes for her marriage, and I doubt she would accept him if she did not possess a true regard for him. Miss Elizabeth is not the type to accept a proposal merely for the sake of securing her own future."

"If she is not, then we must hope that he is determined."

"I believe he is. And I believe her behavior is likely the surest way to secure him in the long run. He likely receives as much attention as he would ever want already from the insipid young women who try to capture a young man only for his fortune."

A sly look stole over the other man's face. "Do you think they need a helping hand?"

"No, indeed," responded Sir William. "In fact, you are the first with whom I have shared these speculations."

"Leave the women to their gossip while we keep our own counsel?"

"Precisely. Young Mr. Darcy seems to me like a young man who knows his own mind, and understands how to get what he wants. I believe they will work it out for themselves—they have no need of oldsters such as ourselves to help them along."

The conversation turned to other more mundane matters, but none of it held any interest for a now-fearful Caroline. She would have laughed at their presumption and audacity had their observations not so clearly mirrored her own, though she had been loath to admit it to herself.

But what to do about the situation? She had tried and tried to comport herself in the proper manner, learning Mr. Darcy's likes and dislikes in an effort to better herself to be the woman who would properly complement him. She had flattered and simpered, become acquainted with his mousey sister, and showed her talent and accomplishments and her abilities as a hostess, and she had nothing to show for it, even though she had spent years in the endeavor.

Had Miss Eliza caught his eye without even trying, by challenging him with her impertinent opinions and the fluttering lashes of her *fine eyes*? It was in every way a disaster—for Caroline knew that regardless of her success in securing Mr. Darcy for herself, she could not allow him to be captured by the likes of a mere country miss. The shame—the mortification—would be too much to bear, especially once it became known in town that an unsophisticated chit had stolen him from her. She would never be able to show her face in London again!

But what could she do? He would be there within the week, and if he so desired, she was ripe for the plucking.

With a sudden start, Caroline peered around the room until her eyes caught sight of her target. Perhaps all was not lost as she had thought. Perhaps there was a way to remove Eliza Bennet from the equation.

It took a good bit of doing, but some minutes later, she found herself in the company of her quarry, ready to put her hastily conceived plan into action. It certainly helped that he had hardly moved his eyes from Eliza the whole time Caroline was watching him.

"Miss Bingley," intoned Samuel Lucas when he noticed her closeness.

Although Caroline had not thought so at the time, their introduction upon her arrival to the room was now the most fortunate happenstance she could imagine.

"Mr. Lucas," she greeted him.

Their conversation was stilted and desultory for some time, as it appeared her companion had little desire to converse with her. In truth, he seemed less than interested in anything other than watching Miss Eliza's form as she conversed with her sister and future brother. The situation was to Caroline's advantage.

"You seem focused elsewhere this evening, Mr. Lucas. Am I that insufficient a conversationalist?"

He turned his eyes to her and bowed slightly. "No, indeed—I am simply contemplating the very great pleasure of renewing old acquaintances, especially with dear friends of one's youth."

"Ah, I assume you refer to Miss Elizabeth Bennet? I heard the . . . conversation between Mrs. Bennet and your mother earlier. They were correct in their conjectures?"

"My mother and Mrs. Bennet," said he with a snort. "They have not a modicum of sense between them. But, yes, in this instance they are correct—I do have a long history with Lizzy. She was a close companion of my youth and has turned into a very fine young lady."

"Then you admire her?"

His eyes became hard, and he glared at her frostily. "I hardly think this is an appropriate topic for two such as you and I who are still largely unacquainted, Miss Bingley."

"My apologies for giving offense. I was merely attempting to help."

She turned to walk away but was immediately arrested by his voice. "You have not given offense, Miss Bingley—I apologize for my harsh words."

Smirking slightly, she turned, schooling her features into a more pleasant expression and peering back at him.

"You mentioned you were trying to help? What do you mean?"

"You seem to hold the lady in high esteem, yet you are unhappy, lingering on the outskirts of the room, watching her as she converses with others. What do you mean by it?"

Lucas grimaced and took a long swig of his drink. "It does not appear that her affections are the equal of my own."

"Then perhaps you do not know her as well as you think. I can tell you she is far from indifferent toward you."

"And how do you know that?" demanded he. "From what I have seen, she is no friend of yours."

"Friends, no—acquaintances, yes. Truly, Mr. Lucas, you have been away for several years, whereas my acquaintance with her is of a much more recent variety. She tends to push people and challenge them rather than flatter them with insincere compliments. Yes, I believe she is far from indifferent to you."

Caroline almost laughed as a thoughtful expression appeared on Lucas's face, but she was not finished. It was time to twist the dagger a little more forcefully and set the bulldog on her rival.

"But I must caution you, Mr. Lucas, that there is another who seems to have taken a fancy to the impertinent Miss Eliza."

"And who might that be?"

"Well, I do not know if you have heard, but my brother's most particular friend, Mr. Darcy, will be joining our party this week. He is a fine gentleman with a large estate in Derbyshire—quite the catch for a young lady from a small town. He has been known to pay her attention in the past, and I have it on good authority that they recently met in Derbyshire and were *very* cozy with one another."

Feeling his gaze bore into her, Caroline nevertheless kept her features placid and pleasant. Her endeavor depended upon his reaction to this piece of news. She wanted him pursuing Eliza Bennet openly and as quickly as possible.

"And I presume that as your brother's *particular friend* you would prefer Lizzy did not steal him out from under you?"

"No more than you would have him steal her from you," said she in a challenging tone.

His quiet contemplations lasted only the briefest of moments before he smirked at her and raised his glass. "I believe, Miss Bingley, that we understand one another perfectly."

He then drained his wine and walked away, leaving Caroline to bask in the warmth of a successful mission. Perhaps Miss Eliza was not destined to be at Darcy's side as Sir William had thought.

Chapter V

*T*he days after Darcy was first called to Matlock house were tense and uncomfortable due to Lady Catherine's continued harangues on the subject of Darcy's future marriage felicity. Everyone had known she was stubborn and difficult, but no one could have predicted the reality of her displeasure. Whenever he was in the house, she hounded him with continual discourse on the subject, never allowing anyone a moment of peace.

Darcy began to avoid going to his uncle's house, as he knew his presence made everyone even more uncomfortable since she could not be silenced on the subject. In turn, this was beneficial for him, as he found that he had many preparations to make for their imminent departure to Hertfordshire. He could better spend his time working from his own townhouse, dealing with some last-minute pieces of business—which would allow him to operate his holdings from a distance and stay in Hertfordshire for several months, if necessary—and generally tying up any loose ends.

Bingley's consent was immediately sought and granted for some additions to his party. It was decided that they would leave London for Hertfordshire on Thursday, and Darcy would be accompanied by Georgiana, Anne, and Colonel Fitzwilliam—although the latter was not certain how long he would be staying. Darcy could almost see Caroline Bingley's raptures at hosting such an exalted company, although her attentions to his person would likely overshadow the rest of the party. Hopefully, the pointed comments he had made about Elizabeth after she and the Gardiners had dined at Pemberley had been enough to dissuade Miss Bingley from her foolish quest to secure him. If not, a more direct approach could be required . . .

Darcy's conversation with Anne when he told her of the extension of the invitation had been illuminating, leading him to understand that though he had visited her home every year for several years, he truly did not know Anne as well as he should.

"Ah, Fitzwilliam, you come bearing tidings, I suspect," greeted Anne as Darcy entered the room.

Darcy peered at her, noting the mischievous glint in her eyes and the slight upturn of the corners of her mouth—Anne was not known for her sense of humor or lightness of mood, and he was not certain he had ever witnessed such an expression on her face.

"Indeed, I do, cousin," said he, putting aside her somewhat unusual behavior. "I wrote to Bingley to request he extend his invitation, and I have just received a response in the affirmative."

The beaming smile which appeared upon her face was yet again one with which Darcy had not had much experience. Could her freedom from her mother have worked such a wonder upon her disposition?

"Excellent, Fitzwilliam. I thank you for your help in procuring this invitation. I shall look forward to meeting this Mr. Bingley of whom you speak and renewing my acquaintance with the impertinent and bewitching Miss Elizabeth Bennet."

Darcy directed a stern glare at her, to which she responded by breaking out in laughter. "Oh, Fitzwilliam, if you could only see yourself when you adopt that stern and impenetrable Darcy mask. Truly, it would take a woman of Miss Bennet's fortitude to get close enough to you to see past it."

Darcy was somewhat affronted. "Surely it is not *that* bad."

"I assure you, cousin, that it certainly can be *that* bad," rejoined Anne, the broad smile still etched on her face. "And given how forbidding your mask can be in the privacy of our family home, I wonder what it is like when you are out in company. It must be a fearsome sight to behold!"

Gazing at his cousin in wonder, Darcy was only able to blurt, "Is that really you, Anne? Where has this playful attitude been all these years?"

"Perhaps you have never taken the trouble to find it, cousin," replied Anne with an arch look.

Immediately, Darcy realized with a certain amount of chagrin that she was correct—he *had* visited his aunt and cousin every year, but he had never taken the time to truly get to know her.

This epiphany provoked him to reflect upon his entire history with his cousin, causing a certain amount of guilt to well up within him. If he was not aware of this facet of Anne's character, how many other things had he missed? They had spoken of their mutual determination that they should not marry, but how had life truly been for Anne living with such a domineering mother? How much had he missed in his pride and arrogance?

"Anne, you are correct, and I fear that I have much to answer for."

She directed an expression of exasperation at him. "Fitzwilliam George Darcy, you truly do have a way of deflecting all the blame back upon yourself, do you not?"

Darcy gaped at her, uncertain what he should say.

"Come, cousin. Perhaps we are not as familiar and well acquainted with one another as we ought to be, given our close family association, but we *are* two separate people, are we not? Perhaps the responsibility for this oversight should rest on both of our heads rather than you assuming it all yourself. I made as little effort as you and must be a partner in accepting whatever blame lies in the situation. To be completely honest, I was comfortable in my little world and even though your visits, along with Richard's, were a source of amusement and change, I did not care enough to broaden my horizons. At times, I felt too ill to bother."

"Then should you be making this trip to Hertfordshire so soon after your recent journey with your mother?"

Anne waved him off. "Oh, do not worry about that, cousin. I have been much stronger these past few years, and all that is wrong with me is that I fatigue rather easily. I shall not expire during our journey to your beloved's home."

"That is not exactly something about which to joke, Anne," Darcy responded with irritated disapproval, ignoring the comment about Elizabeth Bennet.

"Something needs to shake you from your displeasure, cousin. I shall be well—I promise."

Shaking his head, Darcy focused back on his cousin, who was peering back at him with some annoyance. "But surely if I had made some effort to understand your situation, I could have done something to help. Living with your mother could—"

"Stop right there!" she broke in, her earlier annoyance now giving way to full displeasure.

"She has faults aplenty," said Anne, "but she *is* my mother, and I will not have you speaking ill of her. You should know, cousin, that for many years I was quite content living with my mother, and although she has always displayed the tendency toward ordering our lives as she saw fit, I was comfortable with that. Indeed, I do not think I had the strength to have any influence in my own life.

"It has only been these last few years as she has aged, that this so-called agreement between your mother and mine has become more and more of an obsession, and even then, for much of the year, when you and Richard are not present, we are quiet and comfortable, and between her and I, the topic is hardly ever raised."

"Astonishing!" responded Darcy with a roll of his eyes. "I wonder what she is about then—I have always received letters on a monthly basis, reminding me of 'my duty' and how I must 'uphold the family honor' by marrying you. What can she mean by it?"

"I believe she looks on you as the difficult one," replied Anne with a wry laugh. "*I* am the dutiful daughter who will do what she is told. *You* are the man who is master of his own estate and accustomed to getting his own way and ordering his life. That is why she concentrates upon you."

"Except the daughter is not as dutiful or meek as she would have thought," inserted Darcy with a gleam in his eye.

"Of course! You have to admit it was ingenious—by going along with her and not challenging her opinions, I affixed her gaze firmly upon you and was able to continue to live in my home. It would have become unbearable if she were to focus her energies on me as she has on you."

"In that case, I am happy to be of service," responded Darcy gallantly.

He was still somewhat disconcerted at what had been revealed in this little tête-à-tête with Anne, but he had hope that her future would be improved by her change of residence. Regardless of how Anne had been treated, with her newly uncovered defiance, her life would not be comfortable if she were to return to Rosings with her mother.

"I shall look forward to coming to know you better, cousin," said Darcy. "I think we have wasted quite enough time, do you not agree?"

"To be certain, cousin," replied Anne with a bright smile and a hand on his arm.

It was at that moment when the door to the sitting room opened violently and in strode the forbidding personage of Lady Catherine. She glared at Darcy, who rose to face her, before taking in the situation. Her glower instantly transformed into a predatory grin, and she smirked at Darcy with an insolent and triumphant air.

"So, you have finally come to your senses, have you, boy?"

Darcy was tempted to respond with a barb, but considering their conversation of the past few minutes, he was certain Anne would not want to have her mother openly insulted.

"Lady Catherine. No, I have *not* 'come to my senses,' as you suggest, I merely had a brief matter to discuss with Anne. I will now be taking my leave."

"Really, mother, you must not assume such things with no more evidence than walking into a room and seeing cousins sharing a conversation," interjected Anne.

Lady Catherine's fury went beyond anything Darcy had ever seen before—her face became blotchy red, her eyes flared, and she began to rant and storm.

"You insolent whelps! How *dare* you ignore the strictures of duty and honor and the wishes of your elders—"

"Lady Catherine!" bellowed Darcy, cutting her off. "We have been through this before, madam, and I will not allow you to continue this tirade. You will be silent!"

While his aunt stood there sputtering in rage and disbelief, Darcy turned to Anne before making good his escape. "Anne, it has been a pleasure speaking with you. I hope to have the pleasure repeated many times in the future."

"As do I," responded Anne with a warm smile. "Please give my regards to your sister."

Bowing over her hand, Darcy quit the room as quickly as he could, so as to avoid a further display of his aunt's displeasure. As he was leaving, he could hear his cousin begin to berate his aunt; he reflected there was much about Anne he still did not know. He would enjoy learning more about her while he attempted to woo the woman he loved.

Finally, Darcy was unable to further put off the confrontation with his aunt he had been dreading, and once he felt his preparations were as complete as they would ever be, he braved his aunt's displeasure and returned to Matlock house.

It had been decided between Darcy and his uncle that they would confront Lady Catherine together, without the sometimes inflammatory wit of Lord Matlock's youngest son. Richard had complained vociferously at being excluded from such momentous events, but Darcy pointed out that he was not truly a party of what was occurring, and that his presence and propensity to speak irreverently would undoubtedly inflame the situation even more than it already was. Ultimately Richard was forced to yield, though he little liked the necessity.

Darcy arrived at the townhouse and was immediately shown into his uncle's study, where the older gentleman greeted him with a hearty welcome and an invitation to sit. When the pleasantries had been dispensed with, they became serious.

"All your preparations have been made?"

"Yes, Uncle — my business is complete, and invitations have been procured for Anne, Richard, and Georgiana. We depart on the morrow."

"Excellent! In that case, I suppose we should go about our purpose here and have it out with my sister."

Standing, the earl pulled a cord, and when a servant appeared at the door several moments later, he instructed that his sister be sent for, stressing the fact that this was *not* a request.

"Well, the dragon is on her way," quipped the earl. "I do not know about you, but I feel an uncomfortable confrontation looming — a little liquid fortification would not be amiss. What is your pleasure?"

Darcy made a face. "Is it not a little early in the day, uncle?"

"It is at that! But I do not think I can face Catherine without it."

"In that case, I will have brandy," responded Darcy with a smirk.

The earl laughed and moved to the side table. "That is the spirit!"

He returned to the desk and handed one glass to Darcy, taking a sip from the other as he sat in his comfortable arm chair. They drank in silence for several moments, but although nothing was said, Darcy could feel the eyes of his elder relation fixed upon him, making him feel slightly uncomfortable.

"I certainly hope this young lady of yours is worth the trouble, Darcy," Matlock finally said, breaking the silence.

"She is not exactly *my* young lady, Uncle," murmured Darcy into the depths of his glass.

"Then make her your lady!" exclaimed the earl. "She obviously knows of your eligibility and character; now it is up to you to show her that you can be a man upon whom she can depend. Be yourself, Darcy — I will wager she will not be able to resist you if you do that."

"Thank you Uncle." Darcy was not certain it would be as simple as his uncle was suggesting, but he did appreciate the compliments. Heaven knew he needed all the help he could get.

"You are a good man, Darcy. Show her that, and I believe all will be well."

The door opened, and in strode Lady Catherine. She settled into a chair, sitting regally erect, as if she were a queen holding court, her opulent and expensive dress incongruous for a Wednesday spent at home. Of course, Darcy reflected, she never did anything in half measures — he doubted she owned any dresses suitable for simply sitting at home in a parlor. The woman demanded the finest of everything, regardless of the situation.

"Yes, well, then, Catherine, we do not stand on ceremony here," stated the earl, a certain tinge of sardonic amusement coloring his voice. "By all means, be seated and make yourself comfortable."

Lady Catherine directed a withering glare at her brother and sniffed in disdain. "You called me in here, Henry. Perhaps you should attempt to come to the point rather than nattering on in your sarcastic manner and whimsical ways."

"Ah, yes — the point," responded Matlock, apparently enjoying himself.

Darcy was a little concerned. Lady Catherine had shown her ability to throw tantrums and disrupt the lives of the entire family, after all, and he did not want his uncle to make this conversation any more difficult than it was already shaping up to be.

"Darcy and I have spoken, and we have decided that it is now time to end this little . . . farce you have forced upon the family. It is time to make some decisions."

"The only decision *I* will accept is for Darcy to bend his stiff neck and uphold his duty by marrying Anne. Until that time, we have nothing further to discuss."

"And that shall never happen!" stated Matlock, his voice showing the firmness of manner cultivated over more than three decades of being the master of one of the kingdom's largest estates. "Let go of this delusion, Catherine!"

"Why should I?" she screeched in response. "This is not some passing fancy or insignificant matter. With Pemberley and Rosings joined together, we would form one of the most wealthy and powerful families in the kingdom. You cannot be serious about letting him marry some little . . . tart from the country—if he truly means to have her, then let him take her as his mistress and be done. He will tire of her soon enough."

"*Lady Catherine!*" roared Darcy, coming to his feet and looming over her. "Be silent! I will not have you besmirching Miss Bennet or slandering her in any way! If you will be crude and insulting toward a woman of the highest morality and character, then we have nothing further to discuss, and I will bid you good day."

Matlock looked on at his sister with an expression of mixed pity and disdain. "Catherine, you are the only one who thinks such things. It is time for you to let go of this—Darcy and Anne have made their decisions known."

The look that Lady Catherine directed at both men was almost poisonous. "Would that Edmund had lived—*he* would have upheld the family's honor in this matter rather than . . . frittering away our good name and behaving in such an infamous manner. You will drag our proud family name down into the dust!"

"*Enough!*" thundered Matlock.

Darcy smiled in grim satisfaction to see his aunt pale in the face of her brother's fury—uncle Matlock very rarely became angry and raised his voice, but his temper, once roused, was legendary.

"You will not bring *my brother*—my *dead* brother!—into this, Catherine! You will sit and be silent while we tell you what you will do, and if you so much as raise your voice beyond a whisper, I shall have you thrown from this house!'

Pausing, Matlock grasped his glass and drained its contents, visibly fighting to rein in the temper which had erupted so spectacularly. Darcy kept an amused eye on his aunt, noting that she seemed to be struggling to maintain her own countenance—she clearly wished to say something further, but for once, her caution won out, and she uttered not a word.

"Well, now," continued Matlock in a more even tone of voice, "with that settled, we shall tell you what we have decided. It is time for you to return to Rosings, sister; you have disrupted our lives quite enough."

Lady Catherine sneered in response. "Very well. Anne and I will leave on the morrow."

"You misunderstand, Catherine. Anne has declared that she has no wish to return to Rosings, and consequently, she will be staying with us for the foreseeable future."

An unbelieving Lady Catherine stared back at her brother. "Not returning to Rosings? Surely you jest! She shall return to Rosings where she belongs—after all, it is not as if *he*," she jerked a finger in Darcy's direction, "intends to marry her. She belongs with me until he comes to his senses."

"Yet Anne has stated she will not return with you. What do you propose?"

"I propose that she do her duty and behave as an obedient daughter."

"She is of age. She can make her own choices."

"She is a sickly child, *incapable* of making her own choices."

"Only you would call her a child, Catherine. She is now three-and-twenty! She is of age and is more than capable of deciding her own course in life."

Lady Catherine threw her arms up in exasperation. "She is my child, and she is being influenced far too much by her cousins if this is what she professes to wish. I am her mother, and as such, I am intimately aware of all her wants and concerns. She will do as she is told and return with me to Rosings."

Steepling his fingers on his chest, Matlock sat back in his chair and regarded his recalcitrant sister with a certain amount of vexation. Darcy himself was as frustrated with her willful misunderstanding and stiff-necked pride. Was he himself ever that bad? If he had been, then Elizabeth's initial resentment of his manners was not unreasonable.

"Catherine, I wish you to listen very carefully to what I say, for you may not have another chance. You will not force Anne to do anything she does not want— she is of age now and may do as she pleases."

"Then she will find herself disinherited," snapped Lady Catherine.

"You and I both know you have not the power to affect the state of her inheritance," jibed Matlock in response. "Anne is Lewis's heir and you have no say over the state of her fortune or her affairs. Rosings is not even yours to control, although Anne has not as yet seen fit to depose you from it. I suggest you tread carefully, Catherine."

Lady Catherine's face reddened, and her visage became one of true rage. "*How dare you threaten—*"

"No, Catherine, *how dare you!*" interrupted Matlock, his fury matching hers. "You have attempted to rule over this family for years, imposing your will upon everyone and everything, yet you sit here and accuse *us* of not knowing our duty. The world *does not* revolve around you, Catherine, regardless of whether you would wish it to be so.

"Now have done with it. I would suggest you use your time in solitude to reflect upon your relationship with your family and your controlling ways. Perhaps if you were to show some true contrition regarding your treatment of this family, we would be willing to accept you once more into our company."

If Darcy thought that her fury had been impressive before, it was nothing compared to how she reacted to her brother's censure. Darcy could not ever remember being a witness to such utter rage as his aunt was displaying at that very moment. She was quiet for several moments as she struggled to come up with a response to such language as she had likely never in her life heard directed at her.

The truth be told, Darcy was enjoying her set-down far more than he ought—he believed it had been far too long in the making. Perhaps if she came to the conclusion that the rest of the family would not stand for her antics, she would mend her ways. He hardly believed it himself, but one could always hope.

She rounded upon Darcy and jabbed a finger at him, her ranting nearly unintelligible with rage. "This is *your* fault—yours and that chit of a girl you fancy!" she screeched at him. "You would not do your duty, and now you have filled Anne's head with your stupid idealistic mumblings of 'love' and 'affection.'

"And you—you and that . . . lowborn tart of yours," continued Lady Catherine, turning back to the earl. "Our father is turning in his grave at what this family has become. There was a time when we were respected, pure of ancestry and proud to be one of the premier families in all of Britain. My sister Anne married one of the preeminent land owners while I married another, all for the common purpose of increasing our wealth and influence. And now you would both throw it away on a young woman without fortune or connection.

"Well, I *will not have it*, do you hear? *I will . . . not . . . have it!* I will not have you throw away centuries of Darcy, de Bourgh, and Fitzwilliam heritage on nothing more than the mere whim of the heart. How can you, Darcy? How can you pollute centuries of the highest breeding and standards on some impertinent young upstart? Have you lost all sense?"

"*Lady Catherine!*" growled Darcy between clenched teeth, rising to his feet and towering over his aunt.

Now, it must be understood that Lady Catherine de Bourgh was a formidable woman, not easily cowed. But the expression of rage on Darcy's face, the icy tone of his voice, and the manner in which he loomed over her caused the elderly lady to blanch and shrink away from him in fear. She stumbled back and fell into her chair, darting glances between the two men, both of whom regarded her with fury and no small amount of disgust.

When Darcy spoke once again, his anger was controlled, but he allowed all the contempt he felt for this woman color his voice.

"Aunt Catherine, you will cease your baseless attacks on Miss Elizabeth Bennet and never speak them in my presence. If I ever again hear anything of you insulting her, you will consider our acquaintance severed forever!"

Lady Catherine gasped, and her face paled. "You would betray your family for that . . . that . . . *girl?*"

"I would. And I do not consider it betraying my family, but being true to my principles and protecting a lady of the highest quality. She does not deserve your censure or you derision—if anything, *she* is more of a *lady* than *you!*"

"Are you bereft of your senses?" shrieked Lady Catherine. "To think you would compare *her* with *me!* I have never been so insulted in my life!"

"Then I suggest you grow accustomed to it, Catherine," interrupted Matlock, "because you are about to be insulted again."

She spun to face him an angry retort on her lips. But it died when she saw his firm and unyielding glare.

"For years, I have put up with your tantrums and interference in our lives. It stops now! You have belittled *my wife*—the gentlest, sweetest woman of my acquaintance!—for years, referring to her as an upstart adventuress not fit to be Lady Matlock, while lording your own ancestry over those whom you consider beneath you—of course, in your pride and conceit, this includes nearly everyone who walks on the face of this earth. Is it any wonder that few in society can stand to be around you, except for those who believe the same tripe as so frequently spews from your lips?

"Darcy has my full support in this matter, as does your daughter, Anne. And as for your sister, you apparently did not know her as well as you thought—Anne married George Darcy because she loved him, not due to some . . . master plan to bring about Fitzwilliam dominance in Britain."

"I *knew* my sister, Henry, and I can assure you—"

"No, you did not!" shouted Matlock. "Anne was as gentle and well bred as you are abrasive and domineering. She never wished for an important political marriage, nor did she wish for her only son to be forced into a marriage he did not want."

Lady Catherine gazed back at him with a horrified expression.

"Yes, Catherine, I knew about the clause in Anne's will. Would you like me to send for the family lawyer so you can see it with your own eyes? Or have you had enough disappointments?"

"I do not need to see it," snapped Lady Catherine.

"Good—then that is settled. Let it go, Catherine—you will not carry the day in this matter, just as you failed when I married Constance."

"There is one other thing you should know before you leave," stated Darcy, bringing his aunt's attention back to him. "Regardless of whether it *had* been my mother's wish for me to marry Anne, it would never have happened. Anne and I spoke years ago—some years after my mother's death—and decided that we would not marry. I have tried to inform you of this, but you would not listen. You should listen now. Take Uncle Henry's advice and let this go—your schemes never had any chance of succeeding."

For long moments after his final statement, Lady Catherine sat in her chair, her eyes blazing with rage and contempt; Darcy wondered if she would suddenly collapse from apoplexy.

Whatever reflections she had indulged in came to an end when she stood abruptly and made her way to the door, stopping there to round upon her male relations and deliver one final barb.

"I shall not stay in this house one moment longer. You are both determined to facilitate the downfall of this family, and I will not be a party to its decay. I am most seriously displeased!"

She exited the room and slammed the door behind her, and the final sound either of the two men heard from her was the slapping of her shoes as she stalked down the hallway and out of their lives. Although they would never admit it out loud, both men secretly hoped this would be the last they saw of their relation for a considerable amount of time.

Darcy sighed and ran his hand through his hair. "I am sorry, uncle—I had not meant to cause a break over this."

"Yet you knew it was coming," replied Matlock. "We all knew that she would behave in this manner when you made it clear you would not marry Anne. In fact, I find that I must commend your fortitude—I never expected you to last this long with her meddling before you put her in her place."

"It was all about keeping the peace for Anne, uncle. I thought that eventually she would make a break with her mother, and I did not wish to make life any more difficult for her before she made the decision."

"Commendable indeed, nephew. However, unless I am very much mistaken, I believe there is a young lady waiting for your arrival. I suggest you return to your house and make your final preparations—it would not do to keep Miss Bingley waiting."

His uncle let out a loud guffaw when Darcy's face indicated exactly what he thought of the last comment. At that moment, Darcy reflected that it was likely better had he never mentioned anything about his friend's sister to his relations. He was now certain they would never let him forget about it.

Lady Constance Fitzwilliam was under no illusions as to her sister-in-law's opinion of her—Catherine had made her view known at every opportunity during the years of her marriage to the earl. To be honest, the opinion was shared, to the extent that Constance's opinion of Catherine was as low as the reverse—to her, Catherine was a first-rate meddling snob, and she was not shy about letting her husband's sister know it.

Conversely, Constance had never had anything but respect for everyone else in her husband's family, all of whom had always treated her with nothing but affability. George Darcy had been a fair and conscientious man, if a little severe, his wife had been amiable and warm, and all their cousins, whom she perhaps did not know quite so well, were generally genial and friendly. Even Henry's father, who had opposed his marriage as strenuously as Catherine had, had never been anything but scrupulously fair and polite to her, and he had even warmed to her considerably before his death.

Catherine had been the lone hold-out, and Constance had never cared enough for her sister-in-law's opinion to really give any thought to the matter. By contrast, Constance and Anne Darcy had become immediate friends when Constance had married into the family, and they had often spent time together, speaking of their families and hopes for the future while pitying Catherine, who was obviously not as happy as they were in her own marriage.

When Anne had died, Constance had made a promise to her sister by marriage to always look after her children and provide them the support of a surrogate mother, and she liked to think that she had done her best to fulfill that promise. Fitzwilliam and Georgiana had always had a home to come to when overwhelmed by the demands of the world, and it had largely been through Constance's efforts that Georgiana had regained some of her confidence in the aftermath of the disastrous Wickham affair the previous year. She was still recovering, but Constance was convinced she was on the right path—now all she needed was an older sister to look up to.

From everything that Constance had heard, this Elizabeth Bennet of whom her nephew had spoken was everything the Darcy family could want—an intelligent, amiable woman who would challenge Fitzwilliam and guide Georgiana through the painful transition from girl to woman. Constance assisted when she could, but she knew that Georgiana needed someone nearer her own age and close to her as a sister. Given Georgiana's own words of approbation regarding Elizabeth, Constance was certain the perfect woman had been found.

However, that left the matter of Lady Catherine—she had raised such a ruckus and caused such misery in the family that she was in danger of being banished from it, a circumstance which really was to no one's benefit regardless of how difficult Catherine could be. No, she might not want to hear it from a woman she despised, but Constance was determined that Catherine would not leave this house without one further attempt to point out how her behavior was devastating her relationships with her family. It likely would do no good, but Constance felt it incumbent upon her to try.

She stepped up to the door to Catherine's suite and knocked, pausing just a moment before entering the room without being bidden.

The room was a flurry of activity, as Catherine's maid was busy packing away her mistress's belongings while the overbearing Catherine stood over her, demanding she hurry her efforts.

Spotting Constance's entrance, Catherine's face took on an expression of true malice. "*You!* How dare you show your face here! Get out!"

"Catherine," replied Constance, keeping her expression neutral by force of will. "I understand you are leaving today."

"As if you did not already know," snapped Lady Catherine with a sneer. "I suppose you have come to gloat over your victory and enjoy my humiliation."

"Why ever would I do that, Catherine? We have never been friends, but *I* at least have attempted to be civil in the course of our dealings despite *your* behavior."

Catherine's face became even uglier as she stalked forward, a finger raised to point accusingly in Constance's face. "Do not attempt to declare the high road with me, Constance. Henry may be too simple to see your grasping and artful nature, but I know what you are! And now *my* family is about to be invaded by another upstart such as yourself! We are all to be polluted by this . . . this . . . ignominy which you have forced upon us!"

Constance glared back at her sister, unwilling to give an inch. "And what possible reason could I have to be grasping? I was my father's sole heir and did not need to marry for money. What gain could I hope to achieve by acting in such a manner?"

"His title! His prestige! His very respectability, which you have so willfully thrown by the wayside! A woman of no pedigree or family, with ties to trade, becoming the Countess of Matlock, one of the oldest and most respected positions in England! You have not the sense or breeding to understand how ill-suited you are for the role you can by no means fill. You can only serve to bring this family down to ruin!"

"And you have not the wit to understand when you are completely and utterly wrong!" retorted Constance. "I did not marry Henry because of his title or prestige—I married him because I love him. But *that* is something you cannot understand, is it not, Catherine? You talk about duty and honor, but love is something completely foreign to you."

Catherine sputtered in indignation, but Constance was not finished.

"I did not come here today to argue with you, Catherine. I came here to reason with you and give you a warning."

With narrowed eyes, Catherine sneered back at her sister. "I am in no mood to give consequence to your pitiful prattling, Constance. Leave me now, as I wish to quit this place within the hour."

"Not before you hear what I have to say."

Constance could see the shock and fury in Catherine's face—she had never acted thus before, preferring to keep the peace with her sister by maintaining her distance. In this instance, however, she would not yield. Though it might be hopeless, Catherine needed to hear what she was accomplishing with her behavior.

"Do you have any idea what you are doing here, Catherine? You are pushing the entirety of your family away at such lengths that I fear you will never reconcile. We have never seen eye to eye, and you have never concealed your opinion of me, but I would never wish for you to be estranged from your family forever. And this is what you are doing by consistently meddling in our lives and demanding we bend our ways of thinking to match your own. Can you not see what you are doing?"

Catherine paled at the accusations but shook her head angrily. "Of course *you* would think such things. We are Fitzwilliams—we stand together regardless of the circumstances. Darcy will eventually tire of this young slip—he *will* understand the mistake which he has made, no matter how little good it shall do him."

"Like Henry did?" responded Constance, her voice quiet and carefully controlled. "I believe you spoke almost those same words to Henry when he would not accede to your demand that he not marry me. To the best of my knowledge, Henry has never regretted our marriage, and I do not believe Darcy will either."

A sneer stole over Catherine's face, but Constance would not let her get started. "*Look at him*, Catherine! Watch him as he speaks of her, and make your own judgment. You can see it in his eyes, the way he feels about her. He will not regret her, if he should be so fortunate as to secure her hand. You are wrong, Catherine, and I fear that you shall forever be an outsider to this family if you continue on this course you have set. Give it over and forget this madness. You have everything to lose and very little to gain."

Inclining her head, Constance quit the room, feeling she had done as much as she could, but fearing it was not enough. It was all up to Catherine now.

Charles Bingley sat in his study in Netherfield, nursing a glass of port in one hand. His correspondence had been light since he had returned to Netherfield, but the most recent missive he had sent, confirming the extension of his invitation to Darcy to include the other members of his family, had been one which had brought him true pleasure.

He was very aware that some considered him rather simple and easily amused, but the truth was that Bingley simply knew what he liked. And the things which brought him pleasure included friends and family and the society of truly amiable people. And Darcy, for all their differences in temperament and demeanor, supplied companionship and true friendship, the depth of which Charles had never experienced with any other acquaintance.

Thus, it was no imposition in the slightest to host his friend and his friend's relations. Georgiana was the sweetest girl in existence and a true joy to have in the company; Colonel Fitzwilliam, although Bingley could not claim to know him well, was a very gentlemanly, lively sort of man; and Darcy's cousin Anne, although reputed to be sickly and somewhat taciturn, was welcome simply by the fact of her relationship with his closest friend.

Bingley leaned back in his chair and sipped his port, thinking of his friend and the very odd behavior he had displayed since the last year when they had come to Hertfordshire. Darcy had always been taciturn, uncomfortable in company—particularly company with whom he was not well acquainted—and more at ease in small gatherings with people he knew well.

This was why Bingley found his behavior two months ago at Pemberley to be singular for the usually quiet and somewhat reclusive Darcy. The way he had treated Miss Elizabeth Bennet and her relatives that first morning when they had visited her in the inn at Lambton was not the way Darcy was usually disposed to act. It was from that time that Bingley had begun to suspect a partiality for the young lady which Darcy had evidently hidden during his time visiting in Hertfordshire.

After seeing them together at Pemberley, specifically on the evening when she had played and sung for the company, Bingley had become almost convinced there was *something* there. Bingley was aware that Darcy considered him to be somewhat oblivious, but although his friend's opinion did hold somewhat more than a grain of truth, Bingley *did* have eyes, and the look which passed between them could be nothing less than admiration from Darcy's side. It was Elizabeth's regard which was a little more difficult to determine, though at the very least, Bingley could tell she was far from merely indifferent. If it was so, it was nothing less than a fine joke, with Darcy for once being on the receiving end. The irony of journeying from 'not handsome enough' to 'fine eyes' and then all the way to besotted, if Bingley's observations had any truth, was delicious in the extreme!

But therein lay another problem—namely, Charles's sister who was not likely to take kindly to Darcy paying attention to another woman.

Bingley had to roll his eyes, at the thought of the antics of his still unmarried sister. Caroline would be fit to be tied if Darcy continued to show as much favor to Elizabeth as he had at Pemberley, and Charles was not looking forward to the confrontation such attention would almost certainly engender.

It had always been a tightrope for the young man, one which he would have preferred not to walk, but he had almost been forced to due to the actions of others. He was not insensible to the very great favor and opportunity the prospect of a marriage between his closest friend and unmarried sister would bring to his family—a closer connection to the venerable and respected Pemberley family could only improve their position in society, after all.

Yet though Caroline had spent years molding herself into the proper Pemberley wife, taking every chance to show her talents off to its master, Darcy had never shown an ounce of interest in her. Darcy was far too polite to ever say anything, but Charles suspected he considered Caroline to be a social climber and a bother—a necessary evil which went hand in hand with friendship with the Bingley family. In short, as long as Darcy wanted to continue his acquaintance with Charles, Caroline was a part of that friendship, and one which he could not escape.

Charles knew Caroline was every bit as perceptive as he was himself—far more perceptive where Darcy was concerned, to tell the truth. If Charles had seen the attraction between Darcy and Elizabeth, he was certain that Caroline, who was aware of everything Darcy did and said, could not have missed it. And considering the dislike Caroline had always held for Elizabeth, one which Bingley suspected was based upon the interest Darcy had originally showed in Bingley's future sister-in-law, Darcy's visit had the potential for a spectacular showdown between the two women. And if Darcy's feelings for Elizabeth were as fervent as Bingley suspected, such a scene could result in Caroline's banishment from Darcy's presence, an occurrence which would pain Charles, regardless of the fact that he would certainly understand his friend's actions.

And then there was Caroline's behavior since arriving again in Hertfordshire to consider. She had been less than pleased to attend the one engagement he had accepted, though she eventually agreed to attend, yet not without protest. How she expected him to become accepted once again in the community if he did not mingle, he could not understand, but her obvious contempt for the society of his new home was not something which he could countenance.

There was also the confrontation between Caroline and Miss Elizabeth at the Lucas house to consider. Caroline was far guiltier than Darcy when it came to her opinion of her brother's powers of discernment—he knew Caroline considered him to be aware of nothing more than the latest pretty face and the next ball.

But she was as mistaken as Darcy had been. Bingley had been perfectly aware of the confrontation which had occurred between his sister and Elizabeth at the Lucas party, and although he could not know the particulars of their discussion, it did not escape his attention that Caroline had waited for him to move across the room before making whatever comments she had to Elizabeth. And although he may have been concerned, the fact that Elizabeth had left the discussion looking somewhat smug—while Caroline had been nearly apoplectic with fury—had certainly laid to rest any concerns Bingley might have had regarding the outcome of the conversation. It seemed Caroline had not quite learned her lesson with respect to Elizabeth's ability at verbal fencing, and she had once again paid the price for her impertinence. Some might consider this a betrayal, but Bingley knew his sister, and he knew that whatever set-down had been delivered, Caroline was most likely deserving of being the recipient.

Still, there was the fact that she had tried and had waited until Charles had left the vicinity to deploy her verbal barbs—it was behavior toward his new family which Charles could not tolerate. His sister would have to be warned of her behavior, and the consequences of continued missteps would have to be laid out very clearly. Charles owed it not only to his new family and future sister, but also to his own sister by blood—Caroline was doing no one any favors by continuing to act in this manner. Her actions must be curbed.

With this thought and purpose in mind, Charles sent for his sister, welcoming her into his sanctum when she had arrived. He could not help but notice the expression of surprise mixed with curiosity which adorned her face—he had rarely called her into his study and had never reprimanded her as he was about to. Still, there was a first time for everything, and Caroline would need to become acquainted with the new Charles Bingley.

They made small talk for several moments, Charles carefully keeping watch on his sister as she attempted to pry the reason for his summons from him. Deciding it was best to oblige her, he came to the point.

"Caroline, the reason I have asked you to come here today is to clear the air between us."

His sister's expression was carefully neutral. "I was not aware that such a discussion was necessary. To what are you referring?"

"I refer to the events of this past winter. I know of your—and Louisa's—interference with my betrothed and how you conspired to keep her from me."

Caroline's answering bluster was expected, yet somewhat disappointing. "Charles, I do not know of what you speak. I acted in the manner I did because I was concerned that you were rushing into something without due thought. I wished to make certain all was as you imagined before you made any commitments. I have not interfered."

Bingley's anger was aroused, but he forced himself to remain calm. After all, Caroline could not be aware of his knowledge of Jane's visit and Caroline's return call—that information had been given to him by Darcy. Yet it was still another example of Caroline's willful untruths and blatant meddling—at least Darcy had had the decency to admit to his mistake and apologize. As far as he could tell, Caroline felt absolutely no remorse, not to mention her unwillingness to admit she was wrong.

"Jane was in town last winter for several months, Caroline," replied Bingley, taking great care to keep his voice even. "I know she visited my London townhouse and you returned the visit, and although I do not know precisely what occurred, I can only assume you attempted to sever all acquaintance with her."

"I do not know who has been telling you these untruths—"

Bingley cut her off. "Caroline, do not try to deny it. I have this information from more than one impeccable source, none of whom are to be questioned. I understand you behaved in this matter due to a desire to protect me from what you thought was a young woman who did not care for me, and I can forgive you your intrusion on that score. But I will not allow you to continue to deny this, as there is no more need for obfuscation—Jane and I are now engaged, and there is no reason for you to continue this concealment. It is beneath you."

Privately, Bingley knew Caroline's motivations were not so altruistic—he knew her character and her desire to rise above her humble origins. Yet it would not do to bring that old argument into their discussion. Caroline's machinations were at an end, as far as Jane was concerned, and Bingley could afford to be magnanimous in this matter.

When Caroline was silent, Bingley continued. "I believe you have a decision to make, Caroline, and in the interest of resolving this issue and making the situation more comfortable for all concerned, I would like you to make this decision now.

"I understand you hold the neighborhood and certain members of the Bennet family in contempt, and I cannot change your feelings on the matter. But I can demand that you hold your disdain in check and behave with respect and dignity toward them all, including Miss Elizabeth."

As Caroline's imperious mask descended into shock, Charles smiled grimly. "Yes, Caroline, I know of your dislike for her, and I know that something passed between you yesterday evening at the Lucas gathering. I cannot demand that you put aside your feelings, but I can—and will—demand your good behavior. I expect you to comport yourself with grace and amiability and to treat *all* of our neighbors with respect. If you cannot do this, then I shall have no choice but to send you to stay with the Hursts until my marriage."

Caroline's expression became flinty with displeasure. "You would shunt me aside for . . . for . . . your new *wife* and her *family?*"

"I would. You must understand, Caroline, that Jane is about to become *my wife*. My first loyalty must *always* belong to her."

Bingley watched as she digested this new information—although it was something she should have expected—and he was gratified at the sudden paleness of her face at the thought of being sent away in disgrace. He had so rarely challenged her behavior in the past that it would undoubtedly take some time for their relationship to once again settle into a comfortable routine. Until then, she would have to make do, as he had not even the slightest intention of yielding.

"Very well, Charles," she finally capitulated. "I *did* have words with Eliza Bennet last night, and although I consider her to be impertinent and improper, I shall curb my natural disinclination for her."

"And the entire Bennet family," pressed Charles.

"Indeed," responded Caroline with a sniff of disdain.

"Very well, then," continued Charles with a smile. "As you know, Darcy and his relations are due to arrive tomorrow. I suspect you still have some preparations to make, so I shall leave you to them."

"Thank you, Charles," she said, inclining her head.

She stood and made her way to the door, pausing only when Charles spoke once again.

"And Caroline, I suggest you give up your designs toward Darcy and focus on some more . . . interested man. He has never looked upon you as more than my sister the entire time we have known him. Let it go."

Caroline's responding glance was flinty with displeasure, but she kept her temper in check. "I have already promised to behave with decorum, Charles. Please do not tell me how to behave with a man who has been a very close friend for several years now."

With that, she exited the room, leaving Charles wondering how long it would take before he had to reprimand her once again. It was good that Darcy was so strong and resolute—Caroline would try the patience of any man.

Chapter VI

A relieved Fitzwilliam Darcy entered his carriage and sat down with a sigh, grateful to finally be away from his aunt and the repugnance of her society. It had been a trying few days, but it was finally over—he was looking forward to the society of his friends and family, not to mention the added benefit of the presence of a certain dark-haired beauty.

He noticed the amused smiles which passed between his cousins and supposed that they had not meant for him to notice, but at this point, Darcy did not care—he was finally leaving London after far too long stuck maneuvering around his aunt and enduring her rants.

It had been five days of wondering what was happening with Elizabeth, wondering if she was suffering from these so-called rumors which Lady Catherine had reported. *Was* she suffering due to this idle report? And if so, what could he say to her? What could he do to be of assistance and protect her from the gossip hounds who would take delight in her humiliation? He knew there was nothing he could do, short of marrying her, which would restore her respectability if the situation was as he feared, but he was not any more enamored of the prospect of taking her to the altar under the pressure of scandal than he had been a few days earlier.

And if the rumors were nothing more than hearsay, something dreamt up by that idiotic sycophant Collins or baseless gossip perpetuated by Mrs. Collins's family, then what should Darcy do? Strict propriety dictated that as he had been refused once, he should gracefully bow out. But how was he to do that, especially given the way she had reacted at Pemberley? Damn Wickham and his profligate ways, snatching the opportunity to change her opinions of him and causing her this heartache!

No, if there was any opportunity at all to gain her good opinion and her acceptance of his hand, then he would pursue that chance—she was far too dear to him to even think about simply walking away. The existence, or lack thereof, of any rumors of their attachment meant nothing—he would survey the situation, determine whether there actually *were* any rumors, and then decide how to act.

The departure of Lady Catherine from London the previous afternoon had been like a ray of sunshine finally beaming down on the beleaguered family after a long, dark night. She had not departed quietly—no, for his aunt to do that was inconceivable. She had persisted in her ranting and complaining the entire way from the presence of her weary relations until she had entered the carriage, evidently determined to have her say and cause as much trouble as possible before finally leaving.

Knowing her ways and the depths of her vindictiveness, Darcy had met her one last time before she departed, telling her in no uncertain terms what would happen if she should even think about attempting to besmirch Elizabeth's good name. Her final parting shot was to pronounce him unfit to be Georgiana's guardian, declaring that he would not only ruin Georgiana's prospects of marriage by "taking up with that tart from Hertfordshire," but that he would also ensure his angelic sister would end up in the same situation as he. By this time, Darcy was too far gone to care what vitriol spewed from her mouth, and he had bid her farewell, determined to never put himself in her company again. He was done with her.

"I know he is not the most loquacious of men," declared the voice of his cousin, interrupting his ruminations, "but Georgiana, I should think that your brother is silent this morning even by his standards."

With a glance, Darcy discerned Fitzwilliam's amused grin, knowing that he was dangerous to Darcy's peace of mind with such an irreverent expression upon his face.

"In fact, I believe he is already miles away."

"About twenty-five miles, I should think," quipped Anne.

Fitzwilliam let out a chortle. "No doubt his attention is firmly affixed on the very pleasant company which can be found at that twenty-five mile distance. I suppose he finds that company far more agreeable than any that we poor plebeians can offer!"

Although he directed a hard look in their direction, Darcy was not truly displeased with his relations. In fact, ever since her arrival in London, Anne was lighter of spirit than Darcy had ever before observed her to be, and he was more than willing to allow them to make jests at his expense if it allowed Anne's transformation to continue. It appeared that removing herself from her mother's influence had been good for her, and further distance seemed to be improving her mood substantially. He wondered at the difference in her character and wondered whether the situation between them would now be different if she had shown this side of her personality before.

But that was truly a thought upon which he would not dwell. What was done was done, and he was now firmly in love with Elizabeth. Besides, Anne, while perhaps changed by the distance from her mother, was still, in essentials, the same person she had ever been. He believed she was exactly as he had described her to her mother—somewhat taciturn and quiet and in no way a good match for her equally taciturn cousin. And he was certain Anne held no more affection for him than she would for a cousin.

A snicker interrupted his latest thoughts. "It seems we cannot penetrate the fog in which our cousin dwells, Anne. I do not believe I have ever seen him so oblivious to his surroundings as he is now. I would almost say he was in love."

The carriage was filled with the tinkling laughter of his cousin Anne, and even Georgiana hid her face behind her hand as a giggle burst from her mouth.

"Are you quite finished, Richard?" asked Darcy, fixing a glare upon his cousin.

Fitzwilliam's grin only widened. "And lose this divinely appointed opportunity to make sport with my cousin? Never!"

This time, Georgiana was not able to hide her laughter behind her hand, and she joined her cousins as the entire carriage rang out with their mirth.

"Pemberley *is* a very large estate, is it not, cousin?" inquired Anne once the laughter had died down.

Suspicious though he was, Darcy could only answer in the affirmative, allowing his cousin's statement to be true.

"Well, then, you shall need someone of impeccable character and high moral fiber, fearless enough to joust verbally with even the likes of my mother, to become the mistress of such an estate."

"Yes, she will need such attributes to fend off Lady Catherine when she arrives to save the estate and claim what is her own!" exclaimed Richard with a chortle.

Reaching across, Anne swatted Richard. "Now, Richard, I will not have you speak of my mother that way. She was simply brought up in a different time than we, and you must know that she is excessively attentive to all of our family's needs."

Richard again burst out into laughter as the last part of Anne's statement was said in a flawless imitation of her mother.

An amazed Darcy looked on, not quite knowing what to say. Anne had castigated him only the day before for comments about her mother, and now here she was, jesting about Lady Catherine herself.

"Do not give me that look, cousin," declared Anne once she had seen his expression. "She is *my mother*, and *I* am therefore entitled to make sport with her if I should choose to do so."

"I should never presume to dictate to you how you should speak of my aunt," responded Darcy in a deadpan voice.

"Ha!" cried the colonel. "We have finally found his humorous side, which is well, as I am not finished speaking of the lovely Miss Bennet!"

A withering glare was Darcy's response.

"That's it!" exclaimed Anne suddenly, snapping her fingers as if she had been graced with a sudden epiphany. "Miss Elizabeth Bennet! *She* is one who could tame my mother and handle the duties of mistress of Pemberley. I recall her to be quite courageous indeed, which she certainly needs to be if she is to deal with a large estate, not to mention our dour and proper cousin."

"I only knew Miss Bennet for a short time at Pemberley," interposed Georgiana somewhat diffidently, "but she struck me as a wonderful lady. I should love to have her as a sister."

Ignoring the continuing chuckles from his cousins, Darcy raised an eyebrow at his sister, a look which was returned with a smile.

"She appeared to be a very genteel and capable sort of person, brother," continued Georgiana. "I liked her very much indeed.

"And if she can handle Aunt Catherine in the same manner with which she handled Miss Bingley, then I should think she is more than your match."

Richard shuddered theatrically. "Miss Bingley! A more obvious social climber I have never had the misfortune to meet."

"Take care, Richard," admonished Darcy. "We will be staying with Bingley, after all, and it will not do to insult his sister in his presence."

"I know how to behave myself in company, cousin," replied Richard, waving him off.

"I'm sure you do," Darcy murmured in response.

"I'll have you know that as the son of an earl, I am versed in all the social niceties, cousin," replied Richard with an injured air. "I am well aware of how to comport myself with the utmost dignity."

An amused snort met his declaration. "Ah, yes," jibed Anne. "And when were you planning to display this impeccable comportment?"

"About the time Miss Bingley attaches herself to Darcy's arm."

Amused snickers again met this declaration, and although he knew he was the target of Richard's humor, Darcy could only laugh. Miss Bingley had never been subtle, and he knew events were likely to transpire exactly as his cousin had predicted. Hopefully, he would not have to be rude to the woman, but she must understand that her pursuit of him had to end.

Still, it was a problem to be examined later. For now, he had to rein in his overly amused relations.

The journey in the carriage turned out to be a balm to Darcy's somewhat scattered thoughts and troubled state of mind. Regardless of the frustration he sometimes felt for Richard's overly flippant and teasing disposition—not to mention Anne's surprising participation—on this day, it was an immense help, as it distracted Darcy from his heavy thoughts. The discussion was not centered on any one thing—not even the state of Darcy's love life—but Richard was unable to let it go without a dig every so often. Even Georgiana joined in on occasion!

They made very good time, as the weather was still warm and fair, but they also took care to not overtax Anne's strength, stopping in a carriage inn approximately halfway to Netherfield for over an hour. Anne had not been impressed, as she directed an imperious glare at the two men—eerily reminiscent of her mother—when she realized how long they had stayed and divined the reason for it. A moment later, though, she erupted in mirth over the identical looks of studied innocence on the faces of Darcy and Fitzwilliam before telling them in no uncertain terms that although their care was appreciated, she was *not* a porcelain doll they needed to coddle. The party departed rather quickly after her pointed comments.

Thus began the last half of their journey. It was much quieter than the first half, by virtue of both Anne and Georgiana entering the realm of slumber not long after they left the inn. This, of course, left Richard and Darcy to their own devices and allowed Darcy to reflect during the lulls in his cousin's conversation.

The scenery rolled by the window, and though he could never feel it was the equal of his beloved Derbyshire, Darcy found himself contemplating it with newly opened eyes. Little copses of trees dotted the landscape, interspersed among the fields, now harvested of their bounty, creating a patchwork quilt of greens, oranges, reds, and browns of trees slowly losing their summer mantle. There was not much in the way of contours to the land—it was largely flat in this region, completely contrasted with the wild ruggedness of the peaks which were in sight of his manor home.

As for the neighborhood, he *had* advised Bingley to take the estate when they had first visited the previous year, but he had expected—and to his chagrin found—the society to be savage. Of course, he now realized he had only found what he had expected to find and had completely missed the fact that these people were not that much different from some of the smaller landowners he had known in Derbyshire and, without a doubt, in other parts of the kingdom. It was a humiliating realization—Elizabeth Bennet's reproofs had humbled him in more ways than one—but it was one he hoped to show her had made him into a better person. He would interact with the locals with dignity, showing interest in their concerns while he tried to determine the exact state of the rumors which Lady Catherine had insisted were rife in the area.

It was in this manner that Darcy passed the journey, and at about the midpoint of the afternoon, they passed through the town of Meryton, sighting Netherfield through the trees moments later. The ladies, who had both woken up earlier, exclaimed their delight at seeing the manor house, while Richard declared it a good house for Bingley to obtain his start as a landed gentleman.

The carriage pulled up to the front doors of the house, which opened to admit a jovial Bingley, who had a wide smile on his affable face. He descended the steps to the carriage, and without waiting for the footman to disembark, he flung open the door and grinned at Darcy and his relatives.

"Darcy!" exclaimed he. "Welcome once again to Netherfield!"

He stepped back and assisted the ladies from the carriage, shaking Darcy's and Richard's hands vigorously once they had descended.

"I cannot tell you how good it is to see you all again. Thank you for gracing my humble abode."

"Thank you, Bingley," replied Darcy, caught up by his friend's infectious good humor. "You know Richard and Georgiana. Please allow me to introduce my cousin Anne de Bourgh."

"I am delighted to make your acquaintance, Miss de Bourgh! Welcome to Netherfield."

Anne laughed at his excitement and dropped into a curtsey. "I am very pleased to meet you, Mr. Bingley—I have heard so much about you."

"Not too much from Darcy, I should hope," replied the effervescent Bingley with a hint of mischief in his voice. "If so, then I expect you would think of me as a most lazy and idle fellow, determined to be pleased by any and all I meet, whether they have any merit at all."

To say Darcy was mortified by his friend's words would be the severest of understatement, yet Bingley's lightness of tone and the slight rise of his eyebrow in Darcy's direction lightened the sting of the words and brought a smile to Darcy's face.

"I should think not, Bingley," replied Richard, slapping Bingley on the back. "I daresay even Darcy has learned to his betterment that not all diamonds are to be found in the midst of London society . . . and that country manners are not so rustic as he would have thought."

"Indeed?" Bingley's eyebrow rose even higher. "In that case, we shall have to put your newfound tolerance to the test and see how you behave in company."

"Why is it that everyone around me seems intent upon making me out to be ridiculous?" asked Darcy plaintively, much to the amusement of the rest of the company.

Once the laughter had died down, Darcy grasped his friend's hand in his own and shook it vigorously. "Thank you for extending the invitation, Bingley. I daresay we shall be quite content and have ample sources of amusement in Hertfordshire. And let me be the first to congratulate you on your recent engagement to Miss Bennet—she is a lovely young woman and will make you very happy, I am sure."

The rest of the family hastened to give their felicitations and expressed their eagerness to meet Bingley's betrothed, and Darcy noticed with amusement that his friend soaked up with all the eagerness and joy of a man deeply in love. After the months of witnessing the desolation on his friend's face, it was good to see Bingley back to his old self.

"I thank you all and simply cannot wait to introduce your family to my angel—I am to visit the Bennets on the morrow and I believe the family would be pleased to make your acquaintance, though I suppose Miss Elizabeth is already known to all of you."

"Indeed, she is," replied Anne.

"A very singular lady, as I recall," added Richard. "In fact, I must agree with your proposal, Bingley—I should very much like to continue my acquaintance with Miss Elizabeth and compliment her on her prodigious skill. After all, it is not every day one meets a young lady with the fortitude necessary to drive away the most fearsome dragons in the country."

Anne elbowed Richard in the ribs, but that did nothing to remove the wide smile which graced his face. Georgiana giggled slightly, and Darcy rolled his eyes. Bingley merely appeared confused at Richard's irreverent comment, but evidently seeing his mirth and the way the others all reacted, he merely shrugged his shoulders and continued on, no doubt suspecting Darcy would explain at a later time.

"In that case, I am certain the Bennets would be vastly pleased to receive you all at Longbourn."

"Oh, Charles, I'm sure Mr. Darcy's family has better things to do than to become acquainted with the Bennets," Caroline's shrill voice drifted down from the top of the stairs.

Darcy winced, having forgotten how grating her voice could be. He began reflecting on the displeasure she would undoubtedly visit upon the entire company the moment she detected his continuing attentions toward Miss Elizabeth. He was not looking forward to it in the least.

"Oh, I suppose you must introduce your Jane to the company," continued Caroline in a superior voice as she floated down the stairs. "But as for the rest of the family . . . Well, let us simply say that their manners and society cannot be what your family is accustomed to in the circles in which they mingle."

The sight of Richard's feral grin caused warning bells to go off in Darcy's head, but his reply was so quick that Darcy was unable to intervene before his cousin inserted his comments.

"I beg to differ, Miss Bingley," said he. "I met *Miss Elizabeth Bennet* in Kent last March, as did Anne, and found her to be a *delightfully refreshing* young lady well worth knowing. If her family is anything like her, I daresay that Darcy and your brother have managed to find a *jewel* of a family out here in Hertfordshire."

"I also liked Miss Bennet when I met her in Derbyshire," interjected Georgiana's quiet voice into the conversation, preempting Caroline's derisive sniff of annoyance.

The comments, however, did not stop Caroline, and instantly upon hearing Georgiana's voice, she went into full huntress mode.

"Dear Georgiana!" her voice rang out, climbing the octaves and causing more than one of the party to wince. "I am so pleased to see you!"

She approached Georgiana and wrapped her in a familiar hug which elicited a roll of the eyes from Darcy and a slightly uncomfortable tightening of the young girl's frame.

"The desolation I have felt since we were last together in August has quite undone me. It is very good of you to join us at Netherfield!"

"Thank you, Miss Bingley," replied Georgiana, her voice soft and hesitant.

But Caroline had already turned away and approached Anne. "Charles, will you do the honor of introducing me to Mr. Darcy's cousin?"

"Of course, Caroline. Miss de Bourgh, this is my sister, Caroline Bingley. Caroline, Miss Anne de Bourgh."

The two women curtseyed to one another before Caroline plastered a smile on her face. "Miss de Bourgh, I am delighted to make your acquaintance."

Situating herself between the two cousins, she held each by an arm and directed them toward the entrance to the house. "It is so good to have other women in the house; my sister Louisa is currently in Scarborough visiting with family and shall be joining us in a few weeks' time. In the meantime, I am sure the three of us will have ample opportunity to become dear friends."

Georgiana murmured what sounded like an agreement while glancing back at Darcy in distress, and although he could not see her face, Darcy could well imagine the eye roll with which Anne had almost certainly favored her hostess.

For Darcy, Caroline's display had firmed his resolve to speak with her and acquaint her with his opinion of their relationship sooner rather than later. Her tactic was one which he well knew and had seen many times. Many a young lady sought to ingratiate themselves with his female relations, hoping the path to his heart—or, more accurately, his pocketbook—lay through gaining their favor. And though Miss Bingley had attempted this many times with Georgiana, claiming a relationship which was by no means as deep as she intimated, now she was attempting to pull Anne into her schemes. Given Anne's behavior over the past few days, which was disturbingly similar to Richard's, no good could come of giving her the opportunity to make sport with Miss Bingley. He had best have the conversation and get it out of the way immediately.

Glancing over at his friend, Darcy could see that Bingley's face was a mask of displeasure. He wondered if Bingley had finally taken his sister in hand, little good though it appeared to have done.

"Well, the ladies appear to be acquainted and getting along famously," injected

Richard into the silence. "In that case, I think I could use a drink to chase away the dust of the road. What say you, Bingley?"

Shaken out of his thoughts, Bingley grinned at the younger Fitzwilliam son. "Of course. Shall we enter the house, gentlemen?"

If Darcy had considered his resolution to speak with Caroline upon his arrival at Netherfield to be firmly formed, dinner that evening brought the matter to an even more urgent level. Unfortunately, his estimation of Caroline's behavior was accurate, and her attentions to him were by no means over.

The afternoon at Netherfield was quiet and comfortable as he, Bingley, and Richard retired for a drink, after which the travelers retired to their chambers to clean off the dust of the road and dress for dinner. He later discovered that Caroline had proceeded to monopolize Georgiana and Anne's time for several hours after their arrival, only relenting when Anne had reminded her in a most pointed manner that she and Georgiana were fatigued from their journey and would like the opportunity to refresh themselves before dinner. Though Miss Bingley had always been scrupulously proper in the past, especially with regard to Darcy and any of his relations with whom she had come in contact, Darcy suspected that she was now feeling the urgency to secure him and was redoubling her efforts accordingly. Apparently, his display at Pemberley and the pointed words which he had directed to her had not penetrated her consciousness—either that, or she was being willfully obtuse.

The real spectacle occurred at dinner, though, as Darcy should have expected. It was, after all, the one forum where Caroline could control to a large extent the ability of diners to converse with one another by virtue of the seating arrangements. Thus, once the group assembled for dinner, Darcy had to suppress a groan when he realized that Caroline had placed him as her dinner partner, likewise sitting Georgiana with Bingley and Richard with Anne.

When they sat down, she immediately engaged him in conversation, keeping up a running monologue which persisted regardless of the need to actually consume the meal. Darcy sat in wonder, marveling at her ability to continue to speak without needing to take breath, food, or drink. Or perhaps she had trained herself to breathe and swallow her food right through her endless chatter. If so, she was far more talented than he had previously given her credit. He suspected she thought he was attentive to her to the exclusion of all others, never realizing he had no other choice if he wanted to maintain his politeness.

The conversation between the rest of the diners was somewhat stilted and sparse, as all the company was uncomfortable with her display. Bingley's face was filled with exasperation and displeasure, causing Darcy to once again speculate that Bingley had actually spoken with his sister and was now unhappy that his directions were not being followed. Georgiana's expression was filled with consternation—Darcy knew that Georgiana, regardless of Caroline's professions of a close friendship between them, actually felt uncomfortable in Miss Bingley's presence and did not want Caroline as a sister. As for Richard and Anne, they appeared amused and exasperated at the same time. There was no help to be had from that quarter.

After dinner, Bingley encouraged the separation of the sexes, standing with Darcy and Richard as the women left the room and then slumping down in his chair after they were gone.

"I am truly sorry for my sister's behavior, Darcy," said he, casting a guilty glance at his friend.

Darcy snorted and raised an eyebrow at his friend. "I presume you had a conversation with her?"

"I did," admitted Bingley. "I told her I knew of her interference and warned her about her behavior toward the Bennets. I also attempted to tell her that you would not offer for her."

"Well, it certainly appears to have made an impression," quipped Richard, earning a glare from his cousin, which he cheekily returned with a smile and a raised glass.

"I simply cannot understand her," lamented Bingley. "She acts as if she is the Queen of England and considers everyone she meets to be her social inferior — even Louisa is not as snobbish as Caroline can be.

"And the truth of the matter is that Jane is her superior in society, if not in consequence, simply due to her status as a gentleman's daughter. Our money comes from trade, for heaven's sake! We are certainly not far enough removed from our roots to be considered acceptable to high society. How can she think in this manner?"

"I believe that is partially my fault," responded Darcy, causing raised eyebrows from his companions. "I have certainly never encouraged her behavior, but my association with you has raised her expectations and given her hope for an advantageous marriage, the likes of which she never would have aspired if we had not become acquainted. And when you consider my name has given her benefits in society that she otherwise would not have had, I think you have a picture of the means by which your sister has acquired her airs."

A snort from Richard caused Darcy to glance up and then down again in chagrin. Would he never learn to curb his tongue and control his own snobbish tendencies?

"My apologies, Bingley. That must have sounded dreadfully superior and tactless."

Bingley merely waved him off. "Not at all, Darcy — it is only the truth after all. You know that Caroline does not hesitate to use your name to gain admittance to the society events she craves. Your family has held Pemberley for generations and is considered one of the most prominent in England — it is not arrogance to acknowledge that fact. My only consideration is your comfort and that of your relations, which appears to be a difficult objective to achieve with Caroline's ambitions unabated. At this moment, I am seriously considering sending her to reside with the Hursts until the wedding."

The suggestion, although it would have resulted in him spending far less time with Bingley's sister, nevertheless made Darcy uncomfortable. Miss Bingley should certainly not be sent from her brother's home on his account, no matter what her behavior had been.

"Charles, I would prefer that I was not the means of estranging you from your sister."

"I hardly think it is your fault, Darcy — Caroline is the only one who can determine her own actions."

"I quite agree with you, Charles, but perhaps I have been remiss in the matter as well. I should have made it clear to her from the very beginning that I am not interested in a closer connection with her."

A thoughtful expression met his declaration. "Do you mean to speak with her?"

"I do. I owe it to her, if for no other reason than for the years of our acquaintance in which I have not made my intentions clear."

"I believe Darcy is correct in this matter," said Richard. "Perhaps if he clears the matter with your sister, we can avoid any other unpleasantness and spare her the indignity of being sent away in disgrace."

Bingley let out an explosive sigh. "Much as I hope that to be the case, I *know* my sister, and I am afraid that it shall not be that easy. I do think you take too much upon yourself, Darcy, but I cannot fault your logic. If you are determined, then I shall not dissuade you."

"Excellent, Bingley. I thank you for your assistance in the matter."

"I assume you will want to address Caroline immediately?"

"It would be for the best. Send her to the library after we are finished."

"Very well, then, Darcy. Leave the door open so that she does not try to compromise herself with you."

"Come, Bingley," said Richard with a laugh, "Darcy has faced more fearsome huntresses than your sister; I assure you he knows how to avoid entrapment, as he has been doing that his entire life."

A small grin met the flippant statement as Bingley rose to quit the room. "I shall send Caroline in directly."

Caroline Bingley was nervous. Sitting in the drawing room with her two companions, she thought back, wondering if her efforts this day would be rewarded with the result for which she had so desperately hoped since she had met the man and seen his magnificent home. But she was aware of his admiration for that upstart Eliza Bennet and her *fine eyes*. If anything was able to foil her carefully created plans, it was his head being turned by the machinations of Caroline's future sister-in-law. It was not to be born!

She had ensured everything was prepared and had gone out of the common way to ensure that he and his family were welcome, far more than she had ever done before. Georgiana had been as quiet as ever, yet she had shown herself to be appreciative of Caroline's attentions. And Anne, while perhaps a little too like Colonel Fitzwilliam for Caroline's peace of mind (she did not like the man and his propensity for making sport of just about everything), had at least answered her questions and engaged her in conversation, such that by the time they parted, Caroline felt optimistic that she had gained an ally in the sickly young woman. Surely with his relations' approval, Darcy would finally have the fortitude to make her an offer as he should have done years ago.

And then there were their interactions at dinner—Caroline had allowed herself to feel guardedly optimistic, as Darcy's attention was reserved for her and her alone. In fact, he had been attentive to her in a way he had never been before—attentive to the point of ignoring the rest of the company! Perhaps her dreams were finally to be realized! She could hardly wait for the men to rejoin them.

"Miss Bingley?"

Hearing her name roused Caroline from her musings, and she blinked at her companions. "My apologies—I fear I have allowed my mind to wander. May I trouble you to repeat what you said?"

Her companions shared a brief look which Caroline fancied was a confirmation of her suppositions—perhaps Darcy had already shared his intentions with his relations. It would certainly account for the ease with which Caroline had been able to draw the two ladies out.

"I was merely inquiring on your opinions of the neighborhood," repeated Anne de Bourgh with a slight smile. "I understand you spent some time here last autumn, and I assume you are familiar with the locals."

Caroline nearly sniffed in disdain but brought herself up short. She remembered Charles's admonition from the previous day and decided it would be best to be gracious for the moment—there would be time enough after she was married to insist they never spend another moment in this backward society. If Charles wished to visit his sister at Pemberley, he would be more than welcome—even with his unsophisticated and provincial wife—but they would never again visit the Bingleys unless they came to their senses and purchased an estate in a more deserving area of the country. And Eliza Bennet would *never* be allowed to enter the hallowed halls of Pemberley again!

Remembering that Miss de Bourgh was waiting for a response, Caroline flashed her sincerest smile and condescended to speak of the neighborhood. "The locals are friendly enough, I suppose," she allowed. "They are not used to the ways of society in the higher spheres, but there are good people here, if a little simple."

"That is well, then," replied Miss de Bourgh with a smile. "I must admit that the company at Rosings is not the most sophisticated either. And I do appreciate the ability to converse with people who are wholesome and unpretentious, unlike those you would find in town. Do you not agree?"

Her jaw dropped before she could restrain herself, and she wondered that one of the Fitzwilliam clan could be so simple as to prefer the country, even that of Rosings, to that of town. It was most singular indeed!

Still, it would not do to offend Mr. Darcy's cousin before she had secured him—tact was called for.

"Oh, I do agree that there is a time and place for the country, Miss de Bourgh. After all, Pemberley itself is not the center of society, now is it?"

She tittered politely into her hand, watching as her companions once again shared a look before indulging in their own mirth. Yes, things were proceeding very well indeed.

"But I really must warn you, Miss de Bourgh—I think you will find that the provinciality of these people exceeds even what you may find you are used to in Kent. They are at times . . ." Caroline paused, searching for the proper words which would allow her to express her disdain while appearing to appreciate the neighbors for whom she held nothing but contempt. "That is, they can be boisterous and full of life, but their manners are nothing to what you are used to."

"I shall be on my guard, Miss Bingley," responded Miss de Bourgh with a twinkle in her eye. "But I *had* meant to ask you something."

Smiling with aplomb, Caroline nodded her head in assent.

"I had thought to question you regarding one of our acquaintances. Although you have not stated it outright, it is clear you do not have the highest opinion of Miss Elizabeth Bennet."

Caroline noticed Georgiana paling in response to Miss de Bourgh's declaration, and she secretly commiserated with the young girl. Caroline privately could not wait to be forever free of the impertinent county miss.

"As you are aware, Richard, Georgiana, and I have all met Miss Elizabeth. I personally found her to be an intelligent, energetic sort of woman whose conversation was engaging and behavior impeccable. I know that Richard and Georgiana also liked her, so I was wondering at your apparent antipathy for her."

Her smile fading, Caroline wondered at the blindness of this woman. Georgiana was not perhaps to be wondered at, given her youth. And as for the colonel, whoever knew what a man was thinking, and certainly Colonel Fitzwilliam was less easily understood than most. In fact, the brazen Eliza Bennet was exactly the type of woman a rough soldier such as he would find attractive! But surely Anne de Bourgh, as a member of an exalted clan who was brought up with the finest of instructors, should have been able to see through the façade Eliza Bennet put up before the world. How could she not?

Still, Caroline's earlier resolution to avoid antagonizing Darcy's relations came back to her, and she refrained, with great effort, from speaking her mind. Instead, she responded thus:

"I fear you have misapprehended my feelings, Miss de Bourgh. I do not dislike Miss Eliza — she is merely a product of her upbringing, much the same as everyone else in this neighborhood. She is clever, I will grant you, but she has little talent, less fashion, and an impertinence which I find intolerable. In addition, she has a tendency to scamper about the countryside with little or no regard for the dictates of propriety.

"However, she is as she is, and I am quite content to allow her to be so, yet I find little inclination to know her better. She appears quite content in her behavior, and I cannot begrudge it, little though I wish to emulate it."

Her guest appeared to consider her words for several moments, while Georgiana looked on in apparent dismay — the girl was clearly uncomfortable with this talk of Miss Eliza. Caroline determined at that moment to take her in hand at the first opportunity after her engagement and acquaint her with the true particulars of Eliza Bennet's character. It would not do to have her look up to the woman.

"I find your exposition of Elizabeth Bennet truly fascinating, Miss Bingley," replied Miss de Bourgh after some thought. "But I wonder if we are speaking of the same person."

Caroline raised an eyebrow. "Truly? In what way? I have spent several months in the same neighborhood and even several days living in the same house, and I believe my characterization of her is as faithful as can be."

"Hmm, I spent some weeks in which I was often in her company as well, and I must admit I have formed a different opinion of her. She is obviously very intelligent and knowledgeable about many subjects. Her manners were always proper and demure, if a little playful, her conversation engaging, and her performance on the pianoforte, while perhaps not capital, was heartfelt and pleasing and much to be praised."

"Anne, perhaps we should not have this discussion right now," interrupted Georgiana. Anne merely responded by waving her off.

"Nonsense, Georgiana," responded Miss de Bourgh, patting the girl on the hand. "I am interested in getting to the bottom of this disparity of opinions of Miss

Bennet."

Miss de Bourgh turned her attention back to Caroline, who was beginning to develop a feeling of some apprehension regarding this line of conversation.

"We have dealt with her manners and had some conversation about her talents. As for her lack of fashion, she admittedly does not dress in the finest of materials or the most recent designs, but we have already established that she lives in Hertfordshire and is not a frequent visitor to London. And really, she has always dressed in a proper and demure fashion, even if the cut is not the most current. I understand her family's financial situation is what prohibits her family from wearing the finest and most expensive fabrics—you can hardly fault her for that.

"Which leaves us with this scampering around the countryside to which you refer. I understand she is a lover of the outdoors and does tend to enjoy her excursions. Was there a particular incident to which you are referring?"

Warning bells were sounding in Caroline's head, but since she had already offered her opinion, she could hardly refuse to elaborate. She wondered if Miss de Bourgh had set up this conversation on purpose, hoping to discredit her.

Taking a deep breath, Caroline glanced at her companions, seeing the slight smile on Miss de Bourgh's face while noting the still-present expression of unease on Georgiana's.

"I do have a specific instance in mind," began Caroline, choosing her words slowly. "When we were in residence last year, Jane Bennet—Eliza's elder sister—became ill during dinner at Netherfield and stayed the night with us. The next day, Eliza came scampering across the country, in the aftermath of a heavy rain, to arrive to see her sister, her petticoats caked in no less than six inches of mud! It was the most improper display I have ever witnessed. What could she mean by walking all that way to see her sister, who had merely a trifling little cold!"

"Ah, Jane Bennet's illness," replied Miss de Bourgh, a smug expression on her face. "I believe your brother told us of this, Georgiana."

Georgiana murmured her agreement.

"But really, Miss Bingley, does it not show a love and affection for her sister?"

Caroline was horrified. How could a woman of Anne de Bourgh's standing and breeding think thusly? It defied all description!

"I suppose it does. But does it not also demonstrate a deficiency of character in defiance of all propriety? Her sister was in no danger, after all, and she could have waited for her father's carriage to be available rather than rollicking in the mud with the swine!"

The moment the words left her mouth, Caroline knew she had made a mistake—she had allowed her distaste for Eliza Bennet to overcome her judgment and said something she should not have. She could not imagine what means the chit could have used to ingratiate herself to Anne de Bourgh, but whatever she had done, the signs, the defense, all pointed to at least some level of intimacy subsisting between them. Caroline should have seen it. Damn Eliza Bennet and her ability to draw in members of the Fitzwilliam clan!

"Miss Bingley," began Miss de Bourgh in a cold tone of voice, "I understand Miss Elizabeth Bennet is not a friend. I also comprehend that you do not see eye to eye on many things. You are of course entitled to your own opinion. However, she is considered a friend of our family, and I would appreciate it if you did not disparage her in my presence or the presence of any member of my family. In particular, my cousin *Darcy* considers her to be one of his dearest friends and would not take kindly to *any* derogatory words spoken to or about her. I trust we understand one another."

Caroline was speechless, but before she could form a coherent reply, the door to the drawing room opened, and her brother and Colonel Fitzwilliam walked into the room.

"Caroline, may I speak to you for a moment?"

Grateful for the interruption which saved her from having to answer Miss de Bourgh's mortifying speech, Caroline excused herself and approached her brother. His countenance was emotionless (unusual for him!), but she thought she detected a slight tightening of the eyes when he looked at her. Truly, Caroline was unable to account for all the changes in the people around her—it was as if the eldest Bennet sisters had bewitched them all!

"Darcy is waiting for you in the library, Caroline," stated her brother when she had joined him. "There is a matter which he would like to discuss with you."

Caroline's breath caught in her throat. Was this finally to be the day when she realized all her dreams? All thoughts of Anne de Bourgh and the detested Eliza Bennet fled from her mind—they were a problem to be considered later.

As she turned to leave the room, her brother's voice floated after her. "It would not do to get your hopes up. Darcy merely wishes to clarify something with you."

Her brother's voice registered in the back of her mind, but she did not pay any attention to his words—his opinions were as that of a gnat's now that she was finally to become Mrs. Darcy. Caroline Darcy! How well did that sound!

Swiftly, Caroline fled the room and made her way down the hallway, allowing her feet to guide her while her mind was far away, awhirl with possibilities. She paused momentarily outside the library door, collecting herself and ensuring a calm and relaxed attitude—she would meet her fate with the utmost reserve and propriety.

At length, after she had used the time to not only calm herself but also to primp and preen, ensuring she looked to her best advantage, she grasped the handle and entered the room, closing the door behind her; damn propriety—she was about to become engaged! The room was dim, and the sparse collection of her brother's books made it appear barren and unwelcoming—a cold, impersonal space rather than the warmth and comfort like that which existed at Pemberley. Caroline suppressed a shiver and gazed around the room, immediately locating her brother's friend.

He stood in front of one of the windows on the far side of the room, gazing out into the night. Caroline drank in his presence as the excitement began to build once again within her. She had always known he was a tall, well-favored man, but at the same time, she knew that this was a secondary consideration—something akin to the icing on the cake. Pemberley was the real prize.

The tread of her feet on the floor caught his attention, and he turned to face her. His face was an emotionless mask, and his eyes did not glint—it was as if he had prepared himself to deal dispassionately with their interactions. Such an attitude could be either good or bad news, but Caroline by this time was convinced he was about to make an offer of marriage to her. There could be no other explanation.

He noticed the closed door behind her and, with nothing more than a glance, moved past her and opened the door, leaving it slightly ajar. Caroline was puzzled at his actions but accepted them as his scrupulous adherence to propriety. He bowed to her and gestured to a chair, which she gracefully accepted, and he seated himself in a nearby armchair. He took a deep breath and began speaking.

"Miss Bingley, I thank you for your willingness to meet with me this evening—I assure you I will be brief."

Though she was not certain how she managed it, Caroline nevertheless assured him in an almost coherent manner that she was pleased to make time for one of her dearest friends.

His answering smile was perhaps a little forced, but he continued in his discourse.

"I feel it is time for you and I to sit and discuss our relationship. I believe I have failed to make my sentiments known to you, and I wish to clarify matters."

Now, Caroline Bingley was no romantic—it was the end result which mattered, not the manner in which that result was achieved. But now, although her excitement had not abated for a moment, she found herself confused; she knew Darcy was meticulously staid and proper, but really, could he not have mustered a little more emotion for such a momentous occasion? She could hardly credit the lack of excitement in his face, the firmly controlled expression, and the earnest manner in which he conveyed himself. He was good and wealthy, but life with him would undoubtedly be dull if this was the best he could do. Caroline would certainly need to keep to her own pursuits once they were married.

"Of course, Mr. Darcy," she said out loud. "Pray, please continue."

He raised his eyebrow in apparent surprise, but really, considering the manner in which he was articulating himself, could he truly be shocked at her reaction?

"Very well, Miss Bingley," resumed Mr. Darcy. "It is my impression that you may have read more into our relationship than actually exists. It is not my intention to offend or insult you, but I must inform you that what you imagine and hope for can never be. I consider you to be the sister of my dear friend and a friend in your own right; however, I have no intention deepening our relationship any further."

From the heights of ecstasy to the depths of despair, Caroline fell, as if she had leapt from the cliffs of Dover onto the rocks below. How could he be saying this? Her eyes narrowed, and her despair abruptly refocused itself into a blinding rage.

Eliza Bennet! She is the cause of this!

Knowing it would not do to unleash her anger, Caroline kept a tight rein on her emotions, listening to Mr. Darcy's refusal. There still might be a way to salvage this!

"I most heartily apologize for any dismay or mortification this declaration brings to you, but I can do nothing else. I only regret we did not have this conversation some time ago—perhaps that would have made it easier."

A long silence ensued—Caroline had no intention of breaking it, wanting Darcy to squirm as the uncomfortable quiet continued. But Darcy appeared to be quite content to wait for her reaction, spurning her efforts to make him uncomfortable. Finally, when she could stand the wait no longer, Caroline fixed him with a stare and spoke.

"May I ask why I am not considered suitable to be mistress of Pemberley?"

"It is not that you are unsuitable, Miss Bingley. It is merely that my feelings for you are not of the sort necessary to make you an offer of marriage."

"Then what must I do to resolve this? Mr. Darcy, I assure you I will do anything, go to any lengths to repair that which you find insufficient or lacking in me. I merely implore you not to consider this matter closed until I have had occasion to address whatever concerns you might have."

A sigh met her declaration, and he briefly rubbed his temples with one hand. "Again, Miss Bingley, I assure you there is no lack in yourself which compels me to speak in this manner. I am certain you have the skills to make someone a very good wife. That someone, however, will not be me. My feelings forbid it."

Caroline's flash of rage returned, and she stared at the man, barely suppressing it. "So, this is it, is it? After I have spent years of my life endeavoring to improve myself, learning your likes and dislikes, almost *throwing* myself at you, and now you say that your *feelings* will not allow you to propose to me as you ought. You have led me on, sir, all the while harboring feelings for . . . for . . . for a jumped-up chit with nothing to recommend her!"

No longer able to bear sitting and looking at the man, Caroline rose to her feet and began to pace the room. "I simply cannot believe you would allow nothing more than a pair of fine eyes to distract you and seduce you into forgetting everything you have been taught. How can you allow this . . . fascination to induce you to make a proposal of marriage to someone who is your vast social inferior? How can you countenance such a disparity of stations? Eliza Bennet has bewitched you—you and your entire family!"

Darcy surged to his feet, an intense expression on his face as his eyes burned into Caroline. She took an instinctive step back, so intimidating had his mien suddenly become.

"Miss Bingley!" snapped he, his voice hard and cold. "What is this about Miss Bennet? Have you heard something since you came to Meryton?"

Bits and pieces of the conversation between Sir William and his neighbor flashed through Caroline's mind, but she schooled her expression and returned his gaze with an imperious glare of her own which would even do his aunt proud. She would not give him any hope; she would not make it any easier for him to gain the favor of that woman—not even should her life depend on it!

"I can assure you, I have heard nothing. I speak merely from what I have observed myself without regard to anything else. The admiration for her fine eyes seems to have gained hold on you to the point of overwhelming your values and overcoming all your good sense. She is impertinent, improper, and in no way suitable to be your wife. Surely you must see this!"

"*Miss Bingley!*" barked Mr. Darcy, his voice as cold as wrought iron. "I would appreciate it if you would not besmirch the good name of that respectable young woman in my presence!"

Caroline was brought up short, realizing that she had once again said too much. This time, however, she could not find it in herself to care—all of her dreams were ruined, and it was all the fault of that little minx!

"Regardless of your opinions," Mr. Darcy was saying, "I am well acquainted with Miss Bennet's character and am confident in my ability to see her worth, as I am extremely confident in her ability to do anything to which she bends her energy and thought.

"However, my business is my own, and my actions are my own, without reference to you or your estimation of Miss Bennet. I am not certain what societal scale you employ to measure your acquaintances, but I can assure you that she is not as inferior to my position as you seem to think. She is a gentleman's daughter and is therefore my equal in the eyes of society and the world, regardless of her wealth or lack thereof."

A roll of Caroline's eyes met his declarations, but her comments died in her mouth when she witnessed his angry glare. Realizing there was nothing she could do or say at present, she swallowed her words and merely peered back at him angrily.

"Have done, Miss Bingley. I am sorry this conversation has brought you pain, and I am sensible to the fact that it ought have taken place long ago. The fact of the matter remains; I will not make you an offer and would not have done so regardless of Miss Bennet or anyone else. My feelings forbid it in every respect. Do I make myself clear?"

"Perfectly, sir," sneered Caroline. "I apologize, Mr. Darcy, but I find myself somewhat fatigued. I shall leave you now."

No further words were exchanged. Darcy bowed slightly to acknowledge her departure while Caroline, not wishing to give him any satisfaction at all, directed a haughty glare at him, allowing him to see all that he had lost, and swept from the room.

She stalked through the hallways of Netherfield toward her room in high dudgeon, not noticing the servants who scurried out of her way. One thought dominated her mind—if she was not to have Darcy, Eliza Bennet must not be allowed to secure him either!

Silence descended on the room as the echoes of Miss Bingley's footsteps faded away like whispers in the night. The lone occupant left in the library exhaled noisily and, after filling a glass with some of Bingley's brandy from the sideboard, collapsed on a chair and brooded, one thought running through his mind.

That could have gone better!

A mirthless chuckle escaped his lips at the thought—though it had been uncomfortable, it had actually gone much better than he had expected. He had almost anticipated a rage so incandescent that she would have lost all control, shrieked like a harpy, and thrown everything she could get her hands on in a murderous rage. No, he was certain the anger she had displayed was nothing compared to what she was capable of displaying. Perhaps the desire to maintain her welcome at Pemberley and his other properties had stayed her wrath. Was it his lot to deal with incensed females? After recent events, it seemed it was so.

His impression of her dislike for Elizabeth—though she had certainly never concealed it—had been far less than the actuality, and he was certain that dislike had been founded in jealousy. Perhaps he had been wrong to betray his admiration for Elizabeth so openly the previous year, knowing what he did of Miss Bingley's ambitions.

Yet the root of the matter lay in the fact that he had not disabused her of the notion he would some day make an offer to her. For that, he was truly sorry, not only for the tense confrontation which had just occurred, but also because he had no desire to hurt her. Truly, as Elizabeth had made him see, his behavior had been left wanting, and his improvement was slow and still required some effort.

In the matter of Elizabeth, could he have been that transparent in his admiration for her? He had mentioned her fine eyes to Miss Bingley, but, to the best of his knowledge, he had never made any other comment to give her any impression of the extent of his regard. Perhaps his behavior at Pemberley toward her and the Gardiners had been enough for Miss Bingley to fill in the gaps of what she already knew.

The other option, of course, was that Miss Bingley had heard the alleged rumors, which would certainly explain the way she had acted this evening at dinner. Yet how was he to know when the woman denied hearing anything of the kind?

Frustrated, Darcy downed the rest of his brandy. He needed to find out what was being said, by any means possible.

His musings were interrupted by the opening of the door when Bingley stepped into the room. Luckily for Darcy's peace of mind, Richard was not there with him—he was not certain he could countenance his cousin's propensity to make sport with him at this time.

"So, it is done?" asked Bingley, taking a seat on an adjacent sofa.

"It is," acknowledged Darcy with a grimace.

Bingley grinned. "I can only imagine Caroline's reaction, if the stomping I heard going up the stairs is any indication."

"She was not pleased," responded Darcy diplomatically. "I must apologize, Bingley—I should have had this conversation with her years ago. I failed to act and have made the situation much worse than it had to be."

"Darcy, I will not allow you to take this upon yourself. You acted as any man who is sought after for his money and possessions would have, and you cannot take responsibility for any expectations which you did not create. Caroline must take the blame for her own actions."

This new and forceful Bingley was another new development in Darcy's world, but it was not an unwelcome one. His friend was realizing the potential Darcy had always seen in him, and Darcy could only applaud it—perhaps his officiousness had created some good after all!

"Enough of Caroline. I would love the opportunity to introduce your family to my Jane, and I think they would wish to become acquainted with Miss Elizabeth again. I am to visit tomorrow morning; shall you attend as well?"

Darcy smiled, thanking the jovial Bingley for the invitation and promising to accompany him the following morning. They spoke of inconsequential things for a few more moments before they left to seek their beds. The morrow for Darcy was to be an important day—he would finally be in the presence of his beloved, and he was determined to unravel the rumors to which his aunt had referred.

Chapter VII

By way of the intelligence provided by Mr. Bingley on Wednesday, Elizabeth had understood that Mr. Darcy would be arriving at Netherfield on the Thursday of that week (which was the reason Mr. Bingley gave for not visiting on that morning) and would be accompanying Bingley on his regular daily visit on that warm Friday morning. His presence in the area was not a surprise, nor was the fact that he would accompany his friend after his visits before his departure for town almost two weeks prior. Elizabeth had met him and conversed with him with complete poise, though not without a little trepidation, so at least their first meeting after the revelations about Lydia's elopement had passed with little change in his manner. Elizabeth was content with their interactions; it was more than she could have expected of him, sensible as she was of his knowledge of her family's near-fall from grace.

What did surprise Elizabeth was the attendance of his relations. Though perhaps Georgiana's presence could be explained as his desire to keep her with him after their frequent separations, the fact that his cousins had also accompanied him was puzzling. Certainly, the Colonel could likely do as he pleased when not bound to his duty—though his choice of amusements was a subject of some wonder—but Elizabeth understood Anne de Bourgh's movements to be carefully controlled by her mother. Had Lady Catherine agreed to send her to Hertfordshire as a means of forwarding their supposed engagement? She could hardly imagine Darcy's aunt would want her daughter in the company of a "dowerless fortune hunter" who was not sensible of her own place in the world. How had Anne de Bourgh possibly come to be here of all places?

Given this intelligence, it is perhaps not to be wondered at that Elizabeth took her time preparing that Friday morning. Though she was convinced she had lost Darcy's love irrevocably, she still wished to make a good impression on him and keep at the very least his good opinion of her, regardless of what he may think of her family. Of course, there was also the underlying desire to show Anne de Bourgh that her mother's opinions were unfounded. That Miss de Bourgh had heard the accusations was not in doubt; Elizabeth suspected that anyone within miles would have heard Lady Catherine screaming on that morning—someone who had been waiting in the carriage for her return could hardly have missed it. It was not as if the sickly young woman's opinion truly mattered to Elizabeth; it was more the desire to prove that Lady Catherine was an ill-bred, meddling termagant. It was equally important to Elizabeth to prove herself a truly genteel young woman in defiance of Lady Catherine's denunciations.

The visitors were announced—the time of their visit was everything which was proper, Elizabeth noted absently—and they were ushered into the sitting room where Elizabeth, her mother, and sisters were waiting. Elizabeth, by virtue of her position furthest from the door, was able to observe each of their countenances as they entered the room and indulge in her own pastime studying the character, emotions, and feelings of each of their visitors.

The Bingleys were easiest to judge, Elizabeth having taken full measure of their characters previously. Bingley entered the room with his habitual smile etched upon his features, and after greeting the entire room, he focused upon Jane, who received him with pleasure, extending her hands and allowing him to kiss the backs of them, all without displaying the blush which would previously have been her response. By contrast, Miss Bingley noted her brother's greeting with a poorly concealed scowl, raising her nose to unprecedented heights while extending her own greeting with a superior sniff.

After Darcy entered the room with his usual intense look—one which was directed at Elizabeth herself for the barest of moments, causing her heart to flutter alarmingly—he was immediately pressed into service making the introductions of his family to the Bennets due to Miss Bingley's disinterest and her brother's focus on Jane. Mr. Darcy managed the presentation with admirable composure, Elizabeth noted, especially as her mother was rendered speechless at the thought of having *four* progeny of the peerage present in her sitting room.

The good Colonel was as jovial and pleasant as Elizabeth remembered from Kent the previous spring—he greeted the party with pleasure and more than a few friendly remarks, which immediately won him the approval of the entire family. Mr. Darcy's sister was as quiet as Elizabeth remembered from Pemberley, but she appeared to gamely exert herself to say a few words, greeting Mrs. Bennet with a shy smile while merely glancing and nodding at the other Bennet sisters.

But the largest surprise was in the person of Anne de Bourgh, who bore no resemblance to the quiet and withdrawn woman to whom Elizabeth had been introduced in the spring. She entered the room with her cousin Darcy and immediately looked up at him, laughing at something he said before turning her attention back to the Bennets. Gone was the sickly young woman who moved little and said less, and in her place was a young woman who, although still a little pale and thin, was nevertheless of a healthier color. She greeted the assembled Bennets with a pleasure which could not be feigned, expressing her happiness at finally making their acquaintance. Could this amazing transformation be the reason why

Lady Catherine had allowed her only daughter out of her sight? What could Lady Catherine mean by it? After all, she had declared the Bennets to be a family without fortune and connection only days earlier, castigating Elizabeth in particular. What could now have induced her to allow her daughter to make and continue the acquaintance of those she had deemed unworthy only days earlier?

Elizabeth's ruminations were cut short, though, as Miss Darcy and Miss de Bourgh, spying her, moved to greet her, leaving her to store away her reflections for another time.

"Miss Elizabeth!" said Georgiana Darcy in greeting as she curtseyed. "I am very happy to make your acquaintance once again."

She appeared to have picked up a modicum of courage, as her greeting was more confident than the one with which she had favored Elizabeth's family. Elizabeth attributed it to their prior acquaintance, hoping that the young girl saw her as a friend in her own right rather than just an acquaintance of her brother's.

"Miss Darcy," responded Elizabeth with pleasure, "welcome to Hertfordshire. And I must insist you call me 'Lizzy' or even 'Elizabeth' if you must—'Miss Elizabeth' is much too large a mouthful to make it practical."

The young girl glowed in happiness, presumably at the thought of being considered close enough to dispense with formalities. "I shall, but only if you will call me 'Georgiana' or 'Georgie' in return. After all, my name is as much of a mouthful as yours!"

"Indeed, I shall," returned Elizabeth, happy to see the subtle changes in the young girl. Perhaps, with assistance from Elizabeth's sisters, she could be further drawn from her shell.

Anne de Bourgh moved closer to the two acquaintances and gave them a bright smile. "Yet I have a simple name which cannot be shortened, so I suppose you both shall simply have to be content with 'Anne,' if I may be extended the same privilege as my cousin, Miss Elizabeth."

Shocked again at the change in this woman, Elizabeth could only nod her assent, an act which prompted a laugh from the other woman.

"Oh, do not worry, Elizabeth; I am the same as I have ever been. I merely seem to have discovered my voice in my mother's absence."

Confusion reigned in Elizabeth's mind. Miss de Bourgh—Anne—spoke glibly of her mother, yet Lady Catherine could not but know of her daughter's presence here in Hertfordshire. Although Elizabeth knew it was not exactly polite and could be considered impertinent, Anne's smile and friendliness encouraged her to risk requesting clarification. In a tactful manner, of course.

"How is Lady Catherine?"

"Mother is the same as ever, I should imagine."

Anne regarded her with a half smile on her face, prompting Elizabeth to feel slightly uneasy, as if the other woman knew an embarrassing secret about her and was smug in her knowledge. Mr. Darcy could not have told her of their past interactions, could he? She risked a quick glance at Mr. Darcy and saw him engaged in conversation with the Colonel and her mother—a situation which carried its own concerns—and although he appeared to be attempting to follow and participate in the conversation, she could see his eyes darting about the room from time to time, especially in the direction of her and her companions.

"I am sure you are surprised at my presence here in light of what occurred just days ago."

The sound of Anne's voice jerked Elizabeth's attention back to the conversation, and after taking a moment to collect herself, Elizabeth allowed the observation to be true in a manner which she hoped was polite.

Anne pursed her lips in thought. "Let us just say that my mother has had a disagreement with the rest of the family."

"A rather loud and lengthy disagreement," Georgiana chimed in with a wry smile.

"Yes, quite. As a result of this, the family felt it best that my mother return to Rosings in solitude to consider her actions. I was to stay with my uncle Matlock and my cousins, but when I discovered Darcy was to visit Hertfordshire, I immediately jumped at the opportunity to see more of this county and make new acquaintances. And here I am."

A mortified blush blossomed on Elizabeth's cheeks; she should have suspected Lady Catherine in her disappointment would not have left the situation as it stood.

"Anne, Georgiana, I feel I must apologize for being the means of causing such dissention in your family. I never suspected . . . perhaps I should have . . ." She paused fighting for the words which would not come. "If only I had given Lady Catherine the assurance she demanded —"

"Nonsense!" exclaimed Anne. She took Elizabeth's hand and led her to the nearby sofa, sitting Elizabeth down, while Georgiana took up her position on Elizabeth's other side.

"I am certain it is not a surprise to you," said Anne, "but my mother has been attempting to run roughshod over our family for years, and most of us have rarely bothered to challenge her due to our desire to keep the peace. What my mother required of you was disrespectful and frankly none of her concern. You were completely within your rights to refuse her and deny all subsequent entreaties.

"You may not know this," continued Anne after a moment's thought in which she gazed at Elizabeth with a contemplative look, "but although my mother had waxed poetic on the subject of this supposed agreement between her and her sister, Darcy and I discussed it on several occasions and decided years ago that we would not marry."

Elizabeth glanced across the room involuntarily, only to meet the eyes of the man in question, who was staring at her with his typical intensity. Her blush deepened, and she lowered her eyes to the floor.

"So you see, my mother would ultimately have been disappointed regardless," said Anne. "Her displeasure has not been what anyone in the family had not foreseen, and we coped with it as a family. I assure you that none of us blame you or your dealings with Fitzwilliam. He is his own man and may do as he chooses without the high-handed interference of my mother. I urge you, Elizabeth, to think on it no more. I would much prefer to further our acquaintance rather than dwell on my mother, who is not even present."

Plucking up her courage, Elizabeth met Anne's eyes and gave her a wry smile. "I should like that very much."

Elizabeth glanced nervously between her companions and voiced a question which now seemed very important. "Has Mr. Darcy told you of our . . . dealings with one another?"

"Not, I suspect, to the extent you fear," responded Anne with a smile, which was mirrored by Georgiana.

"We know some of it, including his disastrous proposal and a little of how you interacted last fall," said the young girl. "But he has refused to divulge all, much to the consternation of Cousin Richard."

Elizabeth blushed with mortification once again, but her discomfiture was quickly eased by Anne, who was showing herself to be an astute observer in her own right.

"Do not be alarmed, Elizabeth," she soothed. "I, for one, believe you were completely correct in refusing him, although perhaps both of you could have kept your feelings and words under better regulation."

With a little less enthusiasm, Georgiana allowed this to be true, her reluctance in large part, Elizabeth suspected, due to her discomfort at agreeing with any point of view which would appear to be seen as critical to her brother.

"I will not push or pressure you in any way, Elizabeth," resumed Anne, "but I must tell you that neither Georgiana nor I—nor *most* others in our family—would have any objection to you becoming mistress of Pemberley."

Astonished, Elizabeth stared at her companions. "But Mr. Darcy . . . he . . ."

"Do not worry. He has not confided his plans to us, so I cannot tell you what he means to do, nor would I tell you if I knew. I do know he still thinks very highly of you, and I suspect he would not object to continuing or furthering your acquaintance."

Elizabeth shook her head. "I do not think that is possible. Things are . . . complicated between us."

"I have no doubt they are," responded Anne with a reassuring pat on the hand. "Yet I am also certain that they may be worked out to your satisfaction—and undoubtedly his—if you both are willing to try. I will only say that you should not judge Darcy too harshly—he can be somewhat antisocial and highhanded at times, but he is a good man."

"I am aware of that," was Elizabeth's quiet response.

"Excellent! Then let us dwell no longer on this subject and speak of happier things."

With a smile, Elizabeth allowed herself to be drawn into a conversation of Meryton's environs, none too soon she reflected, as she noticed Caroline Bingley move closer to their group, hovering on the edge and obviously listening in while trying to appear as if she were not. She did not seem to be overly friendly with either of the cousins, which was somewhat surprising considering her fawning attentions to Georgiana at Pemberley. Perhaps something had occurred on that front as well.

Pushing all thoughts of Caroline Bingley from her mind, Elizabeth relaxed and allowed herself to enjoy the conversation.

It was generally acknowledged by all of his acquaintances that once Fitzwilliam Darcy put his mind to a course of action, nothing would stand in the way of its successful completion. His legendary determination had lent him an almost celebrated status during his time at Cambridge, earning him much praise. Those whom he called friends had described his determination to be "single-minded," "implacable," or simply "fearsome" in his pursuit of his goals.

Yet in this situation, he found himself wondering how exactly he should go about accomplishing his task. He could not simply approach the young lady in question—particularly since he shared such an unsettled acquaintance with her—and ask her point blank if the rumors which had so incensed his aunt indeed existed. He could almost see the situation now.

"Excuse me, Miss Elizabeth, but my aunt de Bourgh has informed me that she heard rumors of our imminent engagement from her sycophantic and senseless parson, who, as you know, is incidentally your cousin. Would you please confirm or deny the existence of these rumors so I may determine how I should act?"

Darcy almost allowed a humorless chuckle at such a scene to bubble up from his chest. He could well imagine the response he would receive—and deserve—for such an imbecilic application. Doubtless she would begin to think him witless. No, it would certainly not do for him to behave in such a manner; he would of a necessity be required to bide his time and watch her, not to mention those around her, being attentive to all. Surely if such rumors did exist, he would hear them within days.

Mindful of Elizabeth's observations about his behavior in company, Darcy attempted to be attentive toward the conversation between himself, his cousin, and Mrs. Bennet, which consisted mostly of Mrs. Bennet's sense of honor at the thought of having the son of an earl present in her drawing room and Richard's compliments on the comfort of her house, the beauty of her daughters, and the loveliness of the neighborhood.

As for Darcy himself, the presence of the aforementioned earl's son seemed to have thawed Mrs. Bennet's attitude toward his person; much of the coldness and disdain in her manner, which had been barely concealed during his previous visits, was now gone, although he thought he detected once again a predatory gleam in her eye toward the two of them—after all, she did still have three unattached daughters, two of whom were considered to be very handsome. But for once, Darcy was not put off by the thought; he was in love with one of those daughters, and the Bennet matron's attitude was nothing that he would not have encountered in town. If only he had recognized this and acted appropriately when he had first come to Hertfordshire! And it seemed that Bingley's engagement to Jane had blunted some of her desperation, as she appeared much more confident and less shrill than she had in the past. In essentials, though, she was still the same silly woman he had met the previous year, even if her manners did not repulse him now as they had then.

He made a point of speaking to her with more warmth than he had ever before, as befitted the mother of the woman he hoped to eventually marry, after which he and Fitzwilliam moved on into the room. Mrs. Bennet spotted Miss Bingley, and with a zeal and fervor which he was certain was not reciprocated, she attached herself to the young woman, proceeding to speak with her as if they were old friends brought together after a long separation. Darcy shared a grin with his cousin at the look of consternation and barely concealed contempt on Miss Bingley's face, though he secretly hoped that she would not forget herself and in her anger insult the woman, thereby embarrassing herself and her brother.

On the other side of the room, he watched as his two kinswomen sat beside Elizabeth and carried on a conversation in which he ached to participate. He was grateful for their friendliness and attention—it made the task of wooing her that much easier to know that his relations genuinely liked and respected her. He had noticed a slight paleness to Elizabeth's face when Anne led her to the sofa, but they, and Georgiana, now appeared to be getting along famously, each laughing at some anecdote shared by the others. It was clear that whatever their interactions had been at Kent and Pemberley, the three ladies were well on their way to becoming fast friends.

"It does the heart good, does it not, Darcy?" murmured the Colonel from his side. "If only such visions of felicity and loveliness were the rule rather than the exception."

"There is only one vision of loveliness for me, cousin," responded Darcy, prompting a grin from the colonel.

"Ah, yes, the inestimable Miss Elizabeth Bennet. I would caution you, however, to open your eyes and consider what you see before you. Georgiana is growing up, Darcy, and she is very comely in her own right. I daresay it shall not be long before you will have to endure hordes of her admirers all clamoring for her attention."

Darcy frowned as he regarded his sister. He had not been blind to the changes in her appearance, but the past year and the trials she had endured, specifically the incident with that wastrel Wickham, had put the matter of her age and eligibility from his mind. He still tended to see the little girl who had so enraptured him as a young boy when he looked upon her, and he was loath to think of her in any other way. Clearly, that was changing.

"And it may not have caught your attention," continued Richard, "but Anne's escape from Lady Catherine has also effected a change in her manner and appearance. She is still a little pale, but I cannot remember ever having seen her so full of life and laughter. We should have taken up her banner and removed her from her mother's influence years ago."

"Indeed, we have been remiss," whispered Darcy in response, having noticed the changes in Anne for himself. "Still," continued he, remembering their conversation on the day of Lady Catherine's departure, "perhaps she was not ready for such a change at that time. I, too, feel responsible for not acting earlier, but she gave me a tongue lashing when I attempted to apologize, saying the blame was as much hers as yours or mine."

"Too true," agreed Richard. "At least she appears to be happy now. And will continue to be so, if I have any say in it."

"Aye," agreed Darcy, continuing his observation of the three ladies.

The younger Bennet sisters, Mary and Catherine, chose that moment to approach the group, and although Darcy knew Georgiana to hold Elizabeth in high regard, he also knew she was anxious to meet Elizabeth's sisters, particularly as they were closer to her own age.

For the next few moments, he observed as Elizabeth once again worked her magic, introducing his sister to hers on a more intimate basis, coaxing them gently, leading them to interact with one another. Within moments, the three were speaking animatedly with one another in a friendly, if somewhat cautious, fashion. It did Darcy's heart good to see his sister shedding her typical reticence and engaging in conversation. Her heart was at last healing.

"I must hand it to you, Darcy," spoke Richard from his side, "you have kept yourself aloof from the courting rituals of the eligible females of our set, but when you finally fell for a woman, you chose the brightest star I have ever beheld. Look how she draws everyone in to the conversation and makes them all feel at ease. I declare Elizabeth Bennet could charm a cantankerous old boar and have it rolling over at her feet, begging for truffles and a scratch on the chin!"

Darcy could only agree with his cousin, although he did turn and eye him with an unfriendly expression.

Richard's answering chortle did nothing to improve Darcy's mood. "Oh, do not look at me that way, Darcy. There is no need for you to become territorial; I admire Miss Elizabeth greatly, but I have already promised that I shall not intrude in your courting. Just be certain you do it properly this time—she is a rare treasure and should be treated as such."

Darcy's response was quiet and introspective. "Of that, I am aware, cousin."

The colonel gave him a sidelong look before clapping him on the back. "I will tell you once again—just be yourself. Show her the side of you that *I* see daily rather than the one harried by every eligible woman in town and fawned over by their mothers. There is no need to present a front to *that* young woman, and to do so would only damage your suit."

Nothing more than a grunt of agreement met Richard's declarations, for at that moment, the two younger Bennets, having excitedly discussed something for the previous few moments, rose from their seats. Miss Catherine grasped Georgiana's hand and dragged her off to partake in some other amusement while Miss Mary followed at a somewhat more sedate pace. He noted with a smile that his sister did not appear to go unwillingly; she seemed to have become fast friends with Elizabeth's sisters.

Having been favored with the opening he desired, Darcy approached the remaining ladies, noting Richard following behind. Elizabeth's smile as she welcomed them warmed his heart, allowing him the courage to greet her with affection and friendship.

"Miss Elizabeth, it is good to see you again."

He felt a nudge from his companion and let out a long-suffering sigh. "And I suppose you remember my reprobate of a cousin?"

Elizabeth's tinkling laughter met his reintroduction while the colonel regarded him with an injured air.

"Reprobate? I think not, cousin. Personally, I prefer the term 'rascal' coupled with 'devilishly handsome,' as I believe they are much closer to the truth."

By this time, Elizabeth and Anne were laughing gaily at the cousins' antics.

"'Rascal' might be accurate, cousin," Anne managed between her laughter, "but 'devilishly handsome?' Methinks someone has a high opinion of himself."

"Aye, that I do," agreed Colonel Fitzwilliam with aplomb. "Miss Elizabeth, it is truly a joy to see you once again. How do you do?"

"Very well indeed," responded Elizabeth with a sparkle in her eye. "I am happy to see you both again. I hope your journey into Hertfordshire was pleasant and not excessively tiring?"

"No, indeed," responded Darcy. "With these two—along with my sister—for company, there was no lack in conversation or amusement on our journey. In fact, once we left our rest stop in the afternoon and the ladies descended into slumber, I found myself looking for ways to silence my verbose cousin here," he said, clapping Richard on the back. "But alas, as I could not justify opening the door and throwing him out, I was forced to put up with his prattle for the entire journey."

"*Prattle*, cousin? I will have you know I am a member of his Majesty's army and a scion of an old and well respected family. As such, I do not prattle, chatter, babble, jabber, or any other such nonsense. I am always serious, and my opinions are well considered and highly rational."

His irreverent and slightly silly speech was punctuated by a wink in Elizabeth's direction, causing the entire party to laugh.

"Cousin, I do not think I have ever heard such a ridiculous speech issue forth from your mouth, which is saying something, as I have known you my entire life."

"Then you have not spent as much time with him as I have, Anne," said Darcy. "I assure you, this is quite usual for our overly talkative cousin."

"Then I am certain it did you good to have him in the carriage with you, Mr. Darcy," stated Elizabeth with a gleam in her eye. "After all, I am certain *you* could not be accused of being loquacious."

Her light and teasing manner, in addition to the slightly mischievous expression on her face as she made her declaration, removed any sting he otherwise might have felt at her words. Darcy felt himself becoming enchanted by her manner all over again; she could do nothing which was more certain of capturing his attention and increasing his love for her than simply being herself and acting in her arch way.

"Certainly not, Miss Elizabeth," returned he. "No more than you could be considered shy and retiring."

"Touché, Mr. Darcy," responded Elizabeth with a delighted laugh. "I see that crossing verbal swords for you carries as much danger as it ever has."

"But regardless of our irreverent banter, I must say that I am most pleased at seeing you all in Hertfordshire and wish to bid you welcome to Longbourn. I am overjoyed at the prospect of continuing my acquaintance with you for however long you are able to stay in the neighborhood. Do you know how long you will remain at Netherfield?"

"Other than Richard here, who may have to return to his regiment at any time," responded Darcy, "I believe we are all at our leisure. I should imagine we shall stay for some weeks—in fact, Bingley may become tired of our presence before we are actually required to leave for any other reason."

Elizabeth smiled. "I cannot imagine Mr. Bingley ever becoming weary of *any* company, especially yours, Mr. Darcy. I should think there is little to worry about from that perspective."

"Ah, so I see you *have* taken the measure of our inestimable Mr. Bingley," returned Darcy with a smirk.

Another round of laughter met his declaration. Darcy was highly gratified that he was able to converse—and even more, participate in the slightly teasing and animated discussion—with his more effusive companions.

Turning her attention to Richard, Elizabeth continued. "I am sorry to hear that you may be called away, Colonel Fitzwilliam; I greatly enjoyed our conversations in Kent, and I believe you would make a welcome addition to the society of the neighborhood."

"Thank you for the sentiment, Miss Elizabeth," responded the Colonel with no small measure of smugness, "but Darcy does not know as much about my regiment as he thinks he does. I have some weeks of leave accumulated and should not be required to depart for some time. I hope that we shall have many further opportunities for conversation in the coming weeks."

"We shall be vastly pleased to have you, Colonel."

Though he was surprised at his cousin's declaration, Darcy was pleased that Richard would be able to stay in the neighborhood for some time. He and Richard had always been the closest of cousins, and Darcy relied upon him for support and assistance. Richard had worked hard to get to where he was, but in the back of his mind, Darcy had always been afraid of the possibility of Richard being called into the thick of the fight against Napoleon's forces, as had happened in the past. Richard deserved a rest from his labors.

Sitting back, Darcy was able to participate in the conversation, which consisted of discussing the surrounding countryside and the state of affairs in Kent—particularly the news of Elizabeth's close friend, Charlotte Collins—and which gradually turned into a discussion of common likes and dislikes and of the society of the area. In addition, since he had three others to assist in carrying the conversation, Darcy was also able to observe the members of the party, and Elizabeth in particular, while still participating.

Though he watched Elizabeth as closely as possible, he could not detect any distress in her manner other than the blush he had detected when he had chanced to glance in her direction while speaking with her mother. That he attributed to some comment Anne had likely made which referenced him; knowing Anne's newly revealed teasing manner, it had been meant to elicit a response. But other than that, he had not been able to see any distress, which appeared to indicate that all was well and that the rumors which Lady Catherine had reported were either nothing more than idle speculation or had already died down. Still, if they *had* existed, he would still expect that she would feel somewhat uncomfortable in his presence, which did not appear to be the case given their banter. It was a good sign, but far from proof nonetheless. He would also expect the rumors to resurface with his arrival, which would require him to continue to be vigilant.

The conversation continued for some time before the door to the parlor opened up and a servant stepped in, announcing two more visitors. Darcy, concentrating as he was on the conversation, missed the names of the new arrivals, although he did recognize young Maria Lucas, who immediately spied the younger girls and moved to join them. The other visitor was a young man, who he assumed must be another Lucas due to his resemblance to Maria. He greeted Mrs. Bennet and appeared to politely converse with her for a few moments, but his eyes rarely left Darcy's group.

He soon bowed and moved away from Mrs. Bennet, his eyes focused on Elizabeth as he made his way across the room. Darcy happened to glance at Elizabeth as he began to move, and he witnessed her stiffening as her face took on a polite yet distant expression. Darcy was shocked, as he had never seen her act in this manner before—not even when she had sparred with him during the previous year had she reacted with such coldness.

The young man soon joined them and, bowing to Elizabeth, offered his greeting. "Lizzy, how wonderful to see you again. How are you this fine day?"

Though her countenance betrayed no reaction, Darcy fancied he could spy a slight tightening around her eyes.

"I am very well, *Mr. Lucas*," responded she, emphasizing the young man's name.

Darcy instantly understood her remonstration for his overly familiar manner.

"That is well," responded Lucas with a slight bow and a sardonic grin. "Would you do me the honor of introducing me to your friends?"

"Certainly." Elizabeth turned to the cousins. "Mr. Darcy, Colonel Fitzwilliam, Miss de Bourgh, this is Mr. Samuel Lucas, brother to my close friend Mrs. Collins, and heir of our closest neighbor, Sir William Lucas. Mr. Lucas has recently returned to Hertfordshire after completing university.

"Mr. Lucas, this is Mr. Fitzwilliam Darcy of Pemberley estate in Derbyshire; Colonel Richard Fitzwilliam, son of the Earl of Matlock; and Miss Anne de Bourgh, their cousin. Miss de Bourgh is the daughter of Lady Catherine de Bourgh, who is the patroness of your new brother, Mr. Collins. They are visiting Mr. Bingley and will be staying in the neighborhood."

The pleasantries dispensed with, the group fell into conversation once again, although the ease and familiarity of the previous discourse appeared to have been lost with the arrival of Mr. Lucas. Darcy could not account for it; Elizabeth was rarely this way with anyone of her acquaintance, and with someone she would have known for many years, Darcy would have expected that she would be even more familiar in her conversation. Yet for some reason, she appeared to be somewhat coldly formal with him, completely in contrast to the previous warmth she had displayed toward Darcy and his cousins, though she had known them for far less time.

As for Lucas himself, Darcy could not help but be unimpressed with the man. He appeared to be socially adept, his behavior was open and engaging, and he seemed to have some sense and understanding, yet underneath, Darcy thought he could detect something else, as if it were a mask the man wore to conceal his true self. If Darcy were to be asked to account for his reaction, he would be unable to completely explain the reason for his antipathy. The only thing he could compare it to was being in the company of George Wickham. That in itself was an indictment upon the man.

Still, it would not do to be rude to a man who was clearly well acquainted with Elizabeth, so he exerted himself to converse normally in the discussion, watching Elizabeth and her reactions as closely as he could.

For Elizabeth, much of the enjoyment she felt in the conversation disappeared with the addition of Samuel Lucas. His willful disregard of her wishes and his continued use of her more informal appellation offended her, and although he had ceased to do so after her pointed remonstration, she could still feel his insolence and carelessness toward her feelings even as he claimed to hold her in the highest regard. She doubted the cousins had noticed anything amiss—it took one far better acquainted with his character to pick out his mannerisms and understand the way he acted.

The desultory conversation continued for several more moments before Elizabeth suggested they move out into the garden. The weather that day was still as fine as could be expected for the month of October, and the air in the parlor had begun to feel a little close due to the number of people currently occupying it. Her plan was agreed to by all, and once the ladies had gathered their bonnets and coats, they exited the house.

Perhaps unsurprisingly—although she had intended the excursion outside to enable her to escape from Samuel's attentions—she found herself drawn into what she suspected Samuel considered a more personal greeting, away from the companionship of the others.

He stopped her as they exited and, grasping her hand, bowed and bestowed a light kiss on her knuckles.

"*Miss Elizabeth*," he drawled, pointedly emphasizing his formal manner of addressing her, "how nice it is to see you again today. I must say you are looking remarkably beautiful."

He was all insolence, and Elizabeth was immediately repulsed by his intimate manner, even though it was covered by a veneer of formality.

She quickly pulled her hand away and regarded him. "I thank you, Mr. Lucas. Now, if you will excuse me, I must see to our guests."

"By all means," was the response. He bowed and motioned to the door. "I should wish to converse with this Mr. Darcy and his cousin myself. I am certain you and I shall yet enjoy plenty of time to speak with one another."

Narrowing her eyes at his presumption and wondering at his meaning, Elizabeth made no objection to his retreat, relieved as she was over his departure. She stepped from the doorway in which she had been accosted and glanced around the garden. Samuel had already joined Mr. Darcy and the colonel, while Anne was speaking with Mr. Bingley and Jane. The younger girls had gathered near a bench on the far side of the garden and were speaking together in low tones.

The scene was peaceful and tranquil, and it evoked memories of happy times spent with good friends and new acquaintances.

"Eliza."

Elizabeth turned at the sound of her name and found herself face to face with Caroline Bingley, the one person she had not accounted for. The greeting was a little frosty, although perhaps politer than Elizabeth would have expected after their tête-à-tête at Lucas Lodge.

Still, Elizabeth ensured a pleasant expression was on her face and greeted Miss Bingley in kind.

"We seem to be the only ones without a conversation partner. Shall we take a turn around the garden?"

The setting was so familiar that Elizabeth almost laughed aloud, thinking of her stay at Netherfield the previous year and the evening when Miss Bingley had spoken similar words. As Mr. Darcy was some distance away and engaged in conversation with his cousin and Mr. Lucas, she doubted Miss Bingley's motivation was the same as it had been that evening at Netherfield. Of course, this did not assist her in determining just exactly what the woman's purpose was on this particular day.

Still, Elizabeth would be polite, regardless of her aversion for Miss Bingley and the words which had passed between them. She nodded her assent, and the two began walking through the garden. Their conversation was desultory and sparse, and Elizabeth felt some discomfort in the situation. It was not until they had crossed almost half of the circuit around the garden that Miss Bingley stopped and turned to face Elizabeth.

"Miss Eliza, I feel I should apologize for my behavior at Lucas Lodge," said she, surprising Elizabeth greatly. "I have no excuse but to assert that I was fatigued from my journey and did not guard my tongue as I should have."

It was all Elizabeth could do not to gape. Still, she gathered her wits and replied, all the while wondering if Mr. Bingley had somehow discovered their conversation and mandated this apology.

"I fear my behavior was not blameless either, Miss Bingley," replied Elizabeth. "If you are willing to forgive my trespasses, then I should be happy to extend the same courtesy to you."

Though she did not appear to be completely happy, Miss Bingley agreed. "You and I have perhaps never seen eye to eye, but that is no excuse for unpleasantness between us. If you are willing, I would prefer to leave that acrimony in the past and continue afresh."

"I agree, Miss Bingley," responded Elizabeth. She was still suspicious of the woman's motives, but she could not fault her words. "Let us think of it no further."

They continued on around the garden and their conversation, while it did not flow the same way that her earlier dialogue with Mr. Darcy and his cousins had—not that Elizabeth would have expected it to—was nonetheless easier than it had been before. Miss Bingley told Elizabeth of her sister and her husband and her visit to Scarborough, while Elizabeth reciprocated with her impressions of Derbyshire on her previous trip.

They had nearly completed the circuit—while maintaining a civility which they had never before managed—when Elizabeth noticed that the conversation groups, which appeared somewhat fluid, had changed. Mr. Darcy now stood speaking with his cousin Anne.

"Ah, I see you have noticed Mr. Darcy and Anne de Bourgh," said Miss Bingley from her side.

When Elizabeth glanced at her, Miss Bingley continued, appearing to be somewhat unhappy.

"I take it you have not heard?"

Elizabeth shook her head, and Miss Bingley continued. "Nothing has officially been announced, you understand, but I have heard it said that Mr. Darcy has become engaged to Miss de Bourgh."

Shocked, Elizabeth glanced over at the cousins, seeing them conversing amiably, before settling her gaze back on Miss Bingley. The woman appeared to be affecting an unconcerned attitude, but her manner was a little too nonchalant, her expression a little too forced, for it to be genuine. But was this a result of her disappointment, or was there something else?

"In that case, I must offer my congratulations to them and my sympathy for you, Miss Bingley."

Her eyes became hard. "Whatever do you mean?"

"Come, now, Miss Bingley. I am not blind. I am well aware of the fact that you aspired to be mistress of Pemberley yourself. There is no reason to conceal it."

"Do you seek to mock me?"

"Indeed, I do not. I merely thought to commiserate with you over the loss of your dream due to this engagement. I meant no offense."

The hard glare continued for several moments before Miss Bingley finally replied. "In that case, I thank you for your words," she ground out. "I *had* thought Mr. Darcy was interested in me for more than simple friendship—we have known one another for years, after all—but it was not to be. I fear family duty has a greater claim on Mr. Darcy than anything else. I do wish him the best, though."

Her talk of family duty caused Elizabeth's eyes to narrow in suspicion—she knew firsthand that while Mr. Darcy *was* a creature of duty and was perfectly willing to perform any engagements into which he had entered, he did not consider his familial requirements to extend to marrying Anne—nor did Anne, for that matter.

Then there was her conversation with Anne in the drawing room merely a few moments earlier. Either Anne had been prevaricating, or Miss Bingley was outright lying. No, this talk of Miss Bingley's rang false, but Elizabeth could not understand why Miss Bingley would make such a claim if it was untrue. For a social climber such as she, the results of her claim being exposed as a lie were too great to ignore.

"Excuse me, Miss Bingley, but might I ask where you heard this?"

"I must decline, Miss Elizabeth," responded Miss Bingley in a short and clipped tone. "My source does not wish to be revealed."

"In that case, I must give the happy couple my felicitations. Pray, excuse me."

Making to walk away, Elizabeth was stopped when Miss Bingley grasped her arm. She peered back at the woman, looking for the telltale signs of panic that her ruse was about to be exposed. Miss Bingley, however, although she appeared to be somewhat worried, did not look frightened. She either hid it well, or Elizabeth's conjecture was incorrect.

"I would appreciate your silence in this matter, Miss Eliza. As the engagement has not yet been announced, I understand they wish to keep it quiet for now. It is only known to a select few of their closest friends; they would not be happy with me for exposing it to you."

Elizabeth did not miss Caroline's insinuation that she was not considered a close enough friend to know of the supposed engagement, a fact which caused even more suspicion on Elizabeth's part.

"And yet you have told me."

A firm gaze was her response. "You have stated you are not blind, but I can assure you that I am not either, Miss Eliza. I witnessed your interactions with Mr. Darcy here last autumn and during the summer at Pemberley. As Mr. Darcy is a man of consequence, I cannot help but imagine that his attentions may have raised certain . . . expectations on your part. I am merely trying to put you on your guard."

"In that case, I thank you, Miss Bingley," responded Elizabeth, not wishing to carry the conversation any further.

"I have merely acted in the manner of a friend. Mr. Darcy's adherence to duty is so strong that I suppose neither of us ever had a chance to overcome it. I must admit my own disappointment. I am attempting to move past it, and I suggest you do the same."

"I shall try, Miss Bingley," murmured Elizabeth.

She nodded her head and moved away, not wishing to discuss the matter further with the insincere woman. Elizabeth did not trust Caroline Bingley—not in any matter regarding Mr. Darcy—but it was pointless to argue with her. Elizabeth knew in her heart that Miss Bingley was either mistaken or had told her an outright falsehood; Anne de Bourgh would never have spoken the way she had if she was secretly engaged to Mr. Darcy. Still, it would not hurt to continue to watch and determine for herself the true state of Mr. Darcy and Miss de Bourgh's relationship.

What Elizabeth could not determine was her own feelings on the matter. It would take some reflection before she could decipher her own reaction. There was no time at present for her to think on it.

It was not much longer before the visitors had stayed for the polite length of time for a morning visit and excused themselves to return to Netherfield. Before they departed, Miss Bingley reluctantly extended an invitation to Jane and Elizabeth for lunch the next day at Netherfield. Elizabeth almost burst out laughing, as it was clear she had done it at the urging of her brother, who stood over her with a pleasant yet firm expression on his face. Some things never changed.

The invitation was accepted with alacrity, and plans were made to attend the neighboring estate the next day. To Netherfield, they were to return.

Chapter VIII

As the two carriages began to roll down the drive from Longbourn, Darcy leaned back in his seat and closed his eyes, thankful that his first meeting with Elizabeth since learning of the supposed rumors had passed in a relatively successful manner, yet already regretting the loss of her company. Certainly the company in which he now found himself was not one in which he could simply lose himself in conversation without needing to worry about keeping his words under regulation—the presence of Miss Bingley prevented that rather effectively.

The trip that morning had been undertaken along family lines, with Darcy and his relations in one carriage, and the Bingleys following in the other. However, when they had readied themselves to return to Netherfield, Bingley had suggested they trade traveling partners for the journey back so as to vary conversation and company. Privately, Darcy suspected that Bingley just wanted some time away from his sister, as he had no doubt that Miss Bingley had been vocal in her denunciation of not only Darcy's refusal of her, but also the Bennets and her brother's *ill-judged* betrothal. At the very least, if she had been silent, it would likely have been cold and uncomfortable, not at all the sort of atmosphere which would make the effervescent Bingley feel at ease.

As a result, Darcy now found himself in a carriage with Miss Bingley and Anne, while Georgiana and Fitzwilliam traveled with Bingley. Though he would not have chosen to travel with Miss Bingley (especially considering the fact that he had essentially spurned her the previous day), Darcy decided after a moment's reflection that obliging Bingley and taking his sister off his hands for the brief journey was not an imposition. It also helped that the young woman in question was not inclined to speak; Miss Bingley, unsurprisingly, was still furious, and she had not directed two words toward him the entire morning. Darcy found he could bear her silence quite cheerfully and was content to be in her company as long as the current situation persisted. And since Anne was also in a quiet, pensive mood—she sat with her face turned toward the window, watching the scenery as it rolled past—Darcy was able to sit back and think upon the morning.

It was an entirely odd circumstance, he mused, that no hint of his supposed engagement to Elizabeth had been betrayed that morning at the Bennet residence. Or rather, it was odd that the rumor which Lady Catherine had insisted was to be blamed on the machinations of the Bennets was not in evidence at said family's home. It was perhaps conceivable that the family had refrained from discussing it within the hearing of Darcy's family, but that hardly seemed likely given Mrs. Bennet's proclivity for ferreting out the existence of any and all of her daughters' prospective beaux and expounding upon them loud and long, real or imagined. He would have expected her to trumpet such rumors to the world rather than conceal them in any fashion.

The thought immediately embarrassed him; Mrs. Bennet, for all her silliness, had given birth to the woman Darcy hoped to marry, and for that, she deserved his respect and gratitude. He knew he must improve his opinion of her or, at the very least, learn to tolerate her better.

Besides, Elizabeth's reaction did not betray any discomfort, and furthermore, Bingley had made no mention of it. It had been more than a fortnight since they had originally returned to Hertfordshire, and Darcy could not imagine that Bingley had been in society for two weeks without hearing of it. His friend could be somewhat unobservant when focused on Miss Jane Bennet, but Darcy could not imagine him to be that obtuse. Bingley certainly would have said something if he had even heard a hint of any rumors concerning Darcy.

But that did not answer the question of where the rumors had originated in the first place. Lady Catherine's only link to Hertfordshire of which he was aware was her parson's connection through his wife to the Lucas family. Could the Lucases be the source of these rumors? If so, then why had Bingley not heard of them? It was all very vexing, and he knew he was no closer to solving the riddle than he had been that morning. More patience would be required.

Knowing there was nothing to be done at present, Darcy allowed his worries over the task he had set himself to melt away. Instead, his thoughts followed the much more agreeable path of considering his interactions this morning with his beloved and her family.

To be honest, Darcy was astonished at his own behavior. Certainly, he had in the past, when he felt comfortable in company, been far more loquacious and open than he had been when he had first arrived in Hertfordshire, although his behavior at the time had in large part had been due to the problems with Wickham and Georgiana. But for some reason, the combination of being once again in Elizabeth's presence and the company of his relations had loosened his tongue. He had never been as teasing as he had been that morning with anyone other than his close family. Even Bingley and his friendly and agreeable disposition had never induced such a response from Darcy.

He knew himself to be of a very sober disposition. Indeed, many had called him grave, staid, or resolute—although there were those such as Wickham who would not be so kind, he did not doubt—but the world in general did not know the true Fitzwilliam Darcy. He simply did not feel comfortable revealing himself thus before all and sundry. He was a person who valued his privacy, and he preferred to remain that way.

This was why his teasing with Miss Elizabeth was such a surprise, even to himself—surprising enough that underneath the merriment, he had noticed Richard looking at him with questioning glances during their conversation. It was normally Richard who was easy in manners and animated in company. It seemed that the mere presence of Elizabeth Bennet was enough to induce him—Fitzwilliam Darcy—to discard a lifetime of behavior and allow himself to simply relax. She truly was a rare find if she could have this effect upon him mere moments after he had been admitted to her company.

Yet what Darcy did not realize was the fact that not only was Elizabeth Bennet affecting him, allowing him to open up to a degree with which he had never before felt comfortable, but that he was also permitting himself to recognize his feelings for her and seek out her approval which was changing him. In essentials, he was the same man he had always been, and if there had been others directly involved with the conversation, he would never have felt open enough to act as he had. It was now only with Elizabeth being an addition to his family—at least in his own mind—which allowed him to lose his reserve and act in such a carefree manner.

This did not occur to Darcy, although certain members of his close family, along with perhaps the aforementioned Miss Elizabeth Bennet, could possibly have divined the truth. Darcy only knew that, in some manner, Elizabeth had changed him, and that fact made him love her all the more.

A shift in the seat across from him caught his attention and jolted him out of his reverie. Opening his eyes, he peered at the ladies. Miss Bingley was focused upon him, an unreadable expression affixed upon her face, while Anne had given up her contemplation of the passing scenery and was watching Miss Bingley out of the corner of her eye.

Miss Bingley sniffed in arrogant disdain, causing Darcy to reflect with no small amount of amusement that while he had seen that particular form of haughtiness from her in the past, it had never been directed *at him*. Anne, being perfectly aware of what had passed between her cousin and Miss Bingley the previous evening, smirked slightly and rolled her eyes.

"I fear we must have some conversation, Miss de Bourgh," stated Miss Bingley, turning resolutely away from the gentleman. "Otherwise, my brother's suggestion of traveling with new companions will have been for naught."

"I believe you are correct, Miss Bingley," replied Anne, clearly intending to allow Miss Bingley to further the conversation if she so desired.

Miss Bingley appeared to catch her purpose, but although her expression hardened slightly, she betrayed no other reaction.

"How did you find your first introduction to Hertfordshire society?"

"Very interesting. I find I like the Bennets quite well indeed."

Darcy watched Miss Bingley's reaction very closely and was not disappointed, as her expression became haughtier at Anne's statement.

"Yes, I suppose the Bennets could be termed . . . *interesting*."

"They are a good family who clearly hold each other in the highest of affection, Miss Bingley. The younger girls were very welcoming; they made Georgiana feel completely at ease, for which I must thank them. Mrs. Bennet *is* perhaps slightly high-strung, but she was pleasant and a very good hostess. The pastries which were served were delicious, and they would not have been out of place if they had appeared on a breakfast tray at Pemberley itself. Do you not agree, cousin?"

Suppressing a smile at Anne's baiting of Miss Bingley, Darcy was forced to agree—he had thought them delicious as well.

Though she appeared to have swallowed a lemon, Miss Bingley was also forced to allow that the pastries had been very well done.

"In addition, Miss Jane Bennet was every bit as angelic as my cousin and your brother had led me to believe, and you know my opinion of Miss Elizabeth. I count it as a very enjoyable visit—I am eager to continue my acquaintance with all of them."

"Well, I suppose everyone was especially well behaved today. It is unsurprising, as they cannot have the honor of receiving four scions of an earl every day."

"Whatever can you mean, Miss Bingley?" responded Anne, a slight frown upon her face. "I found their behavior to be quite impeccable, although perhaps Mrs. Bennet was a trifle exuberant."

"Well, I have known Mrs. Bennet to be flighty, not to mention somewhat vulgar when she gets excited. Perhaps her daughter's most advantageous engagement to my brother has calmed her nerves now that she does not need to concern herself over her future. What do you think, Mr. Darcy?"

Darcy was not about to become involved in criticizing a woman of whom he had just moments earlier pledged to think better. Besides, he suspected Miss Bingley's words were actually very close to the mark.

"It is certainly an eligible match for both parties," responded Darcy, thinking that an oblique answer would be preferable to outright contradiction. "Miss Bennet obtains security for her future and the future of her children, while your brother secures connections to a gentleman's family—a family which has held their estate for generations, I might add. Of course, this does not even mention the very great benefit to them both for marrying where their hearts are inclined. No one seeing them interact together can doubt their tender feelings for one another."

Miss Bingley did not miss his meaning, but her darkened expression indicated that she thought his statement to be a barb in her direction rather than one in his own as he had intended it to be. Miss Bingley and her sister had merely pointed out the evils of Jane's connections during their conversation the previous November; it had been Darcy who had claimed that Jane Bennet did not harbor deep feelings for Bingley. Now, watching them together, Darcy wondered how he could ever have mistaken their mutual regard. Of course, it was obvious in hindsight that he had seen exactly what he had wanted to see.

"I think the family *has* improved," allowed Miss Bingley with another haughty sniff. "But then, the example of the comportment of superior members of society cannot help but rub off on them, I suppose."

"Indeed," responded Anne softly, while Darcy resisted the urge to roll his eyes.

"And what of Mr. Lucas? What was your impression of him?"

"I was not in his company long enough to form an opinion, Miss Bingley," said Anne.

"And you, Mr. Darcy?"

Though Darcy did not want to get into his thoughts and feelings about Samuel Lucas, he could hardly remain quiet on the subject since he was already part of the conversation.

"Samuel Lucas appears to be an intelligent man," responded Darcy, choosing his words cautiously. "I too was not in company with him long enough to form a true opinion of his character, but what I saw of it, I must admit did not particularly impress me."

A raised eyebrow met his declaration. "Is there a reason why, Mr. Darcy?"

"A feeling more than anything. He was impertinent in his conversation, asking questions and making comments which were not exactly proper, and all the while, he smirked and laughed, as if he knew a great secret which he was unwilling to share."

Miss Bingley sniffed and shrugged. "For my part, I found him a sensible man with very good manners and an engaging way of speaking."

"I'm sorry, Miss Bingley," interjected Anne, "but I do not believe you spoke two words to Mr. Lucas. Were you previously acquainted with him?"

"Yes, I met him at a party at Lucas Lodge a few days before you arrived," confirmed Miss Bingley. "He is a great favorite with the Bennets and can often be found there visiting with them, although I think his purpose is more to visit one of the family in particular."

"Truly?" queried Anne. "I must admit, I did not notice that he paid any special attention to any member of the family, although his address to Miss Elizabeth was somewhat impertinent and overly familiar."

By this time, Darcy had lost all interest in their discourse and was content to allow Anne to carry the conversation. Miss Bingley's next words, however, brought his attention back to the two young women, though he was careful to control his reaction.

"That is because it is she whom he visits."

Casually glancing at the two women across from him, Darcy noted Miss Bingley's attention focused on him, as if she were waiting to hear his reaction. Darcy's blank stare in response caused a grimace, and she once again raised her nose in the air and peered back at Anne.

"Rumors of their courtship are all over Meryton — in fact, Mrs. Bennet and Lady Lucas discussed it at great length only days ago at a gathering at Lucas Lodge. They are certainly excited over the prospect of their families being joined together in such an intimate way. And you know they were best of friends as children. I suppose it should not be surprising that two who have known each other their whole lives should desire a closer connection."

Anne regarded Miss Bingley with an expression of disbelief. Darcy knew that she was thinking of the same thing, namely Elizabeth's rather cold reception of the Lucas heir as he visited that morning. Miss Bingley, who was not part of the group, could not know how they had interacted.

"I must admit, I formed a much different opinion of their interactions," replied Anne after regarding Miss Bingley with an inscrutable expression. "Elizabeth greeted him as an acquaintance, but certainly not a close one. I especially remember her chastising him for his familiar greeting, while she called him *Mr. Lucas*."

"Perhaps," Miss Bingley agreed rather nonchalantly, "but I suspect that was likely because they have not published the fact of their courting as of yet. And as you all left the house before I did, you would not have witnessed their more . . . intimate greeting as they left the house. It was much more familiar than when they were in company and left little doubt as to their feelings for one another."

Although her expression remained skeptical, Anne nevertheless did not pursue the subject any further. "I suppose we shall have to wait and see, in that case."

"Quite," replied Miss Bingley, once again turning her attention to the passing landscape.

Darcy was in a quandary. On the one hand, he knew he could not trust Miss Bingley's portrayal of anything related to Elizabeth Bennet—her enmity for the young woman was entirely too clear for that.

On the other, her mention of specific incidents—the party at the Lucas residence, the greeting between Samuel and Elizabeth of which he had merely caught a glimpse, and the fact that they were old friends—gave him pause.

He had certainly seen nothing in their manner which would suggest a greater intimacy than appeared at first glance. Rather, nothing which suggested a greater intimacy had appeared in *Elizabeth's* manner; Samuel, judging by his greeting and his overly familiar way of addressing her, clearly admired the second Bennet daughter.

But was the sentiment returned? The expression on Elizabeth's face when he had entered the room suggested not—she had not appeared happy to see Lucas at all. Then there was the conversation, which Darcy had already noted was somewhat stilted and cold after Samuel had arrived. Unless Elizabeth was a very talented actress—and Darcy was forced to admit he had misread her reactions in the past—Darcy would have to claim he had seen nothing in her manner which indicated any kind of attachment on her part at least.

But what of Mrs. Bennet? If she had been speaking of a match between the two—and he had no doubt that the match would be met with much approbation, given the two families' close ties and status as leaders in the area—could there be something to this rumor?

Darcy passed a hand over his face, his head beginning to ache with thoughts of rumors, counter-rumors, courtships, and engagements. At the very least, rumors of Elizabeth's courtship with Lucas seemed to preclude the possibility of rumors of Darcy's engagement with her, if this courtship Miss Bingley insisted upon even existed. He forced himself to focus on what he knew.

Elizabeth was an independent young lady, and given what he knew of Mr. Bennet, he doubted the man would make his daughter—especially one as strong-willed as Elizabeth—marry against her will. Beyond that, from what he had seen, Darcy did not think she held Mr. Lucas in great regard.

He was already aware of the fact that she would not marry a man solely for prudence; her refusal of his suit had made that abundantly clear. If this was an idea contained in the mind of Mrs. Bennet alone, Darcy thought he had little to fear. Though pressure might be brought to bear by her mother—and perhaps even Samuel himself—Darcy had no doubt she would resist if it was not what she truly wanted.

The consideration which trumped all others, however, was the source of this intelligence. Miss Bingley was crafty, but she was also ruled by her passions and her dislikes, and in this instance, her dislike was firmly focused upon Elizabeth

Bennet. It was likely her words contained some measure of truth, but he could not put credence in the entire story. There was something about it that did not quite sound right . . .

As the carriage pulled into the Netherfield drive, Darcy decided to do the only thing he could in such a situation—watch and observe. He did not doubt that it would all become clear in due time. Until then, he would have to continue on as he had already determined, though this new development vexed him greatly.

The carriage door opened and Anne de Bourgh watched as her cousin alighted and then helped Miss Bingley and herself down with his offered hand. Miss Bingley immediately let out a disdainful huff and stalked up into the house, her nose held high in the air. Anne exchanged an amused glance with her cousin while they both attempted to stifle the snickers which threatened to burst forth.

"Cousin, I find I am far too restless to enter the house at this time," stated Anne. "Will you accompany me on a short turn through the gardens?"

"With pleasure, Anne," replied Darcy with a smile.

As they walked, the second carriage carrying the rest of the party pulled up to the door, and its occupants descended. The three arrivals directed questioning looks at Anne and her companion, but she waved them off, not wanting anyone else to accompany them and listen in on their conversation. Fortunately, they did not press the issue—they all entered the house, leaving Anne and Darcy alone for their walk.

Anne had something of a dilemma. She had listened to the story spun by Miss Bingley with a growing sense of disbelief; she had seen the reactions of Elizabeth to both Darcy and the Lucas heir that morning, and what she had seen had not matched Miss Bingley's assertions.

She was uncertain of her cousin's reaction. Darcy was in the habit of keeping himself under careful regulation, and as such, it was sometimes difficult to have any insight into his thoughts or feelings. Anne thought Darcy knew Miss Bingley well enough to know that anything she said—especially regarding a woman she considered a hated rival—was not to be trusted. At least, she hoped that was the case. She had already determined to watch the situation closely and approach Elizabeth for confirmation if necessary—she knew *that* course of action to be somewhat impertinent, but her cousin's happiness and the happiness of a young woman of whom Anne thought highly were at stake. There was nothing Miss Bingley could possibly do to keep them apart unless they themselves were swayed by whisperings that Anne suspected only held a kernel of truth. Thus, she was determined to hear Darcy's thoughts on the subject and ensure he heard hers if their opinions did not match.

They wandered around the house and entered the gardens, allowing Anne to feel a sense of peace come over her. Her mother had never allowed her to roam further than Rosings' gardens, and even then, permission was granted infrequently. Anne truly loved nature and loved walking out of doors, but it had always seemed easier to take the path of least resistance and bend to Lady Catherine's will. At least her phaeton had allowed her some means of escape from the house, though she had not been able to use it as often as she would have liked—Lady Catherine had still insisted on her staying indoors most days.

Her recent act of defiance and her break with mother had truly been the first time she had ever openly rebelled against her mother's will, although her discontent had been growing for years. In truth, Anne credited Elizabeth Bennet in part for allowing her the courage to finally do what she had better have done years earlier. Anne had immediately seen Elizabeth as a strong and self-assured young woman, one who was not afraid to hold her own opinions and state them confidently regardless of what others might think. Her admiration had only increased when Charlotte Lucas had let slip the fact that Elizabeth Bennet had refused an offer of marriage from Mr. Collins, one which most young women in her situation—and the aforementioned Mrs. Collins herself—would have felt bound to accept, regardless of how dull or even loathsome the gentleman might be. Her mother's fortuitous journey into Hertfordshire had merely allowed her a convenient opportunity to make her escape, affording her the comfort and support of her relations during the event.

Anne was thankful for Elizabeth's quiet strength and firm beliefs, not to mention her example of what an independent young woman could be, and she was determined to see her newfound friend happy with Darcy. Then, Anne could set about seeking her own happiness in life, whatever that might be.

"Cousin, shall we sit?" queried Anne, gesturing to a stone bench which sat along the path.

An immediate expression of concern came over Darcy's face. "Anne, are you fatigued? Perhaps we should retire to the house."

"I am fine, Darcy," responded Anne with a roll of her eyes. She sat down on the bench, motioning her cousin to sit beside her before continuing. "I am not as fragile as mother would have you all believe, and I think the air of this county, as well as the freedom to move which my mother has never allowed, has done me a great deal of good. Exercise, you know, is very beneficial, and I believe I have suffered from a lack of it. I shall never be of a robust constitution, but I find now that I feel as well as I ever have."

Darcy watched her closely before sighing and leaning back in his seat. "That is well, Anne, but please do not overtax yourself. I am enjoying getting to know you better, and I do not wish you to become ill because you have done more than you ought. For all of our sakes, Anne, please take care."

"I shall," replied Anne with a casual wave of her hand. Her cousins would continue to fret over her until they were certain she was as well as she claimed, and the proof of that would only come with time. She could bear their overly solicitous attitudes because she knew they cared for her.

"Now, I would speak with you, cousin."

Darcy's expression was one of some slight trepidation. "Of what?"

"Nothing so onerous, I assure you. I merely wished to solicit your opinion on the intelligence Miss Bingley divulged during our return."

The trepidation changed to amusement, and Darcy regarded Anne with a slight smirk upon his face. For a moment, Anne almost ground her teeth together—now was not the time for Darcy to emulate Richard's overly flippant manner!

"Now you, too? I knew Richard had an unhealthy interest in my love life, but I had thought you content to leave well enough alone."

A frustrated Anne glared at him. "You know me better than to suppose I would meddle in your affairs, cousin."

"I never thought anything else, Anne," responded Darcy, touching her arm. "I merely find it amusing that suddenly the entire family is interested in my relationship with Miss Elizabeth Bennet."

"You should be happy someone is," admonished Anne. "I mean only to help and want nothing more than your happiness—and of course, that of Miss Elizabeth as well. You know that Miss Bingley, regardless of the veracity of what she imparted to us this morning, has no wish to promote your happiness if it does not include her own."

"Yes, I am aware of Miss Bingley's aspirations and views, Anne, and I can assure you I have thought about what she said, and at this point, I am not discouraged. I saw nothing of Miss Bingley's assertions this morning in Elizabeth's manners or her countenance. Until I do, I shall proceed as I have intended."

"Excellent, Darcy," responded Anne with a nod of her head. "I suspected you would not be drawn in by her claims, but I wanted to offer my support if you were by any means wavering."

"I thank you, Anne. It is comforting to know I have your encouragement."

Anne nodded in response, content with the way the discussion had proceeded. She had been afraid Darcy would continue to hold his feelings close and not divulge them; he was so maddeningly independent and reticent at times that trying to induce him to show his feelings when he was not willing to reveal them was often an exercise in futility.

"Then what do you think Miss Bingley is up to?"

A scowl met her question. "I fear it is one of two possibilities. Either she has heard of Mr. Lucas's interest in Elizabeth—which would not surprise me for an instant, as Mrs. Bennet is not exactly . . . reticent when it comes to her daughters' prospects—or she has invented a blatant falsehood. From what I saw of Miss Elizabeth's behavior, she does not welcome Samuel's attentions, nor does she encourage them."

Anne nodded her head. "My own observations match yours quite closely. Indeed, I have known Miss Bingley for less than twenty-four hours, and I believe I have already taken her measure. I believe Richard put it most succinctly—a more obvious social climber I have never had the misfortune to meet!"

A laugh escaped Darcy's lips, and he returned Anne's gaze with amusement. "Our cousin does have a gift for words at times."

"I would caution you about Miss Bingley, though, cousin, "continued Anne. "I do not know that she has given up her designs upon you. I would strongly advise you to ensure you are never alone with her. And for heaven's sake—keep your door locked at night!"

A laugh met her response. "You *do* know I have been hunted by the likes of Miss Bingley my entire adult life, do you not?"

Anne inclined her head with a grin, satisfied with the response. "So, what do you plan to do about this intelligence?"

"Nothing," replied Darcy. "I shall continue on my course, try to find out if the rumors your mother reported do actually exist, and act based on what I find."

"You could simply ask Miss Bennet, you know."

Darcy frowned. "The thought had occurred to me, but I dismissed it as impertinence. I do not wish for her to think of me as an arrogant imbecile now that I have begun to improve her opinion of me."

"I think it neither imbecilic nor arrogant, cousin. Elizabeth is an intelligent and perceptive young lady, and I cannot imagine her thinking anything less of you for being honest. You are, after all, attempting to protect her reputation."

Darcy gazed back at Anne, evidently considering her words. "You think she will respond favorably?"

"There is only one way to discover her reaction, is there not?"

Her cousin did not seem at all impressed with her flippant response, causing her to giggle softly at his expression. He was changed to a certain extent, but he was in essentials still the same man he had ever been; in short, he still did not respond well to being teased, unless the tease was Miss Elizabeth, of course!

"I apologize, Darcy—I suppose you have had enough teasing from Richard. I believe that as long as you explain yourself properly, Elizabeth will take no offense. Perhaps an inquiry about her relationship with Samuel Lucas *would* be an impertinence, but to ask her about the rumors my mother heard from her parson is not. I suggest you ask."

"Thank you for your suggestion, Anne," said Darcy after a moment of thought. "I will take your advice under consideration."

"You are a good man, Darcy," responded Anne, patting his hand with affection. "I am sure your Elizabeth cannot fail to recognize that fact as well.

"Now," said she, rising to her feet, "I believe I should like to enter the house and freshen up before luncheon."

Darcy also stood and extended his arm, which Anne took with pleasure. The first steps were in place, and Anne was determined her cousin should not fall prey to Miss Bingley's designs.

The young lady who was one of the subjects of the cousins' discussion stood at the window in her bedchamber, gazing down at them, her emotions seething with disappointment and dissatisfaction. She had spent years becoming the perfect Mrs. Darcy, and still he saw fit to spurn her. It was not to be borne!

And yet Caroline was uncertain as to what more she could possibly do to avoid the ignominy which seemed to be speeding ahead with all the momentum of a runaway carriage. She had no friends in the house, and even Louisa, had she been present, would have been hesitant to support her in her quest in direct violation of her brother's instructions and Mr. Darcy's declarations. Even if she was to compromise him in any way, she doubted her brother would seriously insist on Mr. Darcy marrying her; it was for that reason she had never attempted it before. And now, with his newfound confidence—Caroline almost gagged at the thought of her brother not being under her influence—he was assuredly less likely to support her than ever. No, loath as she was to admit it, any chance of becoming mistress of Pemberley was gone.

She was left with nothing more than an act of petty revenge against those who had caused her defeat. As Mr. Darcy and that Bennet chit had ruined her hope of happiness, so would she ruin theirs. It was not much, but it was all she had left—she would not see that *woman* married to Mr. Darcy if it was within her power to prevent it.

Caroline was very aware of the dangerous nature of the path to which she had set herself. Mr. Darcy's power to completely ruin her life and make her unmarriageable by anyone of consequence was not to be underestimated. Part of her wished to wash her hands of the business and retreat to London, intent upon finding herself another man who would take her and her twenty-thousand pounds And perhaps most importantly, a man who had never even heard the name Elizabeth Bennet! But her pride would not allow her to simply leave well enough alone—the country chit would not be allowed to carry the day over Caroline Bingley!

Luckily, she thought she had hidden her tracks well. Mrs. Bennet's loud proclamations from the evening at Lucas Lodge meant that she could plausibly assert that she had merely heard the woman speak of an imminent engagement, and if Darcy were to learn of her words to Elizabeth that morning, she could state that she had misinterpreted their relationship. She had only done this to sow a little confusion between the two of them. If she were fortunate, Samuel Lucas would use the time to his best advantage.

Mr. Lucas, she had no doubt, given his performance that morning, would play his part to perfection. Hopefully—and this was really her only hope, as she suspected both Mr. Darcy and the Bennet girl would learn the truth before long—Mr. Lucas would continue to court Elizabeth, with her permission or without, and then propose. Then, with Mrs. Bennet's approbation and enthusiastic support, Elizabeth would be forced to accept, removing all possibility of her accepting Mr. Darcy.

Caroline almost rubbed her hands with glee. If all went well—though Caroline realized that success in this endeavor was not at all assured—this would all happen while Mr. Darcy and the Bennet chit were trying to sort out what they had heard. By then, it would be too late. Elizabeth would not be happy in a union with Mr. Lucas, and Caroline would have her revenge against both Mr. Darcy and her detested rival.

If only Mr. Lucas would quickly come to the point!

After the Netherfield party departed, Elizabeth entered the house, her mind full of the conversations and revelations of the morning. She was happy to have once again made the acquaintance of Mr. Darcy's relatives, and she felt herself becoming firm friends with all of them. Though she still could not decipher her feelings for the gentleman himself, she was immensely grateful for the opportunity to further her acquaintance and determined to use the time available to better judge her feelings.

As for Mr. Darcy's feelings . . . Elizabeth's thoughts were full of the conversation she had had with Anne and Georgiana. It appeared that, against all rational explanation, Lydia's fiasco had not damaged Elizabeth in Mr. Darcy's estimation, if Anne's assurances were in any way accurate. And she could not imagine that they were not; after all, she had it directly from the man's cousins, and Mr. Darcy *had* after all returned to Hertfordshire, when she would have thought he would avoid her entirely. Elizabeth could not help but feel a frisson of excitement run up her spine at thought of the love she inspired in this man; he, who adhered to propriety and duty, always safeguarding the reputation and credit of his family, had persisted in his feelings toward her in defiance of her petulant refusal of his hand and regardless of her sister's misstep. It was humbling and gratifying at the same time.

Now, if she could only decide her own feelings and to what extent her happiness depended upon his good opinion, not to mention his continued presence in her life.

She had decided to completely discount Miss Bingley's assertions. Elizabeth did not know from where the woman had obtained her notion, but she was certain Miss Bingley could not be correct. Perhaps, as Jane would likely claim — though that was not certain any longer considering Jane's own ill-treatment at the hands of the bitter woman — perhaps Miss Bingley was merely mistaken or had read something into Mr. Darcy's relationship which was not there. It was possible and seemed to be the only likely answer if Miss Bingley was correct — Elizabeth doubted she had been told in confidence as she had claimed, for there had appeared to be little warmth between them.

However, she knew in her heart that Miss Bingley was merely bitter at Mr. Darcy's attentions to herself, as Miss Bingley was the one who had desired them for far longer than Elizabeth had even been acquainted with the gentleman. Her words were almost certainly an attempt to separate Elizabeth from Mr. Darcy, although Elizabeth herself considered it to be a stupid and ill-judged plan — too many things could go wrong, and all had the ability to cause Miss Bingley much distress, if Elizabeth knew anything of Mr. Darcy.

But the woman would act as she would; Elizabeth could do nothing to curb her behavior, even if she had been inclined to make the attempt. As Elizabeth had told Lady Catherine, she intended to act in a manner which secured her own happiness, and if she decided that happiness consisted of a life with Mr. Darcy, the Caroline Bingleys of the world would not dissuade her.

Satisfied with her resolve, Elizabeth returned to her room and divested herself of her bonnet and pelisse before returning to the drawing room to join her sisters.

Upon entering the room, she realized she had failed to account for one of their guests. She had been humming the tune she had played at Pemberley when she stepped into the room and saw Samuel Lucas conversing with her mother. She stopped in shock while the man in question rose to his feet and gave her a slight bow.

Meanwhile, Mrs. Bennet bustled up to Elizabeth and pulled her into the room, clucking at her the whole time. "Where are your manners, Elizabeth? Indeed, I do not know. You must not neglect young Samuel when he has called at Longbourn to see you particularly. Now, come and sit with him."

"I beg your pardon, Mrs. Bennet," Mr. Lucas said, gazing intently at Elizabeth, "but I was hoping to continue walking in the garden as we were doing before the Netherfield party left."

He smiled at Elizabeth, a smile which had quite the opposite effect of one of Mr. Darcy's. "You left so quickly, Lizzy, that I did not get to speak with you. I was hoping for the chance to do so."

Elizabeth ground her teeth at his continuing insolent insistence in not addressing her more formally. "I am sorry, *Mr. Lucas*, but as we have already spent part of the morning outside, I am no longer inclined to walk in the garden. Besides, has the proper time for a polite visit not elapsed already?"

A dark expression fell over his face, but it was nothing compared to the comical look of horror which adorned her mother's features. She immediately hurried up to Elizabeth and, taking her by the arm, forced her from the room, all the while addressing Samuel.

"Do not worry, Mr. Lucas. Elizabeth will be out in a moment to accompany you on your walk. I will ensure she is freshened up and returned to you in a few moments."

The last glimpse of Mr. Lucas which Elizabeth caught as she was led from the room was the return of his unpleasant smirk. Truly, was he not aware of the great disadvantage to his suit that his boorish behavior must bring? Elizabeth was quickly coming to detest the very sight of the man.

She was given no time to think about her unwanted suitor, however, as Mrs. Bennet guided her into the dining room and stopped, confronting Elizabeth with an expression of intense displeasure suffusing her features.

"Elizabeth Louise Bennet!" she hissed. "I will not tolerate your games with young Samuel. He is a perfectly amiable and intelligent man and more particularly interested in you, although with the way you carry on, I cannot imagine why.

"Now, you listen to me, Miss Lizzy! You have already refused Mr. Collins, who was an eligible match for you, and I will not see you acting in the same manner with Mr. Lucas. Samuel may very well be your last chance to marry, and I will not have you squander it—a girl who rejects marriage proposals obtains a reputation, and if you fritter away this opportunity, no sensible man may ever look upon you again. Disappoint me, and I will wash my hands of you; you will need to depend upon your uncle's kindness once your father is dead because I will have nothing further to do with you!"

Elizabeth almost laughed aloud at her mother's words. If only she knew the true state of things! Still, she would not give her mother the satisfaction of a reaction, nor would she illuminate her as to the interest Darcy had shown—and was continuing to show—in her. Her mother might frighten him away!

"You will go up to your room and retrieve your bonnet and pelisse, and then you will accompany young Samuel to the garden. You will be attentive to him in every way, and you will not in any way attempt to dissuade him from his interest in you. Now, go!"

A little push accompanied Mrs. Bennet's words, and soon, Elizabeth found herself on her way up the stairs and to her room. She considered momentarily applying to her father to intercede on her behalf, but—knowing him—he would consider the situation amusing and attempt to make a joke of it. Besides, Elizabeth did not wish to disturb the fragile peace she had with her mother; she would walk with Samuel, but only as far as civility demanded.

Retrieving her things, she returned to the drawing room, although she did take her time, deriving a perverse sort of pleasure for her small act of rebellion. Upon entering the room, Samuel immediately stood—the smirk which had so vexed her before still firmly upon his face—and made to lead her from the room.

"I believe I could do with a bit of air myself," Jane spoke up, rising from her chair as if to accompany them.

Elizabeth glanced at her sister, grateful that Jane was so perceptive. But Mrs. Bennet would have nothing of it.

"No, indeed, Jane," interrupted she. "I do not believe I can spare you. We must use this time to go over the flower arrangements and fabrics for the wedding. I believe Samuel and Elizabeth will simply have to do without you."

Not waiting for another outburst, Mr. Lucas grasped Elizabeth's elbow and ushered her from the room. All Elizabeth could do was to seethe at the machinations of her mother while trying to hold her tongue so she would not say something truly rude and impertinent to her companion.

"I must admit, Lizzy," began Mr. Lucas, pulling her along the garden path, "I thought we would never be alone."

Forced to follow him though she was, Elizabeth determined she would be no more than civil to him. In short, she held her tongue.

"I was quite surprised to see the Netherfield party here this morning," said he, "though I suppose I should not be surprised that Mr. Bingley called. He *is* engaged to your sister, after all. You must be particular friends with Miss Darcy and Miss de Bourgh for them to call on you the very morning after their arrival."

Seeing a chance to discompose the insufferable man, Elizabeth smiled sweetly. "Actually, I only know them a little, though I think we are on our way to becoming very well acquainted. It is Mr. Darcy who is a particular friend."

It was almost comical the way in which Mr. Lucas's head spun around and a deep scowl came over his countenance—exactly as Elizabeth had anticipated. He narrowed his gaze, but she merely smiled impudently in response.

Huffing, he continued to walk away from the house. Though his face resembled a thundercloud, his voice betrayed none of his displeasure.

"I was not aware you were so well acquainted, Lizzy."

"Indeed, I am, *Mr. Lucas*," responded Elizabeth, annoying him even further by her insistence on her formal mode of address. "I spent several weeks in which we were much in company when Mr. Bingley first came to the neighborhood last October. Then there was the time I spent with your sister in Kent. Finally, I do not know if you are aware, but we met again at Pemberley—his estate—in Derbyshire merely two months ago. Have you ever had the good fortune to see his property?"

"I have not had that pleasure," Mr. Lucas ground out.

"It is absolutely exquisite. I do not believe I have ever seen lovelier grounds or a house so beautiful and grand and tastefully decorated. I believe . . . that is to say, my aunt and uncle very much enjoyed our time in Derbyshire—and especially at Pemberley—very much indeed." Elizabeth had nearly said that she would be happy to spend the rest of her life at Pemberley, but she felt that was far too provocative with the mood he was in and the jealousy which was practically oozing off him in waves.

"And Mr. Darcy was so very friendly and accommodating," continued Elizabeth, affecting a complete lack of perception of his displeasure. "He invited us for dinner, you know, and went fishing with my uncle. I have never known a master of such a great estate to be so affable and agreeable."

"And I suppose you know *many* masters of great estates?" Mr. Lucas bit out sarcastically.

"Oh, no, indeed," stated Elizabeth. "But meeting him in his domain was not at all what I had expected. It was a very great surprise. I suppose our friendship, which had admittedly started off somewhat rocky, began to flourish while I was visiting his home. Now we are very much in each other's confidence."

With effort—Mr. Lucas, it appeared, was not a very good actor—he mastered himself and directed a pleasant glance in Elizabeth's direction. "I am very glad you have made such a good and . . . *attentive* friend, Lizzy. But perhaps we have spoken too much of Mr. Darcy today. I wish to speak of other things. After all, we have not reacquainted each other with our doings over the past several years. I should very much like to speak with you of some of the things I have seen and done and hear stories of your own escapades."

It was at that point when Elizabeth realized exactly where he had been leading her—she had not paid any attention previously due to her immense satisfaction in baiting and annoying him. It appeared Mr. Lucas wished to have some very private time with her, as he was leading her to a remote part of the garden, a part which was not visible from the house.

Stopping, Elizabeth removed her hand firmly from where Mr. Lucas had kept it trapped against his arm. She directed an imperious look at her companion and tapped her foot on the ground.

"I am sorry, Mr. Lucas, but I will not leave sight of the house."

A charming smile was etched on his face. "What, Lizzy, you do not trust me?"

Elizabeth was tempted to tell him exactly of what she thought him capable, but she determined it was better not to bait him any further. "It is not proper, as you well know."

"But Lizzy, it is not as if we have never been alone in these woods before today. There was no awkwardness when we played as youngsters."

"We are not youngsters any longer, Mr. Lucas," Elizabeth responded, a hint of steel evident in her voice. "We are now grown and must keep up appearances for propriety's sake.

"Besides," continued she with no small amount of venom in her voice, "I have told you repeatedly not to address me in such a familiar manner, and still you persist in doing so. First names and other familiar appellations are reserved for engaged couples, and we are certainly not engaged. In light of this and the manner in which you have forced me to accompany you in collusion with my mother—and against my will, I might add—do you really think I would trust your intentions?"

A long-suffering sigh met her declaration, and Mr. Lucas shook his head in regret. "If that is the way it must be, then it shall be.

"I apologize for not addressing you more formally, Miss Bennet," said Mr. Lucas with a bow. "I cannot promise I will never do so again—force of habit, you understand—but I shall endeavor to remember it in our future interactions.

"As for your objections to our little outing, surely you cannot begrudge me the opportunity to once again become acquainted with my dearest childhood friend. I will agree to stay within sight of the house, if you feel it necessary, but I would appreciate your continued presence. I have so much to tell you."

Though Elizabeth could sense no significant change in his manner, in this instance she decided it would be better to be polite.

Thus began a long and most difficult time for Elizabeth. Although he had stayed far longer than could be considered polite by any means, he refused to leave, instead regaling her with tales of his days at university and his travels and adventures, half of which, she suspected, was embellished to the point where it bore only a cursory resemblance to any actual events. She tried to hint that he had outstayed his welcome, and when that did not work, she tried to tell him directly. But he all but ignored her, stating that for two such old friends as they, the normal rules of society could be ignored.

She had hoped to finally rid herself of him when the time for luncheon approached, but her mother outmaneuvered her by inviting him to stay for their midday repast. He had accepted with a smirk, his eyes affixed upon her, laughing at the way he had influenced Mrs. Bennet to bend her to his wishes. She was ready to break her plate over his head!

Even her father had had little sympathy for her plight, amused as he was by the antics of his wife. He merely winked at Elizabeth, letting her know he knew of Mr. Lucas's outrageous behavior and found it amusing. Elizabeth's glare had let him know of her opinion of his non-action, but Mr. Bennet had not been offended in the slightest.

It had finally taken Elizabeth's claim of a headache after luncheon to induce Mr. Lucas to go home. Even then, she doubted he would have departed had she not left him standing in the garden as she retreated to her room.

While he walked down the drive from the house, Elizabeth watched him through the window in her room, her anger at him swelling within her breast. How dare the man impose himself upon her in that manner! At least she had been invited to Netherfield the next day. God bless Miss Bingley and the invitation which allowed her to avoid him!

Chapter IX

*T*he next day, the eldest Bennet sisters made their way to Netherfield, both in their own way grateful for the respite the evening would bring from the activities and intrigue to which they were subjected at Longbourn, although their reasons were quite different.

Perhaps unsurprisingly, the past weeks had been trying for even one of Jane's sweet and patient disposition, given the excitement which surrounded Mrs. Bennet's ongoing preparations. Elizabeth did not know how her sister could possibly put up with her mother's incessant prattling about lace, flowers, delicacies for the wedding breakfast, the wedding gown and bridesmaids' dresses, and everything else which her mother deemed necessary for the successful completion of what would, after all, be in essence a very short and simple ceremony.

Yet Mrs. Bennet, seeing an occasion to not only show off her skills as a hostess, but also to display the good fortune of her daughter to the entire neighborhood, had descended into an absolute frenzy of action, oblivious to the weariness which was settling over the entire house. And though it may have been somewhat cynical for Elizabeth to consider it, she knew that her mother's planning and showing included a generous measure of gloating—after all, of their immediate neighbors, several of them still had unmarried daughters, and even those who had married (Charlotte immediately came to mind) could not boast such a conquest.

For Elizabeth, her reasons for wishing to quit Longbourn were due in no small part to her mother, but they were also due to her overly amorous and totally unwanted suitor. Elizabeth wondered if it was her fate to continually be beset by the attentions of those who she preferred would leave her alone. First, Mr. Collins (she could not suppress a shudder at the thought of his obsequious and fawning preference), then Mr. Darcy (although the thought of *his* attentions no longer disgusted her), and now her childhood friend had all seen fit to importune her with dreams of their future felicity, which had unfortunately seemed to revolve around her.

The most amazing thing was the fact that she, rather than Jane, had been the focus of this attention. Jane had always been the one to catch the eyes of young men, not Elizabeth, who, though she was considered pretty and clever, was certainly not the classic beauty her sister was. The situation was so different from anything in Elizabeth's experience—and frustrating in its continued disruption of her life—that it was enough to make her gnash her teeth in aggravation, regardless of how unladylike she knew it would appear.

Her mother's scheming nature was not unknown—her interactions and tacit approval (if indeed that approval was not explicit!) for Mr. Collins's misguided suit had clearly illustrated her desperation to have any and all of her daughters married off, and it really did not signify who their suitors were, as long as they were able to support a wife in some fashion. Yet with Jane's engagement to Mr. Bingley and his five thousand a year, she would have thought that her mother's desperation would have been blunted now that her future was assured. Yet it seemed as if Mrs. Bennet was as she had ever been—the only difference was her focus and the fact that her actions were no longer characterized by the hopelessness which had always been a part of her endeavors in the past. It was obvious that although she was no longer in danger of living among the hedgerows, the need to ensure her final three daughters were married still existed.

Enter Samuel Lucas, whose fortuitous timing in his return to Hertfordshire had put him directly in the path of his childhood friend. How Elizabeth wished he had delayed his return by even a few weeks; it would have given her time to discover her own feelings for Mr. Darcy and bring the matter to a close. Although it was by no means guaranteed that she would accept the gentleman's suit—in the unlikely event that he was still of a mind to extend it—at least she would have had the leisure to make the choice without any outside interference. A part of her even wished she had accepted Mr. Darcy's suit when he had first made his offer; at least she would have been done with it and away from the clutches of Mr. Lucas!

Now Elizabeth did not seriously repine her refusal, not when the offer had been so insulting. And she knew that if Samuel Lucas actually did get around to making her an offer, she could count on her father to support her when she refused him.

At least Mr. Collins had been stupid and easy to deflect; unfortunately, the same could not be said for Mr. Lucas. Elizabeth did not think he was Mr. Darcy's match in understanding, liberality, or cleverness, but he was certainly no Mr. Collins, and as such, she could not employ the stratagems she had used to avoid the parson. It was frustrating in the extreme.

On that particular morning, her frustration level with both her mother and her mother's accomplice had risen to new heights. Mr. Lucas had arrived at Longbourn late enough for it to be within the bounds of propriety (at least in the country), but early enough that it could also be seen as somewhat of an imposition. Her mother of course had been ecstatic at his arrival and had welcomed him to Longbourn, eagerly sending for her second eldest daughter to join them in the parlor.

Elizabeth, however, had not been in her room, having left some time earlier for her morning walk as was her habit, and she had therefore not been present to receive him, much to the chagrin and annoyance of her mother. And though Elizabeth had taken well over an hour before she had finally returned to her home, Mr. Lucas had stubbornly stayed at Longbourn, flattering her mother with his insincere compliments while basking in her delighted exclamations of anticipated marital bliss (or at least the desired ability to flaunt another engaged daughter before the neighborhood).

Upon Elizabeth's return, she had once again been forced to walk with Mr. Lucas and put up with his unwanted attentions to her person. A little time in the parlor had been followed by his artfully stated wish to walk with Elizabeth once again, a wish which her mother, of course, had agreed to satisfy immediately.

Thus began the battle of wills. Where Samuel had been forward, Elizabeth was reserved; where Samuel pushed, Elizabeth retreated and avoided; where Samuel became overly familiar and affectionate, Elizabeth demurred. It had been a supremely exhausting game of cat and mouse which Elizabeth was ill inclined to play.

The most discouraging part of the entire morning, to Elizabeth's mind, was the fact that no matter how evident and pointed her hints — and Elizabeth knew that it was no time for subtlety — Mr. Lucas either misunderstood or willfully ignored them. He was not as mentally deficient as Mr. Collins, so she had little choice but to assume he had comprehended her feelings, yet he had decided to act in favor of reveling in Mrs. Bennet's obvious approval of his suit. Elizabeth could not imagine what he meant by it. Could he really think that she would accept him — once he deigned to make his proposal — merely on the recommendation of her mother? Did he really know so little of her to suppose that she could be worked upon in such a manner? Had he heard nothing of her refusal of Mr. Collins? His improper actions and total lack of understanding of her character disgusted her, and she could not understand how he could miss her obvious distaste for him.

By the time their departure to Netherfield had approached, Elizabeth had descended into a black mood, almost snapping at her suitor in her aggravation. Of course, that failed to deter him in the slightest. On the contrary, he appeared to enjoy her diminishing patience!

The crowning moment of the entire morning, however, had come when she and Jane were preparing to depart for Netherfield. Even now, Elizabeth could not think about the scene without a shudder.

"Jane, could you imagine I could be so happy to leave my father's own house?"

Elizabeth was warmed by the sympathetic look with which her sister favored her and returned the offered hug with affection. "I am so sorry, Lizzy," said Jane "It is distressing to see you so unhappy, but Mama will not hear anything of my deflecting Mr. Lucas's attentions. If I could only accompany you and give you some respite. But each time I try, she has some new detail for me to look over, as if my tastes mattered to her in the slightest!"

The situation, disconcerting thought it was, suddenly struck Elizabeth as amusing, and she was forced to stifle a giggle. Jane saw it and joined in, patting her sister on the back.

"I am happy you can still see the humor in the situation, Lizzy. If even you can lose your good humor, I am sure the rest of us could not maintain it!"

"Indeed, you do flatter me, Jane," gasped Elizabeth between spurts of laughter.

"You are the one who has the sweet and patient disposition. For myself, I find that if I do not laugh, then I shall surely cry. And laughing is infinitely preferable, is it not?"

"I am sure it is, Lizzy."

Though she was tempted to continue and perhaps have a little fun at the expense of her mother—not to mention her overly determined suitor—Elizabeth grasped her bonnet and pelisse and turned back to her sister.

"Regardless of the temptation to continue to make sport with our mother, I believe we should depart; it would not do to keep Miss Bingley waiting."

A roll of Jane's eyes—something Elizabeth doubted she had ever seen before recent events—met her declaration. "Oh, assuredly so. I would not wish to antagonize my future sister before I am married."

"Any further than you already have by agreeing to Mr. Bingley's proposal?" was Elizabeth's arch reply.

A giggling fit overtook her sister again, even as she tried to direct a stern glare at the offender. "Now, Lizzy, I cannot have you causing me to have such unchristian thoughts about Miss Bingley. After all, you know she only wishes what is best for her brother."

"And herself."

The laughter returned, but this time both sisters joined in the mirth.

"Yes, of course you are right," Jane finally gasped out.

Her mien then became serious. "I should hope, though, that her disappointment is tempered by the sure knowledge of our love for each other. Once she realizes that, she can hardly continue to oppose our marriage."

"Oh Jane, I am certain she has resigned herself to your marriage," exclaimed Elizabeth, reaching out to grasp her sister's hands. "She always did appear to hold some affection for you. I believe it was the rest of your family for whom her contempt was aroused. As long as you continue to be as you are, I am certain she can have nothing with which to reproach you. Who could?"

Jane blushed. "I am not perfect, Lizzy,"

"No, Jane, you are not. But I believe you are as angelic a person as exists in the world today. Your new sister, I am sure, cannot help but love you as dearly as I."

"And I you," responded Jane with a fierce hug. "But the hour is swiftly approaching, and I believe we should depart."

The sisters made their way from the room and descended the stairs, out toward the waiting carriage. As they passed by the parlor, Elizabeth noticed that Samuel Lucas was still present and had engaged her two younger sisters—as well as his sister Maria, who had accompanied him—in earnest conversation. Shuddering at the gall of the man, Elizabeth swiftly moved with her sister to escape the house. Unfortunately, they were not fast enough.

"Lizzy!" the voice of her mother rang out through the house. "I have need of you in the dining room."

Elizabeth considered pretending herself hard of hearing—she longed to disregard the order and quit the house—but it was not in her to be so rude to her mother. She sighed and exchanged a glance with Jane.

"Go to the carriage, Jane, I shall be but a moment."

"No, Lizzy," responded a determined Jane. "I will stay here and offer my support if need be."

Grateful for her sister's care, Elizabeth reached out and squeezed Jane's hand before turning back to the interior of the house.

Her mother was the only occupant of the dining room, and her pacing and the wringing of her hands bore testament to her agitated state. But then again, when was Mrs. Bennet *not* agitated?

"Elizabeth," exclaimed she, although her voice was low and furtive, "what are you doing, child?"

Uncertain to what her mother was referring, Elizabeth chose to be blunt. "I was departing for Netherfield, Mama. Have you forgotten the invitation to dinner which Miss Bingley extended only yesterday?"

"That was for Jane," responded her mother with a sniff. "You know there is nothing at Netherfield for you."

Elizabeth remembered another time in which her mother had used almost those same words to her. *This time*, however, she could truthfully state that *there was* indeed something there for her in the persons of her increasingly intimate friends.

"Mother!" Elizabeth's voice was stern. "You know very well that Miss Bingley extended the invitation to include both Jane and myself. And besides, Caroline Bingley is not the only lady at Netherfield. You forget that I am well acquainted with Miss de Bourgh and Miss Darcy."

"And what of it? Your acquaintance may be continued on another occasion. It is Jane who should become better acquainted with the two ladies, as she is now to have a connection to them through Mr. Bingley's friend."

Elizabeth only sighed in exasperation. Her mother was not exactly the most devious person, and Elizabeth well understood why she wished her to remain at home. But Elizabeth was not of mind to humor her whims.

"I sincerely hope you are not suggesting I snub two such prominent young ladies, Mama. After all, a connection and friendship with them could lead to future opportunities, you know."

"To what future opportunities do you refer?" demanded Mrs. Bennet. "You have a perfectly sensible opportunity right in front of you, Miss Lizzy. I do not mean for you to slight the young ladies, but surely we can come up with some reason for you to stay at Longbourn."

"I think not, Mama. I have been invited; therefore, I shall go."

"But young Samuel Lucas has come to Longbourn to see you, Elizabeth," pleaded Mrs. Bennet, "though I do not quite know what he sees in you. I have invited him for tea, so you simply must stay."

Though it sometimes still gave her pain, Elizabeth was used to her mother's careless attitude toward her feelings. She was well aware of the fact that she might never gain her mother's approval, but truly, although she did love her, Elizabeth had long been reconciled to the fact she was her mother's least favorite daughter. It therefore gave her no pause to disabuse Mrs. Bennet of her notions and refuse any repeat of the application to remain at home.

"I have spent the entire morning with Mr. Lucas, Mama. I have had enough of his company, quite frankly, and I wish to see my friends again. I shall go to Netherfield—I am quite determined, I assure you."

Exasperated, Mrs. Bennet clucked her tongue, presumably at Elizabeth's obstinacy and refusal to bow to her wishes. Then a smile of cunning—which caused Elizabeth to shudder violently—came over her face.

"In that case, I suppose it must be. But all is not lost; you must invite young Mr. Lucas to accompany you to Netherfield, where he may still be afforded time in your company."

Aghast at the suggestion that she so completely flaunt proper manners, Elizabeth gaped at her mother in complete consternation, unable to make a response. Fortunately, her response was not required.

"Mama!" exclaimed Jane, walking into the room. "How can you say such a thing?"

Mrs. Bennet directed a dark and disparaging glance at Elizabeth. "I must resort to such devices, as your sister will not encourage Mr. Lucas."

"Whatever schemes you may employ, I will not allow you to embarrass us before my fiancé and his sister with such an ill-judged ploy. How can you suggest we invite someone who was not invited—who is only slightly acquainted with them—and impose upon Miss Bingley in such a manner? I am certain I could not bear the humiliation."

Though her mother's frown deepened, even she was not able to contradict Jane's statement.

"Now, I must insist we leave at once, Mama," declared Jane. "We shall be late if we stay a moment longer."

"Very well. I suppose that is the way it must be," replied Mrs. Bennet with a sniff. "But you mark my words, Jane—if Elizabeth continues in this manner, she shall never be married, and I shall have nothing to do with her once your father is dead. You will be forced to support her once that happens. She will be a burden upon you and Mr. Bingley, much as she is on your father and me."

The venom with which Mrs. Bennet pronounced her opinion caused tears to form in Elizabeth's eyes, for although she had thought her mother had no more power to injure her, clearly she had been mistaken.

"Enough, Mama!" commanded Jane, a sharpness which Elizabeth had never before heard apparent in her voice. "Can you not see that speaking in such a manner upsets Lizzy? If Lizzy should happen to live with us in the future, you can be assured that I will consider it a most fortunate circumstance. She will be most welcome by both myself and my future husband, and she will *never* be a burden upon us. I demand you cease speaking so immediately!"

Mrs. Bennet did not reply; she merely sniffed in disdain while quitting the room.

Jane grasped Elizabeth's hand and led her from the house. Approaching the carriage, she instructed the driver to set a brisker pace than was his wont to make up for lost time, and she guided Elizabeth onto the seat, where she held her in her arms. For Elizabeth, the feeling was incredibly comforting, and she indulged herself in the release of a few tears, although she refused to weep openly. Her mother would get no such satisfaction from her!

Surely Elizabeth was fortunate to have such a sister—Jane was everything in the world to her. Her thoughts of what she would do once her sister was married and had quit her childhood home once again invaded Elizabeth's mind. Surely she could not be happy living at Longbourn with her mother constantly harping on her, forever mortifying her pride with her unthinking comments and ill-judged machinations. Elizabeth was not certain she could continue to bear it, especially once her mother finally realized the disappointment which was sure to come. Elizabeth would not marry Samuel Lucas!

The carriage turned into the drive at Netherfield, and Elizabeth lifted herself from her thoughts. The tears had long since stopped, and her spirits were somewhat restored due to Jane's tender ministrations, but she had spent the entirety of the carriage ride lost in her own recollections.

"Lizzy, are you well?"

Smiling at her sister, Elizabeth reached out and grasped her hands. "I am certainly well, Jane. I thank you for taking such good care of me."

"How could I not? You are my dearest sister."

"And you are mine."

Jane's critical gaze still rested upon Elizabeth, making her feel slightly self-conscious, but her smile belied the stern expression. "Truly, Lizzy, if you do not feel up to the company just yet, I am sure Miss Bingley would oblige you by providing a room in which you can rest until dinner."

Suppressing a shudder at Miss Bingley's imagined reaction to such a request—more sick Bennets imposing upon her hospitality!—Elizabeth was quick to deny any such necessity.

"Dear Jane, I assure you I am well. Do not trouble yourself for my well-being; I am eager to meet with my friends again."

"In that case, I shall not importune you any further, Lizzy."

By that time, the carriage had pulled up to the drive, and the sisters stepped down from the coach, aided by the footman. Determined to put the events of the morning behind her, Elizabeth smiled at her sister and climbed the steps to the house, where they were met by expressions of obvious delight from Anne and Georgiana, not to mention the supercilious sneer of Miss Bingley. Though she was wary of the woman and the tales she told, Elizabeth greeted her amicably while reserving a more affectionate greeting for her other friends. Soon, they were all ensconced in the drawing room, chatting happily.

It was not long before the dinner hour when the gentlemen of Netherfield entered the drawing room and greeted the ladies, having returned from dealing with some estate business. For Fitzwilliam Darcy, the opportunity to be in the company of his beloved without the interruption of her mother or her (alleged) suitor, had been looked upon with great anticipation.

As he walked into the room, he noticed his friend greet the ladies before immediately extending a more personal greeting toward Miss Bennet. However, Darcy's attention was not on the actions of his companions or the occupants of the room save one. His first glimpse of Elizabeth seated on the couch between his sister and his cousin and dressed in a pretty pale green dress caused his breath to catch in his throat. With such visions of loveliness at hand, it was unsurprising that the likes of Caroline Bingley—who was sitting to the side wearing an unpleasant shade of bronze—could not compare.

He approached the ladies, oblivious to the significant looks and muffled snickers of his relations, and favored the second Bennet daughter with a tender smile.

"Good day, Miss Elizabeth. You are looking remarkably well."

With her usual ebullience, Elizabeth responded, "Thank you, Mr. Darcy. I daresay you are looking rather dashing yourself."

At that moment, Anne—rather suspiciously, to Darcy's eye—rose from her seat and, excusing herself, retreated from the trio to speak with Richard. Darcy eyed her for the briefest of moments before smiling once again at Miss Elizabeth and sitting next to her, noting with some confusion as Miss Bingley, who had been walking swiftly in their direction, suddenly stopped and retreated, a dark expression adorning her face. With a mental shrug, Darcy returned his attention to Miss Elizabeth, who was herself directing a quizzical eye in Miss Bingley's direction.

"I hope I find you well this afternoon?" said Darcy a moment later, being somewhat at a loss as to what to say.

"I am well, thank you," responded Elizabeth, her smile seeming to indicate that she understood his hesitation. "I would like to say again what a pleasure it is to see you and your family," here she directed a smile at Georgiana, "back in Hertfordshire. I am certain Mr. Bingley is vastly pleased to have your company and expertise at his disposal once again."

Smiling indulgently, Darcy reflected that Elizabeth always seemed to know what topic to introduce—Bingley and the estate was one thing he could talk of without awkwardness, and he suspected the topic would have some interest for Elizabeth herself and Georgiana as well.

"Bingley is a dear friend, Miss Elizabeth, so it is no trouble whatsoever to offer him my assistance whenever it is required. I daresay my friend finds this part of the country agreeable, and although I was uncertain at first, I have come to find it quite pleasant."

Elizabeth's answering smile was enough to tell him that his oblique reference to his previous behavior, accompanied by the tacit apology, was understood and accepted.

"I thank you for your gracious words, Mr. Darcy," said she, a soft smile adorning her face. "I completely understand that this small corner of the kingdom cannot have the delights and possibilities of town, but I must say that I find its peaceful nature very pleasing."

"I find Hertfordshire quite pleasant," said Georgiana. "Town can be enjoyable, and I do so love going to the theater and visiting with my relatives. But it can become a little overwhelming at times. I think the country suits me well indeed."

"As do I," confirmed Darcy. "Surely Hertfordshire is less wild and its contours softer than many of my favorite places, yet it is pretty and pleasant and has an appeal all its own."

"I must confess, Mr. Darcy, that I am somewhat envious. Although I have seen some of Derbyshire and find the area around Lambton to be beautiful, our tour last summer was necessarily cut short due to my uncle's business, and we were not able to make it to the lakes or see as much of Derbyshire as we had originally proposed. I think I should like to make my way to that part of the country again, one day, and see that which I missed before."

"Oh, you must come, Elizabeth," cried Georgiana. "Next time, you may stay at Pemberley, and we can all journey up to the lakes together."

Secretly, Darcy wished Elizabeth's sojourn and stay at Pemberley would consist of considerably more than a mere few weeks, but now that their acquaintance was finally beginning to deepen, he did not suppose himself in possession of the ability to extend the invitation fortuitously tendered by his sister without betraying his continued high regard for Elizabeth. He desperately wanted her to know of his constancy, but he was uncertain of her returning regard, which necessitated his silence, and he was therefore pleased when Georgiana made the invitation.

Elizabeth gazed affectionately at Georgiana before directing a questioning glance in Darcy's direction. He was, with a modicum of dignity, able to assure her with a look that Georgiana's proposed scheme was certainly welcome to *him.*

"I thank you for your invitation, Georgie," replied Elizabeth. "If I should happen to have the very great fortune to be able to tour that part of the country again, I would be pleased to accept your kind offer."

"Do, please, Elizabeth! We shall have so much fun and be such a merry party if you do."

Elizabeth laughed at Georgiana's antics and patted her hand affectionately. "I daresay we shall. But until then, I shall have to content myself with secondhand accounts of the wonders of the lakes. That is, if you will oblige me with stories of your experiences there."

Her manner was arch, yet it was filled with such innocent joy in the simple matter of learning that Darcy felt himself captivated by her all over again. The talk turned, as she requested, to the country around Derbyshire and the lakes, with the Darcy siblings paying specific attention to the areas near Pemberley which she had not had occasion to see during her sojourn in that part of the country. Of the lakes, they said little, however, as Darcy insisted that she simply must see them for herself; their words simply could not do them justice.

It was not long before they were called in for dinner and their conversation had to end. Yet each promised the other that they would take it up again, and much to Elizabeth's surprise, her friends insisted that she must begin to plan to revisit her northern tour immediately, as there were many places which they wished to show her. Elizabeth was clearly caught off guard and promised that if it was within her power, she would find it most agreeable to take them up on their offer. The matter settled, they suspended the conversation in favor of making their way to the dining room.

Thus began the second part of the evening, which, though it had started off pleasant enough, proceeded with much frustration on Darcy's part. Every circumstance, it seemed, conspired against his desire to continue to be in the company of Elizabeth, and regardless of his efforts, it appeared there was nothing to be done.

It started off in the dining room, where once again, due to her role as hostess, Miss Bingley was able to manipulate the gathering and influence the available conversation at the dinner table. Mr. Bingley, as was his right, sat at the head of the table, while Miss Bingley took her place at the foot. Not having thought about it in advance, Darcy nevertheless found himself unsurprised that he had been placed in the most inconvenient location to continue his conversation with the enchanting Miss Elizabeth. He was seated to Miss Bingley's right, while Elizabeth was to Mr. Bingley's right; thus, he was on the opposite end of the table, with two others to speak across if he wished to converse with her. The party was rounded out by Jane Bennet to Bingley's left, Anne in the middle, Georgiana at Miss Bingley's left, and Richard between Elizabeth and Georgiana.

As they came into the dining room and took their places, Bingley glanced down the length of the table and frowned when he saw where all their friends were seated, but he said nothing, merely directing a glance at his sister before focusing his attention on the two sisters to his either side. Darcy empathized with his friend; Charles certainly saw and understood the goal of Miss Bingley's dinner placements, but since she was acting as his hostess for the moment, there was nothing he could do without a conversation which would undoubtedly be awkward. Therefore, he chose to avoid the unpleasantness which would ensue and did not acknowledge her machinations, although his expression seemed to indicate that a long discussion with his sister may be in the offing for that evening.

Darcy half expected a repeat of his first night at Netherfield, but he was surprised when Miss Bingley, upon sitting in her chair, turned her attention to Georgiana and completely ignored him. Exchanging significant looks with Anne and Richard—Elizabeth's attention was turned to a conversation in which Jane and Bingley had included her—Darcy sighed and attended to his meal.

On the one hand, Darcy was annoyed with Miss Bingley for her blatant interference and what he now saw as her continued attempts to separate himself from Elizabeth. On the other, however, her placements did have the virtue of leaving each of the diners with a natural conversation partner. Bingley, of course, was largely focused on Jane, and although he did attempt to include Elizabeth as much as possible, she was able to converse with Richard on her other side. Richard, it appeared, was quite happy to speak with a woman he considered both intelligent and singular. And Darcy, though he was completely ignored by Miss Bingley, spoke primarily with Anne. The one unfortunate part of this arrangement was that it left Georgiana to the tender mercies of a one-sided conversation with Miss Bingley, which Darcy knew was not agreeable to her in any fashion.

It was left to Richard, who, having somewhat of the devil in him and being, as Darcy was aware, provoked on his cousins' behalf, to disrupt Miss Bingley's schemes. He set to including both ladies on either side of him in conversation, monopolizing them with his witty stories and engaging conversation. And while Georgiana had no wish to offend her hostess, it was also clear she had no desire to converse with her in any more than a polite yet slightly distant manner. Many times throughout the course of the meal, she was drawn into conversation by the persistent and highly amusing colonel, leaving Miss Bingley alone and fuming since she would not speak with Darcy. It was a situation which suited him quite well indeed.

After dinner, the separation of the sexes was brief, as Darcy knew it would be—Bingley's desire to be in the presence of his beloved was as transparent as it was amusing. The gentlemen made their way to the drawing room after a quiet drink and, entering, found the ladies engaged in a most animated discussion. At least, most of the ladies were, Darcy reflected after a moment's thought. Caroline Bingley sat off to one side, only contributing rarely to their discussion, with a look which bespoke her displeasure with the rest of the ladies.

As happy as he was to bask in the pleasure of his beloved's presence, Darcy soon realized there was a drawback to Elizabeth getting along so famously with his female relations. With the ladies' friendship rapidly deepening, it also curtailed *his* ability to be with her. Though he was able to join them from time to time, their conversations were often feminine in nature, and though he could contentedly listen to her voice for hours, it was difficult to have any part in the conversation. It also rendered his desire to speak with her alone a virtual impossibility.

The other part of the frustration was again his hostess. On the rare instances where Elizabeth was not engrossed in speaking with either Georgiana or Anne, Miss Bingley made it her business to be at Elizabeth's side, directing her airy and superior comments at the younger Bennet sister, who appeared as if she could have endured the lack of Miss Bingley's company quite cheerfully.

After the second time in which he was thwarted by Miss Bingley's artifice, a scowling Darcy was joined by his cousin, who directed an amused smirk at the supercilious woman.

"You do realize what she is doing, don't you?" asked Richard quietly.

"A blind man could see through her actions, Richard," responded Darcy. "What I do not understand is what she believes she is accomplishing with her subterfuge. It is not as if behavior such as this will induce me to reassess my decision. She must know that I will not court her, regardless of her desire to separate me from Miss Elizabeth."

"Therein lies the crux, I believe. She seems to be more interested in preventing you from any interaction with Miss Elizabeth—or at least preventing private discourse—than in courting your favor."

An exasperated sigh exploded from Darcy's mouth. "But what can she mean by it? She cannot believe that her machinations will keep me from Miss Elizabeth forever. Even she cannot be so short-sighted as to believe that she always can monitor our movements, especially when I could saddle my horse at a moment's notice and visit Longbourn without her presence."

"Who can tell what nefarious schemes exist in the mind of a lady?"

Darcy's amused chuckle prompted a grin from the colonel, who continued:

"Assuming Miss Bingley's purpose is to keep you from coming to an understanding with Miss Elizabeth, I do not believe her only action would be to keep you apart from her. She has something else up her sleeve, I do not doubt. I would watch her very closely."

"Indeed, I shall," replied Darcy softly, continuing to survey the room.

Before most of the company was willing for the evening to end, the time arrived for the Bennet sisters to return to their home. With a flash of inspiration, Darcy knew how he could arrange for some time alone with Miss Elizabeth, and although it was not exactly proper, neither was it precisely flaunting propriety.

"Richard!" he hissed as they escorted the ladies to the front hall. "Distract Miss Bingley for me."

With a grin, Richard dropped back to where Miss Bingley was walking at Georgiana's side and began a one-sided conversation, talking in an animated fashion while slowing his steps in order to emphasize his points with expansive hand gestures. Though Miss Bingley appeared to be less than pleased by his company, she was hardly able to put him off without being discourteous.

Darcy quickened his pace and arrived at Netherfield's front entrance, where Bingley was engaged in an affectionate farewell with Jane Bennet while Anne and Elizabeth spoke in low tones. Directing a glance at Anne, which she immediately understood as a plea to allow him a few moments with Miss Elizabeth, he approached them and began speaking, even as Anne excused herself quietly and moved away.

"Miss Elizabeth, I wish to thank you for coming to dinner tonight. I enjoyed our conversation."

A brilliant smile met his declaration. "As did I, Mr. Darcy. I hope we shall have the opportunity to have more such conversations in the future."

Darcy could not have asked for a more perfect opening. He phrased his question carefully while ensuring his voice was kept low, so as to avoid being overheard.

"Miss Elizabeth, please forgive my forwardness, but I believe I should like to have an opportunity to speak with you without all the disruptions and interruptions we seem to have suffered tonight."

She was clearly intrigued by his meaning, yet she said nothing, merely smiling at him and nodding in agreement with his words.

"If I may ask you—do you still walk out in the mornings?"

Elizabeth stifled a gasp and peered incredulously at Mr. Darcy. Was he truly asking her to meet him privately during one of her morning walks? What did the man mean by it? Did he intend to propose to her again?

But reason quickly reasserted itself, and Elizabeth forced her suddenly agitated mind to calm. No man with even a rudimentary sense of self pride would ever propose a second time to a woman who had already refused him—especially in the vitriolic and accusing manner in which she had thrown his words back at him. And as she had previously noted, Mr. Darcy's sense of pride was far from rudimentary, although she was again forced to admit it was not the ravening beast she had always thought it to be.

Equally obvious was the fact that though she would have been suspicious of such an application if it had come from Samuel Lucas, she in no way felt any concern at the prospect of being alone on a country path with Mr. Darcy. She had admitted to herself that she had misjudged him and knew considerably less about him than she had thought; yet she was certain that he was the consummate gentleman, and she would be well protected in his company.

"I do, Mr. Darcy," she finally responded, "on most mornings when the weather permits."

His answering smile caused a most disconcerting fluttering to appear in her stomach in its brilliance, and Elizabeth found herself warming even further toward the man.

"In that case, I should like to meet you to discuss a matter of some import. In which direction do you usually walk?"

Elizabeth blushed even as she wondered about what matter he could wish to speak. "I walk in many directions depending upon my mood and the amount of exercise of which I find myself in need. However, on Monday, I will walk out in the direction of Oakham Mount, where you may find me if you wish to speak."

Mr. Darcy's brow furrowed. "You will not walk out tomorrow?"

"I usually try to avoid it on the Sabbath, Mr. Darcy, as it tries my mother's nerves if I am absent when the family is preparing for church."

Though Mr. Darcy appeared to be sensible of her reason for not walking out on Sunday, he could not entirely hide the disappointment at having to wait an extra day for their conversation. The curiosity she already felt at the reason for his application was now aroused to an even higher level. He must wish to speak of something particular for him to have made such an application.

"In that case, I shall ride out on Monday," said Mr. Darcy with a bow. "I shall say farewell until tomorrow at church, Miss Bennet."

The final members of their party arrived and after bidding farewell to their hosts, the Bennet sisters were obliged to leave. Jane and Elizabeth were handed into their carriage by a beaming Mr. Bingley, who immediately thanked them for their company and gave his fond wishes for the pleasure to be repeated. He then stepped back and allowed the carriage to roll away from the house.

Her thoughts filled with images and impressions of the day, Elizabeth sat back on her seat and reminisced about the day's events and Mr. Darcy's application. She did not know how she would restrain her curiosity until the time came for her to meet with him. She found herself quite intrigued at his application.

Another pair of eyes watched as Mr. Darcy parted from the despicable little fortune hunter, clearly after some sort of short private discussion between the two. Caroline Bingley was beside herself in frustration; regardless of her machinations and efforts to keep them apart, they had managed a few moments at the end, and she could not tell of what they had spoken.

She had felt herself successful in her endeavors for most of the day, and though she had not been able to keep them separate when the gentlemen had first arrived, they had been in a drawing room, and it had been easy to keep track of the conversation. She was satisfied it had not been overly familiar, and she did not concern herself over its occurrence. Now, with the contents of their most recent tête-à-tête unknown, she felt her grasp on the situation loosen ever so slightly.

As the Bennet girls (she would never think of them as ladies!) made their way toward the carriage, Caroline risked a disgusted glance around at her companions. Before the gentlemen had arrived, the conversation between the five women had almost solely been carried between the other four ladies, while Caroline had felt herself shunted to the side by their collective indifference to her. In her own home, too! And then that oaf, Richard Fitzwilliam, had distracted Georgiana from conversation with Caroline, leaving her without a companion with whom to converse during dinner. It was not to be borne! To think that she—Caroline Bingley—should be considered less worthy to attend to than some upstart pretentious country nobodies! How dare they think themselves above her!

Still, if Anne and Georgiana were so crass as to ignore her in favor of Eliza Bennet, she would allow them to have their short-lived victory. Once she had succeeded in separating Eliza from Mr. Darcy forever, she would leave this place and never return, ready to find some other rich gentleman who would respect and esteem her for the worth she would bring to him and the elegance she would carry to his home.

Still, it all depended on Samuel Lucas's quick action—if he secured Eliza's hand quickly, then Caroline could leave with at least that satisfaction. But if he waited, all could yet be lost. It was vexatious in the extreme, but all Caroline could do was to continue to play her part. The thought of actually losing to the little miss was too horrible to contemplate.

Chapter X

*M*onday morning dawned clear, and although it was colder than it had been previously — which was more seasonal than it had heretofore been — it was still a fine day for a walk. The woods around Longbourn were still wreathed in the reds, yellows, and golds of the season; the trees were beginning to lose their summer mantles in earnest, and the fallen leaves swirled in the breeze, dancing and swaying to an unseen yet measured rhythm. Through the pale dimness of the morning light, flocks of birds could be seen flying overhead, their sometimes ragged formations and unequal lines belying their single-minded clarity of purpose — the escape from the oncoming winter for warmer climes, where they could shelter in an abundance of food and warmth. If only people behaved with such clarity, such transparency of purpose.

Still, Elizabeth Bennet supposed, much could be inferred in those with whom she spent her days. Several of those of her acquaintances were as panes of glass to her, their motivations and purposes easily read by the discerning eye. She did not always like what she saw, but then again, the motivations of others were often in conflict with her own goals and aspirations. When was life ever easy? But now was not the time to think upon her problems or about those who were the source of those problems.

If asked, Elizabeth would have said she enjoyed the briskness of the weather and the chill in the air. This was the first day in which the approach of winter was evident, and many would have sighed and glared at the skies, noting the coming change in the weather and mourning the loss of summer's warmth.

Elizabeth, however, was not made for melancholy, and through conscious thought, she preferred to think of the changing seasons merely as a continuation of the cycle which had persisted since the beginning of time. Change was a thing to be celebrated, especially that of the climate, as winter, and all that came with it, was a time of great beauty as well, to one who would only look for it. The cessation of her daily walks was a circumstance which she looked upon with some vexation, but at least she still had the environs of Longbourn and the gardens in the back of the house in which to stroll. It was not the same, but it was enough until the promise of spring and finer weather drew her back to her more challenging pathways.

And the chill, far from depressing her, caressed her cheeks, reminding her that she was alive and able to enjoy the frosty air. No, in Elizabeth's mind, the positive aspects of the season must be emphasized; she was determined to look for the good in any situation.

Earlier that morning, Elizabeth had risen from her bed—early even for her—and prepared for the day. Knowing that her unwanted suitor would almost certainly be calling as early that morning as he was able, she swept through the kitchen, gathered a small breakfast for herself, and exited the house, eager to escape before she could be called back. She had no time for Samuel Lucas this morning and would not be dissuaded from her walk.

True to form, her mother had all but forgotten their confrontation when Elizabeth had returned from Netherfield the day she and Jane had dined with Mr. Bingley. Instead, she focused on Samuel Lucas and nattered on about the very great opportunity for Elizabeth to catch a local husband whose character was known to them all. Elizabeth kept her own council with regard to the subject of Mr. Lucas's character, allowing her mother to make herself happy with her conjectures and plans while silently vowing she would never be a party to her schemes.

Elizabeth had already put her mother's final painful words as they had parted earlier that day behind her, resolving to think about them no more. Mrs. Bennet was of such an uncertain temper that Elizabeth knew she tended to speak in vexation, without really considering her words. Elizabeth was aware of the fact that her mother did love her and want the best for her despite her sometimes frustrating and improper way of showing her feelings. She refused to allow her mother's lack of approval of her, which might never be granted, to bother her and make her unhappy.

Her mother's machinations, however, were somewhat more difficult to swallow. The very next day at church, they had barely stepped through the door before her mother was urging her to sit next to the eldest Lucas scion. Elizabeth chose the simple expedient of seating herself between Jane and the end of the pew, earning a scowl from her mother, but also earning her freedom from Samuel Lucas's unwanted attentions, at least for a short time. Mr. Bingley and Mr. Darcy, seated as they were behind them, also provided some measure of protection, as the only seats available after the Darcy party had sat down were behind and on the other side of the aisle. A relieved Elizabeth had been able to focus on the worship service without having to worry about an overly attentive companion.

Of course, as it was Sunday, it was not a day for visitors, which further spared Elizabeth from the young man's presence. Her one glimpse of his countenance had revealed his displeasure at her means of avoiding him, but it had soon been replaced by a smug smirk as he had conversed with Mrs. Bennet after church. Elizabeth was unaware of the substance of that conversation, but she was certain it had something to do with an invitation to visit yet again. Mrs. Bennet was nothing if not persistent.

As a result, after enjoying a Lucas-free day on the Sabbath, Elizabeth was in fine spirits when she departed Longbourn that Monday morning, eager to meet with Mr. Darcy and finally have her curiosity over his purpose assuaged.

The walk was not a short one, and Elizabeth occupied her time in equal parts admiration for the fine woods through which she walked—autumn truly was a time of great beauty and magnificent colors—while thinking about the gentleman, wondering what he could have to say which needed to be said with such a careful eye toward privacy.

No more certain now than she had been when he had first made the application, Elizabeth allowed herself to be cautious about his intentions. He certainly could not be thinking of making her another offer—surely his pride and feelings of self worth would rebel against the very thought!—and Elizabeth could not imagine what else could be so important. It was vexing to be trapped in this condition of curiosity.

She continued to puzzle over the dilemma until, at length, the woods opened up, and she found herself climbing the side of the large hill. She made the crown after a few moments of steady exertion and looked out over the landscape, trying to catch her breath. The magnificent view, of which she never tired, was forgotten for the moment as she searched out the approach of the gentleman.

It did not take her long to spot him. The area toward Netherfield was open for much of the distance, with only a small copse or two to break the emptiness of the plain. Mr. Darcy sat astride a chestnut stallion, cantering toward her position, his progress almost to the base of the mount. Once he had reached it, he dismounted and led his horse up the side on foot, careful as he went to guide the beast safely up the sometimes-uneven slope. His progress up the mount allowed Elizabeth to study him for a brief moment.

That he was a handsome man had never been in question—from the first moment Mr. Darcy and Mr. Bingley had entered the assembly hall in Meryton, he had been immediately acclaimed as the handsomest of the pair. Of course, Mr. Hurst, even if he *had* been single, could not be compared with his companions, as his portly frame and somewhat homely face were nothing to the pleasanter aspects of the pair of friends.

Elizabeth had spent many months considering Mr. Darcy's pleasant features and tall, lean frame—and thinking it unfortunate that it was marred by his proud attitude and disdain for his company. And though he had indeed been proud and had undoubtedly considered himself above the company during those initial months, Elizabeth could only ruefully concede that whatever their relationship had been, she had never been merely *indifferent* to Mr. Darcy; he had always provoked a passionate response in her, whether positive or negative.

Largely negative, she reflected, until he had disabused her notion of his unchristian tendencies. Since then, her opinion of the man had been steadily improving, until now she knew she could only anticipate his company with pleasure. Despite his behavior during the months of their first acquaintance, he had more than overcome her first unfavorable impression of him.

But was it enough? Should he wish to renew his addresses (something which was not at all certain, let alone probable), what should her response be? She now knew him as an amiable man who was uncomfortable in social situations—

particularly when he was not acquainted with the majority of the room—but was it enough to feel confident in a lifetime commitment? Or should she be demure, biding her time, asking him to be patient, but running the risk of pushing him away before she was certain of what her answer would be? It was quite vexing!

"Miss Bennet," he greeted her with a bow once he had reached the summit.

Elizabeth responded with a curtsey and a brilliant smile for her companion, one which was returned unabashedly.

"I am delighted to see you," said Mr. Darcy. "I hope the morning is not overly cool for your taste."

"Not at all, Mr. Darcy. I have walked in much cooler weather, as I am sure you well know."

"I had suspected such, but I still thought I should inquire. After all, I was the one who requested for you to walk out this morning."

"Nothing could have kept me indoors this morning, Mr. Darcy. I urge you to think no more on the subject."

The pleasantries dealt with, Elizabeth could not help but marvel at the magnificent animal standing patiently behind its master. She approached the horse slowly, and when Mr. Darcy had stepped to the side to allow her access, she reached forward and offered it the small wizened apple which she had brought for this purpose. Snuffling at her hand for a moment, the animal accepted her offering and continued its investigation of her once the treat had been consumed.

"He is a beautiful creature, Mr. Darcy. What is his name?"

"Hermes, Miss Bennet."

"Ah, for his swiftness, I presume, though I daresay he would acquit himself in the role of a messenger very well—he has the look of great intelligence."

A beaming smile was her response. "He is very intelligent, and, yes, your conjecture on the origin of his name is quite correct. He is my favorite horse, and I find I ride him twice as often as all of my other mounts combined."

They stood in silence for several moments while Elizabeth allowed the animal to continue to become accustomed to her.

"I think you have quite charmed him, Miss Bennet."

"He is a friendly fellow, Mr. Darcy, and I suspect he is easily charmed by an apple or a carrot or two."

Mr. Darcy laughed, his eyes sparkling with mirth as well as something less . . . defined. His manner was all ease and playfulness, and Elizabeth wished he had shown this side of his character during his time at Netherfield the previous October. Much misunderstanding could have been avoided. And who knew? She might have ended up married to him by now . . .

Firmly putting such fanciful notions from her mind, Elizabeth forced her attention to his words.

"He is indeed. He is eager to please all with whom he comes in contact, yet he is a loyal friend as well—as fine a horse as I have ever had the privilege of riding.

"Excuse me, Miss Bennet," continued Mr. Darcy after a moment's hesitation, "but I was not aware that your interests extended to horses."

Elizabeth smiled. "Not, I admit, to riding, although I do love horses and find them to be beautiful creatures. I am not much of a horsewoman, though that is primarily by inclination rather than any other reason. I am very fond of walking and enjoy the exercise, so I rarely ride."

"But you are able to ride?"

"My father taught me when I was a girl, Mr. Darcy," affirmed Elizabeth. "I have certainly never ridden so fine an animal as your Hermes, but, yes, I am capable."

"In that case, you must join my sister and me on a ride about the countryside. The benefit of a mount is the ability to cover much greater ground and reach a higher vantage point from which to see the scenery. As there are three gentle mares stabled at Netherfield for the ladies' use, I am sure we would be happy to oblige you."

Elizabeth was taken aback by his suggestion for a moment, but his obvious enthusiasm for the plan was such that she could not help but smile in response. "Perhaps we could make an outing of it, Mr. Darcy?"

"An excellent plan. I am sure Bingley and your sister would be agreeable to such a scheme, and Anne, though she does not ride, would love to accompany us in Bingley's curricle, I am sure."

"Is that not a little dangerous, Mr. Darcy?" questioned Elizabeth with a frown. "Curricles are notorious for overturning and causing injury to their drivers, after all. Would Anne be quite safe?"

"She is very skilled, I assure you. She has been driving her own personal phaeton and curricle for many years now about the grounds of Rosings. It was the only exercise her mother would allow her, concerned as she was for my cousin's health."

Resisting any comment on the benefits of exercising using one's own body, Elizabeth nodded her head.

"Besides, we would only be traveling on well-worn paths. I think Anne should be completely safe if she was with the rest of us."

"Very well, Mr. Darcy. You have convinced me. I am agreeable to the scheme at any time convenient."

A bow was her response, and then they lapsed into silence, Elizabeth still stroking Hermes's soft coat while Mr. Darcy looked on with a slight smile. Though she would have been somewhat uneasy at his scrutiny months before, now she felt nothing but a calm acceptance, knowing that his look was not based on disgust but on admiration. She was perfectly capable of feeling pleasure in his company now that she had come to know him better and was sensible of what his feelings had been in the past. As such, the silence was not uncomfortable, merely companionable—a far cry from their interactions and conversations during the previous course of their acquaintance.

"I am sorry, Miss Bennet, but I did ask to meet you for a purpose," said Mr. Darcy at last. "I had hoped to discover what I need to know through observation and conversation, but it seems I have been thwarted at every attempt."

"Yes, Mr. Darcy, it appears you have," replied Elizabeth with an amused laugh. "It seems a certain someone in your party is bent on keeping us as far apart as she can manage—what do you think she means by it?"

"I suppose I should not be surprised to learn that you noticed Miss Bingley's behavior," said Darcy with a rueful smile.

"She is not exactly subtle, Mr. Darcy. It was evident from the place settings at dinner, although her blatant interference after dinner whenever I was left to my own devices also spoke volumes. What I do not understand is why."

He appeared lost in thought for a few moments, during which time Elizabeth took the opportunity to further spoil his affectionate mount. Mr. Darcy would come to the point in his own time; for now, Elizabeth was content to wait.

"Although it may be an impertinence to tell you, it may be a part of my purpose for requesting a meeting with you this morning. If you will indulge me, I will tell you all."

Elizabeth nodded her head while suggesting they make use of the large boulder which had become her personal haunt. Mr. Darcy agreed, and after tying his mount's reins to a nearby branch, being certain to leave enough slack for the animal to graze should it wish, the two made themselves comfortable—or as comfortable as they could be when seated upon a hard, uneven surface. After a moment's additional thought, Mr. Darcy began thus:

"Miss Bingley's behavior is no great mystery to you, I presume. I cannot imagine that you have not noticed her attentions and aspirations toward me, as observant as you undoubtedly are."

Receiving a smile and nod from Elizabeth, he continued.

"What you will not be aware of is a development which occurred merely a few days ago—the day I had arrived back in Hertfordshire from town, to be precise. To be blunt, her attentions to me and her machinations—into which she drew both Georgiana and Anne—were so transparent that I immediately resolved to make my sentiments known to her."

Mr. Darcy's color heightened slightly. "I assure you, Miss Bennet, that I have never encouraged her behavior, nor have I ever been tempted to consider offering for her. The only reason I had not disabused her of her notion before was due to my respect for my friend and my desire to avoid offending his sister. I did my best to let my actions speak for themselves and let her know in a gentle manner of my lack of interest. I had hoped that she would find someone else who was a better match for her, so I would be able to avert any unpleasant scenes which might damage my relationship with Bingley. I now wish I had been more explicit many months ago."

Elizabeth understood the tacit apology in his words, though she was privately aware of the fact that Miss Bingley was quite capable of seeing anything she wished in his manners. The chance that she would have taken any rejection or perceived slight in a rational manner was so vanishingly small as to merit no consideration whatsoever.

"I quite understand, Mr. Darcy," she assured him. "It does you credit that you wished to spare your friend's feelings, and after all, you cannot be held accountable for Miss Bingley's aspirations."

"Thank you, Miss Bennet," responded Darcy with a wan smile. "The day I arrived from town, as I said, I spoke with her and let her know in no uncertain terms that I considered her a friend and that she should expect no further connection between us. Needless to say, she took it rather badly, and considering the fact that she had been aware of my . . . interest in you since last year, it appears she has taken it upon herself to interfere in our interactions."

The final few phrases were finished in a rush, as he clearly felt uncomfortable about referring to their previous dealings in even an oblique manner. Elizabeth felt her face heat up in an instant, feeling his words and his behavior in delivering them were a confirmation of the cooling of his ardor toward her. Still, it was not unexpected, and although Elizabeth felt a moment of loss, she quickly pushed it to the back of her mind for later contemplation and bravely faced her companion.

"But what can she mean by it?"

"A sure understanding of Miss Bingley's actions has not been granted to me, but I suspect, given what I know of her character, that she would consider a successful application to you, after she had failed to obtain an application herself, to be an insult to her pride. She has therefore decided to keep us apart in hopes that she would be spared such ignominy."

Now this was a foible which she could consider with much amusement, and Elizabeth did, breaking out into delighted laughter. "If she only knew!" exclaimed she.

Though Mr. Darcy did not appear to enjoy the irony of the statement—no more than Elizabeth did, if she were to be honest with herself—he smiled and chuckled along with her. Despite the indefinable feeling of loss which continued to plague her, Miss Bingley's absurdity provided a convenient escape from what Elizabeth felt were the consequences of her and her family's actions. Though she felt that she might almost welcome Mr. Darcy's attentions now, it was clearly too late—he would have her as a friend, but there would now never be anything further between them. It was a painful realization, but there it was.

"But this cannot be all," stated Elizabeth once she was finished considering the information he had imparted to her. "Surely it is diverting, but you said you had something to discuss, and reciting your history with Miss Bingley can have nothing to do with me."

"You are correct," Darcy affirmed. "I would not normally relate such a history with you if I did not think it was connected with my main purpose for requesting your company."

"In that case, Mr. Darcy, you had best come to the point. As diverting as Miss Bingley's antics are, I must return to my home at some point."

"Quite right, Miss Bennet; I apologize for taking up so much of your time."

He was so earnest and sincere that Elizabeth's heart could not help but go out to him—it must have been a difficult time for him, what with her rejection of his suit and Lady Catherine's actions, not to mention learning of her family's weakness and her further unsuitability through Lydia's near disgrace.

"Do not think of it any more, Mr. Darcy. I am pleased to oblige you and hear your tale, and I would not have you think otherwise. I am expected at home sometime this morning, but I daresay I have not reached the point that my father will begin to send out search parties."

He chucked at her jest. "No, I do not suppose he would, knowing your fondness for the outdoors.

"The reason I wished to speak to you this morning, Miss Bennet, was to inquire about some troubling piece of news I have received. I was told that there are rumors of our . . . impending engagement running through Hertfordshire. I had heard nothing when I was visiting Bingley two weeks ago, but my source suggested that you knew of the rumors and that they may have sprung up in the time since I left for town. I would like to know if you have indeed heard anything, and if so, what information these rumors contain and to what extent they have spread."

Elizabeth listened with amazement. Knowing he knew of the same idle gossip which Mr. Collins had written of to her father was mortifying. But then again, she supposed it was not to be wondered at, considering Lady Catherine's reaction to hearing the selfsame information. The implication that she or her family could be spreading such stories abroad worried her, and she responded quickly to his query.

"Am I to assume that your source insinuated that I have been spreading these rumors?"

"You are correct, Miss Bennet," Darcy replied, appearing distinctly uncomfortable.

"Mr. Darcy, I can assure you most sincerely that I have neither heard any hint of these rumors to which you refer, nor have I spread them in any way. Everything which has passed between us has remained confidential—I have shared them only with Jane and have the highest assurance of her silence."

Mr. Darcy let out an explosive breath. "I assure you, Miss Bennet, that I had no doubt that you had no part in whatever rumors existed, and I know that you and your sister are to be trusted—I never doubted you for an instant.

"I *was* troubled by the assertions which had been brought to my attention and wished to take stock of the matter as soon as possible, but without overhearing someone speaking of them, I was uncertain as to how I should go about determining the truth of the matter. When Anne suggested I should just ask you, I thought about it and decided that it was the best course. I apologize if I have led you to believe that I suspected your complicity."

"No apology is necessary, Mr. Darcy—you did the right thing in asking me."

He had indeed been correct to ask her. She was gratified by his confidence in her nature, but she could imagine the predicament in which he had found himself—to even have a notion that the woman who had rejected him in so abominable a manner could be capable of trying to entrap him in marriage must have been the severest of disappointments. And although the thought was unchristian, Elizabeth knew that if her mother had gained any knowledge of the failed proposal, it was not outside the realm of possibility that she would have reacted in such a way.

Shaking her head, Elizabeth pushed the thought away, suddenly ashamed with herself. It was true that her mother *was* bent on obtaining a comfortable position for all of her daughters and did not much care how it was accomplished, but she would *never* have stooped to such underhanded methods to achieve her goal.

"May I ask, Mr. Darcy . . . ?" began Elizabeth hesitantly. When he indicated she should continue, she took a deep breath. "May I know from whom you heard these rumors?"

Looking embarrassed, Mr. Darcy turned his head away and responded in such a quiet voice that Elizabeth almost missed his words. "My Aunt Catherine."

Smug in the knowledge her conjecture was correct, Elizabeth smirked at him. "Do not concern yourself, Mr. Darcy; I had suspected it to be so."

He turned and regarded her with curiosity. "Might I know why?"

"My father received a letter from Mr. Collins suggesting that you and I were on the verge of becoming engaged and that your aunt did not favor the match."

At Mr. Darcy's indelicate snort, Elizabeth smiled and continued. "Exactly, Mr. Darcy. Your aunt was clear in her wishes for your future with Anne when I visited Rosings, and it took no great thought to apprehend that any disruption to her plans would be distinctly unappreciated."

"My dear Miss Bennet, I believe that is the understatement of the century."

They laughed together at the expense of their absurd relations, and Elizabeth was secretly glad he could still find humor in the situation. The Mr. Darcy she had known originally at Netherfield the previous autumn would undeniably have reacted in a very different manner.

"But how could Mr. Collins have gotten such a notion? Were there rumors of our tête-à-tête that night at Hunsford, or was there something else? And if there were rumors, why did they only now become known to the master of the parsonage?"

"I do not believe your aunt—or Mr. Collins, for that matter—has ever heard any hint of what happened that night at the parsonage, Mr. Darcy. There was no whisper of anything of the sort during the final week of my stay. I daresay it quite escaped everyone's notice."

"Then from where could it have started?"

Elizabeth was thinking hard about the situation. Surely there had never been any notion of any kind of attachment between Darcy and herself—her former opinions had quashed that idea long before they had been in company long enough for any perceived attachment to have formed. In fact, the only ones who had ever gleaned any hint of admiration from Darcy's manner were . . .

Her eyes shot up to her companion's face and dropped once again demurely as she noticed his eyes intently upon her. Perhaps all of his admiration for her person was not as lost as she had thought.

"I believe I may have an answer to your question, sir," she finally began once she had regained her composure. "I believe we must look closer to home for further insight into this mystery. Mr. Collins does have another connection into the neighborhood, after all. You have recently been in the neighborhood, and Mr. Bingley recently proposed to Jane. It was only then that Mr. Collins made his information known to Lady Catherine and, subsequently, my father."

"You think the Lucases have been spreading this report?" asked Darcy, his brows furrowed. "If so, why has it not swept through the neighborhood?"

"I do not believe it has been discussed openly. Before she left for Kent, Charlotte Collins mentioned a number of times that you looked at me a great deal. Then, while I was visiting her, she teased me several times that you would never have come to visit her so quickly after your arrival if I had not been staying there."

Darcy appeared abashed for a moment, but he quickly shook it off. Elizabeth could only think that Charlotte's conjecture had been correct—Darcy *had* visited the parsonage due to her presence.

"You think she speculated to her husband?"

"I do not believe so," said Elizabeth with a shake of her head. "If you think back, there was another who seemed intent upon throwing us together and congratulating us while dancing."

"Sir William?" asked Darcy, eyes widening.

"The very same. Charlotte is close to her father, and given what she noted to *me*, I would suspect she told her father, or at the very least, he made the same conclusion."

"But I have been in Sir William's company but rarely since Bingley returned to the neighborhood."

"Perhaps. But Sir William may have speculated to his daughter in a letter which

Mr. Collins discovered. You know he keeps nothing from your aunt; it would be a short step from idle speculation to fact in the minds of both my cousin and Lady Catherine."

He was silent for several moments, thinking of her assertions. For Elizabeth, the more she thought of the situation, the more it made sense to her. Sir William had always seemed to be Darcy's champion, and since he considered Elizabeth to be almost as a daughter to him, she knew he would cheer a match between Elizabeth and Darcy as vociferously as Elizabeth's own mother.

"Then why has it not been spread throughout the neighborhood?" asked Darcy at length.

Elizabeth smiled. "Sir William is somewhat pompous and a little too impressed with his knighthood, but at heart he is a good and caring man, and he is excessively fond of me. He loves to hear and speculate about the doings of his neighbors, but he is little inclined to idle gossip. What passes between him and Charlotte he has always kept between them to the best of my knowledge. In this case, I suspect he either remembered his conjecture from last year or saw something in our manners which allowed his imagination to run wild. He likely did not consider the fact that Mr. Collins might catch wind of what he is saying to his daughter. In fact, I'm not sure he has realized that everything Mr. Collins hears will be heard by your aunt as well."

"I suppose it is true then—the existence of an engagement will often breed rumors of another."

The words were spoken quietly, yet Elizabeth could almost feel the irony dripping from his voice. She was not certain what his words referenced, but she was unable to think on it as he continued immediately.

"Once again, Miss Bennet, I wish to assure you that I did not for a moment give any credence to the assertion that you were spreading these rumors."

She smiled at him. "I understand, Mr. Darcy. You would not wish to have your name associated with such improprieties."

"No more than would you."

"Lady Catherine, though, was certain that I or my family was the source of her information and would not be persuaded otherwise. I am not surprised that her next action was to confront you."

Darcy felt his breath still within his chest as he gazed at her with equal parts disbelief and horror.

"Miss Bennet, did I hear you correctly? Do you mean to say that you have spoken with my Aunt Catherine since you left Kent in April?"

Elizabeth's blank stare unnerved him. "Why, did you not know?" was her incredulous query.

"I assure you, I did not," replied Darcy, still trying to wrap his head around the thought. "May I ask when?"

"I believe it was about ten days ago, sir."

"Undoubtedly the very day in which she came to make her demands upon me," he breathed in response. "I fear I must apologize most humbly, Miss Bennet, for the mortification which my aunt must undoubtedly have caused you. I cannot imagine she was any more temperate in her words to you than she was in the demands she made to me."

"Mr. Darcy, I assure you your apology is not necessary. You cannot control your aunt's actions, after all."

"Perhaps not, Miss Bennet," responded Darcy as seriously as he was able. "Yet I must ask you to allow me to make the apology all the same, as I doubt that she will ever be prevailed upon to offer it herself. She was wrong to accuse you and wrong to confront you in the first place. It was not her concern."

Elizabeth inclined her head. "I thank you, Mr. Darcy. Let us just say that we both have relations who make us blush from time to time and leave it at that."

A wry smile crept over Darcy's face, and he acknowledged her point with a nod. Their discussion now completed, they sat in companionable silence for several moments, both reflecting on the situation and the folly of their relations.

At length, Elizabeth rose from her seat and indicated that it was time to return to her home. She had been out for some time that morning, and her mother was likely concerned at her absence.

Darcy agreed, offering to accompany her to Longbourn, and while she assured him she could find the way by herself, he insisted. It was moments later when they began the long walk with Elizabeth's hand in the crook of his arm, while Hermes followed placidly behind, his reins held in Darcy's other hand.

Their conversation during the return to Longbourn was light and unencumbered by the heavy subjects which had characterized it while they sat upon the rock. And although they tacitly steered clear of any mention of their past interactions, Darcy could not help but attempt to see through her words to the feelings which lay beneath. She was not indifferent to him, he thought, but exactly what she felt for him, he could not say. She appeared to accept his conversation with pleasure and returned the compliment with the ease and grace which he associated with her, yet if there were anything further in her manner, it was difficult to detect.

Looking back on their conversation, he remembered the way his stomach had almost entered his boots as she vehemently denied having heard any rumors of their attachment. It was silly, he realized, as her concern seemed to be more the thought that he would seriously believe his aunt's assertion that she was spreading untruths than due to any lingering distaste for himself. In that moment, he was also forced to admit that a part of him—a very small part, to be sure—had almost wished for the rumors to be true so that he could have an excuse to make her another offer, one which would almost certainly be supported by her father in the interest of curbing any further rumors concerning his family. Darcy was still sensible of the very great danger in forcing her to the altar by such means, but he almost preferred a future where he was required to endure her displeasure at being forced to marry him than one in which he had to go through life without her. It was amazing what a few hours spent in her company could do to his outlook on the situation.

At least she appeared to have no knowledge of his actions with regard to her sister. Whatever would happen between them, he had no desire to have her accept him because of nothing more than gratitude for his actions. He wanted her heart. Nothing less than her utter devotion in equal measure to his regard for her would appease him.

When they arrived in the vicinity of Longbourn, Elizabeth turned and smiled at him and spoke in her light and arch manner. "Thank you for your escort, Mr.

Darcy. I can assure you that I am capable of making my way home from here."

Darcy hesitated a moment before smiling and bowing. "I am sure you are eminently capable, Miss Bennet. I wish to thank you once again for indulging me this morning and agreeing to speak with me."

"It was my pleasure, Mr. Darcy; after all, it appeared to be as much for my benefit as yours. I thank you for your care and for your attention to my reputation. It is much appreciated, considering the recent event regarding my sister."

She blushed and turned her head away in obvious embarrassment at her own reference to Lydia's indiscretion, but Darcy, knowing that she could not know of his involvement in the affair, merely smiled, attempting to soothe her discomfiture and restore her good humor.

"Be not alarmed, Miss Bennet. I understand that Mr. Wickham ultimately did the honorable thing and married your sister, so it has all turned out well in the end, regardless of the less than conventional circumstances in which that end was accomplished."

"At great expense to my uncle," muttered Elizabeth.

"Even so," agreed Darcy. "The marriage did take place, which is the important point to recall, Miss Bennet. It does no good to dwell upon it."

Squirming slightly, Elizabeth appeared to be somewhat upset. Darcy wished he could soothe her fears, yet propriety would not allow closer contact; he would have to win her heart to gain that right.

"I shudder to think how close we all came to ruination," she finally said.

"No closer than I or Georgiana," Darcy reminded her. He wanted her to clearly understand that he bore her no ill will for her sister's folly. After all, but for a fortunate circumstance, his own sister would have ended up in the same situation in which Lydia now found herself. And the girl did not even understand her own situation! Darcy hoped for the best, but inside, he knew it was only a matter of time before Lydia became intimately familiar with her husband's habits.

When Elizabeth did not speak any further, Darcy gathered all his courage and spoke once again.

"I would also apologize to you, Miss Bennet, for not making Wickham's character known when I was in the neighborhood last year. If not for my pride and refusal to share my private dealings, I should have branded the man for the libertine he is. Then your sister's elopement could not have taken place. I am most sincerely sorry for not having done more to protect you all."

"I understand your reticence, Mr. Darcy. You wished to protect your sister, and disclosure could have harmed her. While I would have wished for something to have been said, I do not blame you."

A heavy sigh escaped Darcy's lips; that Elizabeth would resent him and blame him for Lydia's downfall had been one of his greatest fears. And now, Elizabeth had absolved him of the blame, at least in her own mind. For himself, he was still unable to reconcile the event.

"Thank you, Miss Bennet. I daresay it shall be some time before I can forgive myself in this matter, but to have your absolution means much to me."

"I should go, sir," whispered Elizabeth.

"Miss Bennet," interrupted a desperate Darcy as she was about to leave. "I admit I have grown very . . . fond of our discussions and would very much like to continue them. May I . . . may I continue to call on you?"

Knowing he had all but declared his intentions to her, Darcy waited with bated breath as Elizabeth first blushed and then looked down. She glanced up at him and gave him a bashful look, something with which he was not accustomed to seeing on the usually unflappable young woman's face. She took a deep breath and gazed at him with a slight smile.

"I believe I would find that very agreeable, Mr. Darcy," said she in a quiet voice.

Darcy felt an expression of heartfelt delight come over his face, and feeling very boyish and light, he reached for her hand, taking it as she extended it, and bestowed a kiss upon it. He had only ever held her hand once in the past, during their dance at Netherfield, and he was both pleased with its strength and surprised at its daintiness.

"I thank you, Miss Bennet. I shall look forward very much to continuing our acquaintance."

"As shall I."

No further words were spoken. Elizabeth turned away and began walking toward the manor. Darcy stood as if rooted on the spot, watching as she walked away, smiling as she turned every so often to glance back at him. Her own smiles as she did so cheered him and spurred him on toward greater flights of fancy. He was closer now, he could feel it!

A short time later, Darcy arrived back at Netherfield and, handing Hermes off to one of the grooms, hurried up the steps of the house and entered, looking for his cousin. It appeared as if breakfast had already been served, and Darcy, excited and giddy as he felt, decided he had no need for food — his interview with Elizabeth had provided all the sustenance he required.

A quick query revealed that Anne had taken a walk in the garden, prompting Darcy to set off for the back of the house straight away. He did catch a glimpse of Miss Bingley, who said nothing, though he could hardly miss the scowl affixed upon her face. Darcy ignored her; she could do nothing to upset his mood, and her schemes were as nothing to him.

Anne was indeed to be found in the garden, sitting on a bench and enjoying the meager rays of the morning sun. A few short weeks earlier, he would have worried for her health, but time away from her mother and the warm clothing she wore caused all concern to depart. Anne was certainly on the mend.

She peered up at him with a smug expression on her face. "You look rather jubilant this morning, cousin. Am I to infer that your encounter with the intrepid Miss Bennet was a success?"

"I believe it was, Anne," responded Darcy, taking a seat by her side. "But I must admit I have learned something which has astonished me greatly, and I am rather surprised that I did not learn of it from you or your mother."

A raised eyebrow met his declaration. "Indeed? Well, do not make me wait, Darcy. What is this astonishing intelligence?"

"Merely the fact that your mother confronted Elizabeth at Longbourn, and neither of you saw fit to inform me."

Anne let out a great peal of laughter at his statement. Darcy was not amused; it was hardly the type of trivial detail which should have been kept from him, after all, and he did not find the matter entertaining in the slightest.

At length, Anne managed to regain control over her laughter, although she had to stifle a few more giggles when she glanced up to look at his face. Darcy was in no mood to indulge her humor on this morning regardless of his euphoria over the success of his interview with Elizabeth.

"Well?" he prompted.

"Oh, Darcy, you do not need to play the imperious master of Pemberley with me," admonished Anne. "You really should practice a kinder, gentler expression in the mirror, you know. I believe it would soften your image."

Darcy scowled. "Can you please come to the point, Anne?"

"Oh, very well. Simply put, yes, my mother did come to Hertfordshire to confront Elizabeth Bennet, and, yes, I knew of it, being here myself. However, I have little knowledge of what was actually said, as I merely waited in the carriage while the dragon attempted to slay the princess. Until this moment, I thought my mother told you of our visit herself."

"I assure you, Anne, that your mother said nothing of her interview with Miss Bennet."

An impish smile came over Anne's face. "In that case, I believe I should credit my mother with more cunning than I had previously thought possible. It seems she was not about to give you any hope in your endeavor, while at the same time making certain she emphasized Elizabeth's perceived scheming nature. If it had not been so hurtful toward a young lady I am swiftly beginning to consider a dear friend, I might almost applaud her."

"You are spending far too much time in Richard's company," complained Darcy. "That speech was worthy of his inability to take anything seriously."

"Or perhaps I have merely found the ability to express my own nature," jibed Anne in response. "Oh, do not distress yourself, Darcy, I shall not embarrass you. Much."

Shaking his head, Darcy decided that a tactical withdrawal was in order. He excused himself after giving Anne the information on his meeting with Elizabeth that morning which she fairly demanded, and then he departed for the house and a change of clothes after his morning ride. It was indeed a very fine day.

Chapter XI

*I*t is amazing how one's perspective can be changed by a single event or conversation. Long-held beliefs or convictions can be overturned with nothing more than a few words, even if the speaker has no intent to provoke such a change. In the case of Fitzwilliam Darcy, Elizabeth Bennet, wary of misinterpreting his actions yet *again*, was loath to assign a motive to his discourse, but she knew that whatever his reasons had been, they had changed her perception and opinion of him once again.

After returning from Oakham Mount in the company of Mr. Darcy—and recalling the glances she had directed back at him on her return to the house—Elizabeth felt herself floating through life in the middle of a fog. Recent events had caused her head to spin and had induced her to question her beliefs. What was she to do if her world kept changing into something unrecognizable every few days? It was too much for her to comprehend.

One thing was certain, though—beyond all reason and all expectation, Mr. Darcy's affections and wishes regarding her had not changed. Despite all which had occurred between them—the misunderstandings, the words spoken in anger, and the events which had conspired to separate them—he still maintained a tender affection for her. How, Elizabeth could not be certain, but she knew his feelings for her still existed, and unless she was very much mistaken, they blazed as brightly as ever.

His concern for her—his care and attention, his insistence in protecting her and her reputation—had survived her sister's treachery, his aunt's words, and even her own voice raised in anger to unjustly condemn him as the worst sort of man. Her rejection of him at Hunsford, she felt, had to have destroyed his good opinion of her forever, and even at the time, Elizabeth had believed that his love was merely infatuation or perhaps related to the challenge of a woman who had spent time arguing with him rather than flattering and complimenting him as he was accustomed to. But his love was of such a sturdy and healthy type that it had conquered all of these things. Elizabeth was humbled and awed at the steadfastness of this man, the constancy of his affection, and the devoted manner in which he had cherished a good opinion of her. It was almost too much.

The hows and the whys of the situation, she could not tell. Despite the disparity in their fortunes and positions in society—indeed, Elizabeth was of the opinion that those things he had so unwisely spoken of during his proposal were the least of the obstacles between them—there were far greater trials he must undoubtedly have overcome to continue in his good opinion of her. Greatest among them, she felt, was his aversion to a closer connection to a man whom he rightly despised, who had used him at every opportunity and then had the audacity to blacken his good name wherever he went. How could he countenance the idea of being a brother to Wickham?

Yet he clearly had every intention of pursuing such a connection; his request to call upon her left very little to the imagination. And Elizabeth knew that *this time* she would welcome his attentions with grateful acceptance. Nothing else made sense. She was not yet certain about marriage to him, but she felt she soon would be aware enough of her own heart to be able to answer even that question. Would that he had acted this way when he had first come to Netherfield! Perhaps she could have avoided her destructive prejudice against him . . .

It was with these thoughts that Elizabeth made her way through the rest of the day, and not even the ever-present and much lamented attentions of her neighbor could induce her from her ruminations. She responded when required and was careful not to allow him to drag her into a situation which could be interpreted as improper, but otherwise, she permitted him to carry the conversation in any manner he saw fit while she allowed her thoughts to wander back to the gentleman from Derbyshire.

Of course, such a situation could not last. Life and the annoyance of her *other* suitor, coupled with her mother's antics, continued to intrude upon her until her other, more pleasant thoughts were overturned, and Elizabeth once again began to feel the exasperation of her situation.

Mr. Darcy *did* call on her the very next day—and every day after—in the company of his friend, yet the presence of the gentleman was lost to her for the most part, due to the actions of others. More than once over the course of the week, Elizabeth had reason to curse those around her, as they appeared intent upon interrupting her and providing her no time with the man whose company she truly desired.

Samuel Lucas, of course, had already made his intentions known, and he watched her, much as a hawk spies on its prey, always on hand to disrupt her conversations and ruin her opportunities to come to know Mr. Darcy better while attempting to flatter her with his own attentions. Her mother was a willing conspirator, constantly throwing them together in company, her shrillness and determination quite the equal of any attempts to persuade her otherwise.

More than that, Elizabeth was absolutely mortified by her mother's behavior toward Mr. Darcy. Mrs. Bennet had a long memory, one perfectly capable of recalling the smallest slight, whether it had occurred the previous day or the previous decade, and she was quite able to bring it up in conversation at the most inopportune time. It was truly too much to ask for her to have forgotten Mr. Darcy's behavior from the night of their first acquaintance, and she let him know on every occasion possible that he was only welcome in her house because he was a friend of Mr. Bingley's. He knew without a doubt that she would prefer he never came at all.

And yet he handled her incivility with great forbearance, never allowing any anger or resentment to gain hold upon him. Elizabeth was prodigiously proud of him and felt offended on his behalf, for even though he had admittedly behaved poorly on that evening the previous year, he had made amends, and his present behavior was irreproachable. Elizabeth's injunctions to her mother against her censure of him were met with an indifferent shrug. Mr. Darcy was still the most horrid and disagreeable man her mother had ever laid eyes upon, and nothing could possibly convince her otherwise. Elizabeth could only imagine what the thought of his ten-thousand pounds would do to her mother's opinion of him if she were learn of his interest in her second daughter.

Elizabeth attempted to apologize to him on her mother's behalf, but Mr. Darcy would not hear of it, claiming instead that her mother had every right to be offended against him considering his earlier manners. He would work to gain her respect by continuing with his changed actions. She could only admire his fortitude, though she wondered if perhaps he underestimated her mother's ability to hold a grudge.

Of course, Elizabeth suspected that Darcy was well aware of the fact that Samuel Lucas was unwelcome and his attentions unwanted. He gave her as much protection from her despised suitor as he was able, taking it upon himself to distract the man whenever he could. That had the unfortunate effect of limiting his own time with Elizabeth, but she thanked him for it all the same.

Of the ladies and Colonel Fitzwilliam, Elizabeth saw nearly as much as she saw of Darcy. Georgiana, having cultivated a friendship with Elizabeth's younger sisters, was not as much in Elizabeth's company as the other two; Anne, however, was another matter altogether. Elizabeth truly felt as if she was forging a deep and abiding friendship with the formerly aloof and unapproachable Miss de Bourgh. In her, Elizabeth found an acute observer, much as she liked to think of herself, as well as a wry and understated sense of humor which meshed with hers quite neatly. Anne was truly a wonderful young woman, and Elizabeth was very happy to have finally come to know her better.

The one of whom Elizabeth saw much and spoke with more than she would have liked was the ever-present and brooding Miss Bingley. She came often with the other residents of Netherfield, and though she had not lost her superior attitude and rarely spoke to anyone if it could be avoided, she kept as close an eye on Elizabeth's conversations as Samuel did himself, and she was always ready to interfere with Elizabeth's ability to speak with Mr. Darcy. Elizabeth took to avoiding her altogether; the almost manic look in Miss Bingley's eye made her distinctly uncomfortable.

This state of affairs continued for the entirety of the week, and by the end of it, Elizabeth was fairly well along the way of being ready to strangle those who were making her life so difficult. Or possibly, she thought, she could hand in her bonnet for a wimple. Surely life as a nun would be much easier!

As uncomfortable as the week had been for Elizabeth, the Sunday church service was doubly so. Though she looked forward to the worship service and the observances in which she took part, it was another opportunity for her persistent and unwanted gentleman caller to impose his attentions upon her.

The day started out much the same as any other Sunday, with Elizabeth waking up much earlier than most of the rest of the household. She took one longing look through her window at the outside world and decided her mother's displeasure was not worth the benefit of a morning walk.

On mornings such as this, Elizabeth's normal routine included a leisurely breakfast and then an hour or two spent in her father's study, curled up with a good book or debating various points with him. This morning was no different in its inception, but it had taken a turn not thirty minutes into her stay in her father's bookroom by the arrival of her mother.

Mrs. Bennet bustled into the room, looking for all the world as if she had experienced some great disappointment.

"Elizabeth, child, what are you doing here?"

Gaping at her mother's insensible question, Elizabeth responded, "Sitting with Father, reading—much the same as I do every Sabbath before church."

"There is no time for that! Come, you must hurry and prepare yourself."

She took Elizabeth's arm and dragged her to her feet, all the while clucking and muttering about recalcitrant daughters and their wild ways.

But Elizabeth was not about to allow her mother to lead her around by the nose, so she dug in her heels.

"Mother, to what are you referring? I am already dressed, as you can see, and only require my bonnet and gloves and spencer before I am ready to depart."

Mrs. Bennet peered at her as if she were a simpleton. "No. That will not do, Lizzy. Your dress is an old one and clearly not sufficient for our church services. You had best change into another gown. Perhaps your dark blue one; indeed, you look very fetching in that gown, and I would not have you embarrassing your parents by showing up to church wearing inferior clothing."

Shooting her father a pleading glance, Elizabeth was disheartened when he winked at her and raised an eyebrow at his wife before shooing them both from his study. Bewildered—although certainly knowing what her mother was about— Elizabeth allowed herself to be led from the room.

An hour later, Elizabeth wondered if her mother had mistaken this morning's services for a grand ball. She was subjected to the attentions of Longbourn's maid, who was directed by Mrs. Bennet to do her hair in an elaborately upswept style, one which may have been appropriate in a ballroom with most of London's haute ton in attendance, but which she knew to be far too pretentious for a simple church service.

Beyond that, her mother insisted she wear her dark blue morning dress, which, although perhaps not a cut to be worn at a major social event, was certainly finer than anything she had previously worn to church. Elizabeth almost felt as pretentious as Lady Catherine, dressed up as she was.

And though Elizabeth protested all these extravagances in her appearance, her mother would hear nothing of changing a thing; her daughter would be showing herself off to her best advantage if Mrs. Bennet had anything to say in the matter. It was not so much the fact of being completely overdressed—church services were, after all, an occasion to dress finely—it was more the difference she knew would be apparent in her own appearance as opposed to her sisters, whom she knew had not been subjected to the same treatment. And this was without mentioning the young gentleman she knew her mother wished for her to impress . . .

Determined to oppose her mother's draconian measures, Elizabeth waited until Mrs. Bennet had left to make her own preparations before instructing her maid to remove the ornate pearls and upswept style her mother had insisted upon. The maid balked, obviously not wanting to incur the displeasure of her mistress, but Elizabeth was firm, informing her that if she did not do it, then Elizabeth would herself. A large sigh met this declaration, and the maid set about changing her hairstyle to a much simpler arrangement. Elizabeth thanked her and swept from the room.

Jane was in her chambers, ready to depart, when Elizabeth stepped in, meeting her younger sister with a sympathetic smile and a hug.

"Mama is determined, is she not?"

"I cannot begin to tell you how mortified I am, Jane," replied Elizabeth with a sigh. "What shall everyone think of me if I arrive at our services dressed for high London society? She does not see in her haste to show me off as a desirable partner that I have no interest in the man she has chosen."

"Yes, Lizzy, I believe I understand your feelings. After all, has Mother not attempted the same with me in the past? You should be glad I have been here to draw her attentions away from you."

Elizabeth laughed, delighted with Jane's wry pronouncement, before pulling her sister into a hug. "I believe you are correct, Jane. I am very grateful for your forbearance; indeed, I must say you are the best person of my acquaintance, having had to put up with this for so long. I do not know how you managed."

Jane was silent for several moments, regarding her sister with an unreadable expression, before she once again spoke up:

"Lizzy, you do know that, should Mama's ways become too much for you, Mr. Bingley and I would be very happy to have you come and stay with us."

"Thank you, Jane," replied Elizabeth, choked up with sudden emotion. She took one of Jane's hands in her own and squeezed it with affection for her sister. Jane was truly too good for the world in which she lived.

"I shall be well, I think," she finally continued, all the while thinking of her earlier ruminations about what she should do when Jane was gone. "I have Papa to help deal with her excesses and my walks should she become too overbearing.

"Besides," Elizabeth resumed after an arch look at her sister, "I had thought you were staying at Netherfield. I should think we both would need to be on the other side of the country to avoid her attentions."

Jane laughed delightedly. "Now, that is my sister Lizzy! And knowing our mother, you are likely correct as usual. Perhaps we should give some thought to Cornwall or Nottinghamshire as a place to settle."

"I am certain Mr. Bingley would be vastly pleased to accommodate you in whatever living arrangements you should propose, dear Jane. I rather doubt him capable of denying you anything."

"Jane! Elizabeth!" rang out Mrs. Bennet's voice from below. "It is time to depart for church. We shall be late."

Suppressing a sigh, Elizabeth smiled at her sister before leading the way down the stairs and into the entrance hall, where the servants bustled and fussed with the family, ensuring they were ready to depart for their morning services.

"Lizzy!" screeched Mrs. Bennet as soon as she caught sight of her daughter. "What have you done to your hair?"

"Nothing, Mama," she replied calmly. "This is a style I normally use when attending church. It is nothing out of the ordinary."

"But child, your hair looked lovely when I left your room, and now you have ruined all my work."

"Mother! I will not attend church dressed as if I were attending a ball in London, while my sisters dress as they usually do. My attire was good enough for you last week; what has changed now?"

Mrs. Bennet did not respond, though she sniffed and turned to allow the servant to help her with her pelisse. "I suppose it does not signify much since you are determined to be intractable.

"Oh, you look well enough, I suppose, and your blue dress truly does do you credit. I only hope you will pay young Samuel Lucas every attention, as he has been very attentive to you."

"Much as Mr. Collins was?" responded Elizabeth evenly.

"Pray do not bring up your actions with regard to Mr. Collins, Miss Lizzy. How you can continue to rattle on in the matter of your future when I have done my best to secure it, I know not."

Elizabeth made no response, knowing her mother would not be deterred. There was little point in arguing, yet she could not permit her mother to have her way in everything. Once again, she was struck by the thought that her mother would be singing a different tune if she had any hint of Mr. Darcy's interest in her second daughter. But wishing though she did for a respite from her mother's attentions, Elizabeth could not bring herself to illuminate Mrs. Bennet concerning the situation which was proceeding right under her very nose; her relationship was too fragile in her own mind to subject Mr. Darcy to her mother's fawning attentions. She might just scare him away.

The walk to the church was completed largely in silence, and as they entered the chapel, the next part of the morning's drama was to be played out. They had arrived just before the start of services, as was their wont, when Elizabeth's sight was immediately arrested by the sight of Samuel Lucas, who was already present at the church. He stood to one side, obviously keeping watch on the door, and his face broke out into a broad smirk as he saw her enter.

Though she would have loved to cut him, Elizabeth's sensibilities were too strong for such unkind behavior, and she curtsied in his direction before turning to her sisters and making her way down to their normal pew. Unfortunately, this was the point where Elizabeth's plans fell apart.

The family moved into the pew, with Kitty and Mary first, followed by Elizabeth. But she noticed as she took her seat that Jane had been prevented from following by her mother's hand upon her arm, and the vacant seat in which she had been intending to sit was immediately commandeered by Mr. Lucas.

Elizabeth gaped at him, noting with some disgust his self-satisfied sneer of triumph while looking at her mother, whose expression was a mirror image of

Samuel's. Jane looked helplessly down at her sister before her mother guided her to a seat next to Mr. Bingley, after which she took up her own position behind Elizabeth and next to Lady Lucas. The service was about to begin, not leaving much time for the neighboring matrons to comment much on the seating arrangements, but Elizabeth could clearly hear a few low exclamations of "Such a charming couple!" and "I daresay they look very well together." That all of this was witnessed by Mr. Darcy was without question, as he sat behind and next to Mr. Bingley. The thought of his being witness to another of her family's improprieties filled Elizabeth with shame.

She directed a dark expression at Mr. Lucas, who returned it with a smirk excessive insolence. Elizabeth bristled in response, and she glowered at him, wondering what she had to do to dissuade him.

"I am very happy to see you this morning, Lizzy," he finally said.

Elizabeth said nothing in return, merely raising an eyebrow at him while she continued to glare.

"Alas, I am sorry, fair maiden," said Mr. Lucas with a laugh after a moment. "I neglected to remember that I must refer to you in a more proper manner. I offer you my most abject apologies, Miss Elizabeth. How are you this fine Sabbath morning?"

"I was quite well until I arrived here, I assure you," snapped Elizabeth. She determined that if he was to continue to be so blind and to pursue her so shamelessly, then he deserved no attention from her.

Mr. Lucas's countenance darkened in response to her rudeness. "Come now, *Miss Elizabeth*, I have apologized. Can you not offer your forgiveness for my unintentional faux pas?"

"I assure you, Mr. Lucas, that your *faux pas*, as you refer to it, was the least of your offenses."

He colored and appeared ready to snap back at her, but the organ started at that moment, indicating the commencement of the morning's services, and he was denied. His dark expression did not change for an instant, but he turned away from her and picked up his hymnal. Elizabeth was exceedingly happy to have been able to escape his attention, at least while the service lasted.

It was a very uncomfortable time for the young Elizabeth Bennet—there could be nothing worse than being forced to sit for the whole of the service by the side of a man she was rightly coming to detest, all the while knowing that he was seething with anger. It was no right state of mind to allow her to attend to what the parson was saying.

After the service ended, Elizabeth sighed with relief and stood, intending to immediately depart from her unwanted companion. Mr. Lucas, however, would have none of that, as he began speaking to her of the service, asking her opinion on the topics which had been discussed, and generally making it impossible for her to leave as she wanted. She heard not a word and attended him not at all, as her gaze was arrested by the sight of Mr. Darcy, who was watching her with some concern upon his face. She smiled wanly at him, a look which was returned with much more warmth, before turning back to Mr. Lucas, intending to remove herself from his presence.

Before she could do so, however, her attention was once again drawn by the loud voices of her mother and Lady Lucas:

"My, my, Lady Lucas, do you see my Elizabeth and young Samuel getting along so famously again?"

"Indeed, I do," was the response. "I should think that we will have wedding bells in the near future for two such eminently deserving and well-matched young people."

Elizabeth colored and looked down, but her trials were not complete.

Mrs. Goulding, hearing what the other two women were saying, cast one look at Elizabeth and Mr. Lucas before turning to the other two ladies:

"Samuel and Elizabeth are courting?"

"Well, nothing is official, you understand," said Mrs. Bennet with a simpering giggle. "But I believe they are well on their way to an understanding. Young Samuel has called at Longbourn every day for the past week in order to see Elizabeth. He appears to be very much smitten with my second daughter."

"Then what you were saying at the Lucas' party was true!" another lady joined in, clapping her hands. "I daresay there could not be a better match. They were such good friends as children; it seems appropriate that their friendship should become so much more now that they have grown. I congratulate you most heartily on this development."

At that point, two things happened simultaneously. Elizabeth, mortified as she was by the loud speculations of the local ladies, directed an imperious glare at the gloating Samuel Lucas before spinning on her heel and marching to confront her mother. At the same time, Sir William Lucas, who had been listening to the ladies' words as closely as had Elizabeth, approached the group as well, a stern expression on his face.

"Lady Lucas!"

"Mother!"

Their voices rang out almost in tandem, startling them both and causing Elizabeth to peer at the country squire in curiosity. Sir William regarded Elizabeth with a sympathetic eye before he bowed to her and spoke up again.

"Miss Elizabeth," said he, bowing but displaying none of his usual pomposity. "Such subjects should not be discussed openly, especially when nothing of any substance has been agreed upon. You have my most heartfelt apologies.

"My dear," continued Sir William, directing his comments toward his wife, "you must cease this conjecture at once. I will not have you besmirching the names of our son or such a fine lady as Miss Elizabeth with such talk. You will create a scandal if you continue, and I will not have it."

Lady Lucas colored and mumbled her apologies, looking suitably chastened by her husband's words, and she excused herself immediately and left with Sir William, who propelled his eldest son from the church. They could not leave before Mr. Lucas once again directed another dark expression in Elizabeth's direction. But Elizabeth was much too focused on the other member of the party who had been speaking so openly.

"Mother, you must cease this immediately. Mr. Lucas has called upon me, it is true, but I do not recall asking him to call or welcoming his attentions when he came, nor has he approached me or my father for permission for a courtship or an engagement. Until such time as that subject is broached, I would very much appreciate it if you would confine your comments to facts and not speculation. Temper your words, Mother, if you do not wish to cause a rift between us which shall never be mended!

"I am now returning home," continued Elizabeth when her mother appeared as if she wished to speak. She then stalked from the church, tears threatening to fall.

On her way out, she noticed Miss Bingley's superior smirk—she had, of course, never directed any other expression in Elizabeth's direction—although she noticed it was tempered this time with a look of some worry. Elizabeth ignored her—Bingley's supercilious and arrogant sister was of no consequence whatsoever. She wanted nothing more than to retreat to her home and suffer by herself.

The scene before him was astonishing, and if Darcy had not seen it for himself, he would never have believed it to be possible. The stupidity of Mrs. Bennet was a thing to be wondered at, and all thoughts of moderating his opinion of the Bennet matron had vanished in the face of the distress she was causing the woman he loved.

Surely this was the origin of the rumor which Caroline Bingley had so gleefully related after his first visit to Longbourn. Whether she believed it was a matter of some conjecture—although Darcy felt that she had embellished it for her own purposes—but it was clear to Darcy that whatever fantasies with which Mrs. Bennet deluded herself, it was clear that Elizabeth was at the very least uncomfortable with such subjects being canvassed openly by all the neighbors.

As for Elizabeth's feelings regarding the Lucas heir, Darcy was reasonably confident, given her words to her mother and her reaction to he man's attentions, that she felt nothing for the man and wished he would leave her alone. Regardless, Darcy was not about to assume anything—he had misjudged her in the past and would not be completely easy about her feelings for Samuel Lucas until she confirmed them with her own mouth.

"This scene puts me in mind of Lady Catherine," the voice of his cousin Richard came from behind. "She is all arrogance and overbearing, while Mrs. Bennet is silly and senseless, but together they somehow manage to discompose those within range of their voices without thought as to how their words and actions hurt those they love."

Darcy grunted in agreement while continuing to focus on the Bennet matron, who was beginning to recover from the set-down her daughter had given her. Mr. Bennet, although he appeared amused at the situation, forestalled his wife's comments on the subject by taking her arm and leading her from the church. What he could find amusing in such a situation, Darcy could not imagine, but he did remember Bennet's sardonic amusement at other times, most notably during the ball at Netherfield, and he felt he did have some measure of the man. That he cared for Elizabeth was unmistakable, but to laugh at such improprieties was more than Darcy could understand.

"I think it is past time that we departed, Darcy," stated Richard. "Perhaps we should take counsel on how best to protect Miss Elizabeth Bennet from the depravations of her mother and Mr. Lucas."

"I will not have you interfering, Richard," snapped Darcy in response. "You will only make the situation worse."

"Do not worry, Darcy; I shall not do anything which would exacerbate things for your Miss Elizabeth. However, I think a certain amount of misdirection and distraction for our good Mr. Lucas is in order. After all, the lady's words seem to be having little effect."

Darcy peered at his cousin and, finding no trace of his usual flippant amusement, nodded his agreement before stalking from the room.

"Perhaps a more direct approach is necessary," commented Darcy darkly once they were all outside and waiting for the carriages. "I should think he would find much greater difficulty in his wooing attempts if he were to go about it on a pair of broken legs."

"And you accuse me of exacerbating the problem!" exclaimed Richard with a delighted laugh.

"Come now, Richard," Anne broke in with a playful smile, "that is the best suggestion Darcy has had since we arrived."

The cousins all laughed at the irreverent comments, and Darcy reflected that he was fortunate he had his family nearby to combat his serious tendencies. Without them, he feared he would have descended into his habitual brooding, which would not have done either himself or Elizabeth any good under the circumstances. It was time to think of her and how to ease her distress—nothing else would do!

Once she returned home, Elizabeth swept past the servants and climbed the stairs to her room, furious at her mother's continued machinations and interference. She motioned for the maid to follow her, and once she had reached her rooms, she proceeded to divest herself of her blue gown and replace it with a simpler garment, all the while forcing herself not to tear the dress to shreds in her anger. It was a favorite of hers, but she could not help but feel it had been tainted by the morning's events.

Shaking her head at her own foolish thoughts, she directed the maid to hang it in the closet and leave her in peace. She stepped toward the window and gazed out, seeing the dull gray light which filtered down through the clouds. It seemed apropos that such events should take place on such a day.

Her agitation was extreme. She would *not* be forced into marrying Samuel Lucas, regardless of what her mother's ill-judged and intemperate words wrought upon her reputation. She would not put up with him! Marriage to William Collins seemed almost preferable in comparison. The mere thought caused her to shudder.

Anxious for some way to resist the seemingly inevitable ignominy which appeared to be set to fall upon her, Elizabeth determined that she must do something to improve the situation. She could not sit idly by while she was ruined in the face of the entire neighborhood.

A short time later, she stood in front of her father's study, knocked forcefully on the door, and entered when she heard her father's voice. Mr. Bennet stood at the window, gazing out at the garden, a troubled expression on his face. His countenance lightened slightly upon seeing Elizabeth enter the room but then became more pensive as he no doubt took in her demeanor.

"Father, you must speak with Mother!" cried Elizabeth. "She is intent upon creating a scandal and completely ruining me."

Her father's countenance took on a tired cast, and he sat down behind his desk. "I understand your concern, Elizabeth, but I think you put too much import into your mother's words. Everyone in the neighborhood knows her and understands her behavior. No one will put any stock in anything she says.

"Besides," he continued with a hint of a grin, "she is far too diverting for me to curb her behavior."

Appalled, Elizabeth allowed her fury to show in her voice as she berated her father. "How can you say such things, Papa? You heard her, and you are well aware of the fact that scandals and damaging rumors have been started by less.

"I should think that you would wish to control your family and protect our reputation and standing after Lydia's disastrous escapade, and yet you make sport of it and laugh at her while saying that no one will take her seriously. I cannot believe you would make the same mistake yet again, Father! I may become unmarriageable due to this situation, and your inaction will be to blame. I have never been so disgusted in my life!"

With one last glare at her father—she noted his shocked expression, reflecting that she had never spoken to him in such a manner before—Elizabeth whirled and stalked from the room, dashing angry tears from her eyes as she once again flew up the stairs to her room and slammed the door shut behind her. She turned the lock and threw herself upon her bed. It was too much to be borne!

For the rest of the day, Elizabeth refused to leave her room, ignoring all entreaties for her to do so. Neither Mary nor Kitty's cajoling, nor Jane's loving voice, nor Mrs. Bennet's demands that she quit her room and join the family for dinner could convince her to open her door. Mr. Bennet did not make an appearance at her door at all, which suited Elizabeth very well indeed, disgusted as she was for his lack of action and interest in the welfare of his children.

She lay on her bed, ignoring the periodic pleas from her sisters while wondering what she could possibly do to alleviate her situation. But nothing came to mind. It could be that she would have to wait until Lucas finally came to the point and made his proposal before she could finally be free of his plotting with her mother. She would publish her refusal of his suit far and wide if necessary, regardless of any pain or humiliation it would cause him. He was the source of her current distress, so it was only fitting that he should feel the effects of his actions himself!

But how would it affect her relationship with Mr. Darcy? Would he, seeing once again the inappropriate behavior and weakness of her family, think better of his suit and quit the area forthwith? After his fortitude with respect to the matter of Mr. Wickham and Lydia, it hardly seemed likely that this would force him away, yet the part of her mind that lacked rational judgment wondered how he could bear to witness this spectacle. Just how much could the man take? Elizabeth doubted that she herself could endure any more before she was fit to be consigned to bedlam—it must have been much worse for a man who had been brought up to be proper in all respects!

She passed the day in this manner, her mind filled with chaotic thoughts and jumbled recollections, until it was dark outside her window, the dinner hour long since come and gone. When the silence of her room was once again disturbed by a light, almost indifferent tapping on her door, she realized she had no conception of how long she had lain with the company of her dark thoughts since the last time someone had attempted to cajole her from her room.

"Lizzy, are you well?" Jane's voice floated through the panels of the door. "Will you not let me in?"

Though Elizabeth was tempted to ignore her and continue to wallow in her solitary misery, an entire day of brooding in her own self pity had exhausted her, and she had not the strength to deny her closest sister.

She rose and carefully turned the lock before sighing and sitting in front of her vanity. The door opened slowly, and Jane peered inside, a concerned yet loving expression adorning her face. She moved into the room and, taking stock of the situation, turned back toward the door and the face of the maid who had followed her.

"Thank you, Sarah, but I will take care of Elizabeth tonight," she instructed the maid. "You may go now."

Sarah bobbed a quick curtsey and moved away while Jane closed the door and gazed back into the room.

"Lizzy, are you well?" asked Jane again.

Tears welled up in Elizabeth's eyes, and she could not quell the shaking sobs which burst forth from her breast. In an instant, Jane was beside her, pulling Elizabeth into a fierce hug and cradling her head against her midsection while Elizabeth, insensible to anything other than the support and love her sister was offering, clung to her and allowed herself the release she desperately needed. They remained in this attitude for some time, Jane stroking Elizabeth's hair tenderly as Elizabeth cried.

When at last her tears were spent, Elizabeth pushed away from her sister and directed a watery smile at her, thanking her for her care and concern. Jane brushed it off, reminding her sister that they had always been there for one another, a condition which would not change, regardless of her impending marriage. Jane moved to Elizabeth's closet and, retrieving a nightgown, urged her to stand so she could change.

"Are you hungry, Lizzy?" queried Jane. "You would not come down for dinner, and I can imagine that you are famished now. Shall I send to the kitchen to bring up a tray?"

Elizabeth shook her head. "I do not think I could eat right now, Jane, but I thank you nonetheless."

Jane gave her sister a severe look but did not comment. She helped Elizabeth with her dress and ensured that she was changed into a nightgown and dressing gown and that her hair was braided for sleep before sitting her down on the bed. She ensconced herself on the other side and directed a stern look at her sister.

"Now, Elizabeth, you simply must tell me what is troubling you. I heard Mother's words at the church, but we have all heard them before, and you have not been bothered by her pronouncements before. What is wrong?"

"*What is wrong?*" demanded Elizabeth. "What is *right?* Samuel insists on showering me with his attention regardless of how many times I tell him I am uninterested in him, Mama and Lady Lucas will not stop speaking of our forthcoming engagement, and I cannot find a moment alone with Mr. Darcy which is not interrupted by Samuel, Miss Bingley, or my mother. I am almost at my breaking point, Jane, and I know not what I shall do."

The surprise on Jane's face was unmistakable, but she managed to control her reaction while turning her sympathetic countenance upon her sister.

"Mr. Darcy? Has your opinion of the gentleman changed so much?"

Elizabeth colored and turned a bashful eye on her sister. "It has. He is a good man. In fact, I am quickly coming to believe that he is the best of men, Jane. I believe we should do very well together if we could only find the opportunity to become better acquainted and gain a stronger understanding of one another. I think Mr. Darcy has been much more discerning of our compatibility than I, and I am ashamed to think of what my former opinion of him consisted.

"And the irony of the situation," cried Elizabeth, feeling the remorse and shame of misjudgments, "is that if I *had* been more discerning and seen him for what he was, then I should not be in this situation now. I should have accepted him at Hunsford and been married to him by now. Then, all of Mr. Lucas's ambitions could have profited him nothing!"

"I am glad to hear that your regard for Mr. Darcy is so much changed," said Jane after a moment. "As you are well aware, Lizzy, I never held him in such low esteem as did you — I am happy you have found such worth in him."

Elizabeth was uncomfortable at Jane's words but gathered herself and smiled at her sister. "Yes, Jane, you were completely correct in this case. I am ashamed at my words and actions before — of how I dismissed your opinion in my arrogance and conceit. Truly, you have been far more perceptive in this matter than I."

"Do not censure yourself, Lizzy," Jane soothed. "I am well aware of the fact that your own discernment is highly superior to my own, and I shall not boast at my being right this one time."

The sisters laughed at Jane's irreverent statement, and Elizabeth drew her sister into an intense embrace once again. "I thank you, Jane, for being sensitive to my need to laugh, even at times such as these. You are too good, and you are much more perceptive than I have ever given credit."

"But this new opinion of Mr. Darcy is not a new occurrence?" It was more statement than question.

"My feelings have grown much more intense of late," replied Elizabeth, "but I must confess that the change in my opinion has been a gradual thing. Now, when I believe I could accept his attentions with gratitude and pleasure, everything appears to be conspiring to separate us. I do not know how much more of our family's ridiculousness he can take. I do not know how much more *I* can take."

Elizabeth lapsed back into silence, her brooding mood once again reasserting its hold upon her; the gloomy thoughts which had plagued her throughout the entire day were back in full force. But it appeared that Jane was not about to allow her to once more descend into her melancholy.

"Lizzy, I fear I must apologize for not giving you the attention you deserved. I had been so focused on my own situation and happiness that I had not recognized that you were going through these trials, and I wish to ask your forgiveness for being so insensitive to your plight."

Elizabeth smiled at her sister — only Jane could be so good. "Jane, you have nothing for which to reproach yourself; only you could blame yourself for being happy. I am fully cognizant of the fact that you are newly engaged to a wonderful young man and that you are focused on your betrothed. This is as it should be."

"Still, I should have given you more support."

"Do not say another word, Jane!" cried Elizabeth. "It is not your fault, and I will not hear of you accepting any blame."

"Regardless, I believe I shall be more attentive to your situation, Lizzy," Jane persisted. "Perhaps we can do something which would alleviate your distress."

"Oh, so you can arrange for Mr. Lucas to be transported to the colonies, can you?" queried Elizabeth with an arch smile.

"I doubt I have such influence," responded Jane in a like manner. "However, I think we can do something to spare you from his attentions, and I am sure Charles would be vastly pleased to assist your courtship with Mr. Darcy. I daresay that the notion of becoming brothers with his dearest friend would be very agreeable to him."

"I thank you, Jane," said Elizabeth with some emotion. "I do not know what I have done to deserve such a wonderful sister, but I am very thankful that I do have you."

They spent the next several hours engaged in earnest conversation. The topics of what to do, Mr. Lucas, or any other similarly distressing subject was not again mentioned by either of them, and by the end of the evening, Elizabeth, although perhaps not completely recovered, felt much more like her old self. Jane had a calming effect upon her for which she was very grateful.

When it came time for them to sleep, Jane refused to leave Elizabeth's side; instead, she pulled back the coverlet and joined her sister in the bed, all the while exclaiming that she would not be dissuaded. She pulled Elizabeth down beside her and drew her close, allowing Elizabeth to fall asleep encircled by the loving arms of her sister. It was a comforting ending to a very unsettling day.

Chapter XII

$\mathcal{I}$t has been said that the most insidious of lies contain, at their core, a grain of truth.

Just how much truth, of course, depends upon the liar, what he is trying to accomplish with his untruth, and what he intends the hearer to believe. For example, a mother might lie to a child as a means of protection or to preserve the innocence of said child, and in such situations, the lie, although perhaps against the Lord's commandment in a literal sense, was not malicious in intent. On the other hand, it is to be admitted that many people tell small untruths—the infamous little white lie—daily, for various reasons. Regardless of their purpose—whether to deceive or protect—such untruths are not necessarily evil in nature.

However, *intentionally malicious* lies are perhaps the most difficult to detect, especially when coupled with other evidence which suggests the lie is in actuality a truth.

For instance, Mr. Darcy's slight against Elizabeth Bennet the night of their first meeting—which the man in question had all but admitted to being a gross untruth!—*did* seem to support the belief of his arrogance and disdain for her feelings in particular and the feelings of others in general. Thus, the offense Elizabeth had felt at his instigation, which was further exacerbated by his behavior at subsequent social engagements and their verbal duels at Netherfield, created in her feelings which made Wickham's untruths all the easier to believe.

Of course, after the knowledge of Mr. Wickham's character and spiteful actions with regard to the Pemberley family were made known to her, his words and falsehoods suddenly took upon a new meaning which she had been unable to discern before. Suddenly, Mr. Darcy was no longer to blame for the circumstances in which Mr. Wickham found himself. Elizabeth could perhaps have wished for a little more discernment which would have allowed her to detect Wickham's untruths, but on the whole, she knew that though she had assuredly wished to believe Mr. Darcy to be capable of such unchristian behavior, there really was very little wonder that she had believed the scoundrel so implicitly. This knowledge still did not make her any less guilty over the thought of her conduct in the matter, especially knowing she *should* have seen through the fact that Wickham, in spinning his story to a complete stranger, was committing a gross impropriety.

Elizabeth awoke the next morning with thoughts of Mr. Darcy and the uncomfortable situation with respect to Mr. Lucas running through her mind. Though she would have appreciated the opportunity to indulge in the pleasure of a long walk, Jane had kept hold of her throughout the night, and Elizabeth was loath to disturb her. She was painfully cognizant of the fact that soon Jane would be married, and when she was, nights such as these, when the sisters talked until the wee hours of the morning and fell asleep in one another's rooms, would cease forever. This closeness with Jane was a thing to be treasured and not to be rushed past, as all would soon be changed.

But that did not stop Elizabeth's mind from engaging in thoughts of the previous months, reflecting upon events and analyzing her own behavior.

Despite Elizabeth's words to her sister the previous night, she was aware of the fact that much as she *now* wished she had accepted Mr. Darcy's proposal in the spring, for her to have *then* accepted it had been impossible. The changes wrought in Mr. Darcy were in large part due to her refusal, she felt, and as such, though his love for her at the time had undoubtedly been genuine, his respect for her had not been. She was well aware that it would have caused hardship for both of them if their marriage had begun under such circumstances. No, it was clear that whatever her current feelings were on the matter, she had been correct in refusing him then.

The other thing particularly which upset her—to which she had alluded the previous evening—was her conduct regarding Jane and her behavior toward her eldest sister, although that had not been a recent thing. Jane was all that was good and lovely, but Elizabeth could admit to herself that Jane's tendency to always look for the good in people had led Elizabeth to unconsciously believe that such a generous and kind soul held little understanding in the true nature of others. This, of course, was something of which Elizabeth had always prided herself. The events of the previous months seemed to call that judgment into question.

Elizabeth specifically remembered the night when she had shared Wickham's falsehoods and a distressed Jane had questioned Elizabeth, asking her if it was proper to believe Wickham so implicitly after so short an acquaintance. Elizabeth had, in her stiff-necked pride and vanity, completely discounted her sister's words, telling her she knew *exactly* what to think about the two gentlemen in question. In light of the truth, which sister had been the more discerning?

And what mortified Elizabeth even further was the fact that the situation in question had not been the first or the last occasion in which she had completely ignored Jane's advice. It was condescending and patronizing, and it had to stop. She did not know how she had come to consider herself so superior in understanding, but Elizabeth would not discount Jane's words any longer. As Mr. Darcy changed to better himself, so must Elizabeth; it was she who must improve to make herself worthy of him, not to mention worthy of her dear sister.

With regard to Mr. Lucas, Elizabeth determined that it was now best to completely avoid the gentleman. He had willfully continued to flatter her and attempt to play upon her vanity while procuring her mother's assistance in wooing her. Jane had promised to help her evade him, and Elizabeth knew she had better begin to enlist the aid of others. If he could use her own politeness against her in order to keep her attention, she could perhaps retaliate and withdraw that courtesy in return while engaging other acquaintances in an attempt to stay away from him. Turnabout was fair play, after all.

Such were Elizabeth's thoughts on that morning. She stayed that way for quite some time, cogitating over her problems and wondering what she could do to resolve them, until her elder sister awoke. She became aware of it immediately when Jane stirred, stretched, and then tightened her arms. Elizabeth felt safe—a sensation she could not remember feeling for some time.

They spoke for several moments—a discussion which consisted primarily of Jane assuring Elizabeth that all would be well—before going their separate ways to complete their preparations for the coming day.

Elizabeth was surprised when she left her room to witness her mother climb the stairs and, after pointedly ignoring her second daughter's presence, sweep into her own bedchamber and close the door rather firmly behind her. Elizabeth gaped after her mother with astonishment—it was singular for Mrs. Bennet to be up and about at this early hour. And lately her comments whenever she saw her daughter had been full of her expectations and excitement over the attentions of young Samuel Lucas. Had Elizabeth's remonstrance from the previous day made that much of an impression upon her? If so, it was a circumstance with which Elizabeth had no experience. Perhaps there actually *was* a first time for everything!

She was joined by Jane in the upstairs hallway at that moment, and after Elizabeth had recounted her mother's actions, Jane merely shook her head and led the way downstairs and into the breakfast room.

However, breakfast was not to be the quiet time to reflect for which Elizabeth had been hoping, as no sooner had she sat down than Mrs. Hill, the housekeeper, entered the room and informed Elizabeth that her presence was required in her father's bookroom. The manner in which Mrs. Hill had phrased his request led Elizabeth to believe that far from this being a simple request; her father had all but ordered her to attend him. This, of course, was in and of itself an oddity, as her father rarely ordered *anyone* to do anything, least of all *her*.

She replied in the affirmative to the elderly lady and—after quickly eating a piece of toast with some preserves liberally slathered over its surface—exited the dining room while accepting Jane's comforting assurances that all would be well. She then made her way toward her father's inner sanctum.

When she knocked and received permission to enter, Elizabeth found her father in a similar state to what he had been the previous day. Yet it was multiplied ten-fold. The lines of worry etched on his face, coupled with the deep frown and slightly wild look in his eyes, suggested his concern and care, something with which Elizabeth was not familiar. Her father's response to troubles was generally to hide in his bookroom and laugh them off—the man before her looked old and careworn. The events of the previous months appeared to have aged him significantly.

When Elizabeth appeared in his room, her father left whatever he was contemplating though the window and crossed to his daughter. Elizabeth felt herself swept up in her father's arms, and for the first time since she was a little girl, she found herself comforted by their strength. Mr. Bennet was not a tactile man, and his physical displays of affection—even with her, his favorite daughter—were generally limited to a kiss on the cheek or a brief grasp of her hand. He must have been very distressed to discard his habitual reserve and show so much affection.

"Come, Lizzy," said he after a moment, taking her by the hand and leading her to one of the two chairs which sat in front of his desk. "I must speak with you this morning, and though the events are somewhat unpleasant, I have found that there are things with regard to this family which I must rectify. Your opinion would be very much appreciated."

He gazed at her appraisingly; Elizabeth blushed and glanced down at her hands, which were folded in her lap. The silence did not last long.

"Before we begin, Lizzy, I feel I must speak to you somewhat to give you the understanding that—regardless of your words to me yesterday—I hold no ill will for you.

"Indeed, you were completely in the right, and you said that which needed to be said. I am well aware of my faults, my dear, and you are absolutely correct that the reputation of our family is somewhat tenuous given the event of Lydia's near disgrace. I must do more to protect you all.

"You know," he continued with a barking laugh, which prompted her to look up at him, "when I returned from London after fruitlessly searching for Lydia, I entertained the notion of being missish and offended that you had somehow seen something which I had not and guessed the event which caused this family so much grief. To know that my daughter was so shrewd in seeing the possibilities in Lydia's sojourn in Brighton where I was not was shaming in the extreme."

His eyes had regained the impudent twinkle which was so familiar to Elizabeth. "Of course, it was merely the work of the moment to discard such a thought. Not only would it be unfair to you, who has shown such greatness of mind, but I simply could not do such a thing to one I hold in so high an esteem. You are to be commended, Elizabeth, for your powers of discernment, which have surpassed those of your father."

"I do not believe I hold the moral high ground, father," said Elizabeth, speaking for the first time. "I have not exactly been the most astute in this matter myself. After all, I liked Mr. Wickham and judged Mr. Darcy to be the worst sort of man, and look how it has all turned out!"

"Hmm, yes, Mr. Darcy," replied Mr. Bennet. "His manners do appear to have softened somewhat, have they not?"

His piercing gaze discomfited Elizabeth, and she once again dropped her eyes to her lap, wondering how much he guessed. Her father was quite perceptive, and it was very possible that Mr. Darcy's preference for her had not escaped his sharp eyes, despite the fact that he had actually spent little time in the man's company.

"Now, Lizzy, I would like you to answer a question for me. I noticed that your manner toward Mr. Wickham cooled somewhat after your sojourn in Kent. Did you learn something about him to give you pause?"

The contents of Mr. Darcy's letter flashed through Elizabeth's mind. There were some things which could not be told to anyone—she would not hurt Georgiana for anything! — but perhaps the less private concerns she could lay before her father. She was somewhat afraid at his reaction, given Wickham's actions — after all, her father could be justifiably angry with her for withholding the information which may have convinced him to change his mind in regards to allowing Lydia her expedition to Brighton.

Still, it was a point which had weighed on Elizabeth since the knowledge of Lydia's actions had become known to her. In spite of her words to Jane, she knew that if she had mentioned Wickham's ill behavior — at least in regards to his propensity to run up debts wherever he went — her father may have been able to do something about it and prevent the elopement. Finally making her confession would bring her some peace of mind, if nothing else.

"I did hear something of Wickham, Papa," began Elizabeth. "Mr. Darcy told me something of his bad conduct which caused me to reevaluate both men."

She then recited what Mr. Darcy had told her with respect to Mr. Wickham's legacy, the money he had received in lieu of the living, his subsequent request for the living when the money was gone, and his betrayal of Mr. Darcy. Of Georgiana's attempted seduction, she said nothing.

Mr. Bennet was quiet after her recitation, his expression introspective. Elizabeth waited for her father's response, wondering what he would make of it.

"Mr. Darcy, is it?" he finally replied. "It seems the gentleman from Derbyshire has a very large role to play in this drama. I had suspected that Wickham's tale was a little too perfect to be believed implicitly, but whatever I had expected, this far exceeds it."

"I am sorry, Papa," said Elizabeth. "I should have made you aware of this when I returned from Kent. Perchance I could have persuaded you to rescind your consent for her trip if I had spoken up."

Mr. Bennet waved her to silence. "It would have done you little good, Lizzy. Believe me — I know myself. I would have stuck to my opinion that she could not be prey to ten such men due to her lack of fortune, never considering the depravity of a young man desperate enough to flee a bad situation and take some . . . companionship along with him. We both know that is what occurred."

"But still — "

"No, my child," interrupted Mr. Bennet, squeezing Elizabeth's hand. "I will not allow you to assume the blame for this. You and I both failed to recognize the specific threat that Wickham posed to Lydia. You did not, after all, suspect any partiality on either side before they left, did you?"

"No, sir, I did not," was her quiet reply.

"Then there is no blame to be had," said he, his voice assuming an uncharacteristic sternness. "Let the blame rest with those who truly deserve it. Perhaps our Lydia is silly and ignorant, but we all have a conscience. I do not know what she was thinking when she ran away with him, but her conscience at the very least must have informed her that what she was doing was wrong.

"And as for Wickham," he continued with a sigh, "given his behavior when they visited, I think I must assume he is an exception to this rule. He certainly displayed no remorse for his actions, and given the way he has treated your friend Darcy, I do not doubt that he is little concerned for his actions or whom they may hurt. On the contrary, he seemed almost smug in the knowledge that his current happy situation is due to your uncle's generosity — if there had been any other way to resolve the situation in Lydia's favor, I would have had him in debtor's prison once we had assumed his debt. He is as self-centered a man as I have ever met.

"Now, Lizzy, I would speak to you of something else—to speak of the Wickhams was not the reason I called you in, after all. I wish to know more of this situation with your mother and young Samuel Lucas. I have known of your mother's ambitions and that you have been sometimes forced into his company, but I would like to know if there is more to it than I am aware of. Has he importuned you improperly, my child?"

"Unless you consider my being forced to endure his company without respect to my own wishes being importuned improperly, then no. I have no physical injuries to resent, Father, from either Mr. Lucas or my mother."

Mr. Bennet's eyebrow rose. "It is *Mr. Lucas*, then, is it? You and Samuel were close playmates as children; I would have expected your address to be somewhat more familiar."

"As does he," responded Elizabeth dryly. "We are *not* children any longer, Father, and as I have no interest whatsoever in the acquaintance becoming any closer than it is now, I judged a more formal mode of address to be more appropriate."

"Good girl!" exclaimed Mr. Bennet. "But come now; tell me what has occurred that has frustrated you so."

And Elizabeth did, relating the history of the previous weeks, including meeting him again at Lucas Lodge, her mother and Lady Lucas' comments—and Mr. Bingley's astonishing defense of her—her mother's machinations and schemes, and the Lucas heir's overly self-satisfied attentions and expectations. She even informed her father of her mother's attempts to persuade her to offend their Netherfield hosts by either ignoring the invitation or insinuating Samuel into the group without an invitation.

When she had finished, her father sat for some time, a half smirk on his face as he contemplated her story. Were it not for the narrowed eyes which accompanied his smirk, she would have been afraid that he was slipping once again into his customary sardonic amusement.

"Your story bears only a cursory resemblance to that which your mother related," said he.

Elizabeth regarded her father with some surprise. "You questioned my mother about these doings?"

"I did," confirmed her father. "I summoned her this morning. She was quite put out with my interruption of her sleep, I can tell you!"

Elizabeth giggled at the thought of her mother's reaction. "So that was why she was up and about so early this morning."

"Indeed, it is. Quite curious, was it not?"

"It was. Might I inquire as to the nature of the conversation?"

"You may," replied Mr. Bennet with aplomb, his expression amused. "Her tale—if it could be called such—consisted of her joy at the prospect of another daughter married, her appreciation for such a fine young man as Samuel Lucas, and a certain disapproval of your determination to make her attempts at pairing you off with him so difficult. I *had* seen some of what was happening, yet I did not know the whole story. I thank you, Elizabeth, for this illuminating conversation."

"And *I* thank *you*, Father, for speaking with her."

He waved her off once again. "It is my responsibility, is it not? Do not forget, my child, that it took your words to induce me to take action. I am heartily ashamed of the fact that I have not taken better care of you particularly, Elizabeth, and I promise to do better in the future. I only wish I could see you so happily situated as is Jane."

A blush crept over Elizabeth's cheeks, and she looked away. She would have wished to be able to share her history and present expectations of Mr. Darcy's regard with her father, but the feelings the man engendered were of such a private nature that she could not find the impetus within her to speak of it. Once the matter was resolved—assuming it *was* resolved in the manner in which she was beginning to long—then she would share with her father the whole of their history.

"I thank you, Father," said Elizabeth at last. "I find myself wishing for that eventuality myself, but only time will tell.

"For now, I will affirm—if indeed there is any doubt in your mind—that I will not marry Samuel Lucas despite my mother's aspirations or designs. I would not suit him, and I believe he has developed other . . . appetites which would make a marriage to him quite miserable."

"I do not doubt he has, and I commend your integrity and steadfastness."

"I must also tell you that I am worried over mother's conduct. With her unguarded way of publishing her wishes before the entire neighborhood, there is no telling what rumors are beginning to circulate. I will not marry him, Father, regardless of what rumors are canvassed or what scandal may erupt."

Mr. Bennet stood and, moving behind his desk, sat in his own chair while gazing at Elizabeth with a pensive expression. "I have spoken with your mother and have directed her to cease in her attempts to force you together with Mr. Lucas. You can well imagine her reaction, I should expect."

Elizabeth rolled her eyes—her mother's response to such a directive could not have been a passive one. In fact, Elizabeth wondered that her displeasure had not been heard throughout the house.

"I should think that your words yesterday, along with Sir William's, will do much to prevent the spreading of any such gossip. But you can be certain that I will quash any such talk whenever I hear it. And of course, young Samuel will obtain no more encouragement in his suit from me than did Mr. Collins."

Father and daughter shared an amused look, each considering the comparison between the two overeager suitors.

"Thank you, Papa," said Elizabeth with some feeling.

"You are a good girl, Elizabeth," replied Mr. Bennet, smiling at her fondly. "I could not live with myself if you were to be hurt by my inaction.

"Regarding your mother, she appears to be truly cowed for now. But you and I both know her silence can only be purchased for a time; I do not doubt that her exuberance will return. If she begins to importune you on the subject again, come to me, and I will set her straight.

"What I am not certain about is Samuel Lucas," continued Mr. Bennet. "I can speak with him, but I wonder if it would do more harm than good. I can well imagine that Sir William—after his words at church—would by now have taken his son aside and had the same conversation I had with your mother. In light of that, I believe I should limit my comments to nothing more than that you will make your own decision and will not have your hand forced by his behavior."

"I will trust you in this matter, Father," responded Elizabeth. "As long as he is not able to monopolize my time with Mother's help, I can handle him."

Mr. Bennet chuckled and shook his head. "I believe you can at that, Lizzy. Without your mother's interference, I do not doubt that Samuel will find you to be a formidable opponent."

Their talk then turned to more mundane matters, and Elizabeth was happy that the situation had been dealt with and that her playful relationship with her father had been restored. When she left the room, she was far more confident about the future. Her father and sister helped banish her feeling of being alone against Samuel Lucas. It was comforting in the extreme.

After the uncomfortable scene on Sunday, the first part of the next week passed much more smoothly than Darcy could possibly have predicted. He was not privy to the details, but it appeared that several changes had taken place, and though he had been concerned over Elizabeth's state of mind, she appeared to have regained her good humor.

The first change was, of course, the resolution Darcy and his cousins had formed during the ride home from the church. Following Richard's advice about Elizabeth, the cousins had determined they needed to step up their efforts to distract the Lucas heir from his quest.

They need not have bothered, at least not on Monday when they had visited the Bennets. In fact, Lucas's demeanor that day was the second change Darcy had noticed. They had entered the drawing room to find the composition of the company slightly altered from every other time which they had visited. Lucas was already there, and rather than sporting the self-satisfied smirk which had adorned his face during every other meeting with him, he instead wore a dark expression of some exasperation.

Elizabeth was, of course, in the room, but she sat on a settee away from the Lucas scion, who was instead being entertained by her younger sisters while Elizabeth conversed with Jane.

The largest surprise, however, was reserved for the presence of Mr. Bennet—who had always eschewed such gatherings before—and the absence of Mrs. Bennet, who they were informed was indisposed that morning. Mr. Bennet's demeanor was that of a watchful guardian, completely at odds with his previous behavior, which had been that of some indolence and amusement, though it was sometimes difficult to determine exactly what amused him. There was nothing of indolence in the man's manner that morning—he keenly watched the entire room with a careful eye and a shrewd air.

They had been greeted by the whole room—Lucas's greeting was little more than a scowl and a nod in their direction—and Darcy had found himself seated next to the Bennet sire and drawn into a conversation about literature and different farming techniques. Darcy found the man to be extremely intelligent and knowledgeable of many subjects, and though he had been disposed to think ill of him due to Elizabeth's suffering, it was not long before Darcy found his opinion improving and his enjoyment of their conversation to be nearly the equal of speaking with Elizabeth herself.

It was not fifteen minutes into their visit when Mr. Bennet astonished them all even further. Lucas had risen from his seat beside Miss Mary and, with a furtive air, approached Miss Elizabeth, who was engaged in conversation with Jane and Anne, when Mr. Bennet spied this and spoke up.

"Ah, Samuel, I see the polite time for your visit has elapsed."

A bewildered Lucas had turned to Mr. Bennet, but his response—whatever it may have been—died on his lips.

"Please give my regards to your father and tell him I shall be by tomorrow to speak to him about the western pasture."

Mr. Bennet then dismissed the young Lucas heir and turned his attention back to Darcy, beginning a discussion about chess. Lucas, left with no choice but to retreat, bowed and bid the room farewell before stalking off in high dudgeon.

Surprised as he was, Darcy could not help but catch Richard's eye, and though Richard winked at him, he was not able to respond, as Mr. Bennet's conversation demanded his attention. He was able to note a short time after that Elizabeth's face held a smile, one which had not faded, though Lucas's departure had occurred almost ten minutes earlier.

It was later as they were returning home when Anne gave them to understand that Elizabeth's father had taken not only Mrs. Bennet in hand but had also spoken to Mr. Lucas and set down the rules of his behavior while at Longbourn. Elizabeth had not gone into any great detail about the event, but her change in demeanor made it obvious that whatever had been said, she was relieved that she now had some sort of protection from the man's schemes, not to mention her mother's desires. And although Darcy was unable to spend more than a few minutes directly conversing with Elizabeth himself, he was comforted and encouraged by the way she and Anne had become famous friends and by how Georgiana was feeling more comfortable in the company of Elizabeth and all of her sisters.

On Tuesday, the matter of Lucas's unwanted attentions was not an issue, as all the Bennet sisters had been invited to Netherfield to spend the day with the ladies. Since Mr. Lucas was not invited, their arrival more than an hour before noon put to rest any thoughts of him importuning Elizabeth with his company. Darcy was given to know from Elizabeth that Lucas had arrived early that morning but had been thwarted in his design by Mr. Bennet informing him that the ladies would not be at Longbourn that day due to a prior engagement. Mr. Bennet had then invited the young man into his bookroom for a game of chess.

Of course, that did not deal with the other conspirator—for Darcy was now quite convinced that Samuel Lucas and Caroline Bingley had some sort of understanding and collusion in the attempt to monopolize Elizabeth's time. However, Caroline's attempts were neatly flummoxed by a bevy of willing assistants, including Anne, Richard, Georgiana, and even Elizabeth's sisters, who ensured the current mistress of Netherfield was not given the opening to impose herself upon Elizabeth. Darcy was therefore able to spend a significant amount of time in conversation with object of his affections, both in the company of others and in the relative privacy of two chairs set near one another, though they were situated in a room full of other people.

That Miss Bingley's face was thunderous at having her designs thwarted was a matter of no concern whatsoever for Darcy. He had already informed her of his disinclination for her, and she was treading on thin ice with her continual intrusions and blatant meddling. Privately, Darcy wished Charles would send her back to town—let her impose herself upon some other unsuspecting dupe, for

Darcy wanted nothing further to do with her.

It was on this day that Darcy, while speaking with Elizabeth, had proposed to set Friday as the date for their equestrian outing. This was immediately agreed upon by all of the party, and—to Darcy's satisfaction—Elizabeth's countenance took on a great beaming smile. He knew he had pleased her by remembering their promise from their walk.

Of equal interest—for some members of the party—was Miss Bingley's displeasure when informed that if she wanted to accompany the party on their excursion, she would be relegated to being with Anne in the curricle, as there were not enough horses for her to take one as well. According to Bingley, his sister had reacted with her typical displeasure and demanded why she should not ride her brother's own horses. The response, which had apparently infuriated her, was that the outing had been planned by Darcy and Elizabeth to give the Bennet ladies a chance to ride. Furthermore, Bingley told her that of the three mares stabled at Netherfield suitable for a young lady to ride, two were owned by Darcy and would be ridden by Georgiana and Elizabeth, while the remaining mare owned by Bingley was reserved for Jane. All further discussion had ceased when Bingley had told his sister she could accept the situation with grace, stay at home that day, or return to London until the wedding, and that it really did not signify to him which option she chose.

On Wednesday morning, Darcy and Richard prepared for a hunt to which Bingley had invited most of the prominent gentlemen of the neighborhood. Miss Bingley made herself scarce, not wishing to be a party to any such male activities, and Darcy, while he would have preferred more time in the company of Elizabeth Bennet, nevertheless greeted Bingley's guests with pleasure and set off in the company of the gentlemen.

The hunting in this part of the country, Darcy had to admit, was very fine. Not only were the birds abundant, but they were delicious when prepared by Netherfield's cook. Darcy could well imagine continuing to join his friend every year at this time to partake in the shooting and the fine catches to be had. All it would take to complete the picture of domestic felicity and bliss would be for Elizabeth to return his feelings and accept his suit. Then, the journey could be undertaken to visit a beloved brother and sister rather than Darcy merely visiting with his friend.

During the walk to the pastures of Netherfield, Darcy found himself next to Mr. Bennet, who, once again contrary to the introverted picture Darcy had of him, had arrived early that morning carrying his hunting rifle as if he knew how to use it. Their conversation from the previous day had given him somewhat of a sense of Mr. Bennet, but he could not claim to truly know the man. Still, if he wanted to be successful in his pursuit of the daughter, gaining the approval of the father was also paramount.

"So, Mr. Darcy," began Mr. Bennet, while they walked away from the manor, "do you have any idea of how long you will remain in the country?"

"At this time, no," replied Darcy. "Our plans are not fixed, though I expect we would return to London before Christmas at the latest. This year, we will likely spend the holiday in the company of Colonel Fitzwilliam's family."

"And you think Mr. Bingley can spare you by then?"

The arch of his brow and the slight smirk on his face led Darcy to understand that Mr. Bennet was jesting. "I expect that Charles can spare me whenever he pleases. When I was here last year, it is true I was very much at his disposal; he had requested my presence in order to assist him while he learned what was necessary to properly run the estate. He now seems much more comfortable with the running of Netherfield, and though he does still ask my opinion and I accompany him on estate business, I do so more to keep myself busy than to render assistance."

"Ah, the wealth of experience," replied Mr. Bennet with a nod. "It is indeed very good of you to be of use to your friend."

Darcy eyed Mr. Bennet, wondering of what he spoke. "I assure you, Mr. Bennet, I am very happy to support Bingley in whatever capacity he requires. Along with Colonel Fitzwilliam, Bingley is my dearest friend, and I would do anything for him."

Mr. Bennet smiled briefly before turning his attention back to the ground over which they traversed. "That is good. My comment was nothing more or less than it appeared, Mr. Darcy—I have seen you and Bingley together, and it is clear you get along famously. I can see you have definitely been of assistance to Bingley, not only with the estate, but also in establishing Bingley as a landed gentleman, not to mention your assistance with his introduction to the ton."

Here, Mr. Bennet's grin became positively feral. "I have been in London, and though I am not a rich man, I know what the sharks in those waters can be like. A man of Mr. Bingley's wealth and disposition would undoubtedly be adept in getting himself into some unenviable situations among those of the upper class."

"You have no idea," responded Darcy with a wry smile. "Bingley is very cheerful and eager to meet people and make friends, and at times, he has difficulty in distinguishing between those who are sincere and those who are anything but. Again, I have been happy to render him whatever assistance was within my power.

"But I would not have you believe that he derives all the benefit from our relationship," continued Darcy. "For myself, I gain a cheerful friend with a very open and honest disposition. Perhaps you have noted the fact that I am not his equal in social situations and can be more than a little taciturn."

"A man after my own heart," rejoined Mr. Bennet. The two men shared a laugh.

"Exactly so," agreed Darcy. "Bingley positively influences me with his animated manners, I daresay, and I am very grateful to have such a friend. Richard—Colonel Fitzwilliam—is very similar, though he is somewhat more satirical in his humor, likely a result of his profession. But he is also away much of the time due to his service in his Majesty's army."

"Then I am happy you both have such a good friend," responded Mr. Bennet.

They walked on for several moments more, Darcy cogitating on the fact that— in temper and inclination—he and Mr. Bennet were very similar indeed. The difference lay in their attention to their duties, Darcy thought, for although Longbourn appeared to be a prosperous, if modest, estate, it did not appear as if Mr. Bennet was making any great effort to improve the productivity—and therefore the profitability—of his estate. Darcy was always searching for better ways of doing things, of means to increase his income. He was by any standard a very rich man, but Darcy was aware of the changes which were encroaching upon his world and the inevitable fact that the world's money was beginning to come from sources other than the land.

Mr. Bennet appeared to be content with his lot, and Darcy could not fault him for this—perhaps he could also rest a little easier once he had secured Elizabeth's affections and taken her to the altar.

"How do you like the area?" asked Mr. Bennet suddenly.

Though he was a little uncomfortable with the question—he had *not* been the most congenial during his previous stay here, after all—Darcy gamely forged on ahead, deciding that the absolute truth was required.

"This is lovely country, Mr. Bennet. Netherfield is perhaps not on the same level as Pemberley, but I believe it a good place for Bingley to learn what he needs to know when he is ready to purchase. Whether he settles down here permanently will of course be up to him, but there is certainly much to be said for the region."

"I am glad you think so. I like to think that though we are only a few miles from London this is a relatively undiscovered corner of the kingdom.

"Are there any other inducements which prompt your presence?"

Startled, Darcy peered at Mr. Bennet, but the man returned his gaze placidly. Had Elizabeth discussed their history with her father? Or had he noticed something of Darcy's regard and decided to determine his intentions toward his favorite daughter?

Somehow, Darcy knew Elizabeth had *not* discussed this with her father, and if the man knew anything, it was through his own observation. Deciding to play his cards close to his vest—nothing had been worked out between Elizabeth and himself, after all—he responded with a brief explanation of Georgiana and Anne's friendship with Elizabeth and said nothing more. Mr. Bennet's frank gaze in response made Darcy somewhat uncomfortable, but the other man allowed the matter to drop.

It was some time later when a conversation of a different nature took place. The movement of the company was fluid, and as they shot, they changed positions, coming into contact with others. In this manner, Darcy exchanged words with Mr. Goulding and Mr. Long—who appeared to be great friends—was greeted by an unusually serious Sir William Lucas, and spoke briefly with both Bingley and Richard.

It was near the end of the hunt when he found himself close to the one member of the party who had been avoiding him—Samuel Lucas. He had felt the other's gaze upon him at certain times during the day, but Lucas had never moved close enough to trade greetings, let alone initiate conversation of any kind. Knowing what he did of Lucas's character, not to mention the distress the man had put Elizabeth through, Darcy was content to allow him his space and maintain the distance. He was not certain that he could hold his temper.

At length, however, Lucas did end up in close proximity to Darcy, and when he noticed this, he directed a cold and somewhat haughty greeting which Darcy returned in a like manner. The dogs flushed out a pair of pheasants, which allowed them the opportunity to shoot rather than speak, and Darcy, aiming his rifle most carefully, was happy to release his shot without having to make small talk.

Once the birds had been felled and the servants sent out to retrieve them, Darcy hefted his weapon and made to return to the house, content that the hunt was coming to a close. What he did not expect was Lucas's presence by his side.

"Your friend is a lucky man in his choice of bride," commented Lucas in the way of making small talk.

Darcy allowed it to be so, hoping the man would cease his attempts at conversation. Lucas did not take the hint.

"Jane Bennet is a beautiful girl, and I have known her most of my life. She will make him a good wife, I am sure—she is so kind and gentle that I doubt she could offend anyone."

"She is particularly well suited for him," responded Darcy. "I doubt he could do much better—seeing as he is gregarious enough for them both, I daresay her calm and quiet nature will be a natural check for him, something he will need in London society."

Lucas smirked. "Oh, I do not doubt that she will rein him in. Jane is so placid and staid that having an outgoing husband will no doubt do her as much good as her nature will do him."

Darcy faltered for a moment, wondering if Lucas's oblique words were a censure upon either of the two young people. He was not allowed to contemplate it much further, though, as Lucas immediately made a comment which set Darcy on his guard.

"She is undeniably beautiful and good-natured, and for a gentleman searching for those qualities in a wife, I daresay they could not find a better specimen than Miss Jane Bennet. However, I find that I much prefer the dark features and liveliness of her sister Elizabeth. Would you not agree?"

Through narrowed eyes, Darcy peered at his companion, wondering what Lucas was thinking to be bringing up such a subject. He had to know—through Miss Bingley's intelligence, if nothing else—of Darcy's interest in Elizabeth. Did he mean to antagonize a potential rival (the thought of the man actually being a rival, given Elizabeth's reaction to him, almost caused Darcy to laugh out loud!) by expressing interest in the young woman Darcy had set his sights upon?

"I agree Miss Elizabeth is very pretty and has a penchant for bringing energy wherever she goes. I believe it is part of her charm."

"She has always been that way, you know. I have known Elizabeth since we were children, after all, and I daresay I can claim to know her as well as anyone outside her family. We played together as youngsters, and I believe our relationship is well on its way to developing into a much closer connection."

Darcy frowned at the other man, wondering if they were speaking of the same woman.

"In fact, I daresay that we shall have a very joyful announcement to make within the next week. After all, Lizzy could not remain unmarried for long after Jane has gone before the altar herself—she is too fine a woman to be left upon the shelf. I am happy to be the man who will sweep her from her feet, as it were—she is worth everything any man can give her, do you not agree?"

His dislike of the other man now extreme, Darcy glared at him. "I wonder if you understand of what you are speaking," he ground out. "I have seen you in the company of Miss Elizabeth, and I daresay that I have certainly seen no such reaction to your presence. In fact, I believe her reaction to be quite the opposite."

"That is because you do not know her as well as I do," rejoined Lucas. "Elizabeth is a singular woman of many fine qualities, but as I stated before, I have known her for as long as I have been alive, and I am well aware of her character. She is a country girl and would not be happy away from the quiet of nature and the walks and hills she so loves. I believe I can give her a good home away from the bustle of the city and close to those people and places she holds dear.

"I am sorry to be blunt, but if you have bent your attentions in her direction, I suggest you look elsewhere for another plaything. I assure you—Elizabeth will be mine ere long, and I will not put up with another confusing her and toying with her emotions."

"I assure you I have no such intentions," said Darcy, holding Lucas in his menacing glare. "And if I may point out, Elizabeth belongs to no one. She is her own person, possessed of a strong personality and decided opinions, and I cannot imagine she would appreciate being reduced to the status of a mere possession."

Lucas barked in laughter and shook his head. "Is that not what all women need? Do they not need to be dominated and owned so they may become of greater consequence in the world? They cannot be what we are, after all—they cannot own land or fend for themselves. They require strong guidance, a firm hand, and unstinting protection from the ills of the world. That is our responsibility, and I assure you that I take this very seriously. Elizabeth will be mine, and I would ask you to respect our wishes in this matter."

"I will respect such wishes when they are made known to me by the lady in question," responded Darcy. "I suggest you follow your own advice and allow the lady to speak for herself. Miss Elizabeth does not appreciate it when another presumes to speak on her behalf."

A shake of his head and derisive laughter was Lucas's response. "For all your wealth and consequence, you do not understand, do you, Darcy? All your possessions are nothing without the right woman at your side. I hope for your good wishes, for I *know* Elizabeth is the woman for me."

He directed a sly look at Darcy before he moved away, whistling a jaunty tune. Darcy watched him as he retreated, his temper seething at the unguarded and blatantly false statements which had spewed forth from the other man's mouth. Surely if he believed his own words, he was delusional!

The most troubling part of the encounter was the almost rabid gleam which had shone in Lucas's eyes as he had spoken of Elizabeth. She was not a possession, nor was she a prize to be won at a game of cards. Lucas's words seemed to indicate that was exactly what she was to him. Darcy determined to be watchful and defend her from Lucas's machinations at all cost. It was clearer than ever before—Samuel Lucas would bear careful watching.

Chapter XIII

$\mathcal{T}$hat Friday morning dawned clear and bright, much to the relief of several of the residents of the neighboring Hertfordshire estates. Late October had, after all, a tendency to be a little fickle; there was just as much chance (or more, the cynical could say) of having rain for days on end as getting one of the warm, fine days which sometimes made the season such a delight. The morning was not especially warm, and there was a crispness in the air which induced one to enjoy the simple pleasure which life brings. Elizabeth, for one, would have considered a much colder temperature to be still agreeable, but others of the proposed party were not necessarily as hardy as she. Jane, in particular, was grateful for the agreeable weather.

For Jane Bennet, in love as she was, the impending outing was very agreeable—Jane loved to ride, and the occasion to ride one of the superior animals owned by her betrothed and his friend had her alive with anticipation. Of course, the possibility of giving her sister the time she required to connect even more deeply with Mr. Darcy was an additional benefit to the already much anticipated excursion.

Jane was not by nature a confrontational person. Indeed, she was determined to see the good in others—though she did recognize that at times they little deserved it—and therefore to attempt compromise, as her younger sister and father were often wont to tease her. She was eminently grateful that her father had stepped in with her mother and put an end to her constant interference in Elizabeth's matrimonial prospects. The events of the previous Sunday, when Elizabeth had collapsed in tears, were so far from the norm that Mrs. Bennet's meddling must truly have upset Elizabeth, and Jane would not have that happen again.

With Mr. Lucas largely out of the way—at least at Longbourn—Jane was able to concentrate her focus on the other bothersome presence—one Caroline Bingley. In her endeavor, she had found willing accomplices; Charles had informed her that he and Darcy's family had seen the problem much as Jane herself had. On their previous visit to Netherfield, it had been quite easy to divert Miss Bingley's attention and ensure Darcy and Elizabeth were able to spend time together without the sister's intrusion.

Elizabeth *would* get her chance with the handsome young gentleman if Jane had anything to say about it! Many thought that in addition to her penchant toward seeing the good in those around her, Jane also had a pliable, relaxed nature. Indeed, she was proud of the fact that she was normally calm and self-possessed. However, "pliable" was *not* the way she would normally choose to describe herself, for Jane was fully willing and able to fight for what she believed to be right or in defense of those she loved. Elizabeth, being her dearest sister, invoked the fiercest of these emotions, and there was literally nothing Jane would not do for her. Caroline Bingley would not deny Elizabeth her due, whatever the woman's reasons and motivations may be—Jane would not allow it!

Jane and Elizabeth prepared that morning—Mary and Kitty had already accepted an invitation to spend the day with Mrs. Phillips and therefore could not attend—with the utmost care, though both would have denied the fact if questioned.

They descended the stairs to the dining room, intent on partaking of a light repast before their departure, which was scheduled for some ninety minutes later. It was already somewhat late in the morning, and as a result, the entire family was already gathered around the table partaking in the morning meal.

Eying their riding dresses suspiciously, Mrs. Bennet wrung her hands and fidgeted, as was her wont when upset.

"Lizzy, Jane, why are you dressed in such a manner?"

The two eldest Bennet girls exchanged a brief glance.

"Why, we are to accompany the Netherfield party on an outing this morning, Mama," answered Jane for both of them. "I am certain we mentioned it on Wednesday when we returned from Netherfield."

Mrs. Bennet surreptitiously glanced at Mr. Bennet, who was eating with apparent unconcern, and smiled at her eldest daughter.

"Yes, Jane, I *do* remember you speaking of it. It is very good of Mr. Bingley to invite you to accompany him, and very sly of you to keep yourself before him so that he does not believe you are tiring of his company."

Jane's directed a disapproving expression at her mother. "Mama, I daresay Mr. Bingley has no doubt of my continued affection and does not need me to 'keep myself before him' to trust in the constancy of my feelings."

"Perhaps," replied Mrs. Bennet, "but one can never be too careful."

She shifted her gaze toward her least favorite daughter, and after another furtive glance at her husband, her gaze hardened. "But why should Elizabeth accompany you? Surely there is no reason for her to put herself before the Netherfield party. I believe she would be better served to remain here to entertain any callers we might receive."

"You would have our second daughter snub Jane's fiancé and his friends, Mrs. Bennet?" interjected Mr. Bennet, a disapproving expression affixed upon his wife.

Mrs. Bennet paled slightly at her husband's tone but gamely continued to make her case. "Of course not, Mr. Bennet. But I daresay they could do very well without her, and I believe I should like to have *someone* with me to entertain anyone who may appear on our doorstep today."

"I shall try not to be affronted by your apparent dismissal of my social skills, Mrs. Bennet," replied the family patriarch in a droll tone. "However, despite your disregard for the lack of importance of our Lizzy to our Netherfield neighbors, among whom number several of her *very* close acquaintances, I believe that Lizzy's attendance in the party is essential today. From what I understand, it was Mr. Darcy, in collusion with our Lizzy, who was the inspiration for their expedition, and not Mr. Bingley or Jane. I do believe several of the party members would be quite disappointed if Elizabeth were *not* to appear this morning."

A superior sniff—very similar to one of Miss Bingley's, Jane thought—was her mother's response. "Oh, very well. I daresay she must go then. She is a willful child and shall do as she pleases—much as she always does."

"I daresay she shall. You know your daughter, Mrs. Bennet, so you should be aware that she will do as she pleases in a matter such as this. I, for one, believe it is good for her to have such fine friends, as their acquaintances can only open up possibilities for Lizzy—and our other unwed daughters, of course."

"Well, then, if you put it that way," said the Bennet matron with a sulk.

"Indeed, I shall, Mrs. Bennet."

He affixed his wife with a frown, causing her to look away and attend to her meal, her apparent unconcern belied by the slightly nervous titter which escaped her lips.

"Mrs. Bennet, regardless of *who* is coming to visit, I do not think any of our daughters should be forced to forego their entertainments and engagements to stay home with their parents and receive callers. The girls shall all attend their various activities while you and I await callers. Besides, it is not as if you are expecting someone to call on Lizzy in particular. Are you, Mrs. Bennet?"

Though she paled slightly, Mrs. Bennet shook her head and kept her attention firmly on her plate.

"Excellent! Jane, Lizzy, you may await your friends in the parlor, I believe."

Having finished their respective breakfasts, Jane and Elizabeth shared a glance before excusing themselves from the dining room.

Once they had made their way to the other room, the sisters collapsed against one another as a fit of giggles overcame them.

"Mama is not exactly the essence of subtlety, is she?" said Jane amidst her laughter.

"Oh, no, indeed," replied her sister before a mischievous expression stole over her face. "I should say she is about as subtle as a certain gentleman's attention for a certain sister of mine."

"Or perhaps his friend's for one of *mine*?" jibed Jane in response.

Elizabeth's cheeks bloomed in response to Jane's words. She playfully slapped Jane's arm and cast a mock-affronted glare at her while Jane shot her an unrepentant grin.

"Please, dear sister—*my* admirer is anything but unsubtle, unlike some admirers I could name."

"Perhaps. Yet I find I enjoy Mr. Bingley's exuberance very well indeed."

Elizabeth smiled at her sister and hugged her. "And I am very happy for you, Jane. He is a good man and shall make you very happy."

Jane basked in her sister's approbation of her chosen partner while at the same time reaffirming her vow that Elizabeth would be allowed her chance at the happiness Jane had achieved. All it would take was a little more time without the disrupting influences of certain of their acquaintances.

The sisters engaged in quiet conversation while awaiting the arrival of the Netherfield party. Mary and Kitty had already departed for Meryton some time earlier—since the weather was fine, it was no trouble for the Bennet sisters to make the journey on foot. Indeed, they had been doing it for many years.

With the younger sisters departed—and their father in his bookroom while their mother had retreated upstairs to her room—Elizabeth and Jane returned to the parlor and waited only minutes before their visitors were announced.

Their five neighbors entered the room, and though Elizabeth was glad to see all of her friends, she had eyes only for Darcy. He looked splendid in his forest-green coat and riding trousers. Indeed, she could not remember a time when he had appeared so handsome and to such great advantage. She never believed she could love him so much as in that moment.

A snicker broke her gaze, and she glanced toward the floor, cheeks blazing at being caught staring at him. The offender came to her immediately, greeting her in his usual jovial manner while telling her that she looked very well that morning. Elizabeth thanked Colonel Fitzwilliam with as much composure as she could muster and gathered herself to welcome the rest of the party, exchanging an embrace with both of the young ladies. Once the pleasantries were past, the sisters donned their outer gear, and the entire party made their way out to the waiting horses.

The first order of business was the introduction of the young ladies to their mounts for the day. Bingley immediately claimed Jane's hand and, with a beaming smile upon his face, led her to a chestnut-colored mare. Elizabeth, however, had eyes for none but the jet-black mare to which the Darcy siblings led her. The horse was a little smaller than the others, with no apparent markings, and she whickered softly as Elizabeth approached. Enchanted by the animal's friendly nature, Elizabeth offered a treat—a few pieces of apple which she and Jane had prepared that morning—to the beautiful animal. The offering was accepted as, with dainty bites, the horse relieved her of the fruit.

"She is a beautiful horse, Mr. Darcy."

"She had better be, or she would fail to live up to her name," was the mischievous reply.

When Elizabeth raised an eyebrow in question, he smiled. "Miss Bennet, please meet your mount for the day, Aphrodite."

Elizabeth laughed. "So, Hermes is not alone, is he, Mr. Darcy? I see you choose names from among the Greek pantheon for your mounts."

"Indeed, we do," replied Darcy with aplomb. "I shall be riding Hermes today, while Georgiana will ride Hera." He pointed to a white mare which was spiritedly shaking her head and stamping her feet as if impatient to be gone.

"I believe you will like Aphrodite," Georgiana spoke up. "She has been my favorite mount these past two years since William purchased her."

Frowning, Elizabeth tried to protest. "Georgiana, I would not appropriate your favorite horse from you. Would it not be better that I ride Hera instead?"

"Please do not concern yourself," declared Darcy. "We have discussed this, and since, as you can see, Hera is a little more spirited, we judged it best that you be mounted upon Aphrodite. She is calm and gentle and not easily spooked."

"William is right, Elizabeth," seconded Georgiana. "I am perfectly content with Hera, and I do ride her on many occasions. I should feel much more comfortable if you were riding an animal better suited to your level of experience. Aphrodite will serve you well."

"In that case, I thank you," responded Elizabeth with a smile for the gentleman and a hug for his sister. "I shall endeavor to be delighted by this fair animal and release her back to you in the same condition in which she came to be under my care."

All three laughed at that comment, to which the colonel joined in as well, as he had approached as they had been speaking.

"I see you have met your mount, Miss Elizabeth," said he, amusement sparkling in his eyes. "And what do you think of this shameful manner in which they name their horses?"

The Darcy siblings rolled their eyes almost as one, and Elizabeth, thinking that perhaps this was some family joke, winked saucily at the colonel. "I assure you, Colonel, that I find their inspiration for names to be quite charming. I supposed yours is named after its physical attributes—or perhaps after some enemy you have defeated?"

The Darcys chortled while the colonel's mien took on an affronted expression. "Of course not. *I* would never injure an animal by naming it in such a cavalier fashion. Only the best of names for *my* mount!"

"If it is so, then perhaps you should share it with me, so I may judge for myself."

"I shall," said he with aplomb. "His name is Jupiter."

As Elizabeth began to laugh, he broke in, amusement glinting in his eyes. "Everyone knows the only pantheon one should use to name their mounts is the Roman!"

This only made the other three laugh louder, to which the colonel responded by joining in.

"Then you must think that your cousins should have named their mounts Juno, Venus, and Mercury?"

"But of course. It is *proper* after all."

Groans and rolled eyes met his declaration, but Elizabeth merely smiled archly at him. "I'm sorry, but I must agree with your cousins, Colonel. I believe the Greek names are far pleasanter and more . . . aesthetically pleasing than the Roman."

"Ah, corrupted already! And I had such high hopes for you."

When their mirth had run its course, Georgiana and Mr. Darcy assisted Elizabeth in mounting, while the colonel approached Anne, who had been speaking with Jane and Bingley, and settled her in her curricle. When all was made ready, the party departed.

Their destination was a good deal further than Elizabeth was wont to walk on her own. To the north and west of Longbourn, upwards of six miles away, lay a small valley which was delightfully forested and popular with many of the riders of the area. A stream ran through the valley, and at the northern end, the remains of an ancient keep could be seen, its foundations overgrown and steadily being swallowed up by the forest. Elizabeth had first visited the site as a young girl after having begged her father to be taken there for a week after she had first learned of its existence. Since that time, she had but rarely visited. The sisters had decided that it was the perfect locale to show their neighbors.

They started off, Mr. Bingley leading the way with Jane, followed by Elizabeth riding beside Mr. Darcy, with the colonel, Georgiana, and Anne bringing up the rear. As the weather was warm and company delightful, they were a merry party, and laughter rang out from various points in the procession as they progressed on their way.

As for Elizabeth, her companion appeared to be equal parts eager and careful. That he was as happy to be there as she had ever seen him was doubtless, and the attention he showed to her made her feel cherished and protected. He was a consummate horseman; his riding appeared to be completely by instinct, as he used his reins, his feet, and even the weight of his body to direct his mount, while he focused his attention on her. He seemed concerned with her safety, as his eyes roamed the pathways, alert for any potential danger, while he stayed close to her, attentive to her level of comfort. As they traveled, he tenderly guided and instructed her, patiently allowing her to deepen her skills while correcting where needed with a gentle and kind hand. His care warmed her heart, and when she happened to catch him looking at her, his regard was easily seen upon his face.

Once they had settled into the routine of their travels, the first thing Elizabeth was concerned with was the absence of one of the Netherfield party.

"Mr. Darcy," said she, "I had understood Miss Bingley was to accompany us in Anne's curricle. I hope her absence is not due to an indisposition?"

"No, indeed," replied Mr. Darcy with a hint of a smile. "The way Bingley tells it, she was somewhat . . . unhappy when she was informed there were not enough horses to go around. As she has been riding for many years, I believe she considers the curricle to be beneath her dignity."

Elizabeth stifled a laugh at his irreverent response. "So she decided not to accompany us?"

A thoughtful expression came over Mr. Darcy's face, and he peered at her as if undecided. "I wonder if I should relate to you the events of the morning."

"If it is private, then perhaps you should not. I am sure I shall not be *too* vexed at not knowing of this mysterious event to which you allude."

"It is not precisely private, merely embarrassing for my hostess." He stopped and considered it momentarily before shaking his head and continuing. "Reconsidering, I doubt she could give three straws if it were to become known to you.

"According to Bingley, after her previous bout of displeasure over the riding arrangements, she demanded to be allowed to use one of his stallions for the excursion."

Somewhat confused over his reference, Elizabeth gazed at him blankly. "Is there some reason why this would not be acceptable, Mr. Darcy? I apologize if my question appears obtuse—"

"No need to apologize, Miss Elizabeth," he assured her. "You are not familiar with the subject, and as such, your ignorance can be attributed to that fact. Not only is a stallion a much larger animal than Miss Bingley would be used to riding, but the only other animal Bingley has stabled here is a large and rather mean gray that is known for bad temper and feistiness. Not only would Miss Bingley be unable to control him, but in a party such as this, that animal would be a menace. I wonder why Bingley keeps him at all—he is a fine horseman, but that creature seems to be intent on killing any who dare to ride him!"

Nodding in understanding, Elizabeth glanced up at the man in question, who was riding close to Jane. The two were so engrossed in their conversation that they appeared to have forgotten they even had companions on this journey. Elizabeth smiled before turning back to Mr. Darcy. He was gazing at her fondly, much as she had seen Mr. Bingley look at Jane many times in the past weeks.

"I understand then that Miss Bingley was not happy with his answer?"

"Not in the slightest. At first she demanded to be allowed to ride the gray, and when Bingley would not accede, she demanded to be allowed to ride his current steed, relegating him to the gray. When Bingley refused every attempt at coercion, she then insisted she be permitted to ride my other stallion. Of course, when Bingley told me of this after the fact, *I* rebuffed the request, even though he had already done it for me.

"The way Bingley tells it, she then declared she would not grace our company on this expedition if she were to be forced to merely ride in a curricle, to which her brother immediately agreed. Once her anger had passed, of course, she attempted to insinuate herself in the excursion again, but Bingley would hear nothing of it, claiming she had declared her intention to stay home."

"Oh, Mr. Darcy, he did not," said Elizabeth, feeling some distress.

It was not that Elizabeth felt sorry for Miss Bingley in any way—the lady was too deserving of being rebuffed due to the way she behaved—it was more the ability she possessed to make the rest of the Netherfield residents' lives miserable that had Elizabeth worried. A small voice in Elizabeth's mind said that Miss Bingley would undoubtedly blame her for her misfortune, yet Elizabeth firmly set that part aside; Miss Bingley was more than adept at creating her own problems, and if she blamed them on Elizabeth, well, Elizabeth had already known the other woman's opinion. Miss Bingley had no power to hurt her if Elizabeth did not give her the opportunity.

She glanced back at her companion, only to find him regarding her with some concern.

"Miss Bennet, I can immediately perceive that you are distressed, and I fancy I know you well enough to see that you consider yourself in some way responsible for this situation. In fact, nothing could be further from the truth."

A sigh escaped Elizabeth's lips. "I do not blame myself, Mr. Darcy. I think it likely that Miss Bingley shall blame me, but that is her prerogative—given what I know of her opinion of me, I do not doubt that if the sun were to fail to rise on the morrow, it would be my fault in Miss Bingley's eyes."

Though the circumstance was not lighthearted, Mr. Darcy managed a wry smile. "I fear I am to blame for her enmity toward you."

"Now *you* are attempting to claim some unwarranted responsibility for another's feelings, Mr. Darcy. Miss Bingley is the only one who can direct her own emotions, and I fear that regardless of her reasons for disliking me, she would, at the very least, have contempt for me and all my family. After all, we are not rich or fashionable enough to suit her tastes, and we are quite content the way we are."

"Though it pains me to speak ill of my host's sister, I believe you are correct."

"Then let us speak of it no further, Mr. Darcy. I should hate to have the specter of a displeased Miss Bingley hanging over our outing."

They shared a laugh, and their talk immediately moved to other more mundane matters. By unspoken agreement, they did not approach the topic of Miss Bingley or any other similar issue which beset them, instead concentrating on merely making conversation, each continuing on the journey toward becoming better acquainted with the true character of the other.

Elizabeth was amazed by the man's ability to make small talk, though she had always considered it one of his most glaring failings. She could truthfully say she understood his reticence better than she had in the past, but none of that was in evidence on that morning. Here was a man who conversed with her almost effortlessly, their conversation weaving here and there, moving along without thought or focus by the two participants. It was a side of Darcy with which she was rapidly becoming more familiar, though she supposed it was another matter about which she had misjudged him. After all, had the colonel not said that he was much different when among the company of those with whom he was familiar?

The one thing Elizabeth longed for did not appear to be forthcoming—at least, not on that morning while they rode to their destination. Feeling confident now as to her feelings for him, she wished he would give some indication as to his intentions—declare himself in some way. She was not certain she was ready to be engaged to him, but she knew she was more than ready to assent to a courtship. If only the man would come to the point.

But there again, her own actions rose to frustrate her wishes. She was now convinced that he still held a tender regard for her, but he appeared determined to conduct himself with every appearance of propriety. In short, he had been refused vociferously once already and would ensure her favorable response before he put himself forward in such a manner again. There was nothing she could do but be patient and welcoming until he finally felt it time to declare his intentions.

At length, the group arrived at their destination, and the newcomers expressed their amazement at the beautiful locale which was so near, yet which was hidden by the contours of the surrounding district. Elizabeth had to agree that it was a beautiful sight, though she thought that it would have been so much more beautiful if the trees still held more than half of their leaves. She determined that if her relationship with Darcy progressed in the manner she now expected, she would have to bring him back during the summer, when the verdant green of the trees and the quiet rumbling of the stream created a haven from the outside world. She was certain he would find it even more enchanting.

The company dismounted their horses at an open clearing about a mile after entering the valley, and after agreeing that the day was sufficiently progressed for luncheon, they began setting up for their midday repast—they would visit the ruins after their meal. A large basket was produced from the back of Anne's curricle, and while the men collected deadwood and dug a pit for a bit of a cheery fire, the ladies spread blankets upon the ground and laid out the picnic lunch while setting aside a pot to brew their tea, which they had brought along for the purpose.

Amazed at the bounty which was produced, Elizabeth could not help but think that the young man from Netherfield was trying to impress his betrothed, and she said so to Jane with a laugh. When Jane protested that it was not only *her* who was present on this excursion, the other three ladies all exchanged raised eyebrows and stifled giggles in their hands. The good-natured ribbing of Elizabeth's eldest sister continued until Anne slyly pointed out that Darcy had had as much input into the contents of the basket as Bingley. Elizabeth's cheeks reddened, and she trained her mock glare on the de Bourgh scion, her gaze accusing her of treachery. Anne said nothing; she merely smiled and turned away to pull another delicacy from the basket, leaving Elizabeth to the snickers of the other two ladies.

In short order, they had everything unpacked, and the men had succeeded in starting a small fire. The pot was filled with water from the river and set over the fire to boil, and the group gathered around the picnic, ready to partake of the bounty.

The picnic lunch was a great success, and the clearing was filled with the conversation and laughter of the party. It was, Elizabeth reflected, an idyllic scene, and one which would remain in her heart and her memory for the rest of her life. She had never been so happy as she now was with Darcy and his friends—even those short days spent at Pemberley now paled in comparison with the feelings and sensations these past days now evoked within her. Even if nothing came of their relationship, she would treasure these memories for the rest of her life.

Eventually, the meal was consumed, the tea was brewed and consumed, and the travelers sat back on the blankets and discussed the next part of the day's endeavors. Elizabeth, as always after a meal, felt the need to exert herself, and she stated her intentions to walk to the stream and rinse off her hands.

"I believe I should like to accompany you, Miss Elizabeth," stated Darcy, rising to his feet.

It did not miss the sharp-eyed Elizabeth's attention that the other members of the party exchanged somewhat smug glances at Darcy's declaration, but she decided to ignore them.

"And I should be pleased to have you accompany me."

They excused themselves and departed from the clearing, heading west into the line of trees, where Elizabeth knew the stream awaited some short distance away. They spoke no words to each other; Elizabeth felt content with his company, and she thought he felt the same. The clearing gave way to the towering, swaying trees, while the forest floor grew clogged with fallen leaves. Mr. Darcy gallantly led the way and held her hand, helping her around the largest piles and clearing them from their path when necessary.

It was a few moments later when they arrived at the stream. It was a narrow and happily bubbling brook which was now, due to the season, somewhat subdued in its merriment. The level of the water was lower than Elizabeth had normally seen it in the summer, yet Elizabeth found a likely spot, and—dipping her fingers into the cool, bracing water—she splashed some on her hands, removing any lingering stickiness from the meal. When she was done, Mr. Darcy handed her a small towel and took her place, dipping his own hands into the water and shaking them dry.

They stood for several moments on the banks of the rivulet, contentedly watching the water flow while the breeze blew up leaves of every color and description, sending them cart-wheeling over the ground, some to enter the stream and join its course, some to catch in the nooks and crannies of trees and other foliage, while some tumbled and danced until they passed out of sight. The songs of hardy birds which stayed in this frozen land throughout the winter months echoed and soared, reminding the land that not all was dead and dreary in the winter months. It was a wonderful scene.

"It is a beautiful prospect, is it not?"

Elizabeth turned to her companion and found him taking in the vista. "Indeed, it is, Mr. Darcy. When I was but a girl, my father brought Jane and I to this place, and we had our picnic in almost the same location as we have done today. I have been in love with this place ever since.

"Alas, it is too far to walk, and I have visited but rarely since. Every time I do, I marvel anew at its beauty and vow to come more often. Perhaps I should take up riding on a more permanent basis, so as to be able to make good my promise."

Darcy directed an expression of mock surprise at her. "Too far to walk? Am I to understand that this location is outside the range of even your prodigious ability to stroll?"

Delighted with his teasing, Elizabeth laughed. "I daresay it is, Mr. Darcy. Even *I* have my limitations."

"I believe, Miss Bennet, that you could do anything to which you set your mind."

"Perhaps so, Mr. Darcy, but I assure you that if I were to attempt to walk all this way, then I had best carry a tent so I should have shelter when it became dark. *And* I should also ensure there was laudanum on hand to calm my mother when she found out what I had done."

Mr. Darcy chuckled in response. "I have no doubt your mother would not be impressed by such a display."

"No, she would not, I assure you."

As they spoke, Elizabeth watched her companion. His manners and decorum were impeccable as usual, but under her watchful eye, she could see the looks that he darted in her direction, the telltale and characteristic intensity evident in his face, and the way he fidgeted slightly with his gloves. They all told her that Mr. Darcy was nervous and agitated—and that he had something to say to her of which he feared the outcome. Willing him to speak, Elizabeth waited to see what he would do.

"Well, this certainly has been a most enjoyable week, has it not?" he finally said, turning to face her.

"Indeed, it has," responded Elizabeth in a quiet voice.

"Quite a change from the previous week, where we could hardly find a moment to speak alone."

"Yes, it appeared as if there were those who wished us kept apart. Their machinations seem to have lost some of their efficacy if that was truly their goal, do you not think?"

A smile stole over his face, and he gazed at her with frank admiration. "I suppose that is so, Miss Bennet. I for one am glad—I do not appreciate the plots of others interfering with my own plans."

Elizabeth's breath caught in her throat, and she wondered how close he was to declaring himself that day, not to mention what her response should be. He almost visibly gathered his courage and gazed into her eyes.

"I must admit, I find it difficult at times to speak the contents of my heart. I have been accused of being a man of actions, not of words. And though I believe I have to a certain extent taken your measure and the measure of your feelings, I find myself being overly cautious, especially given those . . . conspirators, of whom we spoke before."

"Mr. Darcy—"

"Please, Miss Bennet," interjected Mr. Darcy with a hand held out in supplication. "I apologize for my rudeness in interrupting you, but I fear if you stop me now, I shall never have the courage to speak my mind."

Elizabeth drew in a deep breath and nodded her head. "Pray continue, sir."

"Thank you. As I said, I believe I have taken the measure of your feelings and understand the change these past weeks have wrought in them. I must tell you that everything I told you at Hunsford . . ."

Here, his cheeks blushed, and he ducked his head. Elizabeth stepped forward and put her hand on his arm, looking deeply into his eyes when he raised them to hers.

"Please, Mr. Darcy—say no more. It is all forgotten, I assure you."

"By you, perhaps, but I have not found sufficient reason to dismiss what I said or your response. It taught me a great deal—changed me, I believe, to be a better person. I thank you for your candor and your honesty, Miss Bennet, as I doubt I would ever have come to such a realization due to my own faculties."

"Do you also thank me for my frankness and the intemperate manner in which I judged you and deemed you the worst sort of man?"

"In a way, yes," he confirmed. "Your method of delivering those words gave them an air of . . . authority, for want of a better term, that persuaded me to give credence to them, which I never may have done if you had taken thought for my feelings. I assure you, Miss Bennet, I deserved no such consideration."

A smile crept its way over Elizabeth's face. "I believe, Mr. Darcy, that we shall end up quarrelling over who deserves the greater share of the blame and never come to an agreement. Let us agree that we both behaved in ways we do not normally conduct ourselves and return to our previous conversation. I believe you were about to say some words which I would find *very* flattering, and I am loath for you to stop."

Darcy's answering laughter was all she hoped, and he gallantly took hold of her hand and bestowed a kiss upon its back. "You are charming to the last, Miss Bennet. Indeed, I do not know how any man could resist you."

"Now, *that* is more like it, Mr. Darcy," responded Elizabeth with a teasing smile.

"As I was saying," continued Mr. Darcy pointedly, "everything of which I told you pertaining to my feelings remains unchanged. If anything, my regard for you has grown stronger over these intervening months, and I do not suppose I shall ever be free of it, not that I should ever desire to be so. I also believe that in some fashion, your own feelings toward me have been affected and you no longer feel the disinclination for me that you once felt.

"However," he continued when she would have interrupted, "I promised myself that I would never judge my understanding of you to be accurate until I had heard it confirmed from your very lips. Therefore, my dear Miss Bennet, I would confirm to you that I should like nothing more than to renew my addresses to you, but I would like to solicit your feelings in response. If your feelings are unchanged from what they were in April, or if you have an understanding with someone else, I will bow out gracefully."

"Mr. Darcy," chided Elizabeth, "I know you refer to Samuel Lucas. Whatever you have heard canvassed through the neighborhood — or from the mouths of our respective mothers — I assure you there is no understanding between the gentleman and myself, nor shall such an understanding ever exist. In truth, although he *was* a dear playmate from my youth, *now* he only makes me uneasy. You need not concern yourself on that account.

"As for your other question, I assure you that my feelings *have* undergone a material change from what I expressed in Kent. If they had not, I believe you and I should not have enjoyed such tranquil conversation as we have these past weeks."

They both chuckled at her reference to their sometimes contentious discussions the previous autumn, but Elizabeth was determined to move beyond that time. It would do no good to remember the past with anything other than respect and understanding for the lessons learned.

"Therefore, Mr. Darcy, I can assure you of the pleasure your declarations engender, and I must tell you that I await your addresses most breathlessly."

A smile of heartfelt delight suffused his face, and he once again took her hands within his and placed a kiss on the backs of them both. He then looked into her eyes with his usual intensity and declared:

"You must understand my full intentions, Miss Bennet. I mean to openly call upon you as I should have done last autumn and then again in Kent — you deserve every such attention. Then, I shall ask your father for his permission to enter into a formal courtship which shall be announced in town and to the neighborhood. Finally, once I have secured your affections in every way, I shall ask you to marry me and become my wife.

"I assure you, Miss Bennet, I am quite resolute when I have determined my course. *Nothing* shall dissuade me."

A frisson of excitement made its way up Elizabeth's spine at his words, and she gazed back at him unabashedly. "Then I believe, Mr. Darcy, I shall greatly anticipate the time in which you will make good on your promise."

The two now very nearly acknowledged lovers wandered aimlessly, reveling in their newfound understanding of one another. And Elizabeth, though perhaps she may have wished for him to openly declare himself by asking for a courtship, could not fault him for his caution or his desire to make his actions transparent to the neighborhood. After Lydia's debacle, a proper, respectful and open courtship with one of the wealthiest and most respected men in the kingdom would almost completely restore her family's good name. But even more important to Elizabeth at that time were the feelings his impassioned declaration engendered, which warmed her heart and filled her with a sort of childish delight.

At length, they made their way back to the others and endured their good-natured teasing and congratulations when everything which had transpired had been explained. Darcy and Elizabeth bore it all with good grace and happiness, basking in the warmth and support of those who were dearest to them.

The rest of the day passed in a blur of pleasant emotions for Elizabeth, and it would be long before she would be able to focus upon anything other than her companion.

*   *   *

It was late that afternoon when the combined Longbourn and Netherfield parties made their way through the woods after a day riding, talking, laughing, and exploring the beauties of the valley and the remains of the old keep. In their laughter and joy, they did not see the figure of the man who watched their progress from a distance.

Samuel Lucas sat astride his horse, well off the path his vantage point overlooked, seething with indignation and fury. There, below him on the path, *his* Elizabeth was smiling and flirting with that meddlesome gentleman from the north who, it seemed, had not taken his friendly warning with any degree of seriousness. Of course, he had not expected Darcy to be intimidated by his demand, as the man was foolishly self-assured. It was unsurprising that Darcy was able to see Lizzy's lack of response to his suit, so clear it was. The best he had hoped for was a moment's pause from the gentleman—time which Samuel could use to his best advantage.

He had expected Lizzy to be gone from Longbourn that morning when he had visited, and although it *had* been anticipated, the displeasure her avoidance produced was considerable, and he had had difficulty concealing it from the newly vigilant Mr. Bennet.

But why was she behaving in such a manner? They had been the closest of companions when they were young, and Elizabeth *should* have been grateful for his return and attention. Why was she so contrary as to reject his overtures now that he had deigned to make them? And what were Darcy's true intentions? Did he truly care for her, or was he simply playing with her affections, much as Samuel had seen many other rich men do with women?

In the end, it mattered little. Samuel would not be denied—Elizabeth was *his*, and he would not allow this Darcy to best him. She belonged to *him*, and he was not disposed to allow some jumped-up rich man—who had the audacity to waltz into town, flash his money, and assume the entire neighborhood would genuflect when he walked past—to steal his Lizzy out from under his nose.

Cursing the situation, Samuel watched with a glower as he witnessed her laughing and reaching out to lay her hand on Darcy's arm in response to something the man had said. She should be responding that way to *him*!

The party rode out of sight, and he finally turned his horse and began the journey home, thinking, plotting of how he could use the situation to his advantage and ensure his victory over the man he was rightly coming to detest. Regardless of everything else, it was becoming clear to Samuel that time was quickly expiring in his quest to secure Lizzy's hand. Whatever he was to do, it was obvious that the time was now.

He would secure Elizabeth immediately—nothing else would do. Once he had proposed and published it to the neighborhood, Elizabeth would have no choice but to accept him—her sense of duty would allow for nothing else. Then this exasperating flirtation with the rich gentleman would come to an end as it should, and she would take her proper place at his side and live out a happy life in the neighborhood in which she had been born. And Samuel would finally enjoy the fruits of his labors.

Slightly calmed now, Samuel allowed himself to drift off in the thoughts of a life with his Lizzy, and he started whistling as he led his horse down the path toward his father's house.

Chapter XIV

*M*ost of the next week passed very agreeably for Elizabeth.

With Mr. Darcy's declaration the day of their outing, the contented—yet still officially unacknowledged—lovers now openly spent a far greater amount of time in one another's company, communing on that deeper level which presages a true meeting of minds. Though Elizabeth had already felt that their regard was profound, the true familiarity gained by constant interaction and accompanied by the exchange of thoughts and ideas (without their sometimes rancorous interactions of the past) allowed their understanding to deepen rapidly.

In Darcy, Elizabeth found a man who was in some ways much as she had expected him to be, yet in other ways, he was quite different. For example, his passion and intensity had never been in question; their discussions at Netherfield—and even the terrible night of his proposal—had made that fact abundantly clear. She was also aware of his determination, his sense of duty, and his loyalty to those whom he considered friends.

Yet the true Mr. Darcy—the one who had openly acknowledged himself to be in love and who was now unafraid to show it before the entire neighborhood—was far more playful and lighthearted when in the company of those with whom he was comfortable than Elizabeth would have ever believed. He appeared to find great delight in provoking her laughter, and he took every opportunity to do so, his countenance taking on an expression of delight when successful. Invariably, he would even join in with a hearty laugh of his own. He was also tender and thoughtful, her comfort and well-being appearing to comprise his most important goals. In short, he was the perfect lover, and Elizabeth was immensely grateful that they had been able to make their way past the acrimony of the past.

Of course, this freedom to be together was not purchased without a price. Jane and Bingley's assistance was, as ever, invaluable. They slyly suggested walks, planned activities in which they could participate as couples, inserted themselves as conversation partners when necessary, and interfered with those who sought to separate them with their constant meddling. Colonel Fitzwilliam was always present to distract Elizabeth's *other* suitor, while Anne and Georgiana made it their mission to ensure Miss Bingley had no power to separate them. Even her father kept in the game, watching alertly whenever the party was gathered at Longbourn, specifically ensuring Samuel Lucas behaved in a proper, respectful manner.

Not everyone was happy with the arrangements, of course. Mr. Lucas's countenance continued to become darker by the day as his designs were thwarted by the combined efforts of the company. Elizabeth, perhaps, would have felt a certain measure of sympathy for the young man if he had not behaved in such a reprehensible manner those past weeks. However, the memory of his smug expression whenever he had manipulated her mother—and the manner in which he had ignored her wishes and imposed himself upon her—caused any compassion Elizabeth might have felt for him to evaporate.

And though Elizabeth thought she could sense a certain desperation building in his behavior, she decided it was nothing to her—he had no one to blame but himself, after all. She took great care to never allow him the opportunity to be alone with her, a circumstance in which she was assisted by her sisters when their neighbors were not available. And though Mr. Darcy expressed a certain degree of concern for Mr. Lucas's attitude, Elizabeth put him at ease, telling him that she stayed near one of her sisters at all times. She also added, somewhat forcefully, that she would not tolerate Samuel Lucas to curtail her activities or affect her life in any manner. His wishes and desires could not rule her, and she refused to stop living her life as she saw fit.

Assuredly, Miss Bingley was another who appeared to be unhappy at the more open manner in which Mr. Darcy's affections were being displayed. Fortunately, she was unable to express her opinion on the matter, as she was thwarted in the same fashion as Mr. Lucas. In addition, as Mr. Bingley had confided during one of the times in which the two couples had escaped the confines of Longbourn, she had been forbidden from becoming involved in any way, lest she suffer her brother's wrath. Though Elizabeth was not aware of what specifically Mr. Bingley could hold over his sister's head, apparently it was enough to rein Miss Bingley in, as she began avoiding the frequent excursions to Longbourn and generally only appeared when the ladies had been invited to Netherfield. Even then, Miss Bingley appeared to join the company without any enthusiasm and often spent the entirety of the visit sitting by herself, glaring in distaste at the rest of the party. To say that this attitude did not bother the rest of the group was a massive understatement.

The other lone holdout to Elizabeth's good fortune was somewhat of a surprise to her—it appeared that her mother was no happier over the situation than the two conspirators.

Now, it must be noted that while Elizabeth was well aware of her mother's weak understanding and flighty nature, she had a healthy respect for Mrs. Bennet's instincts concerning the level of interest *any* young man held for one of her daughters. Even if Mrs. Bennet's highly honed ability had not existed, Elizabeth could not believe her mother would have been able to miss the marked preference that Mr. Darcy was now showing for her. Elizabeth *would* have expected that this would have thrown her mother into a frenzy of joyous exclamations, anticipatory ramblings, and excited crowing to the neighbors of how one of *her* daughters had secured the *richest man* ever to grace their small community with his presence.

But none of this expected—and admittedly humiliating—joyous anticipation had materialized. When witnessing Mr. Darcy's attentions, Mrs. Bennet had more often than not narrowed her eyes to what was occurring while bemoaning to her daughter of her continued lack of response to the Lucas heir and her destiny to end an old maid if she continued on in such a manner. That she did this often in the presence—and in the face—of Mr. Darcy and his attentions was no less than astonishing. She had even half-heartedly attempted to throw Kitty in the path of the wealthy gentleman a time or two until Mr. Bennet had stepped in and firmly put a stop to that, much to Kitty's—and Mr. Darcy's—obvious relief.

That something was bothering her mother was obvious, but what exactly was causing her to behave in such an uncharacteristic manner, Elizabeth was not able to determine. She should have been jumping for joy at her daughter's good fortune.

Could it possibly be the fact that Mr. Darcy's actions the night of the assembly had forever caused an implacable enmity for the man in spite of his riches? But that certainly could not be the case—after all, Mrs. Bennet had been (rightly) angered at Mr. Bingley's abandonment of Jane, yet she had readily forgiven the young man when he had brought his five thousand a year back to finally engage himself to her eldest daughter. And Mr. Darcy was twice the consequence of Mr. Bingley—surely the mere mention of the man's income alone was enough to ensure Mrs. Bennet's immediate and unconditional forgiveness.

It was perplexing, but even Mr. Bennet was unable to account for her behavior. He informed Elizabeth that he had inquired of her concerning her actions more than once, but he had made no headway in deciphering the reason—Mrs. Bennet became tightlipped whenever he had attempted to question her on her reasons, and she could not be induced to say anything. It appeared, at least for the time being, that Elizabeth's curiosity was not to be assuaged.

Elizabeth, for the most part, continued to live her life in the manner in which she had done her whole life—she pursued her love of reading, studying, and debating the various texts in her father's bookroom (now with the advantage of discussing those same subjects with her suitor!); she indulged herself in the pleasure of long walks when the weather cooperated (which was becoming less frequent as the year waned); and she occupied her time talking, laughing, and immersing herself in her favorite activities, all while enjoying the attentions of her ever-devoted suitor. She had determined that she would still be the same person regardless of the rich young gentleman's interest in her.

"I believe I shall take a walk this morning, Jane," said Elizabeth to her sister one morning late in the week.

As it was still very early, Jane was still in her room, not yet dressed for the day, though Elizabeth had been prepared since before first light that morning. The weather the previous two days had been chillier, with heavy frost overnight which had then been washed away by the rain during the day. Certain that the weather was turning and would soon curtail her love of nature, Elizabeth was determined to escape the confines of the house whenever able in order to store up such moments for the coming winter.

Jane peered up from her vanity, where she was preparing for the day, and smiled at her sister. "Has the brightness of the day stirred up your desire to wander throughout the countryside again, Lizzy?"

"You know me too well," said Elizabeth with a laugh. "Winter is approaching, as you know, and I believe I should enjoy the ability to walk while I am able."

"Is there perhaps another reason for your determination to walk out today, Lizzy?"

"Of what do you speak?"

Jane's appraising smirk caused Elizabeth to laugh out loud. "Do not peer at me in such a manner, Jane! Speak plainly!"

"Nothing, Lizzy," said Jane with a mischievous chuckle. "I was just wondering if perhaps other considerations have caused you to evaluate the amount of time you have left to enjoy your walks in *this* neighborhood. After all, *Derbyshire* is a rather taxing journey from *Longbourn*, is it not?"

When Elizabeth's cheeks pinked at Jane's less than subtle insinuations, Jane once again laughed at her sister and rose to enfold her in a hug.

"Is it not so, Lizzy? Unless my eyes are very much mistaken, Mr. Darcy appears ready to fall at your feet and propose to you forthwith. Am I mistaken?"

"Yes, indeed you are mistaken, Jane," was Elizabeth's cheeky response. "Mr. Darcy wishes to pay court to me in front of the entire neighborhood, and therefore, as that goal has not yet been achieved to his satisfaction, he is not quite ready to propose."

Jane's answering slap on the shoulder caused both sisters to once again collapse in laughter.

"Lizzy! Sometimes you are simply infuriating!"

"I have merely told the absolute truth!" exclaimed Elizabeth.

"Well, I am still very happy for you! He is a very good man, I think, and shall be very good for you."

"Thank you, Jane. I believe he will."

"And of course, Mr. Bingley shall be very happy to have Mr. Darcy as a brother, though it is not perhaps the way that his sister would have wished."

"Indeed, she would not have wished for such a connection," exclaimed Elizabeth with a delighted laugh. "I am glad that you see Miss Bingley for what she is, Jane. You will have to put up with her once you are married, and I believe the best way to go about it would be to ensure she understands that she will not have her way."

"I agree, Lizzy," was Jane's quiet reply. "But I could hardly help but come to an understanding of her character given what she did to separate us. And her behavior since her return to Hertfordshire, especially toward you, has been reprehensible."

"Do not be concerned on my account. Everything is working out the way it should. I believe I am content."

After another hug, Jane stepped away and shooed Elizabeth from the room. "I am very glad you are, Lizzy. But if you are to walk this morning, you had best leave now before Mr. Lucas shows up at our door. You would not wish for him to follow you out into the countryside, after all."

Elizabeth rolled her eyes. "Oh, come, Jane, it is much too early for a visit, even from *him*. I have plenty of time before I should have to worry about that eventuality."

"You never know, Elizabeth. He has been looking increasingly frustrated lately, and I would not put it past him to show up early in an attempt to be alone with you, in the absence of our neighbors."

Elizabeth capitulated, though in all honesty, it was not a hard thing to do. "I shall leave directly, Jane. If I should not return by luncheon, advise Papa to organize a search party—Mr. Lucas may have abducted me, after all."

Another laugh, and then Jane pushed Elizabeth from the room. Elizabeth, eager to leave and indulge herself in her favorite activity, made her way to her own room and, gathering her pelisse and her other winter accoutrements, made her way out of the house and onto the drive. She continued on toward the church, and when she had just passed the comforting old building, she struck out on a small path which would take her along the boundaries of Netherfield and afford her a magnificent view of the manor house. In fact, she thought with a smile, it was this very same path she had been traversing when she had caught her first glimpse of Mr. Bingley and Mr. Darcy the previous year when they had first visited the estate.

With a grin of fond remembrance, Elizabeth skipped along the narrow path, happily humming a tune while reveling in the freedom and sense of oneness with nature she always felt when she walked alone.

She walked, setting a swift pace and swinging her arms with relish, enjoying the hints of birdsong which echoed out over the trees and the feeling of the loose fallen leaves under the soles of her shoes. The air was calm that morning, with nary a hint of a wind, which made the air quite bracing, but not overly cold.

Elizabeth smiled to herself—undoubtedly, Jane, along with the rest of her sisters, would find the morning much too cold for a long walk. But to Elizabeth, who was, in her own estimation, a hardier soul, the morning was perfect.

The views of the day were splendid, and she lingered along the path when Netherfield came into sight, noting the smoke rising from the chimneys and the tiny figures of its staff going about their duties. The sight brought memories of her short time at Pemberley and the grandness of the house and grounds. Netherfield was a fine manor, very comfortable, built and decorated impeccably. Yet it was nothing compared with Pemberley, and Elizabeth was now aware of the very great honor which would be hers if she were to become mistress of that great estate.

She sighed and turned away, thinking of the blindness of the past and her great fortune to learn of her mistakes and be afforded the opportunity to correct them.

The return journey to Longbourn was accomplished in much the same manner as her walk out to her vantage point, yet her mind was far more engaged in reflections of the past and her role in the events which had occurred in the past year. The fact that everything appeared to be about to work itself out to *nearly* everyone's satisfaction was a small miracle—indeed, Elizabeth could hardly account for it.

It is to be supposed that the thoughts of the past year and her steadily growing love for the master of Pemberley were what caused Elizabeth to be so inattentive. Whatever the reason, she was still a quarter of an hour's walk from Longbourn when she suddenly became aware of the fact that she was not alone on the path.

Stopping rather abruptly, her eyes widened in disbelief and then narrowed in displeasure as, to the side of the path, she saw Samuel Lucas leering at her, his manner all insolence and self-congratulatory. Though she would have liked nothing more than to ignore him and continue on her way, Elizabeth doubted that he would take very kindly to such treatment. She bit back several unladylike curses and schooled her expression to a neutral one, inclining her head in greeting.

"Mr. Lucas," was her simple and noncommittal greeting.

Ignoring her less than welcoming attitude, Mr. Lucas smirked and extended an exaggeratedly formal bow in her direction. "Milady! How do you do this fine morning?"

Fighting back the desire to answer him with an insult, Elizabeth answered his question in a monotone, allowing her manner to display her displeasure at his artifice. However he may have been affected by her cold greeting, it did not show in his demeanor—he was all cheerful smiles, apparently feeling superior due to the fact that he had managed to get his own way after a week of frustration. But Elizabeth had no intention of permitting the insufferable man his delusions.

"I am sorry, Mr. Lucas, but I was just returning to Longbourn," said she, letting her voice convey the testiness she was feeling for him. "I really must depart, as we will likely be having certain *visitors* this morning, and I should be present when they arrive. I am sure you understand."

"They could no doubt spare you a few moments, Miss Elizabeth. I will only take a moment of your time."

Certain the best way to get the ordeal over with was to allow him to have his say, Elizabeth inclined her head and waited for him to speak. His next action caught her completely by surprise.

He stepped forward, and before Elizabeth had a chance to fathom his intentions or react in any way, he scooped up her hand and placed a lingering kiss on its back. Straightening, he favored her with a smile—which more resembled that smirk of his which she was coming to detest—and reached for her other hand. Elizabeth, finally finding her wits, pulled herself away from his grasp and edged her way in the direction of Longbourn, suddenly concerned as to what his purpose was.

Mr. Lucas, though, was having none of that, and he forestalled her, stepping forward and cutting her off. "Lizzy, I have sought you out this morning for the express purpose of making my feelings known to you and soliciting your hand, and I shall not be dissuaded from my purpose."

Elizabeth stared at him with horror. He could not *possibly* mean to do what she now suspected, could he?

"I am sensible of the good fortune you must feel by being noticed by me," he began, confirming her worst fears, "but as we have been friends for years, I hardly think that your dissembling efforts to appear as if you do not notice my marked interest and attentions to you could fool me. I cannot even begin to tell you the depth of affection and love I feel for you. You were the dearest companion of my childhood and have grown into a remarkable and wonderful young lady whose beauty inspires me daily.

"Indeed, Lizzy, I do not know what I would do if I did *not* have you in my life. Your wit and vivacity, your common sense, your knowledge and abilities—all these things tell me that you are the woman who is meant to be my wife, and I will do *whatever* it takes to secure your hand and your affections. I promise that you will enjoy *every* aspect of our marriage to the fullest."

His eyes, as they raked over her body at this statement, left no doubt as to his meaning and caused Elizabeth to feel *soiled* by his frank and open appraisal of her person. Though she was fully clothed—and covered by her winter attire in addition to her modest dress—Elizabeth almost felt the need to cover herself and hide from his sight. She gathered her courage and met his appraisal with a disapproving glare, ignoring the nervous butterflies which were beginning to stir within her midsection.

"You simply *must* agree to marry me, Elizabeth," continued he. "I am convinced that we are perfectly suited for one another in every way, and I know that living in the neighborhood so close to your family and your childhood home would fulfill every measure of your happiness. I promise to do everything in my power to ensure your comfort and future as well as the futures of all of our children. You *must* marry me."

Elizabeth felt ill. For the third time in the past year, she had been subjected to the indignity of an unwanted marriage proposal, and though perhaps Mr. Collins had been the most loathsome in his *person*, this particular proposal was far more insulting than even what Mr. Darcy had stated during his attempt. At least they had both had the presence of mind to *ask* for her hand despite the *other* sentiments they had both deemed necessary to secure a favorable answer to their suit. Samuel said none of these things—he merely insisted upon her marrying him and *commanded* her to be happy with him. She remembered telling Mr. Darcy that his manner of expressing himself had spared her any concern she might have felt in rejecting him—this sentiment was doubly felt in response to *this proposal*.

Yet something else disquieted Elizabeth and stayed her tongue for the moment. Though Mr. Darcy's declaration had been unexpected and highly offensive, she had never felt herself in any danger in his company, no matter what words passed between them. Mr. Darcy was proper—the perfect gentleman, despite his perceived faults—and Elizabeth had known subconsciously even then that he would never do anything untoward, nor would he attempt to compromise her in any way in order to obtain what he wanted.

With *this* man, though she had known him most of her life, that surety did not exist; he had been gone for too long, and his behavior since he had returned had been too volatile for her to *not* suspect his motives. Though she considered the option of giving him a bare acceptance and then disavowing it later, she shied away from such subterfuge. He would get no such attention from her in this matter, and she would not allow him to insert his foot in the door in any fashion. Besides, the thought of how Mr. Darcy could misconstrue such intelligence if it were ever to reach him—and she had no doubt Mr. Lucas would publish it to the entire neighborhood as soon as was convenient—caused her to shudder. She would not hurt Mr. Darcy again in *any* way!

She stood there watching him, witnessing his agitation begin as her silence wore on. Finally, it seemed he could take no more. He stepped forward and addressed her, his voice demanding.

"Well?"

"I am sorry, Mr. Lucas," replied Elizabeth, keeping her voice calm and placid. "Do you require something of me?"

"I just asked you a question, Lizzy. Will you not answer it?"

"A question," said Elizabeth with a short laugh. "I can recall no question, I assure you."

An expression of exaggerated patience came over his face, and he smiled at her indulgently. "Lizzy, I just asked you to marry me. I am awaiting your answer."

"No, Mr. Lucas, you did not ask for my hand in marriage," said she. "In fact, as I recall, you simply *demanded* that I marry you, telling me of all the advantages which would come my way if I should *bow to your will*. There was no request of any sort in your speech."

Now exasperated, Mr. Lucas glared at her, his nostrils flaring in anger. "Fine!" he bit out. "Miss Elizabeth Bennet, I find myself unable to live without you. Will you do me the great honor of accepting my hand in marriage?"

"No, Mr. Lucas, I do not believe I shall."

His eyes widened and almost bulged out from their sockets. "You *must!*" he blurted out.

"No, there is no '*must*,' Mr. Lucas," responded Elizabeth evenly, keeping a close watch on his shock-filled face. "As a man, *you* may make a proposal to any young woman you choose, but as a woman, it is *my* right to accept or refuse. Regardless of what *your* feelings may consist, I find that *mine* are quite unequal to yours. You say you can make me happy—your words seemed to insist that I will have no choice *but to be happy*—but I am convinced that I should be miserable as your wife, and I do not doubt that you would not fair much better in the exchange. I will not marry you, Mr. Lucas."

"But Lizzy, how could you possibly say such things?" demanded Mr. Lucas. "We have been acquainted since childhood—we have complementary temperaments. You would be happy to continue to live in Hertfordshire."

"You presume much, Mr. Lucas. How can you stand there and tell me of your sure knowledge of my hopes and desires? For all you know, I may wish to marry a pauper from India and move away from England forever."

"Surely you do not believe me to be taken in by such fanciful talk, Lizzy. I can offer you everything you could ever want—a good home in the neighborhood in which you were raised, security, and respectability. What more is there?"

"Love, Mr. Lucas—even if you could offer me a comfortable situation and a good home—of which I do not doubt—you still cannot offer me love," was her even reply. "Jane and I have always maintained that we would only be induced into matrimony for the greatest and deepest of love. I do not love you, Mr. Lucas."

"I can make you love me."

"How?" replied Elizabeth, exasperatedly throwing her hands into the air. "You will *make* me fall in love with you? You will *force* my feelings to somehow materialize where none such exist? How do you propose to do such a thing?"

Mr. Lucas's face was suffused with an anger the extent of which she had never seen before, and she was once again worried as to the lengths to which he would go to secure her. But despite her continuing uncertainty over the depths of his obsession and depravity, Elizabeth could do no more than be true to herself and her principles. She would *not* give in to him.

"If you would only give me a chance—"

"And I assure you, no such chance exists. I beg you to cease to importune me on this subject, Mr. Lucas. My answer shall never change."

The angry intensity of his gaze upon her unnerved Elizabeth even further, but she fought her anxiety down and raised an eyebrow in his direction.

"I admit I find it hard to believe that you, of all people, can be this stupid, Lizzy," he finally bit out after glaring at her for several moments.

"And I do not believe I understand your meaning or your insult, sir," she shot back. "If *anyone* here is being stupid, *Mr. Lucas*, then I believe that person to be you."

He stepped toward her, rage washing over his face. "You *know* I speak of this *Mr. Darcy*," snapped he. "You are a very intelligent young woman, Elizabeth, and although you have not experienced much of the world, surely you must know that a man of Darcy's consequence paying attention to a young woman of a much lower station, of relatively little consequence in the world, can only mean one thing."

"I thank you for your glowing estimation of my worth, Mr. Lucas," was Elizabeth's sardonic reply. "Given what you think of me, I wonder why you would take the trouble to try to entice a girl of 'relatively little consequence' to be your wife."

"Do not be obtuse, Lizzy," he growled. "You are perfectly sensible of my meaning."

"I am being no more obtuse than you are, sir. But in answer to your question about Mr. Darcy, perhaps his attention means nothing more than his enjoyment of my company. Or perhaps he is an honorable man who means to make me an offer regardless of my lack of dowry. Mayhap it has something to do with the fact that I am very close to his *sister* and his *cousin*! There may be many reasons why I am acceptable as a discussion partner to him."

"Now you are being willfully blind, Lizzy!" ground out Mr. Lucas. "You are well aware to what I refer. This Mr. Darcy, with whom you seem to be so enamored, means to use you and discard you when you have served your purpose. I have been acquainted with many rich men during my time at school, and they are all the same. You are risking your reputation by carrying on with him!"

"*You* are the only one risking my reputation, Mr. Lucas, with your insistence on calling on me when I wish to have nothing to do with you, with your encouraging of our mothers' continual discussion of our *nonexistent* relationship, not to mention your attempts to entice me to be alone with you. I can only wonder at your continued thick-headedness and the manner in which you continually ignore everything I have done to attempt to dissuade you. This does not even account for the manner in which you ignore my father's precise instructions regarding our dealings with one another.

"I must tell you, *Mr. Lucas*, that I feel much safer and more secure in the company of Mr. Darcy than in that of certain *others* I could name. I know his heart and his character, and I am aware of his intentions and his hopes and wishes for his future and my place in it. I thank you for your care and concern on my behalf, but you need not bother yourself any further. I will ask you to stop your meddling and cease your attempts to defame Mr. Darcy's name in my presence."

His eyes flashed briefly, but he visibly calmed himself and allowed a forced smile to appear on his face.

"My dear Lizzy, I regret that we so often seem to find ourselves embroiled in such disagreements of late. I assure you I have nothing more or less than your best interests in mind and would not wish for you to think ill of me. I am determined to carry my point in this matter—you *will* be my wife, and you *will* spend the rest of your life as mistress of my estate and mother to my children."

Elizabeth's anger flared, and she clenched her fists. "And I assure *you*, Mr. Lucas, that you shall never carry your point, and I shall *never* marry you. Can I be any plainer than I already have been?"

At her declaration, Mr. Lucas's person seemed to grow larger and more intimidating, and he stepped forward, looming over her in a most unpleasant fashion. His eyes flashed with his displeasure, and he glared at her.

"I had not imagined you would be this intractable, Lizzy," growled he, his face turning almost purple with his rage. "I had thought to meet an agreeable, intelligent young lady who would see the benefit and sense of my application, yet I find I am confronted by a petulant little girl who believes she understands more of the world than she truly does. I am disappointed in you, Lizzy."

"And *I* am disappointed in *you!*" spat Elizabeth in reply, not backing down an inch. "You have continued upon this doomed quest to pursue me in spite of every indication that I did not welcome your suit. Even my father has declared to you that you shall conduct yourself in a proper and gentlemanly fashion, yet you try to intimidate me. *You* are no gentleman, sir!"

"If I am no gentleman," replied Mr. Lucas in a quiet and threatening tone of voice, "then I believe I should have no reason to attempt to behave as one. Perhaps if you will not agree to marry me voluntarily, I should compromise you. Perhaps then, with the threat of ruin to you and all your sisters—even Jane!—you would come to your senses."

Elizabeth was now frightened, uncertain whether he would do as he had threatened. But recalling her previous words that every attempt to intimidate her brought out her courage, she allowed all the defiance she felt to show in her expression as she glared back at him and drew herself up to her full height, her manner filled with an imperiousness Lady Catherine herself would envy.

"Despite the way you prove your ungentlemanly behavior, sir, I will not be coerced by such means. I was sincere in my refusal. I will tell you that you are the *very* last man who walks on the face of this earth with whom I could even sully myself. If I was faced with a lonely fate as a solitary spinster or marriage to you as my only choices, I would still reject you and seek to put as much distance between us as was humanly possible. You, sir, are a conceited swine, and I may safely say that I have never met a man whose behavior disgusts me as much as yours. And though you defame the good name of the gentleman from Derbyshire, you should know that he is one hundred times the man that you will ever be!"

With one last haughty glare, Elizabeth stalked away, holding her head high with a confidence she did not feel. At any moment, she expected to hear his footsteps following her and his hand reach out to grasp her arm, to wrench her around and carry through with his threat. For whatever reason—whether it was due to some measure of propriety which still existed within him, or whether he was not willing to risk such a violent action, or whether the remembrance of their shared childhood experiences stayed his hand or even the fear of Mr. Darcy's reprisal, she was not certain—but he did not follow.

Once Elizabeth had turned a corner, she risked a glance back and was relieved to see the path behind her held no hint of her assailant. Breathing a quick sigh of relief, Elizabeth fairly broke into a run, intent upon reaching the safety of Longbourn as soon as she could. What was to be done about Samuel Lucas she was not certain, but she knew she could not allow herself to ever be caught in this position again.

When the familiar environs of her home came into view, she almost wept with relief. She was home. She was safe.

Samuel Lucas had never felt such a feeling of utter rage as he did at the moment when Elizabeth Bennet walked away from him. She had refused him! How could she do such a thing? He could not make her out for the life of him, and the problem of her continuing defiance was troubling.

As she neared a turn in the path, he was tempted to follow her and insist upon her acceptance of his suit, but as he considered the matter for a moment, he decided that it was not worth the damage it would ultimately do. If Elizabeth was one thing, she was stubborn, and further importuning her in such a matter at this time could only cause more harm than good. He would bide his time.

Stepping off the path, Samuel walked to where he had tied his horse, untied the reins from the branch, and, mounting, set off for home, carefully considering the predicament in which he now found himself.

Why had it suddenly become so important to win the hand of his childhood friend? Though he could not answer that question with any surety — even in the confines of his own mind — he suspected it had to do with the insufferably self-assured rich man from Derbyshire who was showing an unhealthy interest in *his* Elizabeth. Samuel had met his kind before — had attended an entire school full of gentlemen of Mr. Darcy's ilk — and he felt he had the measure of the man. Wealthy men such as Darcy were interested in one thing only when it came to the likes of a young maiden, and Samuel was certain Darcy was the same as the rest.

In another part of his mind, though, Samuel thought back to his time at school. Though his father had scrimped to give him the best education available, Samuel had always been made aware of his place by those who surrounded him. Though he attended a prestigious university and was the heir to an estate of his own, his consequence was a fraction of what many of them would inherit, and in the end, he was merely the son of a country squire, destined to inherit the same small estate his father lived on, but without the knighthood his father held. Though he had made friends by blending in with them and sharing in their proclivities, he had never been their *equal*.

Perhaps this motivated him more than any other consideration — he would not be bested by a wealthy man again! He would have what the rich man wanted, and he would gloat over the fact, pleased that for once he had managed to gain the upper hand on one of the insufferable fools. No other outcome would do!

But how to go about ensuring the result he so desired . . . ? His attempts to court Elizabeth had failed, she had rejected his marriage proposal, and she had almost run from him. What could he do to salvage the situation?

Was Mrs. Bennet the key? Could he drop a hint with her, further pulling her to his side and forcing Elizabeth's hand as a result? It was possible, he decided — if presented as a fait accompli, then Elizabeth would have no choice but to capitulate to his desires. He would have to stay alert and wait for the opportunity — it was sure to present itself if he was patient enough.

Then Elizabeth would be *his*! The thought made him almost quiver with anticipation. Once she was his, he would break her of her insubordination and ensure she never thought to challenge him again.

It would be sweet, he decided, his mouth forming itself into the rictus of a grin. She would be his, with or without her consent.

* * *

Later that evening, Jane sat on Elizabeth's bed, comforting her after her latest ordeal, an event which had become all too common of late. How her sister managed to get herself into these situations, Jane would never know, but Elizabeth's distress at the ungentlemanly behavior of the Lucas scion was rising to almost critical levels.

"I can hardly believe it," commiserated Jane. "The exact circumstance we discussed so flippantly this very morning! How could Samuel behave thus to one of his dearest and oldest friends? He was such a bright, playful child—what happened to change him so?"

"I know not, nor do I care," was Elizabeth's sighed response. "I only wish to avoid him."

Elizabeth's face darkened, and when she spoke again, her voice was low and almost shaking with emotion.

"His countenance was something which I have never before witnessed, Jane. I almost believed him capable of *anything* at that moment, and I was surprised when he did not follow me. He considers me a mere *possession* and nothing more."

"Lizzy, I think you should consider curtailing your walks," advised Jane gently. "I know how you love the activity, but you must avoid giving him the occasion to importune you again. If your conjectures about him are in any way accurate, I hate to think what he could do to you if given another chance."

"Believe me, Jane," responded Elizabeth with a mirthless chuckle, "I had already come to that conclusion myself. I will not be caught alone with him again."

"That is good, Lizzy. I will do whatever I can to protect you, and I am certain Charles feels the same way. Will you not talk to Papa about it?"

Elizabeth shook her head. "It would do no good, Jane," was Elizabeth's tired response. "All the man actually did was to propose marriage to me, after all, and he cannot be censured for such an application."

"But surely his words and his behavior merit condemnation, Lizzy. His manner of expressing himself was reprehensible, and his attempted intimidation unconscionable—I believe our father should know."

Elizabeth sighed. "Was not Mr. Darcy's proposal also worthy of condemnation, Jane? For that matter, Mr. Collins certainly did not acquit himself with any distinction during his application. It seems it is my fate to be subjected to the attentions of men I find detestable."

"You include Mr. Darcy in this estimation?"

"I did, as you well know," replied Elizabeth with a genuine smile. "That I do not any longer does not change the fact that *at the time* I certainly did not welcome his attentions."

"But Lizzy, surely this is a completely different situation. Papa has been exerting himself to protect you, and he will not take kindly to Samuel's continued pursuit of you. Will you not tell him?"

Elizabeth was silent for several moments, and Jane was left to wonder what she would do if Elizabeth should prove to be stubborn in this matter. Should Jane approach their father herself with her concerns over Samuel's continued persistence? Elizabeth would certainly be angry with her for doing so without her knowledge or consent were she to take such a drastic step, but was Elizabeth's peace of mind and safety not worth the displeasure she was certain to provoke?

At length, Elizabeth once again let out a longsuffering sigh and responded, taking the decision out of Jane's hands. "I will tell Papa, Jane. But I will keep it only to the facts. Samuel proposed and I refused. Further than that, I will only tell Papa that I did not like his reaction to my refusal."

Jane hugged her sister, relieved that Elizabeth saw the importance of such a step. "Thank you, Lizzy—I believe it is the right thing to do."

Elizabeth *did* tell her father of her experience with Samuel, but as she had expected, his response was concern for her, but concern with little or no ability to do anything further about the situation. After all, a man *was* entitled to propose to a woman for whom he felt a tender affection, and as Elizabeth left out the other details, her father's hands were largely tied. Her father did promise to continue to keep an eye on the young man and to discourage any further pursuit in which he indulged, but that was the extent of the discussion.

They were able to share a laugh at the thought of *another* unwanted proposal (Mr. Bennet did not know of Mr. Darcy's application, but Mr. Collins's was enough to amuse both of them), and Elizabeth was able to laugh at herself in the face of Mr. Bennet's gentle teasing. It *was* amusing, after all, and Elizabeth could well understand the humor inherent in the situation.

For Elizabeth, the ensuing days were much the same as the previous had been—she reveled in the time she was able to spend in the company of her desired suitor and was happy with the level of attention and affection he was showing her. Her friendship with Anne continued to deepen, and she could not be happier with the way she and her sisters and Anne were gently drawing Georgiana from her reticent manner and helping her to grow into a more outgoing and confident young woman.

As for Mr. Darcy, she longed—yearned—to tell him of her confrontation with the Lucas heir, but for the next few days, they were much in company, and the inclement weather which descended upon Hertfordshire meant that long walks in his company came to a halt. She was not comfortable informing him of such events in the sitting room at Longbourn or in Mr. Bingley's drawing room. She kept her own counsel as a result, while telling herself she would inform her suitor at the first available opportunity.

It was some relief that Samuel kept his distance for the first few days, leading her to a guarded optimism that he had finally given up. However, it was less than three days before that hope was dashed and he finally appeared at Longbourn again, his eyes searching for her and narrowing when he witnessed Mr. Darcy's close proximity. He said nothing, however, merely seeming content to sit on the far side of the room and brood. If Mr. Darcy noticed his ill humor, he said nothing.

Mr. Lucas's obvious displeasure notwithstanding, Elizabeth forced their confrontation from her consciousness and exerted herself to be happy and content with the man she had come to love. She considered herself finished with Mr. Lucas and would not converse with him any further or give him any notice of any kind. He was now persona non grata to her.

Chapter XV

*F*ear and loathing wound its insidious way through the mind of Caroline Bingley, and she found it was all she could do to maintain the fiction of polite attentiveness. If she could have indulged in the luxury of a scowl at the cause of her grief, she would have done so in an instant—but the woman was in that very room!

Elizabeth Bennet! In her mind, Caroline spat the name like a curse. *She* was the cause of all Caroline's problems! *She* was the reason for Caroline's lost hopes and dreams, the reason why the ignominy which Caroline had so desperately tried to avoid now sped towards her with a seemingly inexorable impetus. The woman destroyed everything she touched, yet she stood there talking and *laughing* with her sister and friends. Why could she not simply disappear into the countryside like a good little country miss? It was not as if she were good enough for anyone but the savages which inhabited this godforsaken place!

The fact of the matter was that Caroline's hastily conceived and executed plan had had little effect—Mr. Darcy now appeared closer than ever to proposing to the country miss if Caroline's observations of the past few days were any indication. How could he be so blind? What power did the infernal woman possess to make her so irresistible to him? How could Caroline possibly avoid the humiliation?

In truth, there *was* no way. The plan she had formulated to remove the Bennet chit from the equation appeared to have failed spectacularly. Beyond the fact that Mr. Darcy was treating her as if he was courting her (the thought nearly caused Caroline to gag!), a chance meeting with Samuel Lucas at a gathering of the locals a few days before had revealed a failed proposal of marriage. Elizabeth Bennet had actually had the audacity to refuse Samuel Lucas's offer! She was a social climber and a fortune hunter, plain and simple. How could she—a penniless second daughter of a man of very limited means—think so well of herself as to consider herself an equal of a man of the stature of Mr. Darcy? The nerve, the absolute effrontery of the woman!

She cursed her brother for forcing this disgrace upon her—his ill-conceived plan for her to show the *other* country miss around her new home, guiding the woman through the very house of which she would soon be mistress. Jane Bennet had not the wit to understand how very ill equipped she was to undertake the role of mistress to Charles's home. Yet Charles had demanded it, and Caroline was forced to agree to this farce. And of course it was necessary to bring along the *other* sister. The two of them talked and laughed through the length of *Caroline's* home, their avaricious gaze resting upon everything which she, Caroline, had done to raise her brother's house in this unfortunate part of the kingdom from the hovel it had been to the more dignified and respectable home it had become. Those Bennet sisters would ruin all her work with their wild and uncivilized ways!

Still, Caroline could do nothing and was forced to welcome the chits into her home, displaying to them all impeccable breeding and sensibility she possessed. Though she would rather have screamed and raged at the lot of them, she would be nothing less than the perfect lady she actually was. They would *not* take that from her too!

As they continued their way through the house, the tension and anger Caroline felt became ever more difficult to bear. The sheer loudness of their exclamations, their unfashionable tastes, the way they betrayed their countrified manners and inability to show anything resembling sense—all these things infuriated Caroline and made her long for the time when she would be able to see their backs as they left. Then she could retreat to her room to nurse her misery in quiet and solitude.

It was perhaps not surprising that the tour of Netherfield manor led to the unfortunate episode which was so mortifying for the entire company.

If she were to be honest with herself, Elizabeth knew she had had no business accepting the engagement to be taken through the house of which her sister would soon be mistress. Because of the way Caroline Bingley had been acting around her—especially within the past se'nnight—Elizabeth had been sorely tempted to refuse the invitation and allow Jane to go by herself. After all, with the presence of Anne and Georgiana, it was not as if Jane would be alone with the shrewish woman.

But two things conspired to make Elizabeth review her reasons for not attending and to ultimately reverse her previous resolution. The first was, of course, Jane's plea for her company. Her sister, though she had very excellent taste in her own right, was nevertheless expected to act as a mistress for the first time in her life. As such, she felt that she needed Elizabeth's support and opinions to feel equal to the task, something which Elizabeth knew was patently false. Still, she did understand Jane's insecurity, and she wanted above all things to be of use to her sister.

The second reason was, of course, the fact that she would very likely be in a position to enjoy the company of her increasingly ardent suitor. Mr. Darcy had been so attentive to her that she was left almost breathless with anticipation at every opportunity to see him. She was certain that he was nearing a resolution—he wanted to display his regard before neighborhood, and she understood his reasons, but on the other hand, she was impatient for him to formalize their relationship. If nothing else, it would put her forever beyond the reach of Samuel Lucas, who, although he had not made any overt attempts to coerce her since his failed proposal, still unnerved her with his dark looks and patent frustration.

So, against Elizabeth's better judgment, she put herself once again within range of Miss Bingley's contempt and accompanied Jane to participate in the tour of Netherfield.

Somewhat surprisingly, the first part of the afternoon was very agreeable for Elizabeth. Jane was wide-eyed and excited at the possibilities for her new home, and Anne and Georgiana were as delightful and pleasant as ever, and though the specter of Miss Bingley and her disapproving glares was ever present, Elizabeth was eventually able to put the supercilious woman from her mind. Soon, she was enjoying herself with her sister and friends, ignoring the woman's steadily worsening mood.

Alas, the cheerful nature of *most* of the party was not to last, and it was an innocuous conversation between Elizabeth and Jane which finally broke through the woman's veneer of good manners and unleashed a storm of words.

They had just viewed the mistress's chambers, thereby completing the tour of the house, and had returned to the drawing room as Elizabeth and Jane conversed about the decorations in the room.

"I am certain the room is quite fine the way it is, Lizzy," said Jane. "I should not wish to change the decorations merely to impress my own stamp upon the house."

"Oh, I agree completely," responded Elizabeth with a fond smile for her self-effacing sister. "If the décor meets with your approval and tastes, then there is little reason to waste resources by changing it. But I was not suggesting any such thing."

"Then why do you think I should make changes to the bedchamber? It seemed very fine to me."

"If you *are* happy with it, Jane, then there is no need to change the furnishings. However, I believe I know you, and the room seems a little dark for your tastes. To be honest, I believe it is more appropriate to *my* tastes than yours, as you usually tend toward lighter and airier arrangements than the room is decorated with at present. It is your right as the future mistress of the estate to make any changes you please, if another arrangement would suit you better."

"And what do *you* know of the matter, Eliza Bennet?" an angry voice broke into their discussion.

Glancing up, Elizabeth understood in an instant that Miss Bingley was angry and appeared to be intent upon provoking an altercation. Wishing to avoid any unpleasant scenes, she tried to take a conciliatory tack.

"My apologies, Miss Bingley, I was merely suggesting that Jane consult her own conscience over whether she should redecorate the mistress's rooms."

"What—is it not good enough for *you*?" was the sneered reply. "I will have you know that I redesigned those rooms myself when I arrived at Netherfield. I think I am far more accomplished and have much better taste in such matters than an ignorant country adventuress such as yourself."

Though Elizabeth's sense of outrage was aroused by the woman's condescending and rude comments, Elizabeth, still hoping to avoid a scene, bowed her head slightly and apologized once again.

"I am sorry, Miss Bingley, but I do not wish to cause a scene."

"By my estimation, you have already caused one! You sully everything you touch and cannot keep yourself from interfering in matters which you cannot understand. You cannot even begin to comprehend your utter unsuitability for the role which you and your sister attempt to fill, and you drag down all with whom you come into contact by your very presence!"

"Miss Bingley!" snapped Elizabeth, incensed at the woman's inability to hold her tongue. "I will allow you to make whatever pointed comments you would like about me, for I do not care three straws for your opinion. However, I shall *not* allow you to speak so of my sister. Jane is one hundred times the lady that *you* will ever be!"

Miss Bingley's answering glare was pure poison, and for a moment, Elizabeth thought the woman would try to physically assault her. However, after clenching and unclenching her fists for several moments, Miss Bingley responded in a voice which carried such animosity that Elizabeth knew she would be lying on the floor at that very moment if she could be slain by a mere glance.

"A lady! That is another presumption which you perpetuate without any understanding of what it means to aspire to such a title. Do you not recall the discussion we had about the merits of an accomplished woman? Neither you nor your sister hold a fraction of the achievements necessary to hold such a title."

"And I recall you, *Miss Bingley*," said Elizabeth between clenched teeth, "in one moment claim that there were only a few women who could hold the title and then in the next breath say you knew many. It seems to me you have no more idea of what it takes to make such a claim than I."

"I certainly know better than you! *You* are no *lady*, Eliza Bennet. In fact, you are the furthest thing from a lady to which *any* could aspire. You prance about and practice your wiles upon Mr. Darcy, enticing him with your *fine eyes*, impertinent nature, and pretensions toward true gentility, but we both know that there is only *one thing* which attracts Mr. Darcy to you, do we not?"

Elizabeth tried to break in, to prevent Miss Bingley from saying something which she would regret all of her life, but the words themselves had taken on a life of their own, and nothing could stop their inexorable delivery. Glancing around, Elizabeth could see the other three ladies caught speechless by the torrent of words, but they appeared no better able to gain control of the situation than she.

"But then again," continued Miss Bingley, finally displaying the full effect of the malice which Elizabeth had always known she possessed, "I suppose that is the only thing for which you are any use, is it not? How many other men have you practiced upon before Mr. Darcy arrived on the scene? I suppose you display yourself to all and sundry regularly in order to perfect your ability to catch the notice of a richer man. I suppose your *mother* has taught you well indeed, for I doubt you shall *ever* be worthy of anything more than being a rich man's whore!"

Anne gasped at the vindictive and foul word, almost in one voice with the rest of the ladies who were a witness to the final retreat of Miss Bingley's decorum and even her sanity. Such a word was not spoken in polite society—especially by a woman who had pretensions toward the highest tiers! An insult of this magnitude could not go unanswered!

"Miss Bingley!" admonished Anne. "How dare you speak in such language?"

The other woman's look of contempt caught Anne by surprise. "*You* are no better, allowing yourself to be taken in by this . . . this . . . thing! I cannot believe a woman of your social standing—the daughter of a woman of the standing of Lady Catherine de Bourgh no less—could be so witless as to be ignorant of what these two trumped-up mannequins truly are."

"You throw my mother's name about most casually, do you not? I would question your meaning, as I do not believe you have even met her. What can you mean by it?"

Miss Bingley threw her hands up in the air. "Of course I have never met your mother! I was speaking in general terms of your mother as the scion of an old and noble family. I am surprised that she did not speak to you of these things, as you certainly appear to have little understanding of the innate quality of nobility."

"And that is where you are wrong, Miss Bingley," retorted Anne. "I have listened while my mother spoke at great length of her superiority of herself and those with whom she associated. Trust me, I have heard everything you have said from those who are much more arrogant—and have much more *reason* to be arrogant—and I have heard much more than you could ever hope to understand."

"Has the entire world gone mad?" cried Caroline.

"No, we have not," Elizabeth cut in, her eyes blazing. In looking at Elizabeth, Anne was struck again by the sense of admiration and affection she felt for this young woman—Elizabeth allowed no one to intimidate her and stood up for her principles in a manner which was rarely seen. Anne could only hope to emulate her in word and deed, and she hoped for the opportunity to be her friend for many years to come.

"You know nothing of true nobility, Miss Bingley. I beg your pardon, Anne, but *I have* been acquainted with Lady Catherine, and I can tell you that I do not agree with her assessment of what nobility truly is."

When Anne waved her off impatiently, Elizabeth continued:

"Lady Catherine is a woman of decided opinions, and, yes, she truly believes herself to possess this true nobility of which you speak by virtue of the accident of her birth. But unfortunately, she quite mistakes that matter. True nobility is determined by one's actions and attitudes, not by the chance of birth."

"Of course *you* would think so," snarled Miss Bingley, her unpleasant sneer making its triumphant return. "Those who are born in squalor, rollicking in the mud with the dogs, must cling to such beliefs to justify their own existence."

Elizabeth's eyes widened, and her countenance took on an expression of true outrage, but Anne, seeking to end this farce of an argument, responded first.

"Upon my word you have a high opinion of yourself, Miss Bingley, considering you are merely the *daughter* of a *tradesman*. By your conduct, one would think that you were the queen herself."

Caroline gasped at the insult and stared at Anne. Anne's response was a glare which conveyed all her contempt and dislike.

"None of us are impressed with your opinions or your person and manners. Now, be silent, and do not continue to prove your utter lack of breeding and intelligence as you do every time you open your mouth!"

Miss Bingley glanced around at the room, taking in all the unfriendly faces— even Georgiana and Jane, both of whom had not said a word, were gazing at her with dislike and contempt.

"Georgiana," begged Miss Bingley, "surely you can see what this woman is doing to your family. *I* should have been your sister—not this pretentious upstart."

"All I can see, Miss Bingley, is a woman who imagines herself to be much higher than she merits and who does not care who she steps over to get what she wants."

"But your brother—"

"*My brother* is no friend of yours," was the pitiless reply. "William has only put up with your airs and your attentions out of respect for *your* brother. There was never any chance of his marrying you. You blame Elizabeth for interfering with your conquest, but my brother never would have offered for you.

"I must tell you how delighted I am that he and Elizabeth are moving closer to an understanding—I cannot wait for her to be my sister. I never wanted you for a sister. My brother never wanted you for a wife."

Anne stood still, shocked at the implacable reply which issued forth from Georgiana's lips, while at the same time proud of her cousin. The words, unkind though they were, needed to be said, and when Georgiana was finished, Miss Bingley almost seemed to wilt.

But then the woman's rage returned, and with a look which almost approached madness, she gazed at each of the others in turn.

"I have *never* been so *insulted* in my entire life!" screeched Miss Bingley, completely abandoning any hint of propriety. "I will *not* be abused in the confines of my own home by those who have proved themselves as witless as sheep!"

She abruptly turned on her heel and strode to the door, and flinging it open, she bellowed for the butler. Anne exchanged glances with the other ladies, wondering what the woman was up to now, but a series of uncomprehending stares met her eyes. It was only a moment before the butler stepped into the room and glanced around, his eyes stopping to rest upon Anne with an expression of puzzlement.

"Roberts!" commanded Miss Bingley. "These *women* have offended me with their behavior, and I will not have it. You will gather up some footmen and have them removed from the house immediately!"

Anne gasped as Miss Bingley made her demand, wondering at the woman's lack of common sense and the departure of any sort of composure. She then glanced back at Roberts, who was staring at her with a questioning look, clearly asking her for directions. Anne had known for some time that the servants in the house had no use for the demanding and rude Miss Bingley, and since Anne was the eldest lady living in the house, he obviously considered her to be the one to whom he could turn for direction.

Surreptitiously, hoping Miss Bingley would not notice the gesture and lose an even greater measure of her sanity, Anne shook her head at the man. It turned out to be unnecessary, though, as he had already turned back to Miss Bingley, an apologetic expression on his face.

"Do I understand you correctly, Miss Bingley?" asked the butler. "You wish me to throw the master's betrothed, her sister, and Mr. Darcy's relations from the house?"

"Are you witless or simply deaf?" demanded Miss Bingley. "I will not have them in this house for an instant longer. I wish them ejected forthwith!"

"Perhaps we should wait for the master to return," responded the butler in a conciliatory tone of voice. "You could then discuss the situation and the affront with him before making any rash decisions."

Miss Bingley's nostrils flared, and she affixed the unfortunate man with an unpleasant glare. "Roberts, you will expel them from the house immediately, or I will have you removed from your position!"

The butler stared at her for several more moments before shaking his head once again. "I apologize most fervently, Miss Bingley, but I cannot comply with your request. Mr. Bingley is the master, and I know that he would never wish for me to order the removal of his beloved from the house. You must wait until the master returns and is able to sort through what has happened here. Now, in the meantime, I will call for the housekeeper and have her conduct you to your rooms, where you may regain your composure while you wait for your brother."

By now, Miss Bingley's eyes were almost popping out of her face. "Roberts, you are hereby relieved of your duties!" she screeched. "You will not receive any recommendation, nor will you receive your severance—leave this house at once! I shall command the footmen to remove them myself!"

"And it will do you little good," interjected the voice of the housekeeper. The woman had entered the room while Miss Bingley had been arguing with the butler, and her face was adorned with a disapproving and distasteful expression.

"Our allegiance is to Mr. Bingley; he is the one who pays our wages. You have *no power* to dismiss *anyone* Miss Bingley. Now, if you will accompany me, I believe some time spent in solitary reflection in your room would do you a world of good. You must regain control of yourself."

Thwarted at every turn and faced with a room of condemning stares, Miss Bingley's face turned an unhealthy shade of red in her utter rage, and she rounded on Elizabeth, jabbing an accusatory finger at the young woman.

"*You!*" shrieked Miss Bingley. "This is *all your* fault!"

Then, surprising the company, she extended her fingers like talons and lunged at Elizabeth.

Fitzwilliam Darcy entered the manor house at Netherfield, eager for the opportunity to see Elizabeth again. The morning had been spent inspecting the drainage of several of the fields on the north side of the estate, and although Darcy had spent many hours at his own estate involved in very similar tasks, the prospect of involving himself in such matters in lieu of the company of his beloved was decidedly unappealing. Knowing Bingley felt much the same way filled him with a grim sort of satisfaction, but they had both exerted themselves to the task of caring for the estate. Of course, Richard, in his typical manner, found their distraction rather amusing and let no opportunity to mock his companions pass him by.

"I believe, Bingley, that Darcy is already basking in the light of his fair lady," stated Richard as they entered the house.

"I do believe he is," responded Bingley with a grin. "I find I wish to join him as soon as may be and indulge in some basking of my own."

"You are both hopeless," said Richard with a forlorn shake of his head. "I daresay love serves no other purpose than to addle the brain and pull a gentleman away from his pursuits."

"Wonderful, is it not?" jibed Darcy. "You should try it, Richard—I do not doubt that the right woman could help even *you* see the light!"

Richard's eyes widened dramatically, and he stared at Darcy with mock consternation. "Who are you, and what have you done with my cousin?"

As Darcy opened his mouth to respond, he suddenly heard the sound of voices raised in anger, and his words died on his lips. Sharing a glance with his companions, Darcy forgot about his dusty clothing and, turning on his heel, began hurrying through the house in the direction of the noise.

It was not long before a great shriek was heard, and Darcy broke into a run, sensing rather than seeing his companions matching his pace. They stormed through the halls and came to the door of the main drawing room, seeing a pair of footmen milling around the door in agitated confusion.

One of the footmen spied the approaching gentlemen and gestured urgently. "Mr. Bingley! Come quickly!"

Not requiring any further impetus, Darcy rushed to the room, stopping when he entered, astonished at the scene which greeted his eyes. On the far side of the room, his beloved stood, locked in a struggle with his host's sister. Elizabeth's pretty yellow gown was ripped and torn about the sleeves and neck, her hair had been pulled out of its coif and sat askew on her head, and angry red welts were beginning to appear through the tears in the sleeves of her gown. She struggled, attempting to extricate herself from the other woman's grasp, but to no avail.

Miss Bingley, by contrast, was shrieking with rage, assaulting Elizabeth in the most reprehensible manner, pulling at her hair, her dress, and anything else she could lay her hands upon, while Anne and the housekeeper attempted to keep her from Elizabeth, and Jane tried to interpose herself between the two women. The butler was wringing his hands, obviously trying to determine the best course to pursue.

Immediately understanding the man's dilemma—he could not, after all, lay hands on a gentlewoman—Darcy exchanged a glance with the other two men and rushed forward, forcing himself in between Elizabeth and Miss Bingley as Bingley grasped his sister's hands and forced them away while shouting at her.

"Caroline!" bellowed Bingley. "What is the meaning of this?"

Miss Bingley, however, was beyond reason, and she screamed all the louder, making even more determined attempts to lay her hands on Elizabeth again, something Darcy would not allow to happen. Mr. Bingley called the footmen to attend, and with their combined assistance—along with that of the unfortunate butler—they manhandled Miss Bingley from the room while she screamed insults at them and fought to free herself from their grasp.

Darcy, though, was insensible of anything but the welfare of the young woman who was now ensconced in his arms. He knew it was not proper for them to be situated that close to one another, but propriety be damned! This was the woman he loved!

"Elizabeth, are you well?"

Sniffling, Elizabeth nodded her head against his chest.

Jane stepped forward and smiled. "I shall care for her, Mr. Darcy," said she, taking her sister from him. Elizabeth clung to her like a drowning woman, and they were soon joined by Georgiana and Anne, who directed the sisters to the chesterfield, murmuring words of comfort.

Seeing that something was needed to calm the nerves and quiet anxieties, Darcy motioned to the housekeeper and instructed her to deliver a carafe of wine forthwith. The woman nodded and left to complete her instructions, and Darcy moved to sit on an adjacent chair, studying the woman he loved.

Like Bingley, Darcy had long suspected Miss Bingley of being behind Mr. Lucas's dogged pursuit of Elizabeth, but he had not known her hatred ran this deep. No matter what had occurred, to think that Miss Bingley would stoop to such cruel revenge and lose her equanimity in such a fashion as to allow her to physically assault Elizabeth . . . well, it was nothing short of astonishing! How could the woman ever have considered herself exalted enough in person, mind, and manners as to be worthy of the first circles? It was truly incredible! He would not marry her, even if she was the *only* option between him and a solitary life!

Richard joined him, sitting in the chair next to him, and he appeared as Darcy felt. They exchanged a glance—Richard's questioning, whereas Darcy's was more of a grimace in response.

The wine was delivered directly, and Darcy instructed the housekeeper to ensure each of the ladies was given a generous portion. It broke his heart to see his Elizabeth. She was usually so calm and self-possessed, but her hands were visibly shaking as she accepted the goblet. She swallowed a healthy portion of the vintage before setting it on the table in front of her and returning to the comforting embrace of her sister. The housekeeper once again appeared, this time carrying a shawl, which she draped around Elizabeth's shoulders, protecting her modesty. Elizabeth gratefully drew the fabric around her like a shield.

He peered at his cousin Anne, noting the anger in her visage, and he raised an eyebrow in her direction.

"Anne, what happened here?"

"Caroline Bingley happened," spat Anne, with considerably more venom than Darcy had thought she possessed. "In all my life, I have never witnessed such a scene, Fitzwilliam—such disrespect, such total lack of propriety, such lack of anything resembling common decency cannot be excused! She abused and insulted poor Elizabeth beyond the limit of anything which anyone should be required to endure. Upon my word, I do not think I have ever met someone as reprehensible as Miss Bingley!"

Though Darcy privately agreed with Anne's assessment, he was interested in facts and not condemnations. He was about to say as much when a noise from the entrance caught his attention, and he turned to espy Bingley, who had apparently just entered the room and was now gazing at Anne with undisguised horror. Anne immediately blushed and slumped slightly in her chair.

"My apologies, Mr. Bingley," said Anne. "I am afraid I allowed my sense of outrage to overcome my tongue. I am afraid I have mortified you."

Bingley immediately composed himself. "Miss de Bourgh, if I *have* been mortified today, I do not think it has anything to do with *you*. Please, think nothing more of it."

"Still," interjected Richard, "I believe we should focus on the facts and leave the emotions behind."

"I agree, Cousin" replied Anne, inclining her head slightly.

Darcy looked around, and seeing that Bingley was still somewhat dazed by the manner in which he had witnessed his sister behaving, he exchanged a glance with Colonel Fitzwilliam and allowed the military man to take charge.

The events of the day were canvassed and discussed, and although Elizabeth appeared too overcome by emotion to add much to the tale, Anne—with Georgiana's occasional help—was more than able to disseminate the pertinent information. And although Richard took charge initially, Darcy was heartened to see Bingley gain confidence throughout the questioning, such that, by the end, he was all but conducting it himself. Whereas Richard had dwelt upon the pure facts of the situation, Bingley tried to delve into the motivations of his sister. As a result, more than words and actions were discussed—Miss Bingley's facial expressions and posture during the events, among other things, were also examined in great detail.

At the end of it all, when Miss Bingley's guilt was all but established by their combined testimony, Bingley rose to his feet and approached the Bennet sisters. Stopping before them, he knelt on one knee and grasped Elizabeth's hand in his own directing an earnest look at her.

"Miss Elizabeth, I fear I owe you a most abject apology for my sister's infamous treatment of you. I know that no apology can ever make amends for the mortification and embarrassment to which you have been subjected, yet I offer it all the same. I cannot imagine what Caroline was thinking to have induced her to act in such a manner."

An impish smile came over Elizabeth's face—an echo of her usual playful self. "Oh, I am sorry, Mr. Bingley. I was not aware that you had changed your name."

Bingley frowned in confusion while Anne giggled and Richard guffawed, both of the having caught Elizabeth's meaning. Seeing Bingley's perplexed appearance, Elizabeth took pity upon him, covering his hand with her free hand.

"Mr. Bingley, I am afraid I cannot accept *your* apologies, as *you* have nothing for which to apologize. You have been everything that is good and welcoming and can have no reason to repine for *your own* behavior."

As he caught on, his own answering grin was brief and lacked its usual gleam. "Even so, Miss Elizabeth, I would that there was something I could have done to prevent this scene from occurring. I had of course known that Caroline held a grudge against you, but I did not suspect for a moment she would act thus to extract her revenge. I am most humiliated by her behavior."

"I am sorry, sir, but we are to be brother and sister. Must you address me in such a formal fashion?"

Darcy was enthralled once again by her resilience and ability to alleviate the tension of the situation and put the company at ease. The smile Bingley directed at her was genuine in its affection and relief.

"Of course, but only if you shall call me 'Charles.'"

"It shall be my pleasure, Charles."

Elizabeth was pensive and silent for several moments, but at length, she peered back at the company and dropped her gaze in embarrassment. "I thank you all for your care and concern, but I am truly recovered. I fear that my first inclination from this morning was correct—I should not have come."

"*That* is where you are wrong, Elizabeth," Bingley contradicted her firmly. "I would not have you feel as if you are required to avoid my home due to the feelings of one of its inhabitants. This is an estate *I* have leased, not *Caroline*, and I would have you feel you are welcome at *any time*."

Bingley paused and sighed with regret. "In fact, I believe that at this very moment, you, my soon-to-be sister, are far more welcome in my house than my own sister by birth."

An expression of dismay appeared on Elizabeth's face. "Oh, Mr. Bingley, please do not break with your sister over this. Her disappointment is keen, and my being so much in evidence cannot be easy for her. I must admit that my own conduct and words since she came to Hertfordshire are not above reproach. I beg of you not to allow this incident to lead to an estrangement."

At this, Bingley's face became stony, an expression which Darcy had rarely seen upon his friend's face. In fact, the only time Darcy had seen it in recent memory was when he had made his confession regarding his actions in concealing the knowledge of Jane Bennet's presence in town. He reflected that his ever-congenial friend did possess the ability to intimidate when he was truly angry.

"With all due respect, Elizabeth, I think I should be the judge of that," was his emotionless response. "Did you ever overtly insult my sister? Did you physically attack or malign her? Did you conspire with anyone to separate her from someone with whom you knew she possessed a mutual regard?"

Elizabeth's eyes darted to Darcy's face, and she blushed before gazing down at her hands. She made no vocal reply, merely shaking her head in the negative.

"In that case, whatever you believe your faults to have been, they cannot in any way compare with what Caroline has done to you this afternoon. She has been a selfish being all her life, wrapped up in her own pride and the meanness of her opinion of everyone she believes to be beneath her. I *cannot* and *will not* allow her actions to go unpunished. If there is to be an estrangement between us, then the fault must lie with her where it belongs—for once in her life, she must take responsibility for her own actions!"

His eyes turned upon the face of his fiancée, and his gaze softened. "And besides, it is my understanding that while her physical assault was made upon you alone, her words were meant to be as cutting to my dearest Jane as to you. Since Jane is to be my wife, she will be under my protection, and as such, Caroline's insults must merit a response. If I do nothing, she will feel as if she may trample all over my beloved however she pleases. I will not have that!"

Elizabeth could only nod in understanding of his points and rest her head once again on her sister's shoulder, clearly feeling drained by all that had happened. Darcy rose to his feet and approached her. Taking the seat on Elizabeth's other side from Jane—he directed a warm smile at his sister who had vacated it in order to allow him to be near his love—he claimed her hands from Bingley, caressing them in a soothing manner. His relations smiled at his actions, clearly approving of them—if there had been any doubt in anyone's mind as to his feelings for Elizabeth, those doubts had, with his display, now been put to rest.

"Which brings us to the next point," Richard spoke up. "I believe it is best to remove the ladies—especially Miss Bennet and Miss Elizabeth—from the premises, as there will almost certainly be more unpleasantness before the day is through."

"An excellent suggestion, Fitzwilliam," replied Bingley, rising to his feet.

He looked at Jane and cocked an eyebrow. The message was instantly received and understood, and Jane, with her typical grace, extended an invitation for the ladies to dine at Longbourn that evening, claiming her mother would love to have them.

After further discussion, it was decided that they would all depart without delay for Longbourn and that Richard would accompany them. Not being

particularly well acquainted with Miss Bingley—or even well liked by the lady!—
he, it was determined, should be absent for the evening as well. For once, the
irrepressible colonel did not press the matter, much to Darcy's relief. Within
moments of the decision being made, a message was dispatched, with one of the
Netherfield footmen leaving to inform the Bennets of the party's imminent arrival,
and the entire group set off for the neighboring estate.

His heart in his stomach, Darcy found a moment's time to converse with his
beloved before she departed, assuring her that all would be well and then
commending her to the care of her sister and his relations and bidding her farewell.
He wished more than anything to accompany her, but his friend needed him—he
would not leave Bingley in this difficult time.

When the ladies had been sent on their way with their escort, Bingley led his friend
back to the drawing room, his mind awash with emotions as he wondered how it
had all come to this. What could he say—what could he *do*—to make everything
right again, not only with his fiancée, but also with the young woman who would
soon be his sister? He was quickly coming to esteem Elizabeth Bennet above
everyone else of his acquaintance other than his dear Jane and his closest friend.
How could he possibly make it up to her?

In the drawing room, Bingley grasped the abandoned decanter of wine and,
taking an unused goblet, filled it and drained it in one swallow. He offered some to
Darcy, who refused, and then he filled his glass again, this time taking measured
sips of the liquid while peering moodily out the window.

"Bingley, I would ask you not to do this to yourself," said Darcy from behind
him.

"My own sister, Darcy," rasped Bingley in response. "I knew she hated
Elizabeth, knew she envied and despised her, but I never imagined she could stoop
this low. How could I have? Caroline has always tried to be scrupulously proper
when in the company of others, regardless of how she behaved in the confines of
our home. How could she do this? How could I allow her to the opportunity to do
so?"

Silence was his response, and at length, when it grew oppressive, he turned to
stare his friend in the eye. Darcy was regarding him with a commiserating
expression, but while he appeared to be compassionate and understanding, his
words were implacable.

"You may not wish to hear this, Bingley, but I have always known what your
sister was and suspected she would go to great lengths to achieve her desires. A
part of me has always been somewhat surprised that she never attempted to
compromise herself with me in order to force a marriage; I suspect she has never
done so because she knows that I would never put up with it and that she would
only ruin her own reputation in the attempt.

"As far as her behavior goes, you cannot force her to behave the way you wish,
nor can you stand over her during her every waking moment in order to force her
good conduct. In addition, it would not be fair to her for you to break with her on
the *suspicion* of her eventual poor behavior. Until recently, she had never done
anything to warrant such censure from you, and though she has not been blameless
in her actions, words, and deeds, your response has been prudent and
appropriate."

"But I *knew* her feelings for Elizabeth," responded Bingley, his hands gesturing wildly as he paced the room in agitation. "With her behavior toward my dearest Jane, I should have extracted some measure of apology from her for Jane at the very least and then left her to stay with the Hursts until the wedding."

"You may remember that I was a party to the offense given to your fiancée, Bingley."

Bingley's answering glare was fierce. "Do not, in any way, attempt to compare your actions with that of my sisters, especially Caroline! You were motivated by a sincere concern for my well-being in the face of what you thought was Jane's indifference to me. Caroline was acting for no other reason than a selfish concern for her own interests and her perceived standing in society. And this does not even take into account her ill-conceived recommendation of Georgiana as a prospective bride. You know her sole purpose in this was to bring a union between her and yourself closer to fruition."

His friend grimaced and shook his head. "My reasons, much as I wished them to be so altruistic, were unfortunately motivated in part by my desire for distance in my own effort to remain unaffected by Miss Elizabeth."

"Much good though it did you," said Bingley with a smirk. "Still, regardless of that ulterior motive, your overall intentions were good—and do not try to deny it, Darcy!"

A shrug was his only response. Bingley sighed and squared his shoulders for the unpleasant business ahead.

"Let us retreat to my study, my friend, so that I may interview any staff who may have knowledge of the event."

The interviews proceeded much as Bingley would have expected. Of the servants who were near enough to have some knowledge of the altercation, the footmen, who were stationed outside the door, could only say that they heard raised voices, while the butler and housekeeper could only discuss what they witnessed once they had arrived. None could speculate upon the genesis of the argument—although the housekeeper did say she thought Miss Bingley had been in a foul temper the entire day—but of the clash which followed, all accounts were very close to what they had already been told by the ladies.

It was hardly surprising, Bingley thought to himself—he had never expected for a moment that the servants would contradict what the ladies had already told them. Anne's sense of indignation and Elizabeth's obvious distress had been genuine—or else they had all been superb actresses!

Bingley was liberal with his praise of the way the staff had handled matters—the butler had been correct in his assessment of Bingley's reaction to Caroline's demands and had acted properly in the face of the difficult circumstances, and the housekeeper had done no less. After a stern caution as to the consequences of any rumors which resulted from the day's events (in truth, he need not have bothered—the servants were all locals who knew the Bennets and held the eldest Bennet sisters in the highest of respect), they were dismissed, leaving him alone with Darcy to consider their next moves.

"Would you like my assistance in confronting your sister?"

Bingley grimaced, understanding immediately—as he suspected Darcy did as well—exactly how *that* scenario would turn out. "No, Darcy, I should think not. In fact, I believe that you should be as far away as possible when I brave the lioness in her den."

Darcy smirked at the analogy before his countenance once again took on a sober cast. "I believe you are correct, Bingley. But there is one thing I must make clear before you leave to confront her."

With a tension Bingley had rarely seen in his friend, Darcy stood and paced the room in front of the desk, and though Bingley felt he knew what was coming, it did not make the actuality—or the necessity—any easier to manage.

"Though it gives me great pain to do this, my friend, it is clear that I cannot overlook the way in which your sister has treated the woman I love. Therefore, I shall have no choice but to sever my acquaintance with her completely. I will convey this to her myself if you wish it, but from this time forward, Caroline will *not* be allowed to use my name in society, nor will she be permitted to enter any of my homes. I will not publish specifically what has happened here, of course, but I *will* publish the fact that she is no longer associated with me in any way.

"*If* she apologizes—sincerely—and *if* Elizabeth specifically requests forgiveness, I may be persuaded to relent."

A slight smile came over his face. "I *have* admitted my fault of implacable resentment, and I would not like Elizabeth to think I have not changed for the better, after all."

Bingley laughed in response, grateful for the lessening of the tension while thinking back to the night of *that* particular argument.

"Regardless, my friend, she will forever be a persona non grata to me if those conditions are not met. I apologize for the mortification this causes you, but I can do nothing else."

"Of course you cannot, Darcy. I believe that I also can do no less. Though Elizabeth was Caroline's specific target, my Jane has not been spared her venom. Your assistance in this matter will not be required—I believe it would do more harm than good for you to speak to her. I will inform her of everything, and she will be gone from the house by first light."

Darcy nodded. "Very well then. I believe you may find me in my chambers until it is time for dinner. What say you to taking our evening repast in my sitting room?"

Bingley regarded his friend with a sly smile. "Oh, come now, Darcy, I believe there is someone else in whose company you would prefer to dine, and I am sure she would be grateful for your presence and support. Why dine with me when you may do so in the presence of another whom you hold in the highest regard?"

"Are you sure, Bingley?" queried Darcy with a slight frown. "I would not leave you to take on this task by yourself—I can stay and provide you all the support you require."

"Which is why you are such a good friend, Darcy. But I believe it would be best for *all* who do not bear the name Bingley to be gone from Netherfield this evening. If you hurry, I warrant that you can still make it to Longbourn in time for dinner."

A relieved-looking Darcy clasped Bingley's shoulder in a gesture of solidarity and support. "In that case, my friend, I believe I shall take the opportunity to do exactly that. I shall change and be on my horse directly."

They clasped hands in silent farewell before Darcy left the room, his eagerness to once again be in the presence of Miss Elizabeth evident in his gait and his carriage. Bingley was left to the brooding silence of his study, steeling himself to make plans for the upcoming confrontation.

Waiting only until he was certain his friend had left the house, Bingley gathered his resolve and made his way up to the family apartments for the expected battle with his sister. He knocked on the door to her rooms, which was opened by a timid maid who looked fearfully at the master.

"The mistress has commanded me to allow no one access to her chambers on the threat of dismissal."

Smiling kindly at the young woman, Bingley reassured her. "I am aware of my sister's temper and her demands, and I will assure your continued employment despite her threats. Please, take yourself to the servant's quarters and speak to Mrs. Jones about some supper. You do not need to be here for this."

A timorous smile met his instructions, and the maid hurriedly curtseyed and departed, as eager to get away from her mistress as Bingley was himself, if he were to be honest with himself.

He entered the room and found his sister reclining on the couch with a wet compress pressed against her head. Her face was still a mask of displeasure, but she appeared to have regained at least her sense of propriety, little good though it would do her at this late stage.

"You know my instructions, Clara," said she without looking up. "Whoever it is, I am not taking visitors this evening. Send them away."

"Your maid cannot keep me from this room, Caroline," admonished Bingley. "I have sent her away to get herself some supper, and if I hear of any ill-treatment of her person, I will remove her from your employ and into my own forthwith."

A deep sigh escaped Caroline's lips, and she opened her eyes and glared at him. With an exaggerated effort, she pulled herself into an upright position.

"Can you not see that I have a headache, Charles? Whatever you wish to discuss, it can wait until morning."

"I do not care if you are on your very deathbed, Caroline!" snapped Bingley. "Given the events of the day, I shall *not* wait another instant to have this discussion, and although I know there is no defending your actions, I believe I owe it to you to hear your version of the events before any decision is to be made."

Caroline's answering scowl might have been more impressive had Bingley not already had a very good idea of her culpability in this matter.

"If I am to be summarily convicted of *whatever* offenses those *ladies* have laid at my door, then why should I bother defending myself to you? You will give little credence to my words while you are tied to the apron strings of that little piece you mean to marry."

"Caroline, be *silent!*" snapped Bingley. "Your very words deepen the hole which you have dug for yourself, and I do not wish to be subjected to your vitriol. I will not force you to tell your side of what happened today, but I would appeal to you to tell me if there is anything which will in part explain what has occurred."

The disdain in Caroline's face was evident, and she sniffed while pushing the compress more firmly against her head. "Eliza Bennet was offensive and rude, as she always is. She insulted my taste and the décor which I have chosen for certain rooms, and she struts about this house as if she and her sister own it."

"That is not what I have been told."

"Obviously, she would wish to slant the matter in her favor — you should have spoken to me first."

"*You* were in no condition to speak to me. And in spite of what you believe, Elizabeth was too upset and shaken to speak to me of the matter—she barely spoke two words the entire time. I have my information from the other ladies."

"Confederates, obviously," said Caroline with a sneer, "her *sister*, who can be counted on to support her own blood in this matter, and Anne de Bourgh, who has been condescending and unpleasant the entire time she has been here. It is no surprise that *they* would support her version of the events."

"And what of Miss Darcy?" demanded Bingley. "You claim the closest confidence and friendship with that young lady, yet she supported Anne's *version* of the events in every particular. What is your response to that?"

"She has been taken in by Eliza. There is no other explanation."

Bingley threw his hands up in disgust. "So, you expect me to believe your version of the events over that of *four* ladies of impeccable manners and decorum, not to mention that espoused by the servants?"

"If your loyalty is to your own blood relations as it should be."

"I believe I must refer back to our conversation about where my loyalties must lie, Caroline," snapped Bingley. "If Jane or Elizabeth owned even the slightest measure of blame for this farce, I would be willing to at least understand your behavior. But regardless of the fact that Elizabeth attempted to take some of the blame onto herself, I know for a fact that it was not her doing.

"What were you thinking, Caroline? To demand that the servants throw *my* fiancée from the house—I can scarcely give credit to it, yet I find there is no way to refute it. I had to soothe ruffled feathers among the staff to keep them from walking out on me. How could you do such a thing?"

"The staff is every bit as impertinent and disobliging as Eliza Bennet—you had best remove them and replace them with others from town."

"Do *not* presume to dictate to me how to handle the staff," said Bingley darkly. "I have the highest confidence in their abilities and characters. But regardless of your opinions of the servants, I will not allow you to turn my attention from this matter—we are here to discuss *your* actions and attitudes, not the abilities of the servants."

The siblings stared one another down until Caroline ultimately looked away. Bingley smiled grimly—there was no way, he knew, that she would be able to shape the events into any form which would allow her to be anything but the sole instigator of the unpleasantness, and though she was his flesh and blood, Bingley would not allow her to escape the consequences.

"So, what do you intend to do, Charles? Of what shall your judgment of the situation consist? Am I to be treated as a disobedient child, forced into penance so that my betters may glory in their superiority?"

"If that is your wish," countered Bingley with a flippancy which immediately had Caroline's nostrils flaring. "Can you give any justification for your actions this morning?"

"None that would matter to you, given the fact that you already appear to believe that tart's version of events implicitly."

"I should have guessed," was Bingley's reply. He paced the room for several moments, agitated at his sister's continued recalcitrance and inability to accept the fault for her own actions. There was only one option.

"In that case, Caroline, you leave me no other option but to send you to stay with the Hursts."

Caroline sneered at her brother even as her anger darkened her complexion. "I could have predicted that you would betray me and throw me aside for these Hertfordshire chits."

"If you would give me any reason at all to defend you, then I would be happy to do so, but your actions in this manner are indefensible.

"And do not think me ignorant of the base words you threw in Elizabeth's direction this afternoon. I cannot tell you how embarrassed I am that my own sister would use such a word to describe the sister of my betrothed—a woman, I might add, who is possessed of the highest character and morality, despite what you have thought of her in your jealousy and envy."

"So it is 'Elizabeth' now, is it? If I did not already possess ample evidence that she has taken *you* in as well, the manner of your address now confirms the matter."

"*Elizabeth* gave me leave to address her so familiarly in the aftermath of your unconscionable assault!" barked Bingley. "*She* possesses the gentle manners to which you yourself ascribe, and she was willing to forgive me for your trespass, though she should perhaps have castigated me severely for not exerting any control over you and preventing her embarrassment!

"Do you know, Caroline," continued Bingley after a moment's silence, "that she actually urged me to forgive you, in spite of what you have done? Rather than focusing on her anger or on any desire for revenge, she begged me not to break with you over this. *That* is exactly how *taken in* I am by my future sister. Save your barbs for someone who deserves them, Caroline—Elizabeth does not!"

Caroline's face colored, but she remained silent, which was, Bingley thought, a change from what her normal reaction would be. His accusatory and sardonic manner of speaking seemed to have finally worked their way through her conceit and superiority, and she now seemed to understand she had passed the point where she could influence him in any manner. Grimly, he turned to leave, not wishing to spend any further time in her bitter and twisted presence.

Before he removed himself from the room, however, he turned and looked back at her. "I do not understand what you have become, Caroline. You were bright and precocious as a child, yet as an adult, you have become mean-spirited and obsessed with your position in society. You had best use your time away to rediscover those qualities.

"And you may forget about a reconciliation between us until you apologize—sincerely—to everyone who was offended by your words and actions today. Until then, you are no longer welcome in my house, nor are you welcome at my wedding. I cannot speak for Louisa, but I have had enough of your disdain for others."

"Such an apology will *never* be offered!" cried Caroline in one last act of defiance.

"Then our estrangement will be of a permanent nature."

He thought once again to leave, but he could not do so before he made the full extent of her situation apparent to her.

"I will also caution you to keep what has happened here a complete secret and not attempt to blacken Elizabeth's reputation in any fashion. Do not underestimate Darcy's power to exact retribution if you try his patience. And do not attempt to use Darcy's name any further in society, as he has decided to cut all ties with you."

That more than anything else seemed to pierce Caroline's hauteur. She blanched in response, understanding the implications immediately—to have an influential man such as Darcy sever his acquaintance with her was no small matter for Caroline's social ambitions. In fact, if Bingley were to be so bold, he would say that it destroyed her aspirations irreparably.

"I will have your dowry released to your control," continued Bingley after a moment of allowing her to reflect on the consequences of her behavior. "If the Hursts do not wish for you to stay with them, then you will be required to set up your own household and live on your own money."

This last clearly shocked Caroline, but before she could speak in response, Bingley stepped from the room, closing the door firmly behind him. He spoke with the housekeeper immediately, instructing her to have Caroline's belongings packed for an immediate departure. Then, with grim finality, he informed the entire staff of the fact that Caroline should no longer be obeyed as the mistress of the house.

Once this had all been accomplished, he retired to his chambers for the evening, partaking of a lonely meal while dreaming of the next time he would be in the presence of his angel.

For Elizabeth Bennet, the return to Longbourn was followed by her immediate retreat to the confines of her room. True to form, her mother had received the note informing her of their imminent arrival and had been in the midst of one of her nervous fits over the reasons for their departure from Netherfield. Their entry into the house had been marked by Mrs. Bennet immediately berating them for whatever they had done to incur the master of Netherfield's displeasure and bemoaning that if Mr. Bingley broke his engagement to Jane, then they would all be in danger of the hedgerows once again. And though the diatribe was not directed at her directly, Elizabeth knew in what direction her mother's thoughts ran—but the presence of her father and his stern countenance in the room had saved her from her mother's discontent.

However, when Mrs. Bennet had discovered the state of Elizabeth's dress and the bruising which was appearing on her arms and neck, her tone changed, and she gazed on her daughter with concern, demanding to know what had happened. Elizabeth, loath to speak of the scene which had occurred at Netherfield, was grateful to allow Jane to relate the events to her parents. Indeed, it had taken the combined efforts of Jane and the colonel to assure Mrs. Bennet that while there had been an incident at Netherfield, all was well, and Mr. Bingley was dealing with the situation. Moreover, he would *not* be breaking his engagement with Jane, nor would there be any delay in the nuptials, though his sister's attendance at the occasion was now in question.

Mrs. Bennet surprised everyone, immediately taking charge of the situation and ensuring that a soothing bath was drawn for her second daughter, clucking all the while about Mr. Bingley and his troubles with his sister. Elizabeth kept her own council, keeping Miss Bingley's reasons for her actions to herself. Even at this late date, she did not wish for her mother to discover her relationship with Mr. Darcy!

Once she had finished her bath, a drained Elizabeth sat in her room and reflected, with little true emotion, on the events of the day. And though she still felt some small measure of culpability over having put herself into a situation which would invite Miss Bingley's bad behavior, she knew that the woman had acted in a truly reprehensible fashion. It would be too soon if she were never to lay her eyes on Miss Bingley again!

Fortunately, Elizabeth was not allowed to wallow in her grief and self-pity for long—Jane and Anne would not permit her to indulge in her melancholy. They arrived in her room soon after she had retired to it and cajoled her out of her ill temper, convincing her to join the party for dinner—while Elizabeth would have preferred to demure, they would have nothing of it.

As it turned out, Elizabeth was glad she had allowed herself to be persuaded—Mr. Darcy arrived just as they were sitting down for the evening repast. Elizabeth, moving quickly, ensured a place for him was set next to hers, and she sat down to dinner, ignoring her mother's dark looks at his placement.

She could not have said what she consumed that evening, for her entire being was focused upon Darcy, and though at other times she might have been embarrassed at the spectacle she was displaying, on this night she did not care. His presence was comforting, and she knew that the last of her reservations had fallen away—there was nothing left to do but to agree to marry him when he asked her again.

After an intimate farewell with her chosen, she retreated to her room for the night, her head filled with expectations and longings. Her dreams that night were a mixture—in part filled with fire-breathing dragons intent upon swallowing her whole and in part with the handsome figure of her knight, who protected her against all who would do her harm. With such comforts even in her dreams, she had no cause to repine.

Chapter XVI

$\mathcal{T}$he next day dawned with some measure of comfort for those inhabiting the two neighboring estates. Charles Bingley, though sorrowful that his sister had become so bitter and twisted, was relieved when the door to the carriage closed behind Caroline and she departed Hertfordshire. She had had nothing to say to him when they had met that morning for the purpose of her exodus, rebuffing his every attempt at to extract any feelings from her, leaving Bingley resigned that her banishment would likely be of some duration.

At Longbourn, the residents there were equally reassured when a short note arrived for Jane from Mr. Bingley—though it could more accurately be said to have been *addressed* to Elizabeth—that Caroline *had* indeed departed and would not return until her good behavior and her apologies were guaranteed. As Elizabeth did not expect Caroline to ever admit her culpability in recent events, she was assured that she would never have to endure the woman's company again. That, in and of itself, was something to be celebrated.

Elizabeth had decided to be philosophical about the situation. She was essentially unharmed by Miss Bingley's actions and words—her bruises would heal quickly, and since they were primarily on her upper arms, they were, thankfully, hidden by her gown—and the woman's opinion of her meant less than nothing to Elizabeth. With Caroline's departure, one of the two main irritants in her life had been removed, and the other seemed to have been successfully cowed by the combination of Elizabeth's refusal and her father's vigilance. Considering what had occurred the day before and knowing how much worse it could have been, Elizabeth felt that for the first time in several days, things were beginning to improve.

Little did Elizabeth know that the storm winds were only beginning to blow.

The Bennet sisters were left with little with which to occupy their time that morning, as the Netherfield party was again expected for dinner that evening. When Anne had tried to cancel their engagement the night before, stating that they could not impose again so soon after their impromptu visit that evening, Mrs. Bennet waved them off, insisting that as Mr. Bingley had not been able to attend, she would not hear of them declining the invitation. The Bennets were happy to have them at their home on consecutive nights, and she would be very pleased if they would keep their engagement. Despite her misgivings, Anne had been forced to leave the engagement intact.

Thus, after a morning in which the four sisters were engaged in their own sundry pursuits, it was suggested that a walk to Meryton in the afternoon would be just the thing to occupy them until their company came for the evening repast. Donning their spencers, bonnets, and gloves, the sisters set out for a walk through the fine afternoon sun, each eager to leave recent events behind and lose themselves in an activity in which they had indulged all their lives.

While Elizabeth was not one to shop with the enthusiasm of her youngest sister—all of their outings to Meryton had become somewhat more sedate and less frenetic since Lydia's departure—on this day she was more than eager to leave her cares behind. They spent several hours perusing the various shops of Meryton, taking time to stop and take tea with their Aunt Phillips while they were in town and even making a few purchases of ribbons, a book for Elizabeth, some drawing pencils for Kitty, and some music for Mary.

They had just emerged from the spice shop—having stopped there on a commission from the cook—when a carriage passed, heading through the middle of town toward the road which led to Longbourn. Elizabeth had just realized it was the Lucas carriage when it suddenly stopped in the middle of street. The door opened, and Charlotte appeared, hiked up her skirts, and fairly ran to greet Elizabeth. A moment later, Elizabeth found herself engulfed in the arms of her dearest friend, who held onto her as if she they had not met for years.

"Charlotte, what—"

"My dear Charlotte, I must insist you step away from my cousin this instant!" the dull tones of her cousin rang out.

An embarrassed blush upon her face, Charlotte pulled away, allowing Elizabeth to see Mr. Collins, whose appearance was made even more ridiculous than usual by virtue of the fact that he was affecting a stern and disapproving visage while nervously mopping his face with his handkerchief. Elizabeth turned her questioning gaze on Charlotte, who returned the look with a sternness not usually present in her friend.

"Lizzy, go home—immediately!" instructed Charlotte.

"Pardon me? Why have you left Kent, Charlotte?"

"Charlotte, I really must be firm in demanding you step away from Cousin Elizabeth."

Mr. Collins then turned his attention to Elizabeth, and he affected a severe, admonishing tone.

"I am truly displeased with your conduct, my young cousin, and your tender years notwithstanding, I feel I must protest the manner of your most brazen attempts at subverting one of the highest personages in the land and acting against the express wishes of his most noble family, especially that of a Lady renowned for her gracious condescension and superior understanding of the world—and one, indeed, who has shown you the greatest of attention. I cannot tell you how mortified I was to discover that another of my Cousin Bennet's daughters has behaved in such a forward and brazen manner, in complete defiance of the dictates of our holy word and the natural order of the classes. You are to be severely chastened and cast out if you will not cease your unnatural actions, and you must believe me when I say I am determined to make your father see reason and carry my point.

"Now, come, Charlotte. We shall not tarry a moment longer. I have business at Longbourn!"

Elizabeth narrowed her eyes and peered at her cousin with considerable displeasure, his long-winded discourse revealing much of his purpose. The rest was relayed to her by her friend, even as she edged away to do her unfortunate husband's demands.

"Go, Elizabeth!" hissed Charlotte in a low voice. "Go back to Longbourn immediately. Lady Catherine sent us away, stipulating that our return was dependant upon our ability to talk some sense into you. Mr. Collins is determined to speak with your father."

"Charlotte, you must come away now."

Mr. Collins's voice sounded more like a petulant whine than one holding the air of authority and command which he was no doubt intending. Charlotte edged away, but before she returned to her husband, she made one last plea.

"I do not know how long I can deflect him, Lizzy. Please, get yourself home and speak to your father, or I cannot imagine the scene he will create!"

"I will, Charlotte," said Elizabeth, finally finding her tongue. "Thank you for the warning!"

Charlotte smiled at her, though it was easy to tell that the smile was forced, before hurrying away to her husband, who had started once again on an incoherent rant about the recalcitrance of young ladies and their improper attitudes and actions. He gave one last glare in Elizabeth's direction before he entered the carriage after his wife, and they once again set off.

Amazed at this sudden turn of events, Elizabeth stood shocked for a moment, wondering at the stupidity of her cousin while feeling some empathy for her closest friend. To be forever caught between the ignorance of Mr. Collins and the superiority and officiousness of Lady Catherine must be vexing in the extreme. Of course, Charlotte had chosen this life of hers with her eyes wide open, but that did not prevent Elizabeth from feeling sorry for her friend.

Elizabeth turned to search for her sisters when she noticed the crowd of onlookers who could not have missed the loud and obnoxious voice of her cousin, and by the looks being directed at her by those gathered, she knew the genesis of certain rumors which would do her no credit had been found in his words. Blushing, Elizabeth instantly determined there was no time to be lost—Mr. Collins must be stopped before the damage he inflicted was beyond salvaging. Though Mr. Collins might wish to go directly to Longbourn to confront her father, she knew that Charlotte would insist on their stopping at Lucas Lodge first in order to refresh themselves after the long journey, so there was at least *some* time before the odious parson could arrive and start voice his demands. However, Lucas Lodge was on the way to Longbourn, and the Collinses had the advantage of traveling in a carriage, while Elizabeth and her sisters would be walking. As such, they had best depart immediately in order to make the journey before Mr. Collins could arrive at Longbourn to spew his patroness's demands.

Quickly gathering her sisters together, she explained the situation with as much brevity as she could manage and then set a brisk pace for home. A part of her noted the struggles her sisters had in keeping up with her—Elizabeth *was* the walker of the family after all. However, the need to arrive at Longbourn and preempt Mr. Collins before he could expose them all to ridicule was paramount. They must hurry!

As the carriage pulled away from the little town of Meryton, Charlotte, positioned as she was in the forward seat, looking back, watched as the figure of her dearest friend receded into the distance, inwardly willing Elizabeth to move as quickly as she was able. Her husband had once again started into his diatribe against those who dared to go against the express wishes of her Ladyship, interspersing it now with his estimation of her duties as a proper wife and his demands to throw Miss Elizabeth off and speak to her no more. As was Charlotte's wont whenever Mr. Collins was speaking inanities or on subjects which held no interest for her—which was nearly always!—she ignored his droning voice in favor of her own thoughts.

Regardless of Lady Catherine's threats, Charlotte was well aware of the fact that a living, once given, could not be rescinded in the absence of extraordinary circumstances which always involved the direct superior of the parson in question. As such, Lady Catherine had no say in the matter of whether Mr. Collins continued in his role of pastor of the Hunsford parish.

However, she was well aware of the lady's ability to make their life uncomfortable—she had no doubt the Lady could make them completely miserable if she so chose. In spite of that consideration, Charlotte was convinced that it was best to stay well clear of any dispute between Lady Catherine and her nephew, as those of lower station, such as Mr. Collins, ran the risk of getting caught up in it and squashed between the two battling titans.

Mr. Collins, though, would hear nothing of it; Her Ladyship was upset with the conduct of his young cousin, and therefore that cousin must be acting in a manner which was contrary to all that was proper—there was no other explanation. His determination to confront that young lady—and her father—was only matched by the insipid attentions he insisted in paying upon his patroness.

In truth, Charlotte was anything but upset with the news that Mr. Darcy was on the verge of making an offer to Elizabeth—in fact, she was very pleased that her friend appeared to be about to make a very favorable alliance. She had always suspected that Elizabeth—with her sparkle, intelligence, and zest for life—was meant for more than the obscure life of a country gentleman's wife.

In addition, the fact that she had been right about Mr. Darcy's interest in her closest friend offered a sense of vindication—she had known all along that the man was in love with Elizabeth! The way he had acted around her, the way his eyes followed her, the manner in which he had visited Hunsford parsonage far more often than politeness required—all of these things had suggested his feelings, but Elizabeth, supremely confident and holding a grudge against the man, would not hear anything of it. It was not often Charlotte was able to claim that she had been right when Elizabeth was wrong, which meant this was a moment to be savored. If only she could persuade her husband to stay out of it!

For Samuel Lucas, the situation with Mr. Collins and Elizabeth seemed it might provide the opportunity he required.

It had started two days previous when they had received an urgent message from Kent requesting the carriage for his sister's immediate removal to her ancestral home. The family had been concerned and confused over the sudden request, but Sir William had immediately assented and dispatched their carriage at daybreak the next day. No one knew of what the situation which demanded their removal consisted, and his mother and father had spent the entire time until their arrival fretting for the well-being of their eldest child.

Upon their arrival, it had taken Samuel the work of a moment to determine that Mr. Collins was in no way sensible and that his sister had settled for the man in favor of a comfortable situation rather than for any regard, despite whatever Mr. Collins imagined she felt for him. In fact, the dark looks and exasperated words she had exchanged with him suggested that her true feelings were much more negative than that—indeed, Samuel felt he could cheerfully strangle the parson, and he had not even known the man for more than a quarter of an hour! How could his sister put up with him every day?

Mr. Collins's ranting and rambling words, however, told Samuel that the senseless man meant to confront Mr. Bennet and Elizabeth for her perceived insults to Mr. Collins's patroness, and Samuel realized he might just be able to use the situation to his advantage. How, he could not fathom at that particular moment, but Samuel was certain that if he were to keep his eyes open and bide his time, there still could be a way to make Elizabeth his own.

In truth, Samuel was more frustrated and angry than he could ever remember being before in his life. The past few days since the proposal had been long and torturous as he was forced to watch as *his* Elizabeth was all but courted by the hated Mr. Darcy while Samuel was kept away by a variety of methods. He had even ridden out every day in an attempt to once again catch her in the midst of one of her long rambles, but it appeared Elizabeth was cagier than Samuel had suspected—he had not thought she would give up her favorite activity merely to avoid him. He could not account for her recalcitrance.

Watching carefully, Samuel observed his brother-in-law as he continued to make his case in a nonsensical manner, and when the man immediately declared his intention to depart for Longbourn, Samuel offered to accompany them to offer his support. It was obvious that Elizabeth had not written to Charlotte to tell her what had happened between them—he knew that Charlotte would be appalled with what had happened and would take Elizabeth's side immediately. Though Samuel had been the playmate of Elizabeth's early childhood, she had grown into a young woman at Charlotte's side, and the bond between them was nearly as strong as that between Jane and Elizabeth.

His offer was accepted without comment, and within a few moments, the entire party was walking down the road to Longbourn, his sister Maria and his parents also in tow. He did not know what he would do to secure her, but failure was not an option. He would have Elizabeth; no other option was to be considered.

*   *   *

Elizabeth spent the walk back to her home alternating between being afraid of what Collins would have to say—and how his insensibility meant it would undoubtedly take the most injudicious form—and being angry at the stupid man's presumption. It had always been obvious that Mr. Collins had no room in his empty head for anything other than Lady Catherine's proclamations, but she had never considered him capable of this. She realized she should have expected such an outcome, as Lady Catherine, by Mr. Darcy's account, was crazed with rage over his refusal to marry Anne.

Her sisters tried to calm her with their presence and support throughout the walk home, but Elizabeth, although grateful for their care and concern, was too caught up in the possibilities to truly pay them heed.

When at last the manor house came into their view, Elizabeth hurried her footsteps to an even greater pace, leaving her sisters behind in an effort to find her father and plead with him to control Mr. Collins. Entering the house, she left her outdoor clothing with the staff and made her way to her father's bookroom without delay, entering once the signal had been given in response to her knock.

Mr. Bennet sat behind his desk with a glass of port and a book, as was his wont, and his delighted smile of greeting turned into a frown of worry the instant he perceived her agitation.

"Elizabeth? Has something happened?"

He rose from his chair and was around his desk in an instant, taking a suddenly breathless Elizabeth's hand and leading her to a chair.

"Here, my child, have a sip of this," declared he as he handed her a glass of port.

Elizabeth did as she was told, and though she was not accustomed to drinking port, she was immediately thankful for the soothing fire as it burned its way down her throat.

"Now, has that rascal Samuel importuned you again?" challenged Mr. Bennet. "If he has, I swear I shall—"

"No, Papa," exclaimed Elizabeth, finally finding her voice. "It is much worse. I have just seen Mr. Collins and Charlotte—they are on their way here."

Her father blinked once in surprise before a sardonic grin suffused his face. "Mr. Collins? What can he be doing here? I have not heard from him since that letter he sent to me concerning your imminent betrothal to Mr. Darcy. I suppose he has come to Meryton to castigate you for using your arts and allurements to ensnare the gentleman."

"Papa! This is no laughing matter. Unfortunately, your supposition is not far from the truth."

A speculative look came over her father's face, and he peered at Elizabeth pointedly. "It seems, my child, that there are certain communications which you have left out of our discussions and that Mr. Collins's words were not the ramblings of a stupid man which I had thought them to be."

Elizabeth averted her eyes, knowing she was now well and truly caught. Her father was far too perceptive for her to avoid telling him all. But knowing of the looming arrival of the Collinses, she decided that brevity was the order of the day—she could inform her father of the particulars at a later date.

Speaking quickly yet concisely, Elizabeth imparted the intelligence she had received when Charlotte had met her in the village. Her father appeared to listen intently, but with growing astonishment.

"He truly is a treasure, is he not, Lizzy?" said he once Elizabeth had ended her discourse.

Unnerved by the situation and fearing the return of the indolent father who was more interested in laughing at the world than interacting with it, Elizabeth's response was sharper than she intended.

"Papa! He will expose us to ridicule and make fools of us if you do not restrain him. I beg you, Father—do not allow him to do this."

A sigh was her response. "Ultimately, Lizzy, if Mr. Collins means to have his say in the matter, I do not know what I can do to silence him, short of breaking my bottle of port over his thick head."

The joke, though the image it provoked would have amused Elizabeth had the situation been different, fell flat for both occupants of the room. Elizabeth raised an eyebrow at her father, and he chuckled at her sign of displeasure.

"Lizzy, though watching Mr. Collins's stupidity is among the most diverting of pastimes, I do agree with you that his connection with us serves to make us look very bad when he displays his lack of sense. Unfortunately, such a display occurs all too often for comfort. I will do what I can to blunt his displeasure and rein in his loquaciousness, but you know as well as I that if he is determined to state his case, then there is little we can do but to refute his words. I will do what I can, and I will brook no criticism of you in spite of whatever foolishness with which Lady Catherine has filled his head.

"Do not worry, Elizabeth," continued Mr. Bennet, patting her hand, "Mr. Collins cannot be taken seriously, even *if* he can manage to put together a coherent sentence. It shall all be well, I promise you."

Knowing there was little else to be done, Elizabeth nodded her head, grateful for the support he was showing her and hopeful that the expected damage caused by Mr. Collins's behavior might be mitigated.

Elizabeth spent several more minutes in her father's library, recovering her equilibrium, until Mr. Bennet instructed her to return to the parlor. He further charged her to send Mr. Collins into his bookroom directly after he arrived so that the man's first pronouncements could be contained. Mr. Bennet would take upon himself the initial expression of the man's displeasure and try to dissuade him from inserting himself any further in the business, not that Elizabeth—much less her father—expected him to be reined in by any means.

Once she had regained her composure, Elizabeth thanked her father for his support and made her way to the parlor to wait for Mr. Collins's inevitable arrival. She opened the door to the room and entered, only to stop dead in her tracks—their guests for dinner that evening had already arrived and were sitting in the parlor speaking with her mother and younger sisters. With the excitement over the Collinses' sudden appearance and the need to speak to her father, she had completely forgotten the imminent arrival of their friends. She barely suppressed a grimace at the thought of what the Netherfield party would think of Mr. Collins's pronouncements and absurd behavior.

Unfortunately, her reaction to their presence did not go unnoticed by the perceptive Mr. Darcy, and he frowned in response. She smiled and attempted to reassure him, not wishing him to think that the sight of him was the cause for her reaction. But before she could speak to him and inform him of the events of the afternoon, she heard voices in the hall signaling the arrival of Mr. Collins and the party from Lucas Lodge.

She turned to greet the new arrivals, noting the various looks of the party—Charlotte was attempting to catch her eye with an apologetic expression adorning her features, while Sir William appeared pensive and worried. Lady Lucas and Maria were subdued, and Samuel—she should have known he would try to insert himself into this madness!—gazed at her with an intensity to rival that which Mr. Darcy customarily displayed. Mr. Collins was his usual unctuous self, but there seemed to be an almost manic gleam in his eye—the prospect of losing Lady Catherine's favor appeared to have almost unhinged him.

Her father's admonition to send Mr. Collins to his study immediately turned out to be unnecessary—the man, upon seeing her, turned his lips up in contempt and stormed from the room, exclaiming that he would speak with Mr. Bennet at once.

Elizabeth watched him go, her heart thumping loudly in her chest. And though Mr. Darcy and his family attempted to speak with her to understand the situation, Elizabeth found her attention was focused upon her father's bookroom. She had not the heart to discuss what was happening with them.

After several moments of failing to obtain any intelligible information from her, Mr. Darcy searched the room, and he abruptly stood and crossed to where Charlotte Collins stood, engaging her in earnest discussion. Elizabeth noted his departure and silently thanked her friend for her support and assistance, all the while praying that Mr. Collins's displeasure might be contained before he exposed them all.

"Lizzy!" Mrs. Bennet's voice rang out. "Come here this instant!"

Cringing at her mother's tone of voice, Elizabeth crossed the room, feeling Mr. Darcy's eyes upon her as she moved.

"Lizzy, what is happening?" queried Mrs. Bennet. "I have heard that the Collinses have been ejected from their home by Lady Catherine because of some association between yourself and *Mr. Darcy*." Her mother spat the gentleman's name almost as if it was a curse, accompanying it with a derisive glower at the man in question.

Intuitively understanding what had occurred, Elizabeth turned a baleful glare on Samuel, who stood nearby, but he only studied her with an expressionless gaze.

"Mama, I do not know to what you are referring, but I can assure you that there is nothing improper or secret going on between Mr. Darcy and myself. *He* is a gentleman," spat Elizabeth, glaring again at Samuel, "and has never behaved in any way but the most proper toward me."

Biting her lip, Mrs. Bennet peered at her daughter. "And what Samuel says about him refusing to marry his cousin?"

"What business is it of Samuel's? For that matter, what concern is it of ours if Mr. Darcy chooses or declines to marry Anne de Bourgh? I suggest we all keep our attention firmly upon *our own affairs*," once again the words were flung pointedly at Samuel, who was beginning to appear angry, "and leave others to their own.

"And though it is none of our concern, Mama, I have spoken with both Mr. Darcy *and* Anne de Bourgh, and they have *both* assured me that there is no engagement between them, that there has *never been* an engagement between them, and that they have never been inclined to consent to a closer association than the one they currently enjoy. *Those* are the facts. Other than that, I do not believe it is appropriate to discuss such matters in company—and certainly *not* in their presence."

Though she appeared to still be concerned and less than happy, Mrs. Bennet reached forward and patted Elizabeth's hand. "Very well, Elizabeth, but I believe I should like to have a talk with you later."

Elizabeth inclined her head and turned to leave. She stopped, however, unable to quit the insufferable Samuel's presence without a parting shot.

"Mama, in the future, I suggest you confirm what you hear before giving credence to the ramblings of bitter and jealous *persons* of our acquaintance."

The thrust of her words could not be misunderstood, coupled as they were with the pointed glare she had directed at her neighbor, and Elizabeth was allowed the pleasure of seeing Samuel's jaw clench in anger. Her mother's assessing and slightly put-out expression directed at the Lucas heir gave her hope that she might finally see him for what he truly was. As for Samuel's anger, Elizabeth did not care a jot for it—she was finished with him, if she had not already been before.

She turned her head and marched across the room, sitting beside Jane while accepting her sister's—and Mr. Bingley's—comfort. She held her head high, determined that whatever these persons who appeared intent upon ruining her happiness did, they would not take away her dignity!

Mr. Bennet was standing by the window in his bookroom gazing out at the grounds of Longbourn when he heard a commotion out in the hall. Knowing the time was at hand and wondering what he was to do to stop Mr. Collins from making his accusations, the master of Longbourn sat behind his desk, pressing a hand wearily to his forehead.

It was only moments later when there was a loud pounding upon his door, and the door subsequently opened, with no opportunity for Mr. Bennet's response. A clearly apoplectic Mr. Collins stormed into the room, his stupid countenance ruddy with fury.

"Mr. Bennet! I insist upon being satisfied!"

Mr. Bennet gazed at the sputtering parson with contempt. He said not a word, however, simply allowing his gaze to bore into the stupid man. Mr. Collins did not take the scrutiny well, and he sputtered and wheezed, mopping his forehead with his handkerchief while bemoaning the indecency of and indecorous behavior of his cousin, his cousin's family, and the world in general. Mr. Bennet was pitiless in his disapproving glare, and it was not long before Mr. Collins began to fidget and twitch, a testament of his being distinctly uncomfortable. Smiling grimly to himself—he wanted the man as discomposed as he could possibly arrange it—Mr. Bennet finally addressed his unwelcome visitor.

"I am sorry, Mr. Collins, but I do not believe I have the pleasure of understanding you." He gazed pointedly at the open door and continued, "But as you have barged into my bookroom unannounced and uninvited, clearly in a tizzy over some matter or another, I suppose I must oblige you with a few moments of my time. However, I shall not do so with an open door, allowing the entire house to become acquainted our discourse. Close the door, Mr. Collins."

The man gaped at him for a moment before obediently turning and closing the door.

"Will you not be seated, Mr. Collins? I would prefer not to develop a stitch in my neck while peering up at you."

Mr. Collins's posterior hit the seat in an instant, his eyes still wide, presumably due to his surprise over the manner in which Mr. Bennet was treating him.

"Very good, Mr. Collins; I did not suspect you capable of behaving in a quiet, restrained manner when you have your hackles up. Now, when you entered my room, you insisted I satisfy you in some manner or another. Since I cannot do so without express understanding of that about which you require satisfaction, I suggest you tell me about this matter which is troubling you, after which we may find some mutually beneficial resolution."

Mr. Collins stared at Mr. Bennet for several moments, no doubt trying to determine exactly what the master of Longbourn had meant, Bennet suspected — the man was not known for his towering intellectual prowess, after all — before he finally opened his mouth. And though he affected a relative veneer of calmness, the tone and the volume of his voice became higher as he continued.

"I thank you for your time, cousin," began Mr. Collins with a florid bow, a very curious affectation, as he was sitting in his chair at the time. "I cannot tell you how wonderful it is to arrive here after such a trying time — and in the face of my delightful patroness's most cruel and unjustified distress — to find you willing to discuss the gross improprieties which must be addressed. Indeed, due to my experience with you and the events with regard to Cousin Elizabeth this past November — about which we had best be silent — I almost expected you to tend toward recalcitrance and avoidance instead of steadfast resolve in dealing with the predicament. You are to be praised, cousin."

"Yes, yes, Mr. Collins. I know all about your patroness and that something is troubling you, but shall you not come to the point?"

"Yes, of course, Mr. Bennet. I am afraid I had forgotten where my thoughts were tending, what with my surprise at your willingness to discuss the improprieties . . . Yes, well, the point . . .

"I am sensible to the fact that you may not be aware of the refusal of your daughter to oblige my patroness in her most sensible demands, but I must make you understand. Miss Elizabeth is most grievously offending the noble Lady Catherine de Bourgh with her conduct, and I simply must insist upon your intervention. You must bring her schemes to an end!"

Mr. Bennet pinched his nose; though he had received letters frequently from the man over the months since Mr. Collins had departed Hertfordshire — and had been greatly diverted by his manner of expressing himself in his letters — he had quite forgotten the very great frustration the man's pompous pronouncements and inability to come to the point could incite.

"Mr. Collins, I assure you that Elizabeth has had very little contact with your patroness since she left Kent in April, and as a consequence, as to the best of my knowledge she has not corresponded with the lady, she can have done nothing to provoke Lady Catherine's displeasure. Perhaps if you could be persuaded to be a little more explicit in the specific accusations you wish to lay at her door, I may better answer you."

Mr. Collins's face darkened in displeasure, as he seemed to sense that Mr. Bennet might not be as supportive to his cause as his initial words had indicated. He sniffed in an exaggeratedly offended manner and continued his demands:

"It is simply not possible, Mr. Bennet, for there to be any misunderstanding. You must cast your daughter from your family, ungrateful hoyden that she is. Having been the recipient of your daughter's wiles myself—"

"Mr. Collins!" interjected Bennet angrily. "I will not have you slandering my daughter's good name! I know for a fact that she did nothing to encourage your suit, nor did she welcome it when you offered for her. I will thank you to keep your fantasies firmly in your head where they belong and stick to the material points. Now, what has you in a lather today?"

"Your daughter, Mr. Bennet," said Collins from between clenched teeth. "She has set her sights high above her station and actively attempted to entrap Mr. Darcy in a marriage which has not been properly sanctioned, and she has done so against the express wish of *my patroness!* I spoke to you of this more than a month ago in my last letter to you. Why have you not taken the appropriate steps to curb this unnatural farce?"

"Is Mr. Darcy not his own man?" Mr. Bennet's voice was implacable.

The question clearly took Mr. Collins aback.

"He is the master of a great estate—"

"And he is not beholden to his aunt for anything? She does not control Pemberley?"

"No, but she is his aunt and the scion of—"

"And the banns announcing this supposed engagement between the master of Pemberley and Miss de Bourgh—have they already been published?"

"That is beside the point, Mr. Bennet."

"No, that is *exactly* the point, Mr. Collins," was Mr. Bennet's unyielding reply. "Your words had concerned me because *I* had not heard *anything* of such conditions on Mr. Darcy's independence. If he is not beholden to his aunt and the banns on an engagement have not yet been read, then there appears to be nothing stopping him from conducting his own affairs exactly as he wishes. I suggest you tend to your flock and allow those of the higher circles to work out their own disagreements in their own way."

"*Mr. Bennet!*" said Mr. Collins, his voice ascending almost to a whine. "How can you say such things? The ancient house of de Bourgh and the noble line of Fitzwilliam—have they not a say in how their closest relations conduct themselves and with whom they align themselves?"

"*If* Mr. Darcy is completely independent as you say, then no—they have nothing to say in the matter. They may advise and demand, but the decision rests in its entirety with the young man in question. Neither you, nor I, nor any of his *relations* has any say in the matter.

"And you may not know it, Mr. Collins, but I have it on very good authority that Mr. Darcy's uncle, the earl, in fact *supports* Mr. Darcy in this matter. *He* is the head of the family, not *Lady Catherine.* You would do well to remember that."

The anger in Mr. Collins's face had Mr. Bennet actually fearing that his cousin would fall dead to the ground—surely the man was about to collapse from his heart giving out due to the sheer rapidity in which the blood was flowing to his face. In fact, if that man were to fall down dead, Mr. Bennet thought, he had best do it—then, they could all have the peace of the afternoon restored to them that much sooner.

"Then you actually *approve of this?*" the man finally demanded. "I believe I understand now—*I* was not enough of a catch for my cousin. She had already set her sights on a much *higher* target and has used her wiles to obtain her goal. I simply do not understand how you can condone this . . . this . . . travesty! She should be happy to stay within the confines of her own sphere rather than attempting to depart from the class in which she was raised."

"I have already once chided you for referring to *my daughter* in such a manner, sir," ground out Mr. Bennet from between clenched teeth. "I will thank you not to do so again. I believe Elizabeth to be among the most morally upright and outstanding individuals whom I have ever had the good fortune to know, and I would thank you to remember it.

"And as for your comments about her sphere, I assure you that the disparity you suggest does not exist. Elizabeth is the daughter of a gentleman—my family has held this estate for centuries—and Mr. Darcy, although far wealthier than the Bennets have ever been, is still just a gentleman. In that respect, there is no inequality."

Mr. Collins gaped, and his mouth opened and closed with no sound emerging, not unlike that of a fish. He sat there, stupidly staring at Mr. Bennet for a long moment, while Mr. Bennet regarded him, thinking that Mr. Collins's father had undoubtedly been a cretin and that his son was cut from the same cloth. Perhaps it was time to sever the acquaintance—surely the man would be unfit for any sort of correspondence after the events of this day.

"You *must* refuse them permission to marry, cousin," Mr. Collins finally blurted. "Without your consent, they may not marry, and this delusion can finally come to an end."

"I shall not, Mr. Collins."

"You were willing to refuse permission of *my* suit, but you will support your daughter in her pursuit of a wealthy man?"

"You are wrong, Mr. Collins," said Mr. Bennet, his own anger now truly taking hold of him. "I did not refuse your suit—*Elizabeth* did! I merely supported her in her decision, one with which I agreed wholeheartedly, I might add. I will not refuse consent in this matter if Elizabeth truly desires it, just as I would not have refused her if she had accepted to *your* proposals, much though I would have questioned her sanity.

"And you forget one other thing—Elizabeth will be of age in another three months, and after that, she may do as she pleases. Even if I should refuse consent, they need only wait until Elizabeth is one-and-twenty and marry then. I will not push my daughter away from me in such a manner—she is far too precious to me."

Silence descended upon the room, and Mr. Bennet watched Collins closely, looking for some sign that his words had made a dent in the man's consciousness, though he thought it an impossibility. He had done about all he could—if Collins persisted and ended up burned as a result, it was his own fault.

"So this is your resolve?"

Mr. Bennet sighed and gazed at the countenance of his cousin. Unfortunately, he was much his father's son, and Bennet could well remember some of the rows he had fought with the elder Collins before their estrangement. "Mr. Collins, if I may, I should like to offer you a piece of unsolicited advice. If you persist in this course, I have no doubt you will incur the wrath of the young gentleman from Derbyshire. Mr. Darcy strikes me as the type of man who knows what he wants, and I suspect he does not allow anyone get in the way of his purpose once he has decided on a course of action. Let it go and keep your own council in spite of your patroness's displeasure—you do not wish to anger Mr. Darcy."

"Very well," spat Collins. "I believe that I shall know what is to be done despite your inability to act in an appropriate manner. I cannot tell you how appalled I am at the sorry state of these affairs and the manner in which your family is conducting itself. Her Ladyship is most seriously displeased, and I cannot be anything else. I take my leave of you, sir."

With that, Collins rose to his feet, and turning to leave—after stumbling inelegantly over one of the chair legs—he departed the bookroom, slamming the door on his way out.

Sighing rather loudly, Mr. Bennet rose to his feet to follow him—he had given his word to Elizabeth that he would do what he could to deter Mr. Collins from this disastrous course, and that did not include sitting in his room while Collins insulted her and questioned her integrity and honor. Besides, if Mr. Bennet's conjecture regarding Mr. Darcy's feelings on the matter and his expected defense of Elizabeth was in any way accurate, it would be amusing to watch Darcy disabuse Mr. Collins of any notion of further interference on his part. Mr. Bennet would not miss *that* for all the world!

Elizabeth waited in the parlor with her hand ensconced in Jane's comforting grasp, a sense of impending doom suffusing her senses. Mr. Collins had been holed up with her father for far longer than she had expected, and though she doubted her father's ability to divert the odious man's intentions, she had begun to indulge in the fantasy of his success.

Mr. Darcy approached soon after his brief conversation with Charlotte, and though he said little other than to state his support, he comforted her with his very presence.

Her mother regarded them together with a half-scowl, which was an improvement in her manner from her actions previous, and Elizabeth had hope that whatever had been bothering her might yet be resolved. Samuel, by contrast, was just as annoyed by her display with Darcy as he had been before, though Elizabeth thought little of it. Charlotte, however, appraised them with a wide, self-satisfied smirk on her face, and Elizabeth was certain she would be subject to her friend's smug assertions of how she had *always known* that Mr. Darcy held her in high regard. At that moment, Elizabeth was prepared to endure all manner of teasing if she could only live her own life without the interference of others. But it was not to be.

The sound of a door slamming reached the parlor, jolting more than one person in the process, and moments later, Mr. Collins stormed in the room, looking, if anything, even angrier than he had when he had arrived. The interview with her father had evidently not gone as anyone had desired.

He marched into the room, and the instant his eyes fell upon Elizabeth, he glowered at her and stood in front of her, his eyes filled with fury.

"Cousin Elizabeth, I simply must protest your improper and wild actions in the matter of Mr. Darcy. You, cousin, have behaved in a shameful manner, continuously throwing yourself most brazenly at a man of Mr. Darcy's stature in defiance of his family's wishes and, indeed, of all decorum. I demand you remove yourself from his presence immediately and behave more in the manner of a gentlewoman, lest the judgment of almighty God himself smite you!"

For a moment, Elizabeth was stunned speechless that Mr. Collins could be that lost to propriety to make such base claims of her. Her father had followed Mr. Collins into the room, but before he could refute Collins's claims or Elizabeth herself could formulate a response, Mr. Darcy arose, his face overshadowed with a deadly calm.

"Mr. Collins, you will cease this dreadful slander immediately," snapped Mr. Darcy, causing Collins to take a step back. "Your opinions are not wanted, and the matter of which you speak exists nowhere except in the fantasies and whimsies of my aunt."

"Mr. Darcy," began Mr. Collins once he had found his voice, "surely you cannot—"

"Are you to be the judge of what I can and cannot do, Mr. Collins?" interrupted Mr. Darcy, his voice carrying a dangerous and unfriendly tone to it which caused Mr. Collins to once again retreat in alarm. His manner was not unlike that of a crab in the way he sidled from side to side in agitation, while his waist almost seemed permanently bowed in deference to the Master of Pemberley. "I assure you, Mr. Collins, that my aunt no more controls me—or my Cousin Anne, for that matter— than do you. Are you completely insensible of the damage you are causing by your inappropriate discussion of these matters before your family, the Bennets, or our party from Netherfield? Are you lost to all sensibility and good manners?

"Now, be silent! You would be best advised to attempt to console my aunt and let go of issues which are not your concern!"

Whatever Mr. Collins was, it was clear that he did not lack courage—any other man who had received such a stinging set-down from a man of Mr. Darcy's stature would have resolved to drop the matter forthwith. But it was obvious that Mr. Collins was desperate, and his desperation did not make him wise, and so, regardless of his continued obeisance, he puffed himself up in what he obviously considered to be a most important and impressive manner.

"Mr. Darcy," he simpered, "please be assured I do not blame you in the slightest in this subject—no, indeed. You cannot be blamed for falling for the shameful advances of my cousin. Indeed, I myself was able to make a very fortunate escape from her vile machinations, a happenstance for which I am ever grateful. I beg of you, sir, do not allow her to draw you in!"

Elizabeth gasped at Mr. Collins's words. In the heat of that moment, she would always remember two things—the expression of utter fury which crossed Mr. Darcy's face and the matching expression mingled with disgust on Charlotte's. It was clear between the pair of them that they would cheerfully have throttled Mr. Collins if they had been able to get their hands upon him.

But the moment was interrupted by the sound of another voice which, with the possible exception of Mr. Collins, was the voice she least wished to hear in that moment.

"Mr. Collins," Samuel Lucas's voice rang out, "you need not concern yourself over Miss Elizabeth's involvement with Mr. Darcy. I have the very great pleasure of informing you that I have recently asked Miss Elizabeth to accept *my* hand in marriage, and she has accepted. We are engaged."

Chapter XVII

$\mathcal{T}$here are times in the life of every person when they are struck by an epiphany, and in some cases, these revelations are such that they change the life of the person forever. This moment proved to hold such a momentous revelation for Fitzwilliam Darcy, and although at that instant he was not certain it would prove to be a life-changing moment, he knew that it *was* significant in several ways.

Though he had known that something *must* happen to make his courtship of his beloved more difficult—indeed, *nothing* between Fitzwilliam Darcy and Elizabeth Bennet had ever been *easy*—Darcy had not quite been certain just what form the proverbial "dead fly in the ointment of the apothecary" would take. His attention had been focused upon the sycophantic and ridiculous person of his aunt's rector, and he had not even considered the presence of *another* of Elizabeth's erstwhile suitors.

As the noise level of the room began to rise, he ignored all the extraneous concerns and focused upon that which truly mattered—the person of Elizabeth Bennet, who was confronting the smirking visage of the man who had just proclaimed her to be his affianced. Her eyes were wide, her mouth open, and on her face was an expression of open incomprehension. It was at this moment that Darcy's aforementioned epiphany—or several of them, to be precise—hit him with a surety of which he could not doubt.

The first—and the most forceful—insight was the fact that Elizabeth's expression of incredulity was not actually that; rather, it was one of surprise and outright horror. Whatever Samuel Lucas may have persuaded himself to believe—and by the insufferable leer which graced his face, *he* clearly expected to have his words believed—Elizabeth's reaction was not one of adoration and respect. Darcy knew this without a doubt, as a similar look had once been directed at *him*—it was a memory he would have preferred to forget altogether, but at this moment, he was almost grateful for the experience, as it gave him a sort of peace. Elizabeth was *not* beyond his aspirations, and she was *not* in any way betrothed to Samuel Lucas.

What exactly had passed between them was a matter of speculation. Knowing Lucas's dogged pursuit of her over the past weeks, it seemed to come down to two possibilities—either he was delusional, or he was downright dishonest. His observation of the man as he approached Elizabeth with a smug grin, suggested that the man was guilty of duplicity. Perhaps he *had* made a proposal of marriage to Elizabeth, but knowing her willingness to refuse an unwanted proposal, Darcy had no doubt how *that* conversation had ended.

The second understanding Darcy gained that afternoon was that—for all of his flowery words to Elizabeth about how he intended to court her openly—he had actually made a colossal error in judgment which would almost certainly cause the woman he loved a certain amount of pain.

Oh, it was unknowingly done, and never could he have predicted the unbelievable claim of a man seemingly without morals or propriety. Darcy's motives, while correct—Elizabeth *deserved* everything he had not given her the first time he had attempted to secure her hand—were misguided. Elizabeth was not a woman who required fanciful pronouncements and open admiration—all she wished for was the love of a good man who would protect and appreciate her as she deserved. If he had asked her for an open courtship that day of the picnic, none of this would have happened—Lucas would have been frustrated in his attempts beyond all recovery, and Darcy and Elizabeth might even now be enjoying the dinner that her mother had no doubt planned so painstakingly.

Still, Darcy was not willing to castigate himself so severely—his motives *had* been good and proper, and he had not been blinded by his pride or by the whims of his nature. However, after this bit of unpleasantness, Darcy would get right down to the business of courting her—it was time to firmly bring her under his protection and the security which a formal announcement of their relationship would bring.

Gazing at the woman he loved, Darcy thought to speak again in her defense, but the growing anger on her face caused him to rethink. The first right of response belonged to Elizabeth, and if her growing indignation was any indication, the coming inferno would be a sight to behold.

It is a difficult thing to relinquish that which you love best into the arms of another, no matter how well suited or well positioned that other is, and Mr. Thomas Bennet, loath though he was to admit it, had no other recourse but to acknowledge the fact that he was not the only man in his favorite daughter's heart any longer. Judging by what he was seeing before his very eyes, he was no longer even first in her heart.

Mr. Bennet followed Mr. Collins into the parlor, intending to defend his daughter before the odious man and heave him from the house by the force of his boot if required. But upon entering the room and watching events play out—Collins's stupid words, followed by Darcy's warning for the man to keep his own council—the lay of the land was now revealed to him as if his daughter and her suspected paramour had announced it in clear terms.

In fact, he was somewhat amused—he was what he was, after all, in spite of his determination to protect Elizabeth and in spite of his exertions of the past weeks on her behalf. The situation was ludicrous in the extreme, a scene out of one of Lydia's favorite novels or directly from the theater in London. Collins was so ridiculous in his comments as to give the Bennet patriarch a most entertaining spectacle and further confirm the man's idiocy. His anger over the "acute misery" of his patroness was not able to completely overcome his proclivity toward flowery speeches and flattering words. Such words of anger and self-righteousness spoken in such a long-winded fashion could hardly be taken seriously, even if they *had not* issued forth from the mouth of the inestimable Mr. Collins.

But Samuel Lucas . . . Mr. Bennet frowned. If the young scoundrel was willing to make such a blatantly untrue statement for the sole purpose of forcing Elizabeth into a marriage, he would bear close watching—in fact, Mr. Bennet was seriously considering banning the man from Longbourn permanently. After all, Mr. Bennet would still have *two* unmarried daughters in the house after this mess was all cleaned up, and he did not relish the thought of losing either of them to Samuel Lucas. He had no doubt Samuel would be a most unsuitable husband—who knew of what the man was capable?

So, Thomas Bennet did what he did best when faced by a situation of such absurdities—he sat down with a grin to watch the idiocy play out, anticipating his daughter's response with unrestrained amusement. He was certain Elizabeth would not disappoint, after all, and would give the Lucas heir all he could handle. *Then*, once Elizabeth was done with him, Mr. Bennet could take the matter in hand. Samuel Lucas was in for a rather rude awakening.

Standing stock still in the parlor of her childhood home of Longbourn, Elizabeth stared at the smirking visage of Samuel Lucas, wondering if she had heard him correctly.

Engaged to that . . . that . . . vile excuse of a man? In truth, Elizabeth would rather marry the old nag in her father's stables than contemplate a marriage to such a villain as Samuel Lucas!

And as for the equally detestable Mr. Collins, who was standing there with a look of shock on his face, though that expression was slowly turning to one of delight and cunning—or as close to cunning as the stupid man could possibly approach—why, how dare he enter her father's home, proclaiming his repulsive patroness's demands as if they came from the Prince Regent himself? Was the man so utterly stupid and subservient that he could not have any thoughts that Lady Catherine had not sanctioned? Apparently, he was—Elizabeth had always known him to be lacking any sense or intelligence, and the past few moments had set his character in stone.

"My dearest Elizabeth," the smooth tones of Samuel Lucas penetrated her thoughts. "I know you preferred to wait before we made our announcement, yet I had no choice but to protect your reputation. Will you not join me in accepting the congratulations of the assembled company for our happy news?"

Her anger flaring white hot at the audacity of the man, Elizabeth opened her mouth to deliver a stinging set-down, only to be interrupted by the less than intelligent exclamations of her father's cousin.

"Oh, my! I must abjectly and most sincerely beg your forgiveness, Cousin Elizabeth, for I fear that I have made a most regrettable error. I was of the understanding that you were cavorting around, attempting to entrap Mr. Darcy in the most shameful and forward manner — and in direct violation of all propriety, good feelings, and the dictates of the Lord himself. The information I heard from sources in the area must have been mistaken — and though I would not shame her ladyship by claiming that her superior understanding and good information were erroneous, I can only assume that whatever she discovered during her sojourn here was without foundation. I can assure you that when the circumstances and resolutions of this afternoon's most regrettable misunderstandings are explained to her, her forgiveness will be swift and complete, for she is truly the pinnacle of Christian generosity and understanding — "

"Mr. Collins, are you an imbecile?" challenged Elizabeth, unwilling to hear a single syllable more of the man's rambling beatifications of his mistress.

His eyes bulging out of his sockets, Mr. Collins's jaw worked soundlessly, as ineffectual as was the man himself.

"I believe you must be, Mr. Collins, if you truly believe such senseless statements. I think you overestimate the affection and loyalty which *anyone* here other than yourself holds for your patroness, and I daresay you cannot go more than five syllables without mentioning that harridan you serve, as if she were the very paragon of virtue!"

At this, Mr. Collins's face became a mottled and furious red, and he gazed at her stupidly, sputtering and attempting to come up with some way of refuting Elizabeth's words.

"Cousin Elizabeth, this is . . . this is highly improper! I cannot imagine by what means you insult not only a lady of the highest quality, but a respected member of the clergy — "

"Respected only in the confines of your own mind, Mr. Collins," snapped Elizabeth. "*And* respected only until you open your mouth. Anyone given the misfortune of hearing you cannot help but understand within your first few words what a small-minded and ignorant man you truly are. You are inserting yourself into a situation which does not concern you in the slightest, and I suggest you cease before you are burned in the process!"

"And *you*, Miss Elizabeth, are playing with fire by engaging in the pursuit of such an exalted gentleman," charged Mr. Collins in response. "My patroness — "

"Your patroness has nothing to do with these proceedings! Despite what she may have told you, Mr. Darcy's precise relationship with myself — or anyone else for that matter — is no concern of Lady Catherine's, and it is certainly of no concern to one such as yourself who is wholly unconnected with him.

"And as for my personal affairs, these are equally beyond your concern — *you* are not my father, Mr. Collins, and as such, you can have no say in the matter of those with whom I associate. In short, Mr. Collins, while you may feel that licking Lady Catherine's boots is acceptable behavior for a clergyman, you are not welcome to spew her vitriol in this house in her stead. I suggest you curb your tongue before my father throws you from the premises into the muck from whence you came!"

With a final glare of contempt at the now apoplectic Mr. Collins, Elizabeth turned the force of her displeasure upon the other perpetrator of this farce. Mr.

Samuel Lucas was staring at her, the smug smile of moments before having been replaced by confusion and apprehension.

As well it should have been, she thought grimly, for when she was done with him, Samuel Lucas would wish he had never crossed swords with Elizabeth Bennet.

Allowing all of her displeasure to show in her face—something which was matched by a heightened sense of hesitation in Mr. Lucas's manner—Elizabeth stepped forward and, once again incensed by the way he reached out as if to embrace her, neatly sidestepped his open arms and slapped his face with every ounce of strength she possessed.

As the sound of Elizabeth's hand connecting with Mr. Lucas's face resounded throughout the room, it was joined by the startled gasps of several of those looking on. And though Elizabeth paid them no heed, she was perversely satisfied with the surprise and alarm which appeared on the faces of some, while she gloried in the looks of satisfaction on the features of those for whom she cared the most.

"And *you*, Samuel Lucas!" hissed Elizabeth. "I thought I had made myself perfectly clear, but perhaps I shall be required to do so again. I will not marry you. I will *never* marry you! In fact, if you and I were the last persons remaining on the face of the earth, I believe I would rather condemn the human race to extinction than to soil myself with you!"

She gazed into Samuel's shocked features, wondering at the man's temerity. She could almost feel pity for him if he had not mortified her and claimed that which was more repulsive to her than anything else she could even imagine. He and Caroline Bingley truly did make a most unsavory pair—they were both so deluded in their own selfish desires that they were incapable of considering the feelings of others. Perhaps it would be best if each were to look to the other for a companion in life!

"Perhaps you would not know, Mr. Lucas, but Mr. Wickham was recently in the neighborhood—he is an unfortunate connection, as he is truly a miserable excuse for a human being. But though I once believed him to be the lowest form of insect to crawl upon the face of this earth, even *he* never tried to claim an engagement which did not exist. I cannot even begin to tell you how much you *disgust* me with your selfishness, your complete disdain for me and my family, and your repellent attentions.

"I would have everyone in the room understand," continued Elizabeth, now addressing the entire room, "that I *did* receive a proposal of marriage from Mr. Samuel Lucas less than a week ago. However, regardless of what *this man* has told you all today, I rejected him and left him without any doubt of my feelings on the matter. Mr. Lucas has deceived you all with his falsehoods and outright slander, and I will reiterate myself—on this issue, I will not ever be moved. I will never marry Samuel Lucas!"

Casting a disdainful glare at her tormentor, who was even now beginning to recover—an angry expression growing on his face—Elizabeth turned on her heel, and holding her head high (she thought Lady Catherine herself could do no better!) she stalked from the room, feeling rather than seeing Jane following on her heels.

Charlotte Collins was beside herself with anger. Not only had her stupid and senseless husband made a scene in the home of her dearest friend after she had warned him of the consequences of doing so, but her own brother had turned out to be possessed of a more degenerate character than she had suspected after his time at university. Charlotte had rarely seen Samuel since he had left, but what she had seen had not impressed her; in fact, the longer he was away, the worse he had appeared to become, although now that she thought of it, she had never been close to him. He had always been selfish and arrogant, though he had little reason for being so.

And now, mortified as she was after her male relations had exposed themselves—she now knew exactly how Elizabeth had felt at the Netherfield Ball!—she was uncertain whether she should grasp her husband's ear and haul him from the premises or let her brother know exactly what she thought of him.

Choosing the latter—speaking with Mr. Collins was akin to speaking with a brick wall, after all!—she approached her brother and stepped in front of him, forcing him to meet her eyes. His countenance was filled with surprise at being accosted by his sister, but it immediately turned to a sneer of contempt.

"Samuel," hissed Charlotte, "what do you think you are doing?"

"You could not possibly understand, Charlotte," said he in response. His sneer of self-righteousness was most unpleasant. "I am trying to save Elizabeth from that damnable Darcy. And *this* is how she thanks me!"

"Of what are you speaking? Lizzy is not in any danger from Mr. Darcy."

"Of course *you* would not understand. I have seen his type before—she may fancy herself in love with him, but he only wants her for one reason, and that reason has nothing to do with marriage!"

Charlotte was aghast. "And you are delusional! Mr. Darcy is not the sort of man to behave in such a manner, and he has admired her since practically the first moment he arrived in the neighborhood. I have watched them in company since he came to Hertfordshire, and I can tell you without a doubt that Mr. Darcy has been in love with Elizabeth for some time now. She will not have you, Samuel; I beg of you to cease this foolishness before you anger Mr. Darcy into taking action against you."

When Samuel roughly removed his arm from her grip, Charlotte recoiled at the venomous glower he directed at her.

"Do *not* become involved with my affairs, *dear sister*. I shall look after my own affairs and will not tolerate any interference!"

With that, he turned and strode from the room, his shoulders resolute.

Angry tears beginning to cascade down her cheeks, Elizabeth stormed from the parlor, intent upon getting away from the house and putting as much distance between herself and the amoral person of her now detested neighbor.

How dare he tell such slanderous falsehoods after all that had been done to discourage his misguided suit! She could hardly believe that someone could be so caught up in themselves as to so utterly ignore the feelings of others, but she appeared to attract that sort of man. Even Mr. Darcy—who was now on the opposite end of the spectrum—had not shown such a complete and utter disregard for her feelings when he had made his own proposal.

Mr. Darcy had undoubtedly cared, but he had simply allowed his nervousness and overblown sense of pride to influence the words he spoke, which turned it into more of a disaster than had been necessary. She would not have accepted him—at the time, her feelings were too negative for that to have happened—but perhaps they could have parted with less acrimony, which could have led to true understanding. It was clear that Mr. Darcy had *always* cared; he simply had not expressed himself properly.

"Elizabeth!"

The urgent call from her sister brought Elizabeth up short, and she tried to dash the tears from her eyes before turning and watching her sister run after her.

Jane enveloped her in her arms, holding Elizabeth tight while speaking soothing words to her.

"Lizzy, I do not think this is the best time to go out walking," admonished Jane, her voice gentle and affectionate.

"I am sorry, Jane, but I need to. I need to get away from . . . from . . . *that man* and think."

Pulling away, Jane grinned and displayed some items in her hands—Elizabeth's spencer, bonnet, and gloves. "How did I know you would say that? But I cannot let you leave in nothing more than your dress, Lizzy. I will not allow you to catch cold."

Elizabeth gratefully accepted the items, wondering how Jane had found the time to fetch them while she was fuming. Her sister did not illuminate her; rather, she continued to caution her as she helped Elizabeth to dress.

"Now, Lizzy, I know this has upset you, and I know how you use your walks to calm yourself, but you must promise me something: do not leave the environs of the house."

When Elizabeth raised a questioning eyebrow at her sister, Jane's voice took on a lecturing tone which Elizabeth had rarely heard from her sister. "Lizzy, it is getting late in the day, and I do not wish for Father to have to send out a search party for you."

"I hardly think that necessary, Jane—I have been walking out my whole life and am certain that I know the paths in the area better than almost anyone else alive!"

"I am certain you do," replied Jane.

But her stern countenance and piercing gaze had not abated a jot, and Elizabeth was feeling like a schoolgirl caught out in a lie under Jane's scrutiny.

"I do not like this situation, Lizzy, and I do not trust Samuel—any more than you do, I suspect. If you stay close to the house, Samuel can do nothing, but I fear for your safety if he is able to come upon you with no one in the vicinity. *Please* Elizabeth, oblige me in this."

"I will, Jane," answered Elizabeth, more to appease her sister than anything else. She did not think that Samuel would be able to escape the confines of the parlor after her revelations, but to keep Jane happy, she would agree to her strictures.

"If anyone wishes to find me, I shall be walking some of the paths in the back of the house."

"Thank you, Lizzy," replied Jane with another hug. "Now, go—I shall attempt to calm the room as we wait for your return."

Reflecting that it was good to have such a steadfast and loving sister, Elizabeth gave her one last affectionate smile before she left the house.

* * *

Mr. Darcy watched the events unfold and was filled with an enormous sense of pride and satisfaction in his beloved—Elizabeth was not one to let anyone intimidate her, and she had proven that fact beyond all doubt with her words against her two antagonists. Seeing her engaged in defending herself—seeing the fortitude and self-confidence with which she held herself and fought back against her attackers—filled him with a sense of admiration and love beyond even that which he had previously felt for her. He did not think it was even possible, but there it was—he was even more in love with her than before.

How could he have ever expected to be able to allow himself to court and marry one of the insipid and colorless young heiresses which the ton held as a proper match? He would have been bored within the first two weeks of marriage to such a woman and would have doomed himself to a life without affection. It would have truly been a dull existence—he shuddered to think how close he had come to settling for it.

His musing was interrupted by the explosion of sound from the matrons' end of the room, and he turned and witnessed the two neighboring ladies commiserating over the scene which had just played out. While Lady Lucas appeared to be accepting the disappointment with tolerable composure, Mrs. Bennet was visibly—and vocally—upset with her daughter's perceived foolishness.

"Oh, Lady Lucas," wailed she, "I am sure I do not know what I am to do with that girl. How does she mean to ever be married if she keeps rejecting every proposal of marriage which comes her way?"

Lady Lucas's answer was quiet and noncommittal; it appeared the manner in which Sir William had reprimanded her in church—and the way he was currently watching them closely—had taught the Lucas matron to hold her tongue. Unfortunately, the same could not be said for Elizabeth's mother.

"I mean, really! First, it was Mr. Collins and his proposal, which would have allowed us to stay at Longbourn, and now it is your son Samuel, whom she has known since she was a child. What can she be thinking? No one cares anything for what I suffer, and Elizabeth in particular has no compassion for my nerves!"

That caught Darcy's attention, and he gaped at Mrs. Bennet. He had known Mr. Collins had been attentive to Elizabeth, but as the man had returned to Hunsford with the former Miss Lucas as his bride, Darcy had thought Mr. Collins had redirected his attentions when Elizabeth's indifference become clear. The stupid man had actually had made *his Elizabeth* an offer of marriage? And Mrs. Bennet had actually supported the sycophantic man's suit? Did the woman not know her own daughter? Darcy could not claim to know Elizabeth as well as those of her immediate family did, but it did not take any great insight to understand that she was poorly suited for the man—their relative levels of intelligence alone were testament to that fact! She would be miserable married to him. Indeed, as Mrs. Collins was an intelligent woman herself, Darcy could not begin to understand how she put up with the man.

"I believe I can accurately predict what you are thinking at this moment, Mr. Darcy."

Darcy nearly jumped in surprise as he turned to face the owner of the voice who had interrupted his reverie. Mr. Bennet was standing behind him, watching his wife and Lady Lucas as the former continued to loudly bemoan her daughter's foolishness.

246 ﹌ Jann Rowland

"Can you, indeed?" responded Darcy with a raised eyebrow.

Mr. Bennet shrugged. "I suspect it is very close to what I am thinking at this moment, to be honest. But I have one advantage over you—though I have not exercised my right to control my silly wife to the extent that perhaps I should have, I still have the option. I believe I shall take it now."

The determined man moved off and approached his wife, and moments later, the noise level in the room dropped precipitously, causing Darcy to shake his head. Mr. Bennet was truly a complex character—studying him would take a lifetime, he suspected. The man was obviously quick-witted, and having saddled himself with a woman who was not in any way his equal must have been difficult. It was another testament to the fact that Darcy had made the correct choice.

Chuckling to himself, Darcy glanced around the room and immediately determined to find Elizabeth. He had delayed long enough—it was time to formalize their relationship and begin actively protecting her against the likes of Lucas.

He was about to leave the room when he realized a matter of great import—it appeared that while he had been distracted by the lamentations of the Bennet matron, Samuel Lucas had also quit the room and was nowhere to be seen. He caught the gaze of Mrs. Collins, who had apparently reached the same conclusion, and seeing the look of concern upon her face—her tête-à-tête with her brother had apparently yielded no satisfactory results—Darcy hurried from the parlor, determined to prevent anything from happening to his beloved.

Out in the vestibule, he found an agitated Jane Bennet, who was struggling with her spencer, the tears rolling down her face speaking volumes as to her fears. Her visage turned to relief when he appeared.

"What is it, Miss Bennet?"

"Lizzy and Samuel," gasped Miss Bennet. "Lizzy left to go walking—she does it to clear her mind, especially after events such as we have witnessed this past half hour.

"But she was not gone a moment before Samuel Lucas came storming out of the parlor. He followed her, Mr. Darcy, and the expression on his face . . . I tried to stop him, but he pushed me aside and left—I fear for her!"

There was not a moment to be lost. "I shall go after them, Miss Bennet. Return to the parlor and send Colonel Fitzwilliam after me, for I may need his assistance."

"Thank you, Mr. Darcy!" exclaimed Miss Bennet as she flung her arms around him.

She pulled away immediately, clearly embarrassed over her impetuous action but smiling at him all the same. "You truly are a good man, Mr. Darcy; I believe Elizabeth now sees that as well. Search for her in the paths at the rear of the house—I shall bring the colonel directly."

Face flaming, Miss Bennet turned and, hiking up her skirts, fairly ran from the room, leaving Darcy feeling slightly bemused. He was reminded of the closeness between the sisters—closer, perhaps, than the bond which existed between Richard and himself—and knew that he would be seeing much of Jane *Bingley* in the future. He was looking forward to it, as there were clearly depths to the young woman which he had never known existed.

But for now, he had best concentrate on the matter at hand; he quickly exited the house and made his way around the back. As he cleared the edge of the manor, he stopped up short, and he caught a glimpse of Mr. Lucas disappearing into the trees at the far edge of the garden. Mr. Darcy immediately broke into a run—Lucas would not be allowed to harm his Elizabeth!

Elizabeth's feet led her out beyond the immediate garden and into the paths which crisscrossed the land behind her father's house as she fumed over the audacity of her former friend. She walked for some time without any thought of where her feet were carrying her, her mind going over and over the incidents of the past days and the humiliation perpetrated upon her by those with no morals or concern for anyone but their own petty grievances.

At length, when she had used some of her pent-up energy, she slowed and began to take stock of her situation. She recognized the location—there was a fallen tree to the side of the path, and it told her that she was still close to the house, but the site was secluded and afforded her the privacy she desperately needed. Emotionally spent, she sat on the log and began to think of the day in a more rational manner.

Foremost among her thoughts were the three men who had been her suitors, and she could not help but compare them. Mr. Collins, the first and possibly the most odious, was an open book—obsequious and stupid, he had been too senseless and sure of his own exalted position of parson to the great Lady Catherine to accept her refusal of him. There had been no malice in his thoughts or actions—malice had come later, after his resentment of her refusal of his suit had built, and then when she had dared to act against the desires of his loathsome patroness.

Samuel Lucas, by contrast, was not unintelligent, and he had known exactly what he was doing during his "courtship." Even if Elizabeth had not already greatly esteemed Mr. Darcy, she knew she would have been repulsed by Samuel's actions and manners—there was *nothing* about him which was remotely appealing to a young woman such as herself.

The thought of Samuel Lucas and Mr. Darcy naturally led her to a comparison of the young men in question, and though she may not have thought so early in their relationship, Mr. Darcy was superior in every single category. Samuel had been pushy and arrogant, never caring for her feelings or wishes and finally committing the ultimate betrayal by claiming an engagement which did not exist. By contrast, Mr. Darcy had been patient and affectionate, allowing his emotions, wishes, and desires to show openly while being sensitive to her need to discover her own feelings. He had not betrayed her—even his unfortunate words at Hunsford were not a betrayal; they had simply been the words of a man who had not tempered his sense of pride. *That* was clearly no longer a part of his character.

Thinking back on their interactions throughout the course of their acquaintance, Elizabeth could not help but once again wish that Mr. Darcy had allowed his feelings to show when they had first met. But she was so very glad that he had done so now—clearly, *he* was a man whom she could accept and respect, and one to whom her father could release her without any fear for her future happiness.

The powerful feelings which she had begun to feel for the man welled up in that moment, and though she had previously admitted to herself that she could accept him and be happy with him, there was no longer any point in denying the very great love which she now felt for him. There was no reason to deny any of it. What had begun in contempt and changed with the true knowledge of his actions and character—and had sprouted and grown at Pemberley—were now the genuine feelings of devotion for the man, and she wanted nothing more than to have the ability to declare it openly to him.

The question was how? A man had complete control of the pace of a relationship, and it would be improper for the lady to make the first declaration. Of course, Mr. Darcy had already made *his*, she thought with a smile. She must respond—by word and deed, he would know of her change of heart and her willingness to deepen their connection to meet his already steady devotion. He would know of her love!

A steadily growing noise caught her attention, and Elizabeth glanced back up the path she had traveled. Whoever was approaching was making no attempt to hide their presence, and Elizabeth, though not normally averse to company, found herself still ill-prepared to speak with any degree of composure with anyone. She stood to remove herself from the path, when the man she least wished to see turned a corner in the path and stalked toward her.

Elizabeth could see the look of rage on his face, and she wondered for a moment exactly what he intended and exactly of what he was capable. But she would not cower in fear before this man—he was not worthy of her consideration, and she would show what she thought of him, if any such mystery remained.

"What are you—?"

"Be silent!" cried Elizabeth, unwilling to allow him to begin his diatribe. "I had not believed you to be as lacking in sense as Mr. Collins, but apparently, I was mistaken. Why do you persist in this fantasy?"

"This is no fantasy, Lizzy!" hissed Lucas. "You are *mine*, and I will not allow some northern man with an exaggerated sense of his own worth to take that which rightly belongs to me!"

"I *do not* belong to you, Samuel Lucas! How dare you even insinuate such a thing! I *will not* marry you! Have you no decency or sense of what is right? What has become of you?"

"*I* am as I always was, Lizzy; it is *you* who have changed. I cannot imagine the companion of my youth now chasing after a man with money simply for the sake of gold and jewels."

"And with those words, you prove that you know nothing of me," jibed Elizabeth. "I *love* Mr. Darcy, and I *will* marry him if he should ask me again."

He stopped, his jaw dropping in surprise at the revelation. "*Again?*" was his stammered reply, clearly uncertain as to whether he had heard her correctly. "Do you mean to say—?"

"Yes, Mr. Lucas; that is precisely what I am saying. Mr. Darcy has already proposed to me once, and I rejected him. It puts paid to your estimation of me as a fortune hunter, does it not? For that matter, I wonder why you would wish to marry a woman who is so obviously interested in nothing more than a rich man and the privilege which comes with wealth. Since you do not possess his riches, you can hardly believe I would be content to be *your* wife, if your estimation of me is correct."

The sardonic glare which crawled over Elizabeth's face was in direct counterpoint to Lucas's own scowl.

"I must admit, though," continued Elizabeth, "Mr. Darcy's proposal was insulting, but it is nothing compared to the total lack of concern for my feelings which characterized *yours!*"

"Perchance, then, the time to compromise you has arrived," snarled Samuel, taking another step toward her. "Then, once the rumors start, you will have no choice but to marry me, not when your reputation lies in tatters and your sisters are ruined by your side."

He sneered most unpleasantly as he approached her. "And what of your dearest Jane? How do you think she will feel when the man she loves rejects her because of the scandal which has engulfed her younger sister? Do you believe she will not curse your name and require you to fulfill your duty as you ought?"

"Your words prove how little you know Jane, Mr. Lucas—indeed, your knowledge of her is as lacking as your knowledge of me. Jane would never wish me married to a man such as *you*, nor would she "require me," as you put it, to marry against my will, regardless of her circumstances. And Mr. Bingley *loves* Jane and would never break off their engagement despite what you believe. Besides all of this, Mr. Darcy *loves me*, and I have every confidence in his constancy—his love is forged in the fires of months of suspense and uncertainty, not some obsession of a delusional mind. Beware your actions here this day, Mr. Lucas, as I believe Mr. Darcy wields a great deal of influence—you would not wish that influence to be brought to bear against you."

Samuel threw his hands up in the air. "What do I have to do to convince you that this is best for you, Lizzy? Your mother is convinced; what more do you need?"

"My mother's approval meant nothing when Mr. Collins proposed to me," responded Elizabeth quietly.

Starting anew at this additional piece of information, Samuel gaped at her.

"Yes, Mr. Lucas, you are indeed the third to have proposed marriage to me. Quite singular, is it not? Even Jane, who is acknowledged as the beauty of the neighborhood, has not received so many applications."

He was silent, clearly trying to process this new information which she had just flung in his face.

"You thought you had it completely planned out to your satisfaction, did you not? You thought to shame me into acknowledging a nonexistent engagement by making your falsehoods public, and you counted on my mother to do the rest. But you did *not* count on my father supporting me despite my mother's wishes—my father would never force me to marry *anyone* against my inclinations, or else I would already be beyond your reach as Mr. Collins's wife."

The purple tint of his face was all the answer Elizabeth needed to know that she had guessed close enough to the truth. His fists clenched and unclenched, and she could see he was in a murderous fury. She would not tolerate his attempts to intimidate—whatever he was to do at this moment, she would hold her head high and remain defiant.

"I will not marry you, Mr. Lucas," concluded Elizabeth quietly. "I suggest you give up this hopeless pursuit and find some other, more willing woman who will have you. I never will."

His only answer was a snarl of utter rage, and as his hands came up to grasp her, Elizabeth smiled—though he was physically stronger than she, she was not at all defenseless.

Chapter XVIII

$\mathcal{S}$triding along the confusing maze of paths which meandered through the landscape behind Longbourn, Darcy fretted. Samuel Lucas was familiar with the area, while he was not, and in the time since he had last glimpsed Lucas passing out of sight, much could have happened. His mind conjured horrific images of his love battered and bruised . . . Or worse . . .

No! It would do no good to dwell upon what might be—he had best focus his attention on finding Elizabeth, and then he could deal with whatever situation awaited him. But if the man had harmed Elizabeth in any way, Darcy swore he would not be accountable for his actions.

The place was truly a labyrinth, with paths that crossed each other frequently, some no larger than a pace or two across, many covered with the shifting leaves of the season. Looking this way and that, Darcy was able to detect nothing more than the mostly bare trees, twisted and stunted underbrush, and the gray of the sky—it appeared as if nothing lived in this wasteland of underbrush and bracken.

Just when his concern began to reach the fever pitch akin to panic, he heard raised voices. He stopped abruptly and cast his eyes about, trying to detect their presence through the thick underbrush. Off to his right, he thought he saw a flash of color, and when the muted sounds once again reached him, confirming what his eyes told him, he was off once again, abandoning all propriety as he sped onwards.

He hurried down the path, hearing the voices become all that much louder, and then the sound suddenly stopped. He turned a corner in the path, seeing Elizabeth struggling with Lucas, who held onto her, leaning over and seeming intent upon pulling her down to the ground.

The sight of his beloved being accosted by another man filled him with rage, and in an instant, he had crossed the intervening distance, grasped Lucas by the shoulders, and wrenched him away from Elizabeth to throw him into the dust where he belonged. But to Darcy's immense surprise, Lucas remained upon the ground, doubled over and in some distress, a look of intense pain mixed with hatred apparent in the glare he was somehow able to maintain.

When Darcy glanced over at Elizabeth, seeking confirmation that all was well, he was greeted with a serene smile. Flummoxed by this strange behavior, Darcy glanced back and forth between the two, noticing the smirk and the sparkle in Elizabeth's eyes and the fact that Lucas appeared to be attempting to catch his breath. It seemed as if . . .

Eyes widening, Darcy turned and stared at Elizabeth. She began to chuckle when she noticed his sudden understanding.

"Elizabeth, did you just . . .?"

She nodded with a smirk. "Thank you for coming to save me, Mr. Darcy, but Mr. Lucas just discovered that I was not as helpless as he thought I was."

Darcy gaped at her for a moment before he broke out into a great laugh—even when he felt he had the measure of this remarkable young woman, she continued to amaze him.

Ignoring the gasping and indignant sputtering from the young man who was even now trying to struggle to his feet, Darcy gazed at Elizabeth, allowing his admiration to show clearly upon his face.

"Very good, Elizabeth! But I am curious—how did you know?"

"Where to hit him?"

At Darcy's nod, she continued:

"That little gem was provided to me by none other than a young Samuel Lucas!"

Darcy gaped at her once again, which caused her to break out in a fit of giggles. "It is true! Before he left home to go to school, he told Charlotte and me how to protect ourselves from rakes who would seek to take advantage of us. Of course, I already had an inkling of what could be done with a well-placed knee, but that session helped us understand the exact location and the precise amount of force required. In fact, I seem to remember a similar scene when I became too enthusiastic for his tastes . . ."

Glancing at the man now gaining his feet, Darcy turned back to Elizabeth with a grin. "It appears his instruction was most effective."

Elizabeth merely smirked in response. Lucas, it seemed, was not as amused by the situation.

"How dare you!" rasped he, glaring at Elizabeth with vengeance written upon his brow. "I cannot believe the common harlot you have become chasing after *this* —" he jerked his thumb at Darcy, "man!"

"I suggest you take great care in choosing your words," said Darcy in a menacing tone. "I will brook no criticism of Elizabeth in my presence when you are the one who has behaved most abominably."

"Perhaps, then, the two of you are meant for one another," replied Lucas with a sneer. "She, a scarlet woman chasing after the closest rich man, while *you* merely wish to bed a spirited woman—not that I blame you, considering the inducement," he leered at Elizabeth, "not to mention the insipid heiresses the ton produces."

He turned the full force of his glare back upon Elizabeth, causing Darcy to move between them to protect her.

"I am not some common brigand you can treat in such a manner, Lizzy," said Lucas. "Why can you not—?"

"That is *exactly* what you are, Mr. Lucas!" was Elizabeth's forceful statement.

She moved to Darcy's side and directed the full force of her displeasure at Lucas, something with which Darcy was not unfamiliar. The way her eyes sparkled with the rays of the setting sun filled him with admiration for her courage and determination. Yes, if Darcy were to secure her hand, he would undoubtedly be getting the better end of the bargain.

"How do you think I should react when set upon by a worthless man who has stated his clear intention to compromise me? Truly, Mr. Lucas, I believe you are so lacking in propriety that you cannot determine reality from your fantasy world. Certainly, your brains appear to be addled if after all this time you are still unaware that I know exactly what I want and that I will not be persuaded by your manners—which do not impress me—nor your determination—which frankly disgusts me. What do I have to do to make you understand?"

"Elizabeth—"

"No!" Darcy broke in forcefully. "You, sir, are no gentleman and do not deserve to be treated as such. Now, you will end your misguided pursuit of Miss Bennet, or I will be forced to call you out!"

An unpleasant smirk appeared upon Lucas's face—it appeared as if the man was hoping for this outcome, though why, exactly, Darcy could not say. He would learn a grim lesson if he persisted. He was not aware of Lucas's skill with pistol or sword, but he was confident of his own and knew there were few who could best him.

"I accept."

"*No*, you do not," interrupted an angry Elizabeth. "I am not some trophy to be won in some beastly male ritual for dominance!"

"Elizabeth," Darcy began gently, "I *will not* allow him to treat you in this manner, nor will I allow his continued harassment to continue. If it means I must defend your honor in the manner of a gentleman—though *he* can certainly not claim the title—then I shall. I will allow *nothing* to come between us."

"And I am telling you it is not required." Elizabeth's words were quiet and forceful, and her attention was fixed upon him, her gaze soft, but unyielding. "*Please*, Mr. Darcy, do not do this—*he* is not worth it. I have no wish to risk becoming a widow before I have even had the chance to become a bride."

Darcy's breath caught in his throat, and he stared at Elizabeth in astonishment and wonder. Had she just declared what he thought she had declared? Her calm yet determined gaze in response confirmed her meaning in every particular, and Darcy almost swept her up in his delight. Only the sound of Lucas's shocked and outraged gasp stopped him.

He glanced over at the other man, noting the fact that Lucas's fists were clenched at his sides, and with the gritting of the young man's jaw and the fire in his eyes, Darcy believed at that moment they were about to be attacked by the delusional Lucas when a shout rang out from the path through which he had just traveled.

As one, the three antagonists turned and witnessed the long-awaited (on Darcy's part) support in the form of his cousin. But what he had not expected was for Jane Bennet to bring an entire company with her—in addition to the aforementioned Colonel, he saw Jane herself, Bingley, Mr. Bennet, and Sir William, all striding down the path, each appearing extremely angry.

Jane Bennet fairly flew in to the arms of her sister, accompanied by her father, who hovered over his daughters protectively. Darcy could hear Elizabeth assuring her family that she was well and had not been harmed. Bingley and Fitzwilliam moved to stand side by side with Darcy, facing down the Lucas scion.

"We understood you could use some help, Darcy," stated Bingley as he turned an unfriendly eye on the aggressor.

"Believe me, Bingley—your presence is most welcome, indeed."

It was the presence—and countenance—of Sir William which was the most surprising. His demeanor spoke of an incandescent rage, the likes of which Darcy had never seen nor even imagined on the face of the usually ebullient man.

"Samuel Lucas!" roared he. "What do you think you are doing?"

Lucas stared at the visage of his enraged father momentarily before his countenance became a sneer. "I have just accepted a challenge from Mr. Darcy, Father. I shall prove I am the better man, over his body if necessary."

"No! Mr. Darcy is truly well within his right to call you out considering the way you have behaved, but I will not allow this to continue. You will not drag our family name through the mud, regardless of whatever insanity has taken hold of you."

Turning to Darcy, the Lucas sire bowed low and continued:

"Mr. Darcy, I wish to apologize most profusely that one of my family has conducted himself in such a disgraceful manner. I have apparently been remiss in his education as a civilized gentleman, but you may rest assured that the oversight shall be remedied immediately. In the meantime, I beg you to retract your challenge and allow me the opportunity to correct my wayward son."

Darcy bowed low, indicating his agreement, before stepping back and standing beside Elizabeth. He placed her hand in the crook of his arm and held onto it possessively.

But Lucas was not yet finished. "This is no business of yours, Father," he snapped. "You have no right to interfere with a challenge which has been made and accepted."

"It is not? *I do not?*" thundered Sir William, now fairly apoplectic with fury. "How can it not be my business when my own son—and *heir!*—behaves in such an infamous manner, spouting words not fit for a common rowdy, to a girl I love as well as my own daughters? Your actions and words have shamed me acutely; I never thought it possible that my own son could behave thus. I do not know what has happened to you at that school, but I begin to regret ever sending you there.

"Now, you will return to Lucas Lodge forthwith, and you will wait there for me to arrive so we may discuss your conduct. I have business at Longbourn, after which I shall join you directly."

"I shall do no such thing, Father—"

"Yes, you shall!" interjected Sir William. "If you do not, you shall find yourself disinherited forthwith!"

A gasp escaped the startled man's lips. "You would not dare—"

"I would indeed, my son." Sir William was pitiless and implacable. "I have two other sons, Samuel—either may inherit after I am gone."

"But . . . but James . . . he is young," Lucas sputtered, only to be cut off mercilessly by his father.

"James is approaching the age you were when I sent you off to school, Samuel, and if I were to make him my heir, it would afford me the opportunity to start afresh and teach him, since I have so obviously failed with you."

The young man visibly deflated at the sight of Sir William's imperious glare. "I *am* in earnest, Samuel—if you do not return now to the house, I shall disown you and cast you from the family. Go home!"

His face white and his mouth working, though creating no sound, Lucas did the only thing in his power at that moment—he turned on his heel and stalked off.

Sir William let out a sigh of relief—the confrontation had clearly taken something out of the jovial man, and he wilted slightly. The day's events—indeed, even those of the previous weeks—appeared to have taken their toll upon him.

He turned to the group—the young ladies were gaping at him as if they had never seen him before—and a ghost of his former character returned.

"Bennet—my good friend—Mr. Bingley, Colonel Fitzwilliam, I believe we should return to the house." He turned to Elizabeth and winked at her. "It appears as if we are interrupting something very personal and important between Mr. Darcy and Miss Elizabeth. Shall we?"

Richard, true to form, let out a loud chortle and slapped Darcy on the back before joining Sir William as he retreated toward the house. Bingley smirked at his friend and flipped him a jaunty salute as he gathered Miss Bennet's arm—she had apparently assured herself that her sister was well and was now smiling at the couple—and followed the other two gentlemen down the path.

"Yes, I believe Sir William was correct," stated Mr. Bennet with a smirk. "It seems we *are* interrupting something of a most delicate nature."

His smirk became a pointed look of expectation at his second daughter, and Elizabeth, in response, blushed fiercely. "I believe you have been keeping something from me, Elizabeth," he said. "I shall anticipate an accounting from you in the very near future.

"And as for you, Mr. Darcy," continued the Bennet sire, shifting his gaze, "I shall reserve an appointment for you in my library *the very moment* you return to the house."

Murmuring his acceptance, Darcy waited until the man—whose smirk had returned in full force—had departed before turning to the woman at his side. She was regarding him out of the corner of her eye while she dug the toe of one boot into the dirt of the path. Darcy gazed at her—gazed at *his* Elizabeth—for he was certain that she was now—or about to become—*his*. He fondly noted the playful smile on her face and the contented air about her. Her eyes sparkled and danced, and amusement—amusement!—flashed across her face. The woman was bewitching, but Darcy did not mind in the slightest to be caught irrevocably in her web—he had gone too long wishing, hoping, and praying to be caught—and was determined to catch her in return. Cognizant that this was the moment for which he had longed, he took a deep breath and focused his attention upon her.

"Did I understand you correctly, Miss Elizabeth?" queried he, his heart in his throat. "Please tell me I did not imagine your words or misconstrue their meaning."

Elizabeth's expression fairly glowed with amusement and mischief. "Come, now, Mr. Darcy—you must know me well enough by now to know that I *never* profess opinions which are not my own. Do you not?"

Darcy threw back his head and laughed, feeling all of the tension and anxiety evaporate in the wake of her saucy answer.

"So, am I to understand that I am no longer *the last* man on earth you could ever be prevailed upon to marry?"

"Touché, Mr. Darcy," she responded with a laugh. "Indeed, I may say that you have made a remarkable recovery and that your previous position of infamy is now held by a most deserving young man, though I must admit that there may be another—or dare I say *two* young men!—of our acquaintance who have only been defeated for the position by a hair's breadth."

Affecting a knowing air, Darcy responded:

"Ah, but you have only said I am not the last. You have not explained where I stand in that horde of young men. Might I perchance occupy a position closer the top of that prodigious list than the bottom?"

The smile on Elizabeth's lips never faded, and she cocked her head to the side as if deep in thought. "I daresay that the recovery I have mentioned is complete; from *last* to *only*, and all in less than a year. You are truly a remarkable man, sir."

Feeling a happiness he had never experienced in his entire life, Darcy stepped toward her and grasped her hands in his while bestowing his most grateful smile upon her. "In that case, I should wish to redefine our relationship, Miss Elizabeth.

"I believe you know my feelings, but let me restate them so there will be no mistake. I love you more than life itself. I have been your devoted servant for so long that I cannot remember—nor would I wish to remember—what it was like before you came into my life. I *love you* ardently, passionately, and completely, and I will do anything to convince you we belong together. Will you do me the great honor of accepting my hand and becoming my wife?"

"I believe I should like that very much, Mr. Darcy."

Trembling with emotion—and noting that Elizabeth was in a similar state—Darcy raised both of her hands and bestowed identical kisses upon them. Within, Darcy could feel a font of happiness that he had never known or imagined could exist. As it welled up, he reflected that all of the months of uncertainty, pain, and heartache had been well worth the experience and the lessons they had taught to him. Whatever may come, he was finally home.

"Bennet, may I have a moment?"

Mr. Bennet had been walking in silence as the rescue party—as he jokingly called the group in his own mind—made their way back to Longbourn. Looking up, he noticed that they were nearing the house and that Jane and her fiancé, as well as the valiant Colonel, had outstripped him and were even now entering the gardens behind the house. Sir William, who was now addressing him, had slowed to allow the young folk to pass him by, presumably in order to speak to his neighbor and make his apologies for his son. Bennet's conjecture was immediately confirmed by the man's next words, and he reflected that a sober and serious Sir William was not a common sight, nor was the man half so enjoyable when weighed down by the cares of the world—nor, it would seem, by worry over a wayward son.

"You must allow me to apologize in the most animated means possible for the offenses my eldest has committed against Miss Elizabeth. I am most mortified by his behavior and threats, and I wish to assure you that Samuel will be kept under my direct control until Elizabeth has joined her young beau in marriage."

An amused smile was his response. "Are you not putting the cart before the horse, my friend?"

A hint of the jovial neighbor he had known for years emerged. "The way those two were regarding each other when we departed? Come, now, Bennet—we have been friends and neighbors for years, and I know you are not blind."

"Indeed, I am not," replied Bennet, a wistful feeling coming over him. "I have just given Jane permission to leave me merely a few weeks ago, and now I shall lose Elizabeth. I find that I am less than eager at the prospect, though I know their young men make them happy."

He sighed before continuing. "I suppose it is merely the selfishness of a foolish old man."

"If it is foolishness, then we are fools together. At least you may be comforted by the thought that your two eldest will be marrying men of the highest character and intelligence, both with splendid fortunes. I admit I felt much the same when I let Charlotte go away with Mr. Collins, and though the man is hardly a paragon of good sense, I knew *she* felt herself a burden upon the family and wished for her own situation. Of course, *I* could *never* have felt her to be a burden and would have welcomed her presence in my home all her life had she chosen to remain unmarried."

After a moment's reflection, he continued. "Of course, Samuel has changed so much that I cannot guarantee that she would be welcome after my death. I feel as if I do not know him any longer—he is not the son I sent off to school."

Bennet forbore mentioning that Samuel had not changed in essentials. Even though he and Lizzy had played together as children, he had always been insistent on having his own way, and his sense of entitlement had not diminished with time.

"Unfortunately, it is not uncommon for young men to come away from their university experience changed for the worse," said Bennet aloud. "There are so many things to tempt them—gaming, women, and the freedom of being their own masters—that it is a wonder that any of them turn out well. I had several close friends who drifted away under the pressures of their pursuits at university.

"And you must understand that though you were able to send him away to learn, he does not come from the first circles, nor did he have access to the kind of funds that many of his friends and acquaintances undoubtedly did. That can make a man bitter, Lucas, and change them beyond recognition."

"You think this is what happened to Samuel?"

"It is possible," replied Bennet with a shrug. "He certainly seems to resent Darcy, who we know is a very wealthy man. He deliberately set himself in direct confrontation with the man in regard to my Lizzy and would not be deterred. If Darcy had not been on the scene, would he have taken Lizzy's rejection with a little more grace? It is hard to say. But the fact that his childhood playmate preferred the rich man could not have helped."

Sir William was silent. Bennet knew that the man had not ever been to school himself—he had started out a shopkeeper and had made his fortune and earned his knighthood through service to the crown. He had followed the tradition of sending his son to school as the gentry did, but Bennet understood that Sir William was not truly of the gentry and had found it necessary to navigate his way through their sometimes complicated society through trial and error.

Still, he was a good and honest man, if prone toward simple-mindedness and a certain pomposity, and though he had provided Bennet with many amusements in his behavior over the years, Bennet truly liked him and had been more than willing to help him become accustomed to his new situation when he had purchased Lucas Lodge. His son, however, was not cut from the same cloth, and Bennet suspected he never had been, for all that Lucas had tried to mold him into a proper gentleman.

"Regarding your apology," continued Mr. Bennet after a moment, "inasmuch as an apology is required, I heartily accept it and hold no ill-will toward you for the actions of your eldest—and I can tell you that Elizabeth will also hold no grudges."

"I thank you for that, Bennet. You are truly a good neighbor."

"It is the least I can do. But I must inform you that I do not believe the situation is in any way due to any failing of yours—Samuel is the one who should apologize, not you."

A morose expression came over Sir William's face. "Perhaps you are correct, but I feel I should extend my apologies as the head of my family—he *is* my son, after all.

"Also, I doubt Samuel himself would ever extend the apology himself, and since he will not do so, I will on his behalf."

"You are a good man, Sir William, and I count you as one of my friends. As for Samuel, you may be correct. But I must warn you—due to his actions, I cannot welcome Samuel at Longbourn. Elizabeth may leave soon with her young man, but I still have two daughters left at home, and I will not risk the same thing happening with them. I suspect that Mary and Kitty will not prove to be as adept as Elizabeth at protecting themselves."

"I understand, and I cannot blame you for your caution. One of the stipulations I will impose upon Samuel's behavior is that he may not come to Longbourn at any time, nor will he be allowed to approach any of your family—and Elizabeth in particular, of course."

"In that case, I thank you, Sir William—a lesser man might have supported his son regardless of the circumstances."

Sir William nodded and smiled. "I can do no other, Bennet. Samuel will not trouble you any longer—this I pledge."

They had almost reached the house by that time, and Bennet, looking forward to a little peace and quiet, immediately picked up on the noise which was emanating from the parlor in which his family sat with their guests. Unwilling to brave the cacophony, he turned to Sir William and invited him to his bookroom:

"How about a little fortification before we return to the parlor, my friend?"

"I believe that would be most welcome," responded Sir William.

The two men bypassed the noise of the parlor and entered the bookroom. Sitting behind his desk with his neighbor for company, Bennet reflected that the noise of the house, which had continued for some weeks, would likely remain at a high level for the next few weeks due to Elizabeth's imminent engagement. He would bear it, however, and bear it cheerfully—his favorite daughter would be gone once it was finished, and the days of his comfortable life with Jane and Elizabeth near him would end. These were days to be savored, not to be looked upon with trepidation.

Their declarations completed and the proposal accepted, Elizabeth and Mr. Darcy wandered the paths of her home for some time, allowing themselves to simply enjoy each other's company while attempting to adjust to their new situation. And though Elizabeth knew herself to be happy, the primary emotion she felt at this time was relief—she had been moving toward this for some time, after all. The man by her side was so ardent and passionate that she could not help but understand the strength of Mr. Darcy's feelings for her and the devotion which he conveyed with his every glance.

As a young woman who had sometimes despaired of ever meeting a young man whom she could both love *and* respect, Elizabeth found herself experiencing a sense of contentment which she had never before felt. Mr. Darcy truly was a man who was her equal in every sense, and she could not help but rejoice in the happy chance which had allowed her to meet him, not to mention the fortitude he had displayed in continuing to love her and pursue her in the face of what had passed between them. She was very grateful to him—of that, she was certain.

Their conversation consisted of light and playful banter interspersed with periods of quiet contemplation for both, neither conscious of where they were walking, nor the advancing hour.

They continued in this attitude until Elizabeth, curious as to his unflagging devotion in the face of intense disappointment and adversity, decided to voice a question which had been nagging at the back of her mind their whole time together.

"Mr. Darcy, if I may, I should like to ask you a question."

"You may ask me anything you like," was the response, "as long as you agree to call me by my given name—I should not like to continue to be merely 'Mr. Darcy' to you."

Elizabeth made a face. "I should like that, but 'Fitzwilliam' is so pretentious. What possessed your parents to bestow your cousin's family name upon you?"

Darcy affected an injured air. "It is not pretentious—it is distinguished."

He grinned when Elizabeth rolled her eyes.

"In answer to your question, my beloved, it is a family tradition to name the firstborn Darcy son with his mother's maiden name."

"Bennet Darcy?" asked Elizabeth.

"If it pleases you."

"I suppose it is better than some. Our eldest son will be thankful my family name is not 'Hollingberry.'"

A laugh met her declaration, and Darcy squeezed her hand. "Yes, a fortunate happenstance, indeed. As for how to address me, Georgiana usually calls me simply 'William,' and I would be happy if you did the same."

Elizabeth made a great show of mulling it over in her mind before she finally nodded. "While I do not know if I find you to be simply 'William,' I suppose that moniker works as well as any. As for me, you have my leave to call me 'Elizabeth' or 'Lizzy'—but, please, I beg you to refrain from addressing me as 'Eliza.'"

"Caroline Bingley?" queried he.

"Indeed," confirmed she. "Not only does she address me in that manner almost exclusively—and few others have *ever* done so even in passing—but it is the condescending tone she uses which has induced me to hate the appellation."

"Condescending tones are Miss Bingley's specialty," responded Darcy with an air of affected pomposity, causing Elizabeth to giggle in response.

"But please, Elizabeth, I believe you had a question for me?"

"Indeed, I did . . . William," began Elizabeth, feeling a hint of hesitancy. She had little desire to bring up the past, but she felt that in order to close that chapter of her life, she must.

"I was merely wondering . . . That is to say, after my behavior in Hertfordshire last autumn, not to mention the abominable way in which I abused you at Hunsford . . . what made you retain your esteem for me, when by all rights you should have hated me?"

The manner in which he abruptly halted threw Elizabeth off balance, and fearing she had angered him, she nevertheless raised her eyes to meet his. His gaze, though tender and affectionate, was still somewhat stern, and he appeared to be considering something for a few moments before he undertook his answer.

"I will answer you, Elizabeth, but on one condition."

"I believe I must hear the condition before I can agree to it, William," was her saucy reply.

His answering grin transformed his face, and Elizabeth reflected that one of the most important duties in her new life with him would be to induce him to smile more often.

"Once we have canvassed this subject, I would wish never to bring it up again. The memories are . . . painful in some instances, and I should much rather move on to happier times together with you rather than continually dredge up the mistakes of the past."

"William," admonished Elizabeth, "I understand some of our past interactions are painful—especially for you, who have been emotionally attached longer than I—but we cannot ignore the events which did indeed happen. I would prefer to look back on those times and respect the mistakes made while remembering lessons well learned."

"What you say is true, dearest, but I would not have us continually speaking of this subject throughout our marriage. The lessons learned have indeed been valuable, but I wish to remember the joy this time has brought me and look forward to our future together rather than always be reliving the past."

Affected profoundly by his words, Elizabeth reached up and cupped his jaw in her hand while smiling lovingly. "On this, we can certainly agree, William. I also have no wish to dwell on the mistakes we both made during our previous dealings. However, I should prefer to have the discussion and settle everything between ourselves rather than wait—let us put this behind us now."

A soft smile came over his face, and he took the hand which was upon his face and bestowed a tender kiss upon it. "I had no idea the woman to whom I had pledged myself was so wise. I shall answer your question, Elizabeth, and then you can answer mine, and we shall return to the house. I believe it has become somewhat late."

Startled, Elizabeth looked to the sky and discovered the lengthening shadows of the setting sun—the time had passed more swiftly than she had imagined. She took her fiancé's arm and directed him toward Longbourn.

"Then let us walk as we speak."

Mr. Darcy—no, William now—fell into step beside her, his free hand caressing hers absently as he walked and as he thought about the answer to her question.

"To be honest," he finally said, "I cannot completely answer your question. After that evening at the parsonage, I had fully intended to return to my home in London and forget our argument, forget Hertfordshire, and forget *you*, but it did not exactly happen in that manner.

"I am sure my sister and my cousin worried for me, and I expect it appeared as if I were cast down into the depths of despair." He smiled at her affectionately. "And in a certain sense, I was. I spent a disproportionate amount of time alone— more than even I am usually wont to do—and I believe Georgiana and Fitzwilliam thought I spent much of that time in my cups, though in truth, I only overindulged once or twice. I was far too involved in trying to decide upon the importance and level of truth in your words to imbibe freely. In time, I began to understand your meaning, and when I had examined my life to that point, I realized that there was much in my behavior which could be changed for the better. Then, of course, I began to be weighed down by a sense of my own failures, not only in the matter of our 'courtship,' but also in the manner in which I had behaved throughout the course of my life."

"William . . ." Elizabeth began to admonish him, embarrassed for her own words, but he would have nothing of it.

"No, Elizabeth—I know you are about to say that your words were merely prompted by your misunderstanding of me. In a sense, you are correct—for you did misunderstand my intentions and my character—but your words also had a large measure of truth in them. I *have* been a selfish being during the course of my life, and though I have been a liberal master and have not neglected those who are less fortunate, I have at the very least in my *thoughts* looked down upon those whom I felt to be lower than myself in importance."

His face took on an introspective look, and though Elizabeth felt he was perhaps too hard on himself—much as he had been overly prideful before—still, Elizabeth felt it was necessary for him to purge himself of his feelings of guilt in order for them to move on from their past.

"After I had admitted my own culpability and examined my life, I discovered a great desire to improve myself and do better. I will acknowledge that one of my reasons for doing so was to prove that I was not the complete scoundrel which I had been deemed by a young woman with whom I had desperately fallen in love."

His playful words and cheeky grin did nothing to halt the deep blush Elizabeth felt burning on her cheeks. At the same time, she gazed at this man in wonder—her words alone had brought out such a change in him, and she readily confessed to herself that she had fully expected him to angrily refute her words, causing whatever feelings he cherished for her to be swallowed up in the onset of his resentment. Had he been any other man, they undoubtedly would have, but clearly, *her Fitzwilliam Darcy* was cut from a different cloth than most.

"The other—and more important—reason was that I did not wish to have experienced what I had in vain. You humbled me, Elizabeth, and rightly so—I was in desperate need of humbling, for I had forgotten the lessons of my youth and needed someone to tell me in no uncertain terms that I was not the man I had thought I was or that I had desired to be."

Silence reigned over them for several moments. The fingers of William's free hand continued their light caressing of her own gloved hands, which held on to his arm, and though they were still covered by the soft fabric, Elizabeth could feel her skin tingle at his touch. If he could do this by merely stroking the back of her hand, the passion that would subsist between them would truly be a marvelous thing.

"I was taught as a young man to be proud of my heritage and to uphold the Darcy honor and family legacy, but my parents were truly good people who looked on all about them as valuable in their own right. When you meet my uncle, you will find a man who is about as unpretentious as any member of the upper circles you are likely to meet—he is truly a good man who loves his wife and thinks that many of the opinions held by the upper crust of the ton are ridiculous and worthy of being laughed at. In fact, I suspect your father and my uncle will get along famously, as they are quite similar in temperament and the way they view the world . . .

"*My* failing was an overabundance of pride, which began as the pride of family and heritage but also grew to a tendency to look down on those whose pedigrees, fortune, and societal standing were not the equal of mine. It was not something my parents had ever intended when they had taught me of my heritage."

"But William," interrupted Elizabeth, "that cannot be completely true. After all, you welcomed Bingley as a friend when he is clearly not your equal in society and consequence."

"That is true," responded William. "But Bingley is rather the exception than the norm.

"I think you may have noticed," he now said with a rueful smile upon his face, "that I do not make friends easily. Many people mistake my reticence for aloofness, but in truth, I am merely uncomfortable around people I do not know. Bingley was easy to befriend—though perhaps the opposite is closer to the truth—because of his engaging and open manners, and once I came to know him, I could not turn away from him. I have had few friends in my life, and once I make them, I tend to do anything I can to keep them.

"But as I left Kent, I began to understand your words and my own behavior, and I resolved upon improving myself, but I had one preeminent thought in mind—to show you, should our paths ever cross again, that I *had* heard and understood your words and that I had taken steps to correct your reproofs which, though they may have been founded in misunderstanding and the lies of a certain acquaintance of mine, were still to a great degree deserved."

"Was that why you were not angry when we met at Pemberley?"

"Angry at finally witnessing my greatest wish come true?" retorted he. "Elizabeth, I had dreamed of seeing you walking the paths of Pemberley, sitting with me in the music room, playing with your passion, singing with that angelic voice of yours. I could never be angry at seeing you there."

Elizabeth felt the fire creep back over her cheeks and was surprised at his words all over again. For a man who considered himself ineloquent and awkward in company, he could certainly reduce her to blushes with naught but a few words!

"I am flattered, William, but please do not bestow me with praise which I have not earned."

"And I say you *have* earned it, Elizabeth," contradicted her fiancé. "I am perfectly serious when I say that I have rarely heard anything which gave me more pleasure than hearing you play and sing. You are perhaps not as technically proficient as some I have heard, but you have a way of putting your entire heart and being into your performance which renders me absolutely and utterly in your power. You truly underestimate your own worth in this matter, Elizabeth.

"Besides," continued he with a mischievous smirk, "your lack of technical perfection may, I believe, be remedied with a dedication to practicing."

Elizabeth slapped his hand at the reference to their sparring at Rosings, which did little to wipe the impudent grin off his face.

"I am in earnest, Elizabeth—you play and sing with such passion . . . I believe it was that passion, coupled with your playfulness and ability to put everyone with whom you come in contact at ease, which encouraged my feelings for you to develop with such strength.

"As for our meeting at Pemberley, once I had felt that I had begun to deal with some of my faults, I had seriously begun to consider seeking you out again. I had not made a certain decision—I did not know how you reacted to my letter, after all—but the fact that my affections never wavered taught me that what I had been feeling was no passing fancy and that the possibility of further rejection was worth the opportunity to show you the changes I had made and to perhaps pursue my fondest wish in a more proper manner."

"You were actually thinking of seeking me out again?"

"Perhaps not consciously," said William with a shrug. "But, yes, I believe I was beginning to lean in that direction. Of course, your presence at Pemberley when I arrived provided me with the excuse I needed."

A sly smile stole over his face as he continued. "You may not credit it, but my surprise at seeing you at Pemberley lasted for all of thirty seconds or so. I immediately began to plan how to keep you there and how to fulfill my other desire of seeing you in the music room at the pianoforte I had recently purchased for Georgiana. And I was able to accomplish both, if only for a short time, much to my pleasure and delight."

Elizabeth rounded on him with an expression of mock accusation. "You mean you instructed Georgiana to issue that invitation for dinner?"

"I did no such thing," replied William with a certain smugness. "I thought it likely that she might extend an invitation—especially if you put her at ease, which you certainly did—and she obliged me in a most satisfying way. She had heard all about you in my letters to her last autumn, and she clearly understood that your continued presence would bring me pleasure."

Hearing of his thoughts and machinations brought a delighted laugh to Elizabeth's lips. Would she ever obtain the measure of this man? A part of her hoped not, as she was enjoying immensely the surprises he continually had in store for her.

"I must confess—I had no idea I was marrying such a manipulative scoundrel. To be using poor Georgiana to further your attempts at wooing—for shame, sir!"

"I hope there are many more things you will learn about me, Elizabeth, and I hope to spend a lifetime learning of you."

"I am sure you shall," replied Elizabeth, gazing up into his eyes. She was certain he could see her heart in them, as the look he returned was tender and conveyed the depth of his regard.

"I do have a question for you, however, if you will allow me."

At Elizabeth's acquiescing nod, he continued:

"I must admit that though I was hoping for a softening on your part, I had never expected such a dramatic transformation. Can you please account for the great change in your feelings for me?"

Thinking back upon the past months, Elizabeth considered his request, wondering at the best way to respond to his query. Though she was not necessarily certain in her own mind how the change had come about, she knew he deserved an answer, and she determined to do her best to satisfy his curiosity.

"Your letter was the genesis of my change in feelings," declared Elizabeth after some thought. They were approaching the back gardens and she felt that she needed to answer him before they entered the house, yet she did not rush to answer—he had taken great care to answer her question, and she wished to extend the same civility to him in return.

"My dislike had been formed in no small part by our initial meeting and my resentment of your words there."

He groaned and made to respond, but Elizabeth would not allow it. "William, please allow me to finish, and let those regrettable words fade into the past as they should. I was offended by your words and, at the time, carried that grudge as if it were a crutch, propping up my dislike of you. I realize *now* that the words were spoken to Bingley for some other reason than to insult me, and as I look back on it now, I comprehend the fact that you never really even looked at me when you spoke."

"You are correct, but that does not make the offense any less."

"I daresay it does not," Elizabeth agreed, "but it *does* make it understandable. And your actions since that time—even the regrettable words at Hunsford—have completely disproved the implication of those words. I find now that I have no reason to repine.

"But at the time, what I had heard took on a life of its own, and as I had already, in my cleverness, taken a decided disliking to you, Mr. Wickham's words of accusation found fertile ground in which to grow. Perhaps I should have been suspicious of his perfectly prepared story—not to mention his motives—but in my resentment I took his tale to heart as a justification for my dislike.

"Thus, your letter, in laying out your actions, showed me a different person than I had fancied I had seen, and it also showed me that my judgment was not infallible, as I had, in my arrogance, begun to feel was the case."

"Was it difficult for you to accept the letter for the truth?"

Elizabeth turned away and allowed her free hand to brush against the mostly bare branches of some of the shrubs along the path. This accounting had been harder than she had thought it would be, but she was glad she had insisted upon it now rather than waiting—once they were finished, they could focus fully on the future, taking no more thought for the mistakes of the past.

"I was not of a mind to accept it at all when I first read it—in fact, I thought it was the grossest of falsehoods, particularly the piece concerning Mr. Wickham. It did not take long, however, before rationality began to assert itself, and through a combination of remembrances of Mr. Wickham's words, actions, and manners, and the words in your letter, I became convinced that you were telling the absolute truth and that Mr. Wickham was exactly as you had described him.

"Your actions and motivations regarding Jane took much longer to reconcile. I could immediately understand and accept your account with respect to your friend, but that did not make your account of the failings of my family any easier to hear."

"I hope to never disappoint you again in such a manner," declared William. His earnest expression and loving smile nearly took Elizabeth's breath away, but she would not allow him to deny that which had been truth, despite how difficult it had been to accept.

"And I am sure I have noticed your attempts to get to know my mother better, William," responded Elizabeth. "I love you all the more for it, especially since she has seemed to be especially hostile to you—even more than she was wont to be in the past. You have truly been persistent, and I believe you may have begun to win her over."

"I should hope so," agreed he. "She will be my mother-in-law, after all."

"She shall indeed."

The lovers were silent after that declaration, and entering the garden, they walked the path toward the house, each thinking of the things they had shared and the future, which now appeared bright and filled with the promise of love, laughter, and a family to cherish. Elizabeth reflected that it was more than she had ever expected, and she was grateful all over again for the happy manner in which their situation had been resolved.

They spoke not a word as they entered the house and divested their outer wear into the waiting arms of the servants. The babble of noise from the parlor met them as they journeyed into the house, and they looked at each other with some amusement as the shrill voice of Mrs. Bennet rose over the rest.

"Are you ready, Elizabeth?" queried William with a fond smile.

"I believe I am, William. Though most of the room undoubtedly already knows or suspects, I believe we should make them wait no longer."

"Then we had better go to it."

With that, they walked down the hallway toward the parlor, noting the growing noise of the room. They truly had returned to Bedlam.

Chapter XIX

As they moved to open the door and enter the parlor, Elizabeth could not deny the feeling of apprehension which knotted in the bottom of her stomach. Her prior feelings for the man at her side were, after all, well known to her family and, indeed, to the entire neighborhood, as she had not been shy about sharing them. And now to have those feelings completely reversed in a matter of months . . . Well, suffice it to say, Elizabeth was concerned over the reactions of her family. William had not hidden his courting by any stretch of the imagination, but still, being a private person, he had not exactly displayed his feelings upon his sleeve either. Surely her family — outside of Jane and her father, who were both now well acquainted with the new situation — suspected some measure of her change of heart, but it was a long distance between tolerating a previously intolerable man and loving him with all her heart. She expected a certain amount of convincing to follow their entrance.

The reaction of the neighborhood was less of a worry. Certainly there were those who, remembering her previous abuse of this man, would suspect that she had been shifted to this change of heart for purely mercenary motives, and she could not but admit that their thoughts would be, although untrue, at least understandable. She was, however, confident in her ability to sway the naysayers — all they needed to do was watch her together with her beloved, and she was certain they could not help but perceive the regard between them. If they did not, she decided, it was no concern of hers.

They stopped in front of the door, where her fiancé turned to regard her, an eyebrow raised in question.

"I am perfectly fine, William — there is no need to worry for my wellbeing."

"Elizabeth, you are, indeed, the most resolute and courageous person of my acquaintance, but these past few days have been trying. Are you certain you would not rather avoid this and retire with me to your father's bookroom instead?"

"No, William." Elizabeth was firm. "I will not allow either Mr. Collins or my mother to intimidate me when we have done nothing wrong.

"Besides," continued Elizabeth, smirking at him, "I could not possibly deprive my father of the opportunity to exact his revenge upon you for stealing me away from him. I am sorry, but you are on your own with regard to your meeting with Papa."

"Minx!" hissed William, placing an affectionate kiss on the back of her now bare hand. "I imagine you are enjoying the prospect, are you not?"

Elizabeth grinned. "I know my father, William, and I do not believe that you can escape his sardonic tongue, even if you should be inclined to try."

"I assure you I have no intention of attempting to avoid your father. I am certain facing him can be no worse than facing an irate young woman whose hand in marriage I had the temerity to request."

Laughing, Elizabeth was heartened by the way he could use that awful night to tease her and by the way the mention of it did not bother her in the slightest.

"You may yet be surprised, sir. However, I do not intend to stand here at the door to the parlor like a thief in the night. It is time we joined the various members of our parties."

With a nod, William resolutely put out his hand and, grasping the handle, turned it and followed Elizabeth into the room.

The thickness of the door which separated the parlor from the hall was surprisingly effective in blocking the sound—the dissonance which persisted in the room impacted them sharply upon their entry. Then, for a brief moment, the room fell silent.

The two main perpetrators of the previous volume of the room had, of course, been her mother and Mr. Collins. And while Mr. Collins was gaping at Elizabeth and her fiancé, his mouth moving much like a fish out of water, Mrs. Bennet's mouth had apparently snapped shut as she glared at the two newly arrived lovers. Her gaze was most certainly not welcoming, causing Elizabeth to once again wonder just what it was that her mother had against Mr. Darcy—it was something which she was determined to discover as soon as may be.

The other occupants of the room were arrayed in small clusters and appeared to be talking quietly with one another in their respective groups. William's relations were in one corner of the room, huddled with Jane and Bingley, and Elizabeth thought she detected a certain wonder in their countenances, no doubt due to Mrs. Bennet's complete lack of discretion in voicing her opinions loudly in the company of those who were not family. Jane, of course, had seen it before, and she appeared her usual serene self. Lady Lucas, meanwhile, sat in close proximity with Mrs. Bennet, apparently trying to console her, while her daughter Maria and Elizabeth's younger sisters looked on in astonishment. The final witness to this folly was Mrs. Collins. Charlotte appeared upset and at her wit's end, and she sat close to her husband, ineffectually trying to curb his excesses. She appeared tired and drained but determined to make her point.

The silence, though golden, lasted only a moment before Mr. Collins stood with an abruptness which startled Elizabeth—his ponderous motions never showing her at any time in the past that he was capable of such quick movement—and began berating her in a loud voice. At almost the same time, Mrs. Bennet—though she did not stand—pushed her nose up into the air and began to voice her own opinions of the affair in a loud and angry tone. And though much of what each said was intelligible, a few of their words filtered over the din and made their way into Elizabeth's consciousness.

". . . such a willful and disobedient daughter, I do not know . . ."

". . . never in my life have I seen such a blatant disregard . . ."

". . . mark my words, Miss Lizzy, if you are determined to continue in this fashion . . ."

". . . my noble lady patroness is most seriously displeased . . ."

". . . you will never marry, Lizzy . . ."

". . . thrown from the bosom of your family as befitting a most shameless hoyden . . ."

And as Elizabeth was beginning to wish she had taken William's council and accompanied him to her father's room, her wonderful fiancé—clearly taking offense to Mr. Collin's last statement—broke into the clamor.

"*Silence!*" thundered he, drawing all eyes in the room to himself.

A shocked stillness met his outburst as the previously reserved Fitzwilliam Darcy exerted his authority. Mrs. Bennet stopped in mid-tirade, and even Mr. Collins was rendered speechless by the sight of his patroness's nephew raising his voice in such a manner.

"Enough of this inappropriate display! I do not believe I have ever witnessed such unseemly manners in my life!"

When he had seen he held their attention, William moderated his voice and calmly continued:

"That is better." He turned to Mrs. Bennet, ignoring the slapping gums of the incompetent Mr. Collins and focusing solely upon the Bennet matron. "Mrs. Bennet, you must cease your lamentations and your worry for Miss Elizabeth's welfare. Your daughter is the most exceptional woman I have ever had the good fortune to meet, and I have the very great privilege to have obtained her acceptance of my hand. We are to be married—therefore, you need not ever worry for her again, as I shall be responsible for her well-being. I assure you that Elizabeth's happiness shall always be my foremost concern."

A stunned Mrs. Bennet was silent in the face of his declaration—she had clearly expected something else, raising Elizabeth's curiosity to an even higher level. Could her mother possibly have thought . . . ? No, there was no sense in speculating—Elizabeth would confront her as soon as the opportunity presented itself and learn the truth.

The company was *not* so fortunate as to have Mr. Collins rendered speechless.

"*Mr. Darcy!*" exclaimed he, and for a moment, Elizabeth almost thought he would expire on the spot, as his face had turned the unhealthiest shade of purple she had ever witnessed upon any human being. "I am most rightly appalled, sir— entirely outraged that you, a scion of one of the most noble and exalted bloodlines—centuries old!—could fall to the disgusting devices of such a scarlet woman as Elizabeth Bennet. How can you possibly betray your family, your good name, and your entire class by stooping to such a level for the basest inclinations of the flesh? I seriously suggest that you—"

"And *I suggest*, Mr. Collins, that you cease this cowardly and unwarranted attack *immediately* if you do not wish to regret it for the rest of your life!"

Although his voice was quiet and modulated, the effect of William's voice, which was fairly dripping with malice and displeasure, was far greater than it would have been if he had raged and ranted. Mr. Collins, though certainly not a sensible man, could hardly miss the dire warning in the man's voice. His words died in his throat, and he gaped as he clearly warred within himself over what he considered his righteous anger—and his patroness's distress—and the clear warning in Fitzwilliam Darcy's tone and words.

"Mr. Collins, do you have any idea who I am or what kind of power I wield?"

"You are Lady Catherine's nephew," managed Mr. Collins in response.

"Indeed, I am, Mr. Collins. But whereas Lady Catherine is *a lady*, and one who has spent much of the past twenty years ensconced in her country home, I am a man who has lived in society; I have many connections, Mr. Collins. I also possess *my name*, which can traced back to the time of William the conqueror. I have many acquaintances, both business and personal, and can wield a great deal of influential power in my own right and through the auspices of my uncle, who is an earl, after all. Among some of those acquaintances which may be of interest to you is not only your bishop, but also your archbishop."

Although Mr. Collins could never be accused of being swift of thought, even *he* could not miss the implications of William's comments or the threat which existed in his words. However, Elizabeth's fiancé did not stop there—apparently, he felt that Mr. Collins was too dim to completely understand the threat if it were not clearly spelled out so there could be no mistake.

"Now, Mr. Collins, although I would never stoop to invent a history for the purpose of exacting revenge, I believe your conduct here today, coupled with your language and your assault against Miss Elizabeth, would be of great concern to your bishop. In fact, I feel very secure in the knowledge that he would take a very dim view of your actions, which are not only unchristian, but are also the very essence of impropriety, maliciousness, and vengeance against a lady who did not feel enough for you to agree to marry you."

"*I* have done nothing wrong," stated Mr. Collins, though his countenance, which had turned chalk-white due to William's threats, belied his blustering. "I have merely stated that which is true—Elizabeth is tempting you into marriage using her arts and allurements. She should be happy to stay within her own class."

"Mr. Collins." The room appeared to descend into the depths of winter from the chill in William's voice. "Are you so dense as to miss the fact that I can ruin you forever? I was completely truthful and sincere in my threat to you if you fail to cease these baseless attacks against my fiancée. The only reason I have not already wielded this influence against you is because I would not have your wife—a woman who has far more sense than you, not to mention much better manners—suffer needlessly for your recklessness."

William turned and bowed at Charlotte, who returned a curtsey distractedly, clearly much more perturbed at her husband than at William's words.

"But *do not* underestimate my resolve, sir," continued Elizabeth's fiancé. "If you do not cease your attacks, I will see to it that you lose your position at Hunsford and that you are never able to secure another parish again throughout the whole course of your life.

"And that includes *any* stain to Miss Elizabeth's character—now or in the future. She is destined to be my wife, and I will not have her reputation suffer due to your stupidity. Do I make myself perfectly clear?"

If Mr. Collins had been pale before, he was positively colorless now. His hands shook with fear, and his gaze had dropped to the floor to avoid the stern eyes of his adversary. He jerkily nodded his head to Mr. Darcy's commands and allowed himself to be led to the couch by his wife, all the while muttering under his breath and mopping his brow with his handkerchief—a most inoffensive piece of cloth, which Elizabeth felt certain was by now completely soaked.

Elizabeth glanced around the room, highly gratified by William's unyielding defense of her person before the odious man. The entire room was silent in the wake of Fitzwilliam Darcy's declaration, and though the expressions varied, Elizabeth noted the new look of wonder and calculation upon her mother's visage. William's words had somehow pierced through whatever her mother had been thinking, and her previous displeasure was forgotten.

Having faced down the hateful Mr. Collins, he fiancé turned to her and gently gathered her hands in his. He bowed and bestowed a tender kiss upon the back of each before leaning forward and kissing her forehead, his countenance apologetic, yet still stern and unbending.

"Elizabeth, I most humbly apologize for betraying our understanding before requesting your father's approval."

Elizabeth's answering smile was radiant. "There is nothing to forgive, William—it was, after all, done in my defense. But I believe you have an appointment in my father's bookroom."

"Indeed, I do, my love."

He kissed her forehead once more before, with a stern glare in the direction of the pompous parson—who completely missed it due to his inability to direct his eyes at anything other than the floor—and left the room. The stunned silence which heralded his exit from the room lasted for some time.

Once the door closed behind him, Darcy stalked some ways down the hallway before stopping and leaning against the wall, willing his stress and fury to depart. It would not do to appear before Mr. Bennet in a rage. Darcy knew from his own dealings with the man—not to mention Elizabeth's description—that he would need his faculties firmly about him to handle this particular meeting.

The *utter gall* of Mr. Collins! If Darcy had not been witness to the discussion himself, he would have scoffed at the thought that so much stupidity could exist in the person of one odious man. It had been all Darcy could do not to throttle him, and he knew that if Collins had persisted in his delusional attacks, he might very well be back in the room strangling the idiot even now. It was completely beyond the pale!

Clenching his hands into fists, Darcy took a few deep breaths, and little by little, he felt the anger and tension drain away. It took no small amount of time, but in the end, he felt better and knew he had done right in ensuring he was calm.

He took stock of his situation, and seeing no one else in the hall, he began to walk toward the bookroom which Elizabeth had pointed out to him before they had entered the parlor.

He had just about reached the doorway when an elderly, plump, motherly sort of woman appeared from the end of the hallway and curtseyed to him. Remembering the description Elizabeth had given him some days previous, he believed she was the housekeeper, Mrs. Hill.

"Is this the door to Mr. Bennet's study?" asked Darcy politely, while already knowing it was.

"It is, sir," was the answer. "Would you like me to announce you to Mr. Bennet?"

"Thank you, but it is not necessary."

Darcy turned to the door, and as he raised his hand to knock on the door, he heard the servant speak once more.

"Begging your pardon, Mr. Darcy, but on behalf of all the servants, I would like to thank you for your defense of Miss Elizabeth just now. She is truly a wonderful girl and does not deserve to be attacked by that man."

Looking back at her, Darcy noted the obvious discomfort in the woman's manner, though she was obviously determined to have her say. Elizabeth was fond of Longbourn's housekeeper—always speaking very highly of her—and Darcy found that Elizabeth's description, as usual, was completely correct.

"It was nothing . . . Mrs. Hill, I presume?"

"Yes, Mr. Darcy," was her confirmation. "And I believe it was not 'nothing.' I have known that girl from the time she was a baby, watched her as she has grown into the fine young woman she has become. I am very glad she has found a fine young man such as yourself who esteems her for her own worth."

Though a blush had suffused his features, Darcy gamely returned the woman's praise with a smile. "I believe I could hardly help but to realize her worth. I hope I will succeed in making her very happy with me."

"I believe you shall, Mr. Darcy. But now, if you will excuse me, I must check on tonight's dinner."

She curtseyed and disappeared, leaving a bemused Darcy standing in front of the master's door, reflecting upon all the lives his beloved touched. The word of this servant confirmed what he already knew to be true, but it was still wonderful to hear affirmation of the suitability of his choice.

Emboldened by the unexpected conversation, Mr. Darcy turned back to the door and knocked, and when he heard a voice bidding him enter, he opened the door and stepped into the room.

Surprisingly, Mr. Bennet was not alone—Sir William was seated across the desk from the master of the house, and given the empty glasses and half-empty bottle of port which sat upon the desk, they had been enjoying a drink in each other's company away from the ruckus in the parlor since their return from the gardens. Darcy could not blame them—Mr. Collins could try the patience of a saint, and that was even without the ever-loquacious Mrs. Bennet.

"Ah, Mr. Darcy, I have been waiting for you to arrive. Come and sit with us, young man."

Darcy stared at the Bennet patron for several moments, wondering if the man intended for him to request his daughter's hand in the presence of his neighbor. Sir William, however, neatly resolved Darcy's conundrum.

"I believe that is the signal for me to be on my way," said he, rising to his feet. "First, however, I believe I should not quit the room before extending my heartiest congratulations to you, sir."

Sir William then winked at him and quit the room forthwith before Darcy could utter a syllable in response. He turned to face Mr. Bennet and saw a smile of true affection for the departed man.

"Ah, Sir William. He is a good man—a little blunt and perhaps overly impressed with his knighthood, but I would not trade his friendship for anything in the world. Now, come, young man. I believe there may be a particularly important question which you would like to ask of me."

Sitting on the chair in front of Mr. Bennet's desk, Darcy marshaled his thoughts, marveling at how the thought of asking for the consent of Elizabeth's father—though the man was already aware of what had occurred—should induce such a feeling of nervousness when before he had been completely composed. He was not normally a man given to nerves, but at this moment, he empathized with Mrs. Bennet and her incessant nervous complaints.

"Mr. Bennet," began Darcy, forcing down his anxiousness, "I wish to ask for your permission to marry your daughter Elizabeth. She has been the object of my admiration and affection these many months, and she has this afternoon agreed to be my wife. I would like to ask you to extend your blessing upon our marriage."

True to Elizabeth's characterization of her father, Mr. Bennet grinned delightedly.

"Very calm and collected, young man. I can imagine what it must have cost you—I remember asking for permission from Mrs. Bennet's father very well myself."

His good humor lasted for only a moment, and he became uncharacteristically serious—at least, given Elizabeth's description.

"Before I can give my consent, Mr. Darcy, I fear I must impose upon you to determine whether you are a suitable companion for my daughter."

Darcy was slightly offended by Mr. Bennet's insinuations. "I assure you, sir, that I love your daughter dearly and will be able to take care of her throughout her entire life, whether she outlives me by fifty years or whether we live a long life together. She will be well taken care of, I can assure you."

"Mr. Darcy, I question neither your devotion nor your finances—both, I am certain, are in excellent condition. But you must understand that Elizabeth is very precious to me, and I cannot let her go without assuring myself of her happiness with you, and in order to do that, I need to go beyond the mere physical needs and the depth of emotional attachment."

Darcy was confused by the man's meaning, causing Mr. Bennet to chuckle at the befuddled expression he assumed must be clearly showing upon his face.

"You must think me daft, young man, but I assure you I am in full possession of my faculties, and I am in earnest. I do not question your devotion for my daughter, but I do question the value you place upon her. You undoubtedly know that I can give her little. She is due only her equal share of five thousand pounds—and that only upon her mother's death. Given the unequal reality of your situations, you can hardly blame my caution and my desire to protect Elizabeth."

Mr. Bennet was silent for several moments, but Darcy, sensing he had more to say and wishing to answer the man's questions all at once, patiently waited for him to finish. He was, Darcy reflected, a bit of an oddity—most fathers in his situation would be ecstatic at the thought of *any* man wishing to take a daughter from him and give her a good home. In fact, Darcy did not think he was exaggerating when he thought that almost any man in the kingdom, regardless of station, would approve of the marriage of a daughter to someone of his standing, let alone the master of a small country estate. It was clear that whatever Mr. Bennet's faults were, a lack of love for Elizabeth—and presumably for all of his daughters—was not one of them.

"I must be frank, Mr. Darcy," continued Mr. Bennet at length. "Elizabeth has always declared she will be married for love, and I believe that in you she has found the love she desires. However, as her father, and knowing her character, I believe that *respect* is equally as important in her situation. Elizabeth is a lively, intelligent, headstrong, and capable young woman, and though others might think me delusional in my love for my daughter, I do not believe there are five such women in all of England who are her equal."

"You will receive no argument from me on that score, Mr. Bennet," replied Darcy, finally understanding the thrust of Mr. Bennet's concerns.

The Bennet patriarch peered at him for several moments before continuing:

"I daresay you do, Mr. Darcy. What I am attempting to say, Mr. Darcy, is that for Elizabeth to be happy, she must respect her partner in life, and it is *equally* important for her to receive that respect in return. It is that which I wish to clarify. I understand the first throes of love very well, Mr. Darcy, and what those feelings can do to a man. However, as the years pass and the routines of life impose themselves upon you, and you realize what you have lost by marrying a penniless country miss—no matter how exceptional you believe her to be—will you come to resent her and wish you had chosen differently?"

Darcy's respect for Mr. Bennet increased immeasurably with the man's determined and insightful questions. This was a man who, though perhaps he had not filled his stewardship with regard to the estate as well as he could have, knew his daughter intimately and understood her needs and character better than any other. At once, Darcy was humbled at the thought that this man was about to entrust his most precious daughter to another man—it must be a painful experience indeed. Never—not in all the months of his soul searching after Hunsford—had he been so determined to provide Elizabeth with everything she required to ensure her happiness.

"These are all valid concerns," began Darcy slowly. "I must admit to being somewhat bemused at this whole line of questioning, Mr. Bennet. I doubt there are five such men in the kingdom who would go beyond the most basic of questions if I applied for their daughter's hand, and I do not believe that is my pride speaking when I say it."

Mr. Bennet's answering chuckle was the epitome of the man—somewhat sardonic and with a hint of playful indolence. "I do not doubt you are correct, Mr. Darcy."

"Be that as it may, I can only respond and declare to you the constancy of not only my love for your daughter, but also my respect for her. Indeed, I believe that was one of the first things which caused my attention to be diverted in her direction. She did not behave in the manner in which I was accustomed; for all of my adult life, I have been chased by the young ladies of the ton, all of whom were intent upon capturing Pemberley and becoming its mistress, and there has been no end to the arts by which such ladies would base their attempts to be noticed and win the prize. Miss Elizabeth did none of that—in fact, she paid me no deference, treated me in much the same manner as she would anyone else, and challenged me with her own opinions rather than agreeing with every word which issued forth from my mouth.

"It was most singular behavior, and though I do not believe I initially behaved in the proper manner of a man interested in a lady, my respect for her person and abilities has never wavered in the slightest. I know that with Miss Elizabeth as my wife, my life will never be dull—indeed, that is the primary reason why I have never sought a wife from among the ton. I can also tell you that in the matter of her lack of dowry and connections, I am perfectly indifferent. Miss Elizabeth is in the end such an exceptional lady that I believe I am coming out ahead in the bargain—her worth is far more than any dowry can provide, and the happy fact of the matter is that Pemberley's coffers are well able to weather the lack of dowry in my wife, even if I cared for such things.

"You may also be concerned about the ton's acceptance of Miss Elizabeth's position as my wife." Mr. Bennet's expression told him that the man had indeed considered that aspect of the situation. "I can assure you, Mr. Bennet, that there is no cause for concern. Not only do I wield significant influence in my own right, but I have the full support of my uncle, the earl, in this matter. In fact, he found himself in much the same situation when *he* married my aunt, and he has never regretted it for a moment. I can assure you that I am the same way. If there are—and I cannot doubt there will be—those who disapprove of my choice, their opinions do not concern me in the slightest. Beyond all this, though, is the fact that I am convinced that Miss Elizabeth herself shall win over all but the worst critics. I am certain she can handle herself with those unfortunate souls."

Mr. Bennet laughed heartily. "I do not doubt she can, Mr. Darcy."

His mirth continued for several moments, but Darcy could see he was still mulling the situation over. His eyes caught Darcy's several times, and Darcy thought he could detect a hint of understanding in them. In his manner, Darcy could see a hint of his beloved—this man had formed her, in large part, into the woman she had become, and for that, he could only be grateful.

"Yours was a most passionate and eloquent argument, Mr. Darcy," said Mr. Bennet at last. "I am convinced of your sincerity and know from my Elizabeth that you are a man of integrity and honor. We spoke before of Elizabeth and said that there were only a few ladies who were her equal—I believe I may confidently state that there are only a few *men* who are worthy of her, and I declare that you are one of them."

Darcy heaved a great sigh of relief and reached over the desk to clasp the hand of the man who was to become his father-in-law.

"I approve of your request for the hand of my daughter and welcome you into the family, Mr. Darcy. Now, what is your pleasure? Shall we partake of a glass of port together, or are you eager to have your engagement announced to all and sundry?"

Coughing lightly, Darcy glanced guiltily at Mr. Bennet, concerned he should be displeased at Darcy's impetuosity. "I am afraid I have already announced it, Mr. Bennet."

"Oh?"

It was a single word which could have contained anger, but Darcy was immediately relieved when he could only detect curiosity and amusement in the man's tone and manner.

"When we entered the sitting room, Mr. Collins and Mrs. Bennet immediately began a diatribe against Miss Elizabeth based on their perception of her poor behavior. I interrupted and told your wife of my offer and Miss Elizabeth's acceptance to calm her. Then, I was required to threaten Mr. Collins to induce him to cease his attacks."

"In that case, I wish I had been there to witness his set-down," replied an amused Mr. Bennet. "In light of that fact, I believe we can take a few moments and enjoy a glass of port while you impart the details of Mr. Collins's disgrace. Then we can repair to the sitting room and 'formally' announce your coming nuptials."

Darcy laughed at the droll way in which Mr. Bennet had phrased his words. He was happy to have found such a kindred spirit in his beloved's father, and although he was aware that they were different in many respects, he felt that he would manage very well with Mr. Bennet as a father-in-law. Accepting a glass from the other man, he settled in his chair and began to recount the events in the parlor, which, now that his anger had cooled, highlighted the absurdity of Mr. Collins quite humorously indeed.

Mr. Darcy had only been gone from the room for a moment when Elizabeth's presence was demanded by her mother. Still curious over her behavior and eager to discover the reason, Elizabeth approached her, noting the fact that Lady Lucas had excused herself to give mother and daughter a chance to speak in private.

"Lizzy!" was her mother's sharp query. "Mr. Darcy has proposed to you? Are you absolutely certain that it was a proposal *of marriage?*"

Shock at her mother's words arose within Elizabeth, and she gaped in astonishment. "*Mama!* Just what exactly are you suggesting?"

Her outburst drew the attention of the rest of the room, and Elizabeth, embarrassed and not wishing for the rest of the room to be privy to what was turning out to be a most improper discussion, sat close to her mother and fixed her with a stern eye.

"You cannot possibly be thinking what I suspect, Mama," hissed she.

"But, Lizzy," protested Mrs. Bennet, looking unsure of herself and, for once, highly discomfited, "Mr. Darcy is a rich man, whereas we are poor . . ."

"Mr. Bingley is wealthy, is he not, Mama?" asked Elizabeth, almost in disbelief that she was even having this conversation with her mother. What could she be thinking? "By your estimation, Mama, Mr. Bingley must also be untrustworthy. I can assure you that Mr. Darcy asked me to *marry him.* Now, can you tell me what this is all about?"

The discomfort in Mrs. Bennet's manner became even more pronounced, but Elizabeth was unwavering in her will to get to the bottom of this odd behavior. While she had never been especially close to her mother, she now realized that the past weeks of her mother throwing her in the path of Mr. Lucas had been odd even for her. The statements of the past few moments had shed some light on the situation—and she had begun to suspect Samuel's hand in the matter—but she wished to hear it directly from the source.

"But Mr. Bingley is open and friendly to all, while Mr. Darcy is silent and proud."

"I assure you, Mama, that Mr. Darcy has no improper pride," was Elizabeth's prim reply. "And a prideful man is not necessarily an immoral man. Did Mr. Lucas warn you of Mr. Darcy's intentions?"

"He did," replied Mrs. Bennet in a very quiet voice, looking obviously uncomfortable with Elizabeth's censure. "He told me stories of his time at school and of the other young men with whom he became acquainted and of how the rich men chased after young women with the purpose of having their way with them."

Elizabeth's displeasure grew with every word which issued forth from her mother's mouth. Her annoyance must have shown on her face, as her mother appeared to become more nervous as she continued.

"I was afraid for you, Lizzy!" exclaimed she, wringing her hands nervously. "Mr. Darcy has always been so cold and severe, and Samuel's words concerned me — it all seemed so believable, and I could not allow you to fall prey to such a man. Since you have known Samuel for so long, I felt that a marriage to him would be agreeable and keep you in the area, not to mention protect you from Mr. Darcy's attentions."

"Then why did you push Kitty toward Mr. Darcy if you suspected him of having immoral tendencies?"

Mrs. Bennet waved her off impatiently. "A man of Mr. Darcy's stature would never pay much attention to Kitty. I merely wished her to distract him from you so I could arrange to have you settled with Mr. Lucas."

"That was very foolish indeed, Mama," reprimanded Elizabeth. She peered at her mother, certain that she was still hiding something — her furtive glances and continuing reticence was telling.

"Is that all, Mama?" Elizabeth demanded.

Her mother had the grace to appear abashed. "I admit it did occur to me that since Lady Lucas has a daughter who is to be mistress of *this* house, it would only be just if one of my daughters were to become the mistress of *her* house."

Though she wished to be angry at her mother's interference and lack of insight, Elizabeth was in fact somewhat amused — it was quintessentially her mother, after all, to wish for revenge upon her neighbor in such a manner. The other consideration which stayed her anger was that her mother, despite her misguided actions and unremitting meddling, truly *had* possessed good intentions, no matter what actions those intentions had provoked. She did not ever think they would completely understand or agree with each other, but the evidence of her mother's care for her was heartening.

"I have always been concerned for you, Elizabeth," continued Mrs. Bennet when Elizabeth remained silent. "I have never understood you — your love of books, your sense of humor which is so similar to your father's, your determination to forever be walking the countryside . . . You have always seemed somewhat of a bluestocking to me, and there are few men who can put up with a wife who is their superior in intellect."

"Well, you may rest now from your concern, Mama," responded Elizabeth, a slight primness entering her voice. "Mr. Darcy *has* proposed, and I *have* accepted, and we shall be married. And I am truly not Mr. Darcy's superior in intellect — as a matter of fact, I rather think that we are well matched in that respect.

"And really, Mama, you should have considered with *whom* you were speaking when Samuel Lucas recounted his lies and slander. Mr. Darcy has never been anything but proper in my presence, while Samuel has not. In fact, Samuel threatened to compromise me in order to force me into marriage, and that was not the first instance in which he tried to intimidate me. Does that sound like a man to whom you wish to marry a daughter?"

"He did?" Mrs. Bennet's voice was flinty with displeasure. Her mother was many things, but that did not include an insensibility to her daughters' wellbeing, despite of what she often considered that wellbeing to consist. In an instance such as this, Elizabeth knew she could count on Mrs. Bennet to be rightly offended by Lucas's actions. Perhaps Elizabeth had been wrong to keep these things from her parents—if she had confided more in them from the beginning, many of her trials with Mr. Lucas could have been prevented. It was something upon which she determined to contemplate.

"He did, Mama," confirmed Elizabeth. "But even if he had behaved as a perfect gentleman, I had already bestowed my affections upon Mr. Darcy—there was nothing Mr. Lucas could have done to affect a change. He would not accept that fact, and he had to be threatened with disinheritance before he would cease his pursuit of me. If he had been a true gentleman, he would have stepped back gracefully."

Mrs. Bennet appeared to consider this for several moments before a sly expression came over her face. "So, you are indeed engaged to Mr. Darcy?"

At Elizabeth's affirmation, a look of utter bliss came over Mrs. Bennet's face.

"Oh, Lizzy, I am so happy!" exclaimed she, her countenance instantly transforming to one held in the throes of rapture. "I am simply beside myself—he is so handsome a man and so tall and rich. You will have the best of everything—dresses, jewels, carriages, and more pin money than you will ever be able to spend!"

Acutely mortified, Elizabeth glanced around surreptitiously, wishing she could moderate her mother's tone of voice and volume to a more manageable level of ecstasy. The other conversations in the room appeared to have continued in spite of her mother's raptures, but she thought she caught a twinkle in the eyes of the Colonel and a smirk from Anne, though she could not be certain. Wondering how she would ever make it through the period of her engagement, Elizabeth listened to her mother as long as she was able, from expressions of the greatness to which her daughter would ascend to the plans she would need to undertake in order to prepare for a wedding which must be of the highest quality. After all, since her daughter was marrying a man who was the nephew of an earl, everything *must* be perfect—Mrs. Bennet would accept no less.

After listening for several moments—and feeling the appropriate amount of dread for the coming months of wedding planning—Elizabeth moved away to give herself some space. She knew that her mother would hunt her down, and she would be engulfed in planning sooner or later—but she preferred that it be *much* later.

The door to the parlor opened, and Sir William entered the room, his countenance once again that of the jovial, good-natured neighbor she had known most of her life. He appeared to have recovered from the unpleasant scene with his son, and upon seeing Elizabeth, his smile grew wider.

He immediately approached her, and bowing low, he reached out and took hold of her hand. "Miss Elizabeth, I cannot tell you how truly happy I am for you and your young man. Though I could boast at my own cleverness for having discovered Mr. Darcy's feelings for you some time ago, I believe I shall dispense with the smugness and settle for simply exclaiming my delight. You are as dear to me as my own daughters, and I wish for nothing more than your felicity in marriage."

"Thank you, sir. I believe I shall be very happy indeed," replied Elizabeth, reflecting that Sir William had always seemed to hold her in great esteem.

"You are a wonderful woman, Miss Elizabeth, and I cannot help but suppose you will do Mr. Darcy proud and grace his home and his position in society as you grace us with your presence here. I commend you, my dear.

"However, I also wished to take this opportunity to apologize to you for my son's reprehensible behavior—I cannot express the depth of my mortification at what he has done in his misguided quest, and I assure you that he shall not bother you again!

"No, no, I know you would tell me that it was not my fault," continued Sir William when she would have interrupted. "Samuel will never, I fear, apologize for his own actions, so I wished to do so in his stead."

"Sir William, you are truly a good man, and I thank you for your words. Please believe me when I tell you that I hold no blame for you or your family, nor do I hold a grudge of any sort."

"I thank you, Miss Elizabeth," stated a clearly grateful Sir William with another low bow. "Now, I fear a long overdue discussion with my eldest son awaits me, and I would trespass upon your family's hospitality no longer. I shall bid you farewell."

After exchanging farewells and accepting congratulations from Sir William and his family, Elizabeth saw them to the door as they made their way home. She returned to the parlor directly, and she was accosted by Charlotte upon entering the room.

"Lizzy, I would speak with you," said Charlotte as she took Elizabeth's hand and dragged her to an empty corner of the room. Glancing around, Elizabeth noted the look of disdain from Mr. Collins, but she shrugged the stupid man off—Mr. Collins's opinion meant less to her than that of a gnat, after all.

"First, Lizzy, let me congratulate you on your engagement," began her friend, drawing her into a warm embrace which Elizabeth returned with equal fervor.

"I suppose I should not gloat, but I seem to remember remarking on several occasions how Mr. Darcy appeared to pay particular attention to you. However, much as I would like to continue to remind you of my perceptiveness, I shall content myself with voicing it just this once and speak no more on the subject."

Charlotte's glee was unmistakable, and Elizabeth laughed in spite of herself— she had missed these times with her closest friend and wished Charlotte was not tied to the odious Mr. Collins. A glance in the man's direction revealed an almost palpable anger, presumably at his wife for her feelings on the matter, Elizabeth for having the temerity to follow her own heart, and the world itself for not obeying his mistress's commands with alacrity.

Noticing her glance, Charlotte pulled on her hand, commandeering her attention once again.

"Elizabeth, I must tell you that I am concerned over the situation. Lady Catherine instructed us never to return if we did not separate you from Mr. Darcy, and though the lady does not have the authority to take away the living, I fear for her ability to make our lives miserable. And as for Mr. Collins, I do not know to what lengths he will go to keep his position and favor with Lady Catherine, but I do not think he will be easily silenced."

"You think he will continue to make trouble?"

The thought was bothersome, though Elizabeth did not suppose that there was anything Mr. Collins could truly do to separate them. The man could be an irritant at the very least. And if he did not moderate his opinions and tone of voice, his words could give rise to scandalous rumors which would be difficult to suppress. Elizabeth was already keenly aware of the sometimes improper behavior of certain members of her family, and she was greatly desirous to prevent any trial of her future husband's patience.

"I do not know, but I think it likely that he has not finished with his objections. At this moment, it is only fear of Mr. Darcy's reaction which is keeping his discontentment at bay. Once Mr. Darcy and his intimidating fury are no longer before my husband, I do not think he can be induced to keep his own council."

Wondering if the never-ending obstacles to her happiness with Mr. Darcy would ever cease, Elizabeth was about to respond when Anne joined them.

"Mrs. Collins, I apologize for my eavesdropping, but I heard your words regarding my mother. I believe there is something we can do to alleviate the problem, but we shall have to wait until my cousin Fitzwilliam returns to discuss the matter."

Curious though she was concerning Anne's meaning, Elizabeth, understanding that it truly did not concern her, kept silent. The three women lapsed into conversation, much of it excited musings regarding her engagement to Mr. Darcy. Elizabeth was immediately gratified that Anne truly had not ever had any intention of marrying her cousin and that she was happy for Elizabeth's good fortune. In Miss de Bourgh, Elizabeth felt she had gained a true friend who would remain such for the rest of their lives.

At length, Mr. Darcy entered the room with her father, and upon the expected announcement—which was by now about the worst-kept secret in Longbourn—the approbation and congratulations for the couple flowed freely, causing Elizabeth to blush at the attention and praise. A glance at her new fiancé confirmed that he was as ill at ease as she—*he* was the reticent one, after all.

The only member of the company who did not join in the general air of celebration was the dour parson, whose expression of utter loathing for the young woman whom he considered the root of all his troubles became even darker and more petulant than it had already been.

But Anne, noticing this, had already drawn her cousin to the side of the room, and with Elizabeth and Charlotte's help, she explained the situation to Mr. Darcy.

"My plan is this, cousin," continued she once she had explained Charlotte's fears. "Unless I am very much mistaken, I believe I am the rightful mistress of Rosings, am I not?"

Mr. Darcy smiled, appearing to immediately understand the thrust of her design. "Indeed, you are, Anne. Sir Lewis stipulated in his will that you were to inherit Rosings in its entirety either upon your marriage or when you turned one and twenty. All that is required for you to take your true place is your signature on a few official documents—and of course, our uncle's signature, as he was the executor of Sir Lewis's estate."

"Your mother will not be pleased," Colonel Fitzwilliam broke into the discussion, his usual grin lighting up his features. "I daresay that having suffered so many setbacks lately could well bring about an attack of apoplexy."

"What have I told you about making sport with my mother?" demanded Anne while swatting him. The Colonel's smirk only grew wider.

Anne merely rolled her eyes and continued: "In any case, I believe our path is clear—I shall take control of Rosings with uncle Matlock's assistance, and if necessary, I will remove mother to the dowager house. With mother out of the way, Mr. Collins may keep his position without fear of her disapprobation."

Elizabeth was amused by Anne's plotting against her mother, but she was destined to become even more diverted. Anne stopped and seemed to consider the situation for a moment before turning her attention to the still-scowling Mr. Collins. As her attention on the man lengthened, her face grew pensive, and she requested Charlotte bring the parson to her for a chat. Moments later, the sycophantic man stood before his—although he had no idea as yet—new patroness, a subservient and oily smile once again plastered upon his face. It was also patently false.

"Mr. Collins, I understand you have had some trouble with my mother which prompted to you leave Kent. Is this so?"

The man had the temerity to sneak an accusing glance at Elizabeth—which she returned with an amused smirk, causing his lips to tighten—before he focused his attention back on Anne. He allowed her statement to be true with a note of petulant irritation in his voice.

"Then you may be happy to know that *I* am mistress of Rosings, *not* my mother, and I shall be assuming my position upon my return to Kent."

Mr. Collins's eyes almost bulged out of his head. "But Miss de Bourgh, how can you . . . why . . . what about your lady mother? How can you shunt her aside when she is the most noble and wisest person in all the land? Surely there must be some misunderstanding—Lady Catherine is clearly the mistress of Rosings and shall continue to be for a great many years, God willing."

"I assure you, Mr. Collins, that not only is Rosings mine by legal right due to my father's bequest," said Anne, somewhat testily, "but that there is no mistake. Indeed, you should be happy to know that I shall be your patroness henceforth, for it renders my mother's edicts regarding your continued residence at Hunsford moot, now, does it not?"

Once again, Mr. Collins proved his lack of anything resembling intelligence by saying nothing. He stood there, staring at Anne in consternation and confusion. Privately, Elizabeth wondered if the man's brain had simply stopped functioning.

Anne, however, was regarding the parson as if he were an insect . . . or an unpleasant irritant to be tolerated. "But I must warn you, Mr. Collins," continued she, "that I have some conditions for your continued employment as parson at Hunsford. Shall I relate them to you?"

Displaying a remarkable resemblance to a deer caught in the sights of a hunter's rifle, Mr. Collins did the only thing he could. He nodded for Anne to continue.

"Very well. My conditions are as follows. First, you must cease informing my mother of everything which happens in the parish. The people of Hunsford rely upon you to be the mouthpiece of God, Mr. Collins, and anything they say to you must be kept in the strictest of confidence. Second, you must cease all objections immediately to my cousin's betrothal to Miss Elizabeth—I support them both in this, Mr. Collins, and your misguided efforts on my mother's behalf do *not* coincide with my own opinion on the matter. Finally, you must agree to apologize to Miss Elizabeth forthwith for your behavior. These conditions are not negotiable, and if you feel you are unable to fulfill them in any way, you must tell me immediately. I shall arrange for you to leave the parish and be installed in another living away from the influence of my mother. But I cannot countenance a continuation of your behavior. You must both agree to these terms and apologize to Miss Elizabeth forthwith, or you will leave Hunsford."

Mr. Collins was not happy—Elizabeth could see it in the tightening of his jaw and the narrowing of his eyes. But it was a credit to him that he understood the severity of his situation and the chance which was being offered to him. And though she suspected that he still could not imagine that his "noble patroness" was capable of anything resembling wrongdoing, he immediately gave his assurances in the flowery and overblown language to which she was accustomed. He then apologized to Elizabeth in a manner which was almost desultory in comparison to his usual loquaciousness.

Satisfied with his promise, Anne dismissed him, and soon he and Charlotte departed for Lucas Lodge. Elizabeth shared a teary farewell with her close friend, extracting a promise that Charlotte would attend her wedding when the time arrived. Knowing that there was little Mr. Collins could do to forbid her—not with the multiple set-downs he had endured that evening—Charlotte accepted with pleasure. It was, Elizabeth reflected, as good of an outcome as she could have ever expected.

The company relaxed with the departure of the Collinses and was soon called in to dinner. They were a merry party with much to celebrate, and for the two principles of the merriment, the evening seemed to pass in a daze. It was their first as an acknowledged couple, and though both would have liked to remember it in greater detail, they found themselves concentrating too much on each other to ever truly recollect what had occurred on that evening.

When it came time to part, Darcy and Elizabeth shared a private and intimate farewell, both reveling in the wonder and glory of their mutual love and esteem. They had traveled a very great distance, and together, they knew they could overcome any obstacle which was placed in their path. They spoke of their amazement at their very good fortune and promised, each to the other, to do anything required to make the other happy in their future life. It was truly a magical evening, and after all the heartache and uncertainty they had endured, it was sweeter still for being so hard won. They would be together forever from that time forward, and they both looked forward to the rest of their lives with anticipation.

Epilogue

$\mathscr{E}$lizabeth Darcy sat in front of her vanity as her maid fussed about, putting the final touches on her hair in preparation for the night's festivities. The softness of her gown rustled as she moved, the sensation of the tawny crushed velvet upon her skin luxurious, making her feel like a queen about to hold court. Downstairs, the grand ballroom of Pemberley was festooned with ribbons and bows, softly lit lanterns, and strategically placed candles, lending the room a romantic air, as intended by the estate's mistress. The kitchen staff was hard at work, preparing the vast quantities of the finest delicacies to tempt the palates of the guests which would descend upon them that evening.

Searching her face in the mirror, Elizabeth was struck at the appearance of the woman who gazed back at her, marveling at the changes which life had imprinted upon her visage. The face in the mirror was one of a young woman in the full bloom of life, one which made men stop and take notice, though there was only one man whom she truly wished to attract. *He*, flatterer that he was—at least where she was concerned—was wont to comment upon how married life agreed with her and how she had blossomed into the mistress of Pemberley and into a true force to be dealt with in her own right. Her father, in his satirical and amusing way, had told her several times that the love of a good man—and the confidence it brought—had transformed her into a beautiful woman—one who rivaled even Jane. William, of course, agreed with her father wholeheartedly.

However it had come about, Elizabeth now *felt* herself to be the mistress of Pemberley rather than merely an upstart claimant to the title, and though she and her husband spent much of their time at their estate, eschewing the hypocritical and shallow society of the ton, Elizabeth knew that she had impressed most of the naysayers of society and now could wield a considerable amount of social power of her own, if she so chose. Such things did not interest her, however, and she was content with her family and her life the way they were; she would leave the political and social intrigues to those who cared for that sort of thing.

"There," murmured the maid, stepping back and surveying her handiwork. "I believe you are ready, ma'am. You will outshine all the other ladies at the ball tonight."

"I daresay she shall," said William as he entered through the adjacent door. "But then again, she always does."

Elizabeth blushed, but the maid merely smiled—she had seen her mistress and the master interact many times in the past, after all, and she knew the extent to which they doted upon one another.

"Thank you, Alice. I think you have outdone yourself again," said Elizabeth.

She stood and smiled at the young woman, who was beaming at her with pleasure. "I believe that will be all for tonight. You may go to the servants' feast now. And remember—it is a condition of your employment that you enjoy yourself!"

Alice dropped into a curtsey with a large, genuine smile. "Thank you, ma'am." She curtseyed to William as well before departing from the room, a bounce in her step, Elizabeth noticed with amusement.

"You, sir, are a flatterer!" accused Elizabeth, the twinkle in her eye and the struggle to keep the smile from her face belying the severity of her tone.

An insolent grin—not unlike one which a certain rogue from William's past would often display—lit up his face as he approached her and, taking her hands in his own, kissed her cheek.

"And *you* say that far too often. I never exaggerate—I only tell the absolute truth, as you know. What can I say when confronted by perfection? I *must* speak nothing less than the absolute truth!"

Rolling her eyes, Elizabeth playfully swatted him. "Perfection, indeed! You shall make me into a most conceited and superior woman, sir, if you keep saying such things. I am well aware of my faults, thank you, and would not have you gloss them over."

"In that case, milady, your wish is my command. After all, if my compliments are destined to turn you into such a woman, I must desist. I spent too much time and effort avoiding the noose Miss Bingley had set for me, and I cannot have you turning into her."

Elizabeth laughed. "Indeed, you could not, sir. I am sure it would be most unpleasant to live with her every day—even by proxy!"

Caroline Bingley. She was an object of some ridicule between the couple—one which they were very careful *not* to indulge in discussing when Charles was present. The poor man had suffered enough from his relationship with the lady, and though he had apologized on her behalf many times, they were adamant in ensuring he understood that neither held the actions of his sister against him.

Caroline herself was also somewhat of an object of pity, little though she deserved it. She had never apologized for her actions. Rather, she had persisted in claiming that she had done nothing wrong while blaming Elizabeth for acting as a scarlet woman and entrapping a good man with her wiles. As a result of Caroline's continued defiance, she had been banned from her brother's wedding and had had little contact with him since the time of their estrangement. After five years, the distance between them appeared destined to be a permanent one.

Though her outburst at Netherfield and her attack on Elizabeth had been successfully kept from the knowledge of society, her life had been anything but easy since leaving her brother's house. She had stayed for a time with the Hursts in London, but ultimately, even Mr. and Mrs. Hurst could not tolerate her mean-spirited, vitriolic attacks against Elizabeth, and worrying that she would in her anger say something to expose the entire family to ridicule—or worse, something to draw Fitzwilliam Darcy's retribution—they had ultimately shipped her off to Scarborough to live with her aunt. Upon learning that even the reliable sister whom she had always been able to dominate had grown weary of her, the abuse which she heaped upon the entire family and anyone who did not agree with her had been beyond anything which even the most sainted soul could endure. The Hursts, therefore, stood firm, and she was packed up and on her way within a day of the decision being made.

After more than a year in Scarborough, she *had* managed to convince Mrs. Hurst to let her return to London to stay with them, but the damage had already been done; her return to London society was decidedly anticlimactic. She attempted to insert herself back into the circles in which she had formerly found some acceptance, but she found that all doors had by then been closed to her—her pretensions had been exposed, and William's public disavowal of any acquaintance with her had put to rest any claim she possessed to the highest circles of society. She had immediately found herself on the outside of such society looking in.

Still, she could have made a marriage with someone of less prominence if she had tried—she *did* possess a dowry of twenty-thousand pounds, if nothing else—but her pride would not allow her to enter into what she considered to be such a degrading connection. She was therefore relegated to the fringes of the society she desired, but barred from participating and unwilling to move with those who were at a closer level to the one to which she herself could claim by her own birthright.

She remained unmarried and, having reached her thirtieth birthday, was now firmly on the shelf. The Hursts, who had become closer to the Darcys once Caroline's influence had largely been removed, reported that she was bitter and becoming more twisted by the year. Her society had become so uncomfortable that they had finally requested that she set up her own household, paid for by her own money, which Charles had had released to her. She appeared doomed to end an old maid and had largely withdrawn from the relationships with her own family and from those with whom she had associated in the past—at least those who still wished to have anything to do with her. Of *that* faction, there were only a few.

Thoughts of Caroline always engendered thoughts of Lady Catherine, for their ultimate fates were similar in their bitterness and their vindictive belief in their being ill-used by their families.

Lady Catherine had ended much as William and Anne had said she would. Incensed at Anne's betrayal and livid that her final schemes to keep Elizabeth from marrying her nephew had failed, Lady Catherine had had to be removed forcibly from Rosings to the dower house and threatened with Bedlam before she could be moved on to cease her continuing attempts to regain control of Rosings and impose her will again upon her daughter. And though Anne had acquitted herself well in standing up to her mother—indeed, by the time Anne had left Hertfordshire, she barely resembled the timid and quiet young lady she had been previously—the support offered her by the entire family, especially William and Lord Matlock, had been invaluable in imposing her control upon the estate.

Lady Catherine had finally been left at the dower house with only a few servants to see to her comfort, servants who were paid by Anne and instructed upon the proper way to run the lady's household and curb the lady's extravagant spending. Her family, after a few attempts to bridge the gap, had finally left her alone when her diatribes and abuse of anyone who dared show their face had taken their toll. She was deemed better off left to her own devices, and though not forgotten, she was completely ignored by her family. In the end, Lady Catherine had only Mr. Collins to comfort her, for the parson, infatuated by the idea of her infallibility, had remained steadfastly loyal to her. Whereas he rarely visited Anne at Rosings, he could be found waiting on the Lady almost daily, listening to her tales of woe and agreeing with her in his ingratiating and insipid way.

Alas, the lady had only lived three years after the marriage of her nephew when she died suddenly in her sleep. The doctor who had been called in to examine her body had determined that she had succumbed to a weakness in her heart, a condition doubtlessly made worse by her tantrums and moments of utter rage against the world and the willfulness of her relations. Her death was unfortunately met with pity for the most part, not to mention some relief, as she had been almost impossible in the last years of her life.

As for Mr. Collins, his part in the story ended even before that of his beloved patroness. Though he had scrupulously followed the letter of his promises he had made to Anne the day of Elizabeth's engagement—although Anne could never be certain he stopped telling Lady Catherine all which happened within his parish—he had never truly reconciled himself to the manner in which his patroness had been treated, nor was he able to forgive his wife for her support of Elizabeth and William, which he saw as a betrayal. Charlotte's presence at the wedding of her dearest friend—an event which he refused to attend—was seen as the final treachery, and one which he could never forgive. They lived separate lives after that day—as they had since returning from Hertfordshire after Elizabeth's engagement—rarely speaking more than a few words to each other and never spending any more time than was absolutely necessary in each other's company. Even during mealtimes, often one or another would take a tray in their room or another room in the house. Their estrangement was a matter of common knowledge within the parish, but few could fault Mrs. Collins for the way her marriage had turned out—not when she was trapped with such a man for a husband.

Of course, the lack of any sort of relationship between the two had far-reaching consequences. In short, Mr. Collins did not visit his wife's bedchamber after their return to Kent, and therefore, he did not beget the needed heir to secure his family's possession of Longbourn. Mrs. Collins took this change in her relationship with her husband philosophically, as she would not have welcomed him into her bedchamber even if he *had* been willing—she was so disgusted with his behavior in the matter of Elizabeth and Mr. Darcy that she even began to wish she had never married him, regardless of her desire for her own situation.

Sadly, Mr. Collins, when visiting his good patroness the following spring, made a decision which would result in his death. The spring rains had been heavy that year, and after a night of an especially heavy deluge, a portion of the path to Lady Catherine's residence was submerged in a torrent of swiftly moving water. Undeterred—for he *could not* miss his visit with the great lady—he set about fording the flood, lost his footing, and was washed downstream. It was two days later before his body was discovered some miles down the river, rendering Mrs. Collins a widow less than eighteen months after she married. Though Anne was kind and considerate, offering to allow Charlotte to stay at Rosings as long as she liked—for the ladies had formed a fast friendship—Charlotte did not feel right accepting her friend's charity and returned to live with her family in Lucas Lodge.

With the death of Mr. Collins, the final heir within the terms of the entailment departed life without leaving an heir of his own. The terms of the entailment were thus broken, and it was determined that Jane's eldest son would become the next master of Longbourn. Sad though she had been for Charlotte's suddenly uncertain situation, Elizabeth could not be unhappy that the spawn of such an odious man would never take her family's place at Longbourn. And of course, Charlotte had not fared poorly in the end . . .

"Woolgathering, my dear?"

Elizabeth turned to face her husband and took in the amused smile and the tenderness in his eyes.

"Should I be concerned that after a mere five years of marriage, I have lost the ability to hold my wife's attention?"

"I do not think you should worry about my attention, husband. This day always brings thoughts of the past, as you well know."

"Ah, I do indeed. Dare I hope the thoughts were pleasant?"

Elizabeth made a face. "Not all, unfortunately—I was considering some of the villains in our little tale."

Her husband mirrored her expression. "I suppose the villains had the part to play, though the part was not precisely a happy one."

"It was not," agreed Elizabeth. "But they have paid for their actions in large part, I should imagine."

"They have indeed." William's look was a considering one. "Has Charlotte told you the latest of her brother?"

"She has."

"And has he managed to find a wife?"

Elizabeth's answering smirk was positively vindictive. "From what I understand, Sir William was obliged to journey to a neighboring county and negotiate a betrothal contract with an acquaintance, as Samuel's actions toward me ensured that no woman within fifteen miles of Meryton will have anything to do with him. The man, having heard of Samuel's antics, was absolutely ruthless in dictating terms for the marriage, including the penalties should Samuel mistreat her. In fact, according to Charlotte, the man would likely not have betrothed his daughter to Mr. Lucas if she had had any other prospects. Apparently, she is close to being considered 'on the shelf.'"

A laugh was his response. "Then it is a case of poetic justice, indeed! Has Charlotte met the young woman?"

"She has," confirmed Elizabeth. "Though she has very little contact with her brother, she still visits her family occasionally and writes to her father assiduously, and during a visit a month ago, the young lady was visiting as well."

The knowing expression on William's face told Elizabeth that he was aware that she was not telling him the whole story—if, of course, he had not already heard it himself.

"Minx! You delight in teasing me so! So what does Charlotte think of the lady?"

"Well, if you must know . . ."

Her husband's stern look promising retribution caused Elizabeth to laugh. "Oh, very well. Charlotte considers the woman a shrew. She is from a family very similar to Sir William's in consequence, yet she insists upon looking down her nose at everyone she meets. According to Charlotte, she has managed to insult almost every prominent family in Meryton, and Samuel, though he tolerates her in public, shows no inclination for her and actually avoids her whenever they are together in either of their families' estates."

"It appears Mr. Lucas has his own 'Caroline Bingley' after all," said William.

Elizabeth was well aware of his opinion of the Lucas heir, and she knew that he almost wished he had followed through with his threat to challenge Lucas to the duel and teach him a lesson. Elizabeth was grateful she had been able to stay his hand—she was not certain she could have sat quietly by as her fiancé had risked his life for her.

"It appears they were made for each other, and though I cannot find it in my heart to wish him well, I am at least content that he will receive his just desserts— undoubtedly, they will make each other miserable."

"Indeed, they shall," agreed Elizabeth. "He is *not* a happy man according to Charlotte—he spends much of his time in the local tavern, drinking himself into a stupor, and he has been seen exiting houses of ill repute on more than one occasion. His father's restriction on discussing *me* has apparently held, as he never mentions names, but he has been known to complain to all and sundry about his 'ill-treatment at the hands of a jezebel.' Sir William is apparently at his wit's end— the betrothal contract was an attempt to finally settle his son into some semblance of a proper life. I daresay that if Samuel Lucas does not mend his ways soon, he will end up being disowned after all."

All trace of humor gone from his countenance, William gazed at her with a fierce love and protectiveness etched upon his features.

"All this is nothing less than he deserves, Elizabeth, and though I try to feel some degree of pity for him, I find I cannot. Whether he eventually reforms is his own concern, but if he *ever* importunes you again, he shall not escape my wrath."

Elizabeth smiled and, wrapping an arm around her husband's waist, used her other hand to pull his head down to hers in a chaste but loving kiss.

"Dear William, do not concern yourself with Mr. Lucas. I was never anything more than a challenge for him, one which he could use to prove he was your equal. I have no doubt that he will never bother me again. Please, put it from your mind."

He gazed into her eyes, and the emotions contained therein, ones which Elizabeth had seen so many times throughout the course of their engagement and marriage, caused her to catch her breath. His words confirmed what she already could see in his eyes.

"Oh, how I love you, my Elizabeth," breathed William.

"And I you, William."

"I could stay here and listen to you say that forever," said he before he leaned in and quickly kissed the end of her nose. "I think, however, our guests would prefer our presence at a gathering to which we have invited them. What say you to joining them now?"

"Once we have looked in on the children."

He smiled at her, and Elizabeth felt his love wash over her again. She knew that he was happy and impressed with her dedication to their children and her disdain for those of the upper classes who brought their children out to show and then sent them off with the nursemaids, never to be thought of again until the next time they were required. Elizabeth was not willing to completely turn over her children's upbringing to another—she was determined to continue to be a part of their lives as they grew and learned.

The nursery was just down the hallway, and the couple soon entered their children's domain, happy to see their little ones playing so well with the other children who were now in residence. In addition to the Darcy and Bingley children, little Fitzwilliams played with Ramsays, and Hardwicks, all with a bevy of nursemaids from various households to keep them in check.

A squeal heralded the arrival of their eldest, and soon, little Cassandra Darcy threw herself into the arms of her mother. She was a bright, dark-haired girl of three who was playful and mischievous—and an exact replica of Elizabeth at that age, or so Mr. Bennet attested. Cassandra Jane kept the estate staff busy with her antics and could often be found splashing along the banks of the pond or attempting to capture some poor frog from its rest.

By contrast, her brother, little Bennet James, was a quiet and serious boy, recently turned a year old. He had just started walking and was actively being recruited by his elder sister in some of the escapades her young and active mind was already beginning to formulate. But whereas she was bright and carefree, quick to laughter and a friend to all and sundry, Bennet was very thoughtful and deliberate, even at his young age. It took no great insight to determine which child was the more difficult for the nursemaids to tend.

The door opened behind the Darcys, and in stepped Jane and her husband, coming to look in on their own children. Whereas Elizabeth had had two children over the space of almost five years—one of whom was the all-important heir—Jane already had three, and the gentle swell of her belly bore testament to the presence of another imminent addition. However, unlike Elizabeth, Jane had produced only girls thus far—an older girl, Sarah Elizabeth, and a younger pair of twins—prompting Mrs. Bennet's fears of another Bennet woman bearing only girls.

Of course, Bingley, in his good-humor and even-tempered manner, routinely insisted that if they should have nine such daughters, it was all the same to him; his estate was not entailed after all, meaning there was no need to worry about providing for his children after his death. No one missed the pointed look his wife directed at him at the mention of *nine* children.

The Bingleys greeted their close family with relish, and Elizabeth and Jane hugged, still as close as sisters could possibly be. They shared everything with one another—their triumphs as well as their disappointments, and their love and society had only become stronger when Charles had purchased an estate less than twenty miles from Pemberley. Ultimately, giving up Netherfield had not been a difficult decision for them, as it was both too close to Longbourn—and more importantly to Mrs. Bennet!—for the young couple's sanity and, too small for Charles's dreams. The estate he had purchased, with Darcy's assistance, was perhaps not as great a property as the fabled Pemberley, but it more than met his needs, both from an income perspective and a complexity of management standpoint.

The one thing the sisters had not shared, however, was a wedding day, though they had dreamed of sharing even that as young girls and even as women out in society. That particular discussion had been one which had been difficult for Elizabeth, even as she admitted its necessity.

"But, Elizabeth do you not wish to share our wedding day?" said Jane once Elizabeth had completed the task of informing her sister they would not be married on the same day. "We have dreamed of it for many years and have shared everything else since we were young girls—would not being married on the same day be the culmination of all of our dreams?"

Grasping her sister's hand, Elizabeth smiled at her, thinking of how she would answer Jane, taking care not to hurt her feelings. Elizabeth's reasons truly had nothing to do with her sister, but stating it in anything but a precise manner might bring about that eventuality.

"Indeed, we have, Jane," replied Elizabeth at length. "And if the situation were anything other than what it was, I should be happy to be married on the same day as you and Charles."

"Situation, Lizzy? Of what do you speak?"

A sigh forced its way past Elizabeth's lips. "Think, Jane—you and Charles have been engaged for more than a month, while it has been less than two days for William and I. If we were to marry on the same day, then it would look as if we are rushing to the altar, and it would breed rumors of every sort."

"So we move the date back—Charles and I would be vastly pleased to accommodate you."

"Jane, I think you and Charles should marry according to your original plan and not base it on when Fitzwilliam and I are ready. There are other concerns . . .'"

There was no reply to her assertion, only Jane's bewildered countenance.

"Think on it Jane. You spent two months becoming acquainted with Charles last year, and now you have had the time of your engagement to come to know him better. What have William and I had? During the time you were becoming acquainted with Charles last autumn, I was crossing verbal swords with William, convinced that he was the worst man on the face of the earth.

"Then, when we were together in Kent, we spent more time arguing, culminating in his disastrous marriage proposal. The only time we have spent together where we were not at each other's throats was the few days in Derbyshire and whatever time we could steal together since his arrival with his sister."

"You feel you need more time?"

"Indeed, I do. I am in no rush to get to the altar, Jane, and I know that William is of like mind. I wish to use this time to get to know him properly and have him come to know me. You must have your day, Jane—I shall have mine when the time is right. I do not wish to rush into marriage and discover we should have taken more time to understand one another."

Jane was silent for several moments as she thought of what Elizabeth had said, leaving Elizabeth to her own thoughts. She did not specifically oppose a double wedding with her sister, but she did not want one at the expense of having Jane postpone her own. Besides, Jane had been waiting for so long and had such a sweet and angelic disposition—Elizabeth truly believed that Jane deserved to be the focus of her special day and not have to share it. Elizabeth would then have her own after the appropriate time to get to know her betrothed had elapsed.

When she looked back at Jane, her sister was regarding her with a most unusual smirk upon her face. Elizabeth did not know what to think—she did not think she had ever seen such an expression on the face of her sister before.

"You do know this will leave you as Mama's sole focus once I am gone," said Jane, her voice clearly almost breaking from suppressed laughter.

Elizabeth paled as she thought of the consequences of *that* particular item, which she had completely neglected to entertain.

And so, Jane was married early in December, as per her original plans. During their wedding trip, William and Georgiana had continued to stay at Netherfield, allowing them to be in company with Elizabeth every day. The relationship between Elizabeth and William, already a loving and tender one, had truly blossomed from that time forward, and it had been early in March when they had finally met at the altar to be joined in holy wedlock.

As it turned out, Elizabeth had not had to deal too much with an overly exuberant Mrs. Bennet. William, wonderful man that he was, insisted that no special arrangements be made for their wedding, regardless of his status in the world. *His* parents' wedding had been a simple affair, after all, focusing on their shared love rather than on the trappings of society, and nothing less would do for his nuptials. Though not entirely pleased with that particular development, Mrs. Bennet had been forced to accede to his wishes. And though she took liberties in a few instances—most notably, the wedding breakfast, which was as fine as Meryton had ever seen—all involved agreed that it was a beautiful ceremony in its simplicity. Elizabeth had been more than content, especially with the way her betrothed had deftly handled Mrs. Bennet and had excused Elizabeth from some of the more onerous dealings which her mother deemed necessary.

Having looked in on the children, the two couples took their leave and made their way from the room, talking and laughing as they descended the stairs to their waiting guests, meeting with the other couples in residence as they entered the front hall.

Elizabeth looked on at those in attendance, her heart full of the peace and joy brought by the company of those one truly loves. Her father and mother had made the trip to Derbyshire this year, bringing Kitty with them, as she had been staying at her ancestral home these past few months. Mr. Bennet was much as he ever was, and though at times it had caused her grief in the past, his satirical outlook on life was now dear to Elizabeth, though she thought he had mellowed some since her marriage. He stood now speaking with the earl, each looking over the group with an affectionate yet sardonic eye. William's assertion of their similar temperaments had been highly accurate, and the two could be found together at any such gathering, laughing and drinking port. Elizabeth found that she could cheerfully do without knowing the particulars of their conversation, as she was aware that her father's temperament was much more sarcastic than her own, and the earl was not much better.

Mrs. Bennet, by contrast, was still flighty and uncertain in temperament, though Elizabeth felt she also had settled somewhat in the intervening years, no doubt due to the fact that she had managed to marry off nearly all of her daughters. She was currently in the company of the countess and some of William's other older female relatives, and in such an august company, her mother was quieter and almost deferent, though Lady Fitzwilliam was clearly attempting to put her at ease. Elizabeth had finally made her peace with her mother, and though the Bennet matron could still be counted on to make statements which were not exactly the model of propriety, Elizabeth was content in the knowledge that her mother did not truly mean to offend.

Kitty had changed to a certain extent since the fateful events of the summer of her younger sister's marriage, but in essentials, she was still the same spirited young woman. Gone were the days when she would flit about in Lydia's shadow, emulating her sister's poor behavior, but Kitty was, and always would be, a follower, and teaching her the appropriate behavior expected of a young gentlewoman had at times been an effort in futility. She had spent much of the intervening five years living with either Jane or Elizabeth, so at least she had constantly been under the watchful eye of someone much better able to calm her exuberant tendencies than her mother, who was, after all, rather excitable herself. Kitty was the only Bennet daughter as of yet unmarried—perhaps surprisingly so—but that was a situation which was about to change. A Mr. Edwards from the neighboring county of Leicestershire had been introduced to her six months earlier at a dinner party held at the Bingleys' estate. Mr. Edwards was a sensible young man—and not deficient in understanding—so it could be considered a surprise that he had formed an attachment to a girl such as Kitty. Fortunately for Elizabeth's younger sister, he appeared to love her regardless of her faults, and following a whirlwind courtship conducted both in Derbyshire and Hertfordshire, he had proposed and been accepted. They were to be married in the small parish church at Longbourn where *all* of her other sisters had said their vows.

Close by Kitty's side stood Georgiana, looking every inch the young and pretty heiress she was. Elizabeth was by now as close to Georgiana as if they were truly sisters rather than just related by marriage, and Elizabeth had endeavored with patience and kindness to guide the young woman in the society to which she herself was now accepted. Georgiana had indeed blossomed, firmly putting the damage that the cad Wickham had done to her in the past where it belonged. Georgiana, too, was still unmarried, yet there had been no end of suitors for her hand; however, she appeared content to wait for a man who could make her truly happy, following the advice and example of her brother. Elizabeth had a suspicion that Georgiana was warming to a young man from Lincolnshire who had recently made her acquaintance, but she had not as yet made any mention of her true feelings to her family.

Mary had made a most advantageous marriage for her own particular outlook on life. Though her husband was the least wealthy of the sisters' husbands, Mr. Hardwick was a devout young man who had been intended for the church until his elder brother died in a carriage accident, and he complemented the serious Mary quite excellently. Mr. Hardwick's estate in Staffordshire was small, yet it was well-maintained and prosperous, and Elizabeth had always felt comfortable and welcome by the Hardwicks when they visited.

Perhaps the largest surprise of all the Bennet sisters was reserved for the youngest of them. Lydia had improved substantially over the past years after her ill-fated marriage with Wickham had come to an abrupt—but not unwelcome—end, and she was now married to a pleasant man, whom Darcy had known as a student at Cambridge, by the name of Ramsay.

Of her dark days with Mr. Wickham, Lydia was rarely induced to say anything of substance, but it was obvious that theirs had not been a happy marriage. Of course, knowing what she did about Mr. Wickham, Elizabeth could not imagine *anyone* being happy with that villain for a husband. He had not physically mistreated her—*that much* Elizabeth had been able to pull from the tight lips of her sister. However, not a month had passed before Lydia had discovered her husband's infidelity, and the blazing argument which had ensued had left Lydia bitter and more than a little afraid of her husband. What had concerned Lydia even more were the resentful mutterings she had heard from Wickham while in his cups; he had apparently complained of Darcy's perfidy, Elizabeth's inconstancy, and what he would do to them if he ever crossed their paths again.

Thankfully for all concerned, Wickham was shot by an irate husband while fleeing the bed of the man's wife, ending the story of "one of the most worthless young men in England," as Mr. Bennet liked to refer to Wickham. Needless to say, Elizabeth could not think of a single person in all of England who truly mourned the passing of the young man.

Left with what little money Wickham had not managed to gamble away from the bribe he had received from William—which Elizabeth had discovered some time after her marriage, much to her surprise—Lydia returned home a changed woman. Her experiences with her husband had opened her eyes, leaving her a bitter and cynical young woman who had sworn never to enter into the marriage estate again. It had taken many months for the love of her entire family to pull her from the wreckage of her former life and to encourage her to once again take interest in her future.

A chance meeting with Mr. Ramsay, who had lost contact with William after Cambridge, had produced an invitation to visit Pemberley, where Lydia had been staying, and it had not taken long before her still-spirited youngest sister—who now possessed the manners and sense of propriety to check her exuberance—had captivated the young man. They were married—properly this time!—at Longbourn parish, and Lydia, understanding the true nature of a healthy relationship with a man, now had her future secured with someone who actually loved her rather than someone who falsely professed a love he did not feel in order to lead her to do things which she ought not. Her time with Mr. Wickham had fortunately not resulted in a child, and thus it was her firstborn son, of age with Elizabeth's, who played in the nursery with the other children.

"Elizabeth!"

Elizabeth turned to look back up the stairs she had just descended, noting her two closest friends rushing down the stairs to join her.

"Charlotte! Anne!" exclaimed Elizabeth as she rushed to embrace the two women. "When did you arrive?"

"While you were upstairs primping and preening for tonight," said a beaming Anne.

"We actually met in the last rest stop before Pemberley and journeyed here together," added Charlotte.

"But Charlotte, I thought you were unable to be here."

Charlotte smiled and put a hand on her rounded belly, under which her second child slept. "I have had such an easy time with this one that I was able to persuade my husband," she directed a raised eyebrow at the man who had descended behind her, "to allow me to make the journey."

"Are you certain that was wise?" asked Elizabeth, concerned for her friend. Charlotte had experienced a truly difficult time bringing her son into the world, and all had been concerned for the state of her health.

"I am well, Elizabeth," assured Charlotte. "After Henry, this one has been no trouble at all."

"And I could not very well refuse my beautiful wife when she was so persuasive, now could I?" asked a smirking Richard Fitzwilliam.

That had been the other true surprise. Unbeknownst to Elizabeth—or even Darcy, a circumstance for which he had been truly put out—Richard had resigned his commission in the regulars before journeying to Netherfield the autumn Elizabeth had become engaged to William. His father had always kept his mother's estate in trust for Richard, but being a young man determined to make his own way in the world—and having had a certain wanderlust, according to William—the former Colonel had entered the regulars against his parents' wishes. After he had met Elizabeth at Rosings that spring, he had decided that he had had enough of life in the regulars and agreed to take over the estate as its master.

Richard had likely never given Charlotte Collins a second thought—she was the wife of his aunt's parson, after all. However, after the unlamented Mr. Collins had passed, Charlotte, not wishing to stay at Lucas Lodge with the uncomfortable presence of her brother, had been a frequent visitor at Pemberley. It was during one of those visits that Richard had come himself, as was his wont, and remembering a young Mrs. Collins as a steady, handsome woman, he had immediately set about trying to capture her heart. His success in the undertaking was as obvious as the adoring, slightly silly expression which the two were even now directing at each other. It was that match, along with the matches found by Lydia and Kitty, which had caused Mr. Bennet to laughingly refer to Pemberley as a house of matchmaking. Elizabeth certainly could not refute the fact that love did appear to be in the air of Pemberley, though her husband would obviously have groaned at hearing such melodrama voiced by his wife.

"We should step back, Elizabeth," the voice of Anne Ashdown said in a stage-whisper. "Now that they have both gotten *that* look on their faces, they will undoubtedly each bask in the presence of the other for some time before we can pry them apart. I, for one, would prefer to be somewhere else while they do so."

Richard merely smirked at Anne, and with a wink at the three ladies, he departed, joining William and Anne's husband, Mr. Ashdown, whose presence Elizabeth had not noticed when she had previously surveyed the room.

"You ought to know the expression yourself, Anne," teased Charlotte in response. "After all, it appears on your face every time you stare at *your own husband.*"

"That is merely a brief glance of affection," said Anne airily in reply. "Come, let us sit for a few moments before Elizabeth's guests descend upon us. Given last year's soiree, I suspect they likely number everyone of consequence in Derbyshire!"

Laughing, the two women followed Anne, who was as large as Charlotte, though expecting only her first child. As she walked behind her friend, Elizabeth reflected upon Anne's recovery, which was astonishing, to say the least. Though Elizabeth was too polite to say it, she suspected that Lady Catherine's controlling ways and insistence on Anne's inactivity had been more the cause of Anne's prior sickliness than any true affliction. It was the truth that Anne was not blessed with a robust constitution; she was not the walker Elizabeth was, nor was she at her best during long journeys or any other times of strenuous exercise. She was, however, completely healthy and able to live the life she had mostly been denied as a young woman, culminating with her ability to bring a child into the world, an event which was only a few months away. Mr. Ashdown, her husband, was a second son whose eye she had caught some months after her return to Kent. Never having thought of herself as particularly desirable—or even marriageable—it had taken Anne some time before she could reconcile herself to the young man's interest. It had taken a journey to Pemberley where the confused young woman had confided to Elizabeth that she had never thought she would marry, before Elizabeth was able to help her see that the picture she had built of herself—in no small part through her mother's influence, due to Lady Catherine's insistence that she marry none other than William—was in no way a reflection of the truth. In the end she had succumbed willingly to her husband's efforts to secure her hand. Elizabeth was truly happy for her dear friend and could not help but think she had never seen Anne as contented as she was now.

With Jane, her friendship with Anne and Charlotte had grown to the point where the four women considered each other closer than mere sisters. Their families spent a significant amount of time together and were quickly becoming known as a most fashionable clique within the ton—one which many others were desperate to enter. Of course, none of the friends cared for such things, any more than they cared for those who wished to become close to them merely for their connections.

The event that evening was an unmitigated success, but so were all of the Darcys' gatherings—Fitzwilliam Darcy had always been an accepted member of society, and Elizabeth had gained a reputation of being a consummate hostess. There was food, music, and even dancing aplenty, and guests were heard to remark on the fineness of the table Mrs. Darcy kept and the wonderful atmosphere the décor engendered. It was truly a wonderful evening for all concerned. And the good feeling experienced in the company of friends and family filled the manor house, which had remained largely empty for far too long. Pemberley was once again alive with the love and fellowship of her residents.

That evening, once the guests had returned to their homes and their families to their rooms for the night, Elizabeth shared an intimate embrace with her husband, marveling at the strength of the man she had married and the strength of their devotion to one another. They had had their share of hardships, but they had met and overcome them together while forging a life for their family. She did not believe she could be any happier than she was at that moment.

"William?"

"Yes, dearest?" came the sleepy voice of her husband.

"Thank you."

"You are welcome," replied he, as he instinctively tightened his arms around her once again. "May I ask what prompted your little display of gratitude?"

"You loved me," said Elizabeth. "You kept on loving me and pursuing me, though you had little reason for doing so. Now you have given me a wonderful life and a beautiful home and three beautiful children. How can I not be grateful?"

William chuckled. "I believe it is I who ought to thank you, dearest. You have given *me* all these things, though my behavior did not merit it. You are the brightest star in the sky, beloved, and I am happy to give you whatever you desire, as you well know.

"But I think your mother's excellent punch—or perhaps the lateness of the hour—has addled your thoughts. We have only two children—little Cassie and Ben."

"I did not misspeak, William."

The silence lasted for all of a moment before William drew away and searched her eyes, a half-smile already forming.

"Elizabeth . . . are you suggesting . . . ?"

"No, William, I am telling. In another seven months or so, I believe we shall have another addition to our family."

A joyous expression came over his face, much the same as the one which had suffused it when she had accepted his proposal. He cradled her to his chest contentedly, stroking her hair as he placed delicate kisses upon her brow.

"Have I ever told you that I love you, Mrs. Darcy?"

"Not in the past few moments," was Elizabeth's sleepy reply.

Just as she began to drop off to sleep, Elizabeth heard the final words from her husband that night.

"I love you, Elizabeth, but you are not as devious as you thought. I already knew."

About The Author

Jann Rowland was born in Regina, Saskatchewan, Canada. He enjoys reading, sports, and he also dabbles a little in music, taking pleasure in singing and playing the piano.

Though Jann did not start writing until his mid-twenties, writing has grown from a hobby to an all-consuming passion. His interest in Jane Austen stems from his university days when he took a class in which *Pride and Prejudice* was required reading. *Acting on Faith* is his first published novel, but he envisions many more in the coming years, both within the *Pride and Prejudice* universe and without.

He now lives in Alberta, with his wife of almost twenty years, and his three children.

229

29918133R00171

Made in the USA
Lexington, KY
11 February 2014